The Eyes of the World

Harold Bell Wright

The Eyes of the World

ISBN: 978-1-61895-812-9

Contents

Chapter I
His Inheritance

It was winter—cold and snow and ice and naked trees and leaden clouds and stinging wind.

The house was an ancient mansion on an old street in that city of culture which has given to the history of our nation—to education, to religion, to the sciences, and to the arts—so many illustrious names.

In the changing years, before the beginning of my story, the woman's immediate friends and associates had moved from the neighborhood to the newer and more fashionable districts of a younger generation. In that city of her father's there were few of her old companions left. There were fewer who remembered. The distinguished leaders in the world of art and letters, whose voices had been so often heard within the walls of her home, had, one by one, passed on; leaving their works and their names to their children. The children, in the greedy rush of these younger times, had too readily forgotten the woman who, to the culture and genius of a passing day, had been hostess and friend.

The apartment was pitifully bare and empty. Ruthlessly it had been stripped of its treasures of art and its proud luxuries. But, even in its naked necessities the room managed, still, to evidence the rare intelligence and the exquisite refinement of its dying tenant.

The face upon the pillow, so wasted by sickness, was marked by the death-gray. The eyes, deep in their hollows between the fleshless forehead and the prominent cheek-bones, were closed; the lips were livid; the nose was sharp and pinched; the colorless cheeks were sunken; but the outlines were still delicately drawn and the proportions nobly fashioned. It was, still, the face of a gentlewoman. In the ashen lips, only, was there a sign of life; and they trembled and fluttered in their effort to utter the words that an indomitable spirit gave them to speak.

"To-day—to-day—he will—come." The voice was a thin, broken whisper; but colored, still, with pride and gladness.

A young woman in the uniform of a trained nurse turned quickly from the window. With soft, professional step, she crossed the room to bend over the bed. Her trained fingers sought the skeleton wrist; she spoke slowly, distinctly, with careful clearness;

1

and, under the cool professionalism of her words, there was a tone of marked respect. "What is it, madam?"

The sunken eyes opened. As a burst of sunlight through the suddenly opened doors of a sepulchre, the death-gray face was illumed. In those eyes, clear and burning, the nurse saw all that remained of a powerful personality. In their shadowy depths, she saw the last glowing embers of the vital fire gathered; carefully nursed and tended; kept alive by a will that was clinging, with almost superhuman tenacity, to a definite purpose. Dying, this woman would not die—could not die—until the end for which she willed to live should be accomplished. In the very grasp of Death, she was forcing Death to stay his hand—without life, she was holding Death at bay.

It was magnificent, and the gentle face under the nurse's cap shone with appreciation and admiration as she smiled her sympathy and understanding.

"My son—my son—will come—to-day." The voice was stronger, and, with the eyes, expressed a conviction—a certainty—with the faintest shadow of a question.

The nurse looked at her watch. "The boat was due in New York, early this morning, madam."

A step sounded in the hall outside. The nurse started, and turned quickly toward the door. But the woman said, "The doctor." And, again, the fire that burned in those sunken eyes was hidden wearily under their dark lids.

The white-haired physician and the nurse, at the farther end of the room, spoke together in low tones. Said the physician,—incredulous,—"You say there is no change?"

"None that I can detect," breathed the nurse. "It is wonderful!"

"Her mind is clear?"

"As though she were in perfect health."

The doctor took the nurse's chart. For a moment, he studied it in silence. He gave it back with a gesture of amazement. "God! nurse," he whispered, "she should be in her grave by now! It's a miracle! But she has always been like that—" he continued, half to himself, looking with troubled admiration toward the bed at the other end of the room—"always."

He went slowly forward to the chair that the nurse placed for him. Seating himself quietly beside his patient, and bending forward with intense interest, his fine old head bowed, he regarded with more than professional care the wasted face upon the pillow.

2

The doctor remembered, too well, when those finely moulded features—now, so worn by sorrow, so marked by sickness, so ghastly in the hue of death—were rounded with young-woman health and tinted with rare loveliness. He recalled that day when he saw her a bride. He remembered the sweet, proud dignity of her young wifehood. He saw her, again, when her face shone with the glad triumph and the holy joy of motherhood.

The old physician turned from his patient, to look with sorrowful eyes about the room that was to witness the end.

Why was such a woman dying like this? Why was a life of such rich mental and spiritual endowments—of such wealth of true culture—coming to its close in such material poverty?

The doctor was one of the few who knew. He was one of the few who understood that, to the woman herself, it was necessary.

There were those who—without understanding, for the sake of the years that were gone—would have surrounded her with the material comforts to which, in her younger days, she had been accustomed. The doctor knew that there was one—a friend of her childhood, famous, now, in the world of books—who would have come from the ends of the earth to care for her. All that a human being could do for her, in those days of her life's tragedy, that one had done. Then—because he understood—he had gone away. Her own son did not know—could not, in his young manhood, have understood, if he had known—would not understand when he came. Perhaps, some day, he would understand—perhaps.

When the physician turned again toward the bed, to touch with gentle fingers the wrist of his patient, his eyes were wet.

At his touch, her eyes opened to regard him with affectionate trust and gratitude.

"Well Mary," he said almost bruskly.

The lips fashioned the ghost of a smile; into her eyes came the gleam of that old time challenging spirit. "Well—Doctor George," she answered. Then,—"I—told you—I would not—go—until he came. I must—have my way—still—you see. He will—come—to-day He must come."

"Yes, Mary," returned the doctor,—his fingers still on the thin wrist, and his eyes studying her face with professional keenness,— "yes, of course."

"And George—you will not forget—your promise? You will— give me a few minutes—of strength—when he comes—so that I can tell him? I—I—must tell him myself—George. You—will do—this last thing—for me?"

"Yes, Mary, of course," he answered again. "Everything shall be as you wish—as I promised."

"Thank you—George. Thank you—my dear—dear—old friend."

The nurse—who had been standing at the window—stepped quickly to the table that held a few bottles, glasses, and instruments. The doctor looked at her sharply. She nodded a silent answer, as she opened a small, flat, leather case. With his fingers still on his patient's wrist, the physician spoke a word of instruction; and, in a moment, the nurse placed a hypodermic needle in his hand.

As the doctor gave the instrument, again, to his assistant, a quick step sounded in the hall outside.

The patient turned her head. Her eager eyes were fixed upon the door; her voice—stronger, now, with the strength of the powerful stimulant—rang out; "My boy—my boy—he is here! George, nurse, my boy is here!"

The door opened. A young man of perhaps twenty-two years stood on the threshold.

The most casual observer would have seen that he was a son of the dying woman. In the full flush of his young manhood's vigor, there was the same modeling of the mouth, the same nose with finely turned nostrils, the same dark eyes under a breadth of forehead; while the determined chin and the well-squared jaw, together with a rather remarkable fineness of line, told of an inherited mental and spiritual strength and grace as charming as it is, in these days, rare. His dress was that of a gentleman of culture and social position. His very bearing evidenced that he had never been without means to gratify the legitimate tastes of a cultivated and refined intelligence.

As he paused an instant in the open door to glance about that poverty stricken room, a look of bewildering amazement swept over his handsome face. He started to draw back—as if he had unintentionally entered the wrong apartment. Looking at the doctor, his lips parted as if to apologize for his intrusion. But before he could speak, his eyes met the eyes of the woman on the bed.

With a cry of horror, he sprang forward;—"Mother! Mother!"

As he knelt there by the bed, when the first moments of their meeting were past, he turned his face toward the doctor. From the physician his gaze went to the nurse, then back again to his mother's old friend. His eyes were burning with shame and sorrow—with pain and doubt and accusation. His low voice was tense with emotion, as he demanded, "What does this mean? Why is my mother here like—like this?"—his eyes swept the bare room again.

4

The dying woman answered. "I will explain, my boy. It is to tell you, that I have waited."

At a look from the doctor, the nurse quietly followed the physician from the room.

It was not long. When she had finished, the false strength that had kept the woman alive until she had accomplished that which she conceived to be her last duty, failed quickly.

"You will—promise—you will?"

"Yes, mother, yes."

"Your education—your training—your blood—they—are—all—that—I can—give you, my son."

"O mother, mother! why did you not tell me before? Why did I not know!" The cry was a protest—an expression of bitterest shame and sorrow.

She smiled. "It—was—all that I could do—for you—my son—the only way—I could—help. I do not—regret the cost. You will—not forget?"

"Never, mother, never."

"You promise—to—to regain that—which—your father—"

Solemnly the answer came,—in an agony of devotion and love,—"I promise—yes, mother, I promise."

A month later, the young man was traveling, as fast as modern steam and steel could carry him, toward the western edge of the continent.

He was flying from the city of his birth, as from a place accursed. He had set his face toward a new land—determined to work out, there, his promise—the promise that he did not, at the first, understand.

How he misunderstood,—how he attempted to use his inheritance to carry out what he first thought was his mother's wish,—and how he came at last to understand, is the story that I have to tell.

Chapter II
The Woman with the Disfigured Face

The Golden State Limited, with two laboring engines, was climbing the desert side of San Gorgonio Pass.

Now San Gorgonio Pass—as all men should know—is one of the two eastern gateways to the beautiful heart of Southern California. It is, therefore, the gateway to the scenes of my story.

As the heavy train zigzagged up the long, barren slope of the mountain, in its effort to lessen the heavy grade, the young man on the platform of the observation car could see, far to the east, the shimmering, sun-filled haze that lies, always, like a veil of mystery, over the vast reaches of the Colorado Desert. Now and then, as the Express swung around the curves, he gained a view of the lonely, snow-piled peaks of the San Bernardinos; with old San Gorgonio, lifting above the pine-fringed ridges of the lower Galenas, shining, silvery white, against the blue. Again, on the southern side of the pass, he saw San Jacinto's crags and cliffs rising almost sheer from the right-of-way.

But the man watching the ever-changing panorama of gorgeously colored and fantastically unreal landscape was not thinking of the scenes that, to him, were new and strange. His thoughts were far away. Among those mountains grouped about San Gorgonio, the real value of the inheritance he had received from his mother was to be tested. On the pine-fringed ridge of the Galenas, among those granite cliffs and jagged peaks, the mettle of his manhood was to be tried under a strain such as few men in this commonplace work-a-day old world are-subjected to. But the young man did not know this.

On the long journey across the continent, he had paid little heed to the sights that so interested his fellow passengers. To his fellow passengers, themselves, he had been as indifferent. To those who had approached him casually, as the sometimes tedious hours passed, he had been quietly and courteously unresponsive. This well-bred but decidedly marked disinclination to mingle with them, together with the undeniably distinguished appearance of the young man, only served to center the interest of the little world of the Pullmans more strongly upon him. Keeping to himself, and engrossed with his own thoughts, he became the object of many idle conjectures.

Among the passengers whose curious eyes were so often turned in his direction, there was one whose interest was always carefully veiled. She was a woman of evident rank and distinction in that world where rank and distinction are determined wholly by dollars and by such social position as dollars can buy. She was beautiful; but with that carefully studied, wholly self-conscious—one is tempted to say professional—beauty of her kind. Her full rounded, splendidly developed body was gowned to accentuate the alluring curves of her sex. With such skill was this deliberate appeal to the physical hidden under a cloak of a pretending modesty that its charm was the more effectively revealed. Her features were almost too perfect. She was too coldly sure of herself—too perfectly trained in the art of self-repression. For a woman as young as she evidently was, she seemed to know too much. The careful indifference of her countenance seemed to say, "I am too well schooled in life to make mistakes." She was traveling with two companions—a fluffy, fluttering, characterless shadow of womanhood, and a man—an invalid who seldom left the privacy of the drawing-room which he occupied.

As the train neared the summit of the pass, the young man on the observation car platform looked at his watch. A few miles more and he would arrive at his destination. Rising to his feet, he drew a deep breath of the glorious, sun-filled air. With his back to the door, and looking away into the distance, he did not notice the woman who, stepping from the car at that moment, stood directly behind him, steadying herself by the brass railing in front of the window. To their idly observing fellow passengers, the woman, too, appeared interested in the distant landscape. She might have been looking at the only other occupant of the platform. The passengers, from where they sat, could not have told.

As he stood there,—against the background of the primitive, many-colored landscape,—the young man might easily have attracted the attention of any one. He would have attracted attention in a crowd. Tall, with an athletic trimness of limb, a good breadth of shoulder, and a fine head poised with that natural, unconscious pride of the well-bred—he kept his feet on the unsteady platform of the car with that easy grace which marks only well-conditioned muscles, and is rarely seen save in those whose lives are sanely clean.

The Express had entered the yards at the summit station, and was gradually lessening its speed. Just as the man turned to enter the car, the train came to a full stop, and the sudden jar threw him almost into the arms of the woman. For an instant, while he was struggling to regain his balance, he was so close to her that their garments touched. Indeed, he only prevented an actual collision by throwing his arm across her shoulder and catching the side of the car window against which she was leaning.

In that moment, while his face was so close to hers that she might have felt his breath upon her cheek and he was involuntarily looking straight into her eyes, the man felt, queerly, that the woman was not shrinking from him. In fact, one less occupied with other thoughts might have construed her bold, open look, her slightly parted lips and flushed cheeks, as a welcome—quite as though she were in the habit of having handsome young men throw themselves into her arms.

Then, with a hint of a smile in his eyes, he was saying, conventionally, "I beg your pardon. It was very stupid of me."

As he spoke, a mask of cold indifference slipped over her face. Without deigning to notice his courteous apology, she looked away, and, moving to the railing of the platform, became ostensibly interested in the busy activity of the railroad yards.

Had the woman—in that instant when his arm was over her shoulder and his eyes were looking into hers—smiled, the incident would have slipped quickly from his mind. As it was, the flash-like impression of the moment remained, and—

Down the steep grade of the narrow San Timateo Canyon, on the coast side of the mountain pass, the Overland thundered on the last stretch of its long race to the western edge of the continent. And now, from the car windows, the passengers caught tantalizing glimpses of bright pastures with their herds of contented dairy cows, and with their white ranch buildings set in the shade of giant pepper and eucalyptus trees. On the rounded shoulders and steep flanks of the foothills that form the sides of the canyon, the barley fields looked down upon the meadows; and, now and then, in the whirling landscape winding side canyons—beautiful with live-oak and laurel, with greasewood and sage—led the eye away toward the pine-fringed ridges of the Galenas while above, the higher snow-clad peaks and domes of the San Bernardinos still shone coldly against the blue.

In the Pullman, there was a stir of awakening interest The travel-wearied passengers, laying aside books and magazines and cards, renewed conversations that, in the last monotonous hours of the desert part of the journey, had lagged painfully. Throughout the train, there was an air of eager expectancy; a bustling movement of preparation. The woman of the observation car platform had disappeared into her stateroom. The young man gathered his things together in readiness to leave the train at the next stop.

In the flying pictures framed by the windows, the dairy

pastures and meadows were being replaced by small vineyards and orchards; the canyon wall, on the northern side, became higher and steeper, shutting out the mountains in the distance and showing only a fringe of trees on the sharp rim; while against the gray and yellow and brown and green of the chaparral on the steep, untilled bluffs, shone the silvery softness of the olive trees that border the arroyo at their feet.

With a long, triumphant shriek, the flying overland train—from the lands of ice and snow—from barren deserts and lonely mountains—rushed from the narrow mouth of the canyon, and swept out into the beautiful San Bernardino Valley where the travelers were greeted by wide, green miles of orange and lemon and walnut and olive groves—by many acres of gardens and vineyards and orchards. Amid these groves and gardens, the towns and cities are set; their streets and buildings half hidden in wildernesses of eucalyptus and peppers and palms; while—towering above the loveliness of the valley and visible now from the sweeping lines of their foothills to the gleaming white of their lonely peaks—rises, in blue-veiled, cloud-flecked steeps and purple shaded canyons, the beauty and grandeur of the mountains.

It was January. To those who had so recently left the winter lands, the Southern California scene—so richly colored with its many shades of living green, so warm in its golden sunlight—seemed a dream of fairyland. It was as though that break in the mountain wall had ushered them suddenly into another world—a world, strange, indeed, to eyes accustomed to snow and ice and naked trees and leaden clouds.

Among the many little cities half concealed in the luxurious, semi-tropical verdure of the wide valley at the foot of the mountains, Fairlands—if you ask a citizen of that well-known mecca of the tourist—is easily the Queen. As for that! all our Southern California cities are set in wildernesses of beauty; all are in wide valleys; all are at the foot of the mountains; all are meccas for tourists; each one—if you ask a citizen—is the Queen. If you, perchance should question this fact—write for our advertising literature.

Passengers on the Golden State Limited—as perhaps you know—do not go direct to Fairlands. They change at Fairlands Junction. The little city, itself, is set in the lap of the hills that form the southern side of the valley, some three miles from the main line. It is as though this particular "Queen" withdrew from the great highway traveled by the vulgar herd—in the proud aloofness of her superior clay, sufficient unto herself. The soil out of which Fairlands is made is much richer, it is said, than the common dirt of her sister

9

cities less than fifteen miles distant. A difference of only a few feet in elevation seems, strangely, to give her a much more rarefied air. Her proudest boast is that she has a larger number of millionaires in proportion to her population than any other city in the land.

It was these peculiar and well-known advantages of Fairlands that led the young man of my story to select it as the starting point of his worthy ambition. And Fairlands is a good place for one so richly endowed with an inheritance that cannot be expressed in dollars to try his strength. Given such a community, amid such surroundings, with a man like the young man of my story, and something may be depended upon to happen.

While the travelers from the East, bound for Fairlands, were waiting at the Junction for the local train that would take them through the orange groves to their journey's end, the young man noticed the woman of the observation car platform with her two companions. And now, as he paced to and fro, enjoying the exercise after the days of confinement in the Pullman, he observed them with stimulated interest—they, too, were going to Fairlands.

The man of the party, though certainly not old in years, was frightfully aged by dissipation and disease. The gross, sensual mouth with its loose-hanging lips; the blotched and clammy skin; the pale, watery eyes with their inflamed rims and flabby pouches; the sunken chest, skinny neck and limbs; and the thin rasping voice—all cried aloud the shame of a misspent life. It was as clearly evident that he was a man of wealth and, in the eyes of the world, of an enviable social rank.

As the young man passed and repassed them, where they stood under the big pepper tree that shades the depot, the man—in his harsh, throaty whisper, between spasms of coughing—was cursing the train service, the country, the weather; and, apparently, whatever else he could think of as being worthy or unworthy his impotent ill-temper. The shadowy suggestion of womanhood— glancing toward the young man—was saying, with affected giggles, "O papa, don't! Oh isn't it perfectly lovely! O papa, don't! Do hush! What will people think?" This last variation of his daughter's plaint must have given the man some satisfaction, at least, for it furnished him another target for his pointless shafts; and he fairly outdid himself in politely damning whoever might presume to think anything at all of him; with the net result that two Mexicans, who were loafing near enough to hear, grinned with admiring amusement. The woman stood a little apart from the others. Coldly indifferent alike to the man's cursing and coughing and to the daughter's ejaculations, she appeared to be looking at the mountains. But the young man fancied that, once or twice, as he

10

faced about at the end of his beat, her eyes were turned in his direction.

When the Fairlands train came in, the three found seats conveniently turned, near the forward end of the car. The young man, in passing, glanced down; and the woman, who had taken the chair next to the aisle, looked up full into his face.

Again, as their eyes met, the man felt—as when they had stood so close together on the platform of the observation car—that she did not shrink from him. It was only for an instant. Then, glancing about for a seat, he saw another face—a face, in its outlines, so like the one into which he had just looked, and yet so different—so far removed in its expression and meaning—that it fixed his attention instantly—compelling his interest.

As this woman sat looking from the car window away toward the distant mountain peaks, the young man thought he had never seen a more perfect profile; nor a countenance that expressed such a beautiful blending of wistful longing, of patient fortitude, and saintly resignation. It was the face of a Madonna,—but a Madonna after the crucifixion,—pathetic in its lonely sorrow, inspiring in its spiritual strength, and holy in its purity and freedom from earthly passions.

She was near his mother's age; and looking at her—as he moved down the aisle—his mother's face, as he had known it before their last meeting, came to him with startling vividness. For an instant, he paused, moved to take the chair beside her; but the next two seats were vacant, and he had no excuse for intruding. Arranging his grips, he quickly seated himself next to the window; and again, with eager interest, turned toward the woman in the chair ahead. Involuntarily, he started with astonishment and pity.

The woman—still gazing from the window at the distant mountain peaks, and seemingly unconscious of her surroundings—presented now, to the man's shocked and compassionate gaze, the other side of her face. It was hideously disfigured by a great scar that—covering the entire cheek and neck—distorted the corner of the mouth, drew down the lower lid of the eye, and twisted her features into an ugly caricature. Even the ear, half hidden under the soft, gray-threaded hair, had not escaped, but was deformed by the same dreadful agent that had wrought such ruin to one of the loveliest countenances the man had ever looked upon.

When the train stopped at Fairlands, and the passengers crowded into the aisle to make their way out, of the characters belonging to my story, the woman with the man and his daughter went first. Following them, a half car-length of people between, went the woman with the disfigured face.

11

On the depot platform, as they moved toward the street, the young man still held his place near the woman who had so awakened his pitying interest. The three Overland passengers were met by a heavy-faced thick-necked man who escorted them to a luxurious touring car.

The invalid and his daughter had entered the automobile when their escort, in turning toward the other member of the party, saw the woman with the disfigured face—who was now quite near. Instantly, he paused. And there was a smile of recognition on his somewhat coarse features as, lifting his hat, he bowed with—the young man fancied—condescending politeness. The woman standing by his side with her hand upon the door of the automobile, seeing her companion saluting some one, turned—and the next moment, the two women, whose features seemed so like—yet so unlike—were face to face.

The young man saw the woman with the disfigured face stop short. For an instant, she stood as though dazed by an unexpected blow. Then, holding out her hands with a half-pleading, half-groping gesture, she staggered and would have fallen had he not stepped to her side.

"Permit me, madam; you are ill."

She neither spoke nor moved; but, with her eyes fixed upon the woman by the automobile, allowed him to support her—seemingly unconscious of his presence. And never before had the young man seen such anguish of spirit written in a human countenance.

The one who had saluted her, advanced—as though to offer his services. But, as he moved toward her, she shrank back with a low—"No, no!" And such a look of horror and fear came into her eyes that the man by her side felt his muscles tense with indignation.

Looking straight into the heavy face of the stranger, he said curtly, "I think you had better go on."

With a careless shrug, the other turned and went back to the automobile, where he spoke in a low tone to his companions.

The woman, who had been watching with a cold indifference, stepped into the car. The man took his seat by the chauffeur. As the big machine moved away, the woman with the disfigured face, again made as if to stretch forth her hands in a pleading gesture.

The young man spoke pityingly; "May I assist you to a carriage, madam?"

At his words, she looked up at him and—seeming to find in his face the strength she needed—answered in a low voice, "Thank you, sir; I am better now. I will he all right, presently, if you will put me

12

on the car." She indicated a street-car that was just stopping at the crossing.

"Are you quite sure that you are strong enough?" he asked kindly, as he walked with her toward the car.

"Yes,"—with a sad attempt to smile,—"yes, and I thank you very much, sir, for your gentle courtesy."

He assisted her up the step of the car, and stood with bared head as she passed inside, and the conductor gave the signal.

The incident had attracted little attention from the passengers who were hurrying from the train. Their minds were too intent upon other things to more than glance at this little ripple on the surface of life. Those who had chanced to notice the woman's agitation had seen, also, that she was being cared for; and so had passed on, giving the scene no second thought.

When the man returned from the street to his grips on the depot platform, the hacks and hotel buses were gone. As he stood looking about, questioningly, for some one who might direct him to a hotel, his eyes fell upon a strange individual who was regarding him intently.

Fully six feet in height, the observer was so lean that he suggested the unpleasant appearance of a living skeleton. His narrow shoulders were so rounded, his form was so stooped, that the young man's first thought was to wonder how tall he would really be if he could stand erect. His long, thin face, seamed and lined, was striking in its grotesque ugliness. From under his craggy, scowling brows, his sharp green-gray eyes peered with a curious expression of baffling, quizzing, half pathetic, and wholly cynical, interrogation. He was smoking a straight, much-used brier pipe. At his feet, lay a beautiful Irish Setter dog.

Half hidden by a supporting column of the depot portico—as if to escape the notice of the people in the automobile—he had been watching the woman with the disfigured face, with more than casual interest. He turned, now, upon the young man who had so kindly given her assistance.

In answer to the stranger's inquiry, with a curt sentence and a nod of his head he directed him to a hotel—two blocks away.

Thanking him, the young man, carrying his grips, set out. Upon reaching the street, he involuntarily turned to look back.

The oddly appearing character had not moved from his place, but stood, still looking after the stranger—the brier pipe in his mouth, the Irish Setter at his feet.

Chapter III
The Famous Conrad Lagrange

When the young man reached the hotel, he went at once to his room, where he passed the time between the hour of his arrival and the evening meal.

Upon his return to the lobby, the first object that attracted his eyes was the uncouth figure of the man whom he had seen at the depot, and who had directed him to the hotel.

That oddly appearing individual, his brier pipe still in his mouth and the Irish Setter at his feet, was standing—or rather lounging—at the clerk's counter, bending over the register; an attitude which—making his skeleton-like form more round shouldered than ever—caused him to present the general outlines of a rude interrogation point.

In the dining-room, a few minutes later, the two men sat at adjoining tables; and the young man heard his neighbor bullying the waiters and commenting in an audible undertone, upon every dish that was served to him—swearing by all the heathen gods, known and unknown, that there was nothing fit to eat in the house; and that if it were not for the fact that there was no place else in the cursed town that served half so good, he would not touch a mouthful in the place. Then, to the other's secret amusement he fell to right heartily and made an astonishing meal of the really excellent viands he had so roundly vilified.

Dinner over, the young man went with his cigar to the long veranda; intent upon enjoying the restful quiet of the evening after the tiresome days on the train. Carrying a chair to an unoccupied corner, he had his cigar just nicely under way when the Irish Setter—with all the dignity of his royal blood—approached. Resting a seal-brown head, with its long silky ears, confidently upon the stranger's knee, the dog looked up into the man's face with an expression of hearty good-fellowship in his soft, golden-brown eyes that was irresistible.

"Good dog," said the man, heartily, "good old fellow," and stroked the sleek head and neck, affectionately.

A whiff of pipe smoke drifted over his shoulder, and he looked around. The dog's master stood just behind him; regarding him with that quizzing, half pathetic, half humorous, and altogether cynical expression.

14

The young man who had been so unresponsive to the advances of his fellow passengers, for some reason—unknown, probably, to himself—now took the initiative. "You have a fine dog here, sir," he said encouragingly.

Without replying, the other turned away and in another moment returned with a chair; whereupon the dog, with slightly waving, feathery tail, transferred his attention to his master.

Caressing the seal-brown head with a gentle hand, and apparently speaking to the soft eyes that looked up at him so understandingly, the man said, "If the human race was fit to associate with such dogs, the world would be a more comfortable place to live in." The deep voice that rumbled up from some unguessed depths of that sunken chest was remarkable in its suggestion of a virile power that the general appearance of the man seemed to deny. Facing his companion suddenly, he asked with a direct bluntness, "Are you not Aaron King—son of the Aaron King of New England political fame?"

Under the searching gaze of those green-gray eyes, the young man flushed. "Yes; my father was active in New England politics," he answered simply. "Did you know him?"

"Very well"—returned the other—"very well." He repeated the two words with a suggestive emphasis; his eyes—with that curious, baffling, questioning look—still fixed upon his companion's face.

The red in Aaron King's cheeks deepened.

Looking away, the strange man added, with a softer note in his rough voice, "I thought I knew you, when I saw you at the depot. Your mother and I were boy and girl together. There is a little of her face in yours. If you have as much of her character, you are to be congratulated—and—so are the rest of us." The last words were spoken, apparently, to the dog; who, still looking up at him, seemed to express with slow-waving tail, an understanding of thoughts that were only partly put into words.

There was an impersonality in the man's personalities that made it impossible for the subject of his observations to take offense.

Aaron King—when it was evident that the man had no thought of introducing himself—said, with the fine courtesy that seemed always to find expression in his voice and manner, "May I ask your name, sir?"

The other, without turning his eyes from the dog, answered, "Conrad Lagrange."

The young man smiled. "I am very pleased to meet you, Mr. Lagrange. Surely, you are not the famous novelist of that name?"

15

"And why, 'surely not'?" retorted the other, again turning his face quickly toward his companion. "Am I not distinguished enough in appearance? Do I look like the mob? True, I am a scrawny, humpbacked crooked-faced, scarecrow of a man—but what matters that, if I do not look like the mob? What is called fame is as scrawny and humpbacked and crooked-faced as my body—but what matters that? Famous or infamous—to not look like the mob is the thing."

It is impossible to put in print the peculiar humor of pathetic regret, of sarcasm born of contempt, of intolerant intellectual pride, that marked the last sentence, which was addressed to the dog, as though the speaker turned from his human companion to a more worthy listener.

When Aaron King could find no words to reply, the novelist shot another question at him, with startling suddenness. "Do you read my books?"

The other began a halting answer to the effect that everybody read Conrad Lagrange's books. But the distinguished author interrupted; "Don't take the trouble to lie—out of politeness. I shall ask you to tell me about them and you will be in a hole."

The young man laughed as he said, with straight-forward frankness, "I have read only one, Mr. Lagrange."

"Which one?"

"The—ah—why—the one, you know—where the husband of one woman falls in love with the wife of another who is in love with the husband of some one else. Pshaw!—what is the title? I mean the one that created such a furore, you know."

"Yes"—said the man, to his dog—"O yes, Czar—I am the famous Conrad Lagrange. I observe"—he added, turning to the other, with twinkling eyes—"I observe, Mr. King, that you really do have a good bit of your mother's character. That you do not read my books is a recommendation that I, better than any one, know how to appreciate." The light of humor went from his face, suddenly, as it had come. Again he turned away; and his deep voice was gentle as he continued, "Your mother is a rare and beautiful spirit, sir. Knowing her regard for the true and genuine,—her love for the pure and beautiful,—I scarcely expected to find her son interested in the realism of my fiction. I congratulate you, young man"—he paused; then added with indescribable bitterness—"that you have not read my books."

For a few moments, Aaron King did not answer. At last, with quiet dignity, he said, "My mother was a remarkable woman, Mr. Lagrange."

The other faced him quickly. "You say was? Do you mean—?"

"My mother is dead, sir. I was called home from abroad by her illness."

For a little, the older man sat looking into the gathering dusk. Then, deliberately, he refilled his brier pipe, and, rising, said to his dog, "Come, Czar—it's time to go."

Without a word of parting to his human companion with the dog moving sedately by his side, he disappeared into the darkness of the night.

All the next day, Aaron King—in the hotel dining-room, the lobby, and on the veranda—watched for the famous novelist. Even on the streets of the little city, he found himself hoping to catch a glimpse of the uncouth figure and the homely, world-worn face of the man whose unusual personality had so attracted him. The day was nearly gone when Conrad Lagrange again appeared. As on the evening before, the young man was smoking his after-dinner cigar on the veranda, when the Irish Setter and a whiff of pipe smoke announced the strange character's presence.

Without taking a seat, the novelist said, "I always have a look at the mountains, at this time of the day, Mr. King—would you care to come? These mountains are the real thing, you know, and well worth seeing—particularly at this hour." There was a gentle softness in his deep voice, now—as unlike his usual speech as his physical appearance was unlike that of his younger companion.

Aaron King arose quickly. "Thank you, Mr, Lagrange; I will go with pleasure."

Accompanied by the dog, they followed the avenue, under the giant pepper trees that shut out the sky with their gnarled limbs and gracefully drooping branches, to the edge of the little city; where the view to the north and northeast was unobstructed by houses. Just where the street became a road, Conrad Lagrange—putting his hand upon his companion's arm—said in a low voice, "This is the place."

Behind them, beautiful Fairlands lay, half lost, in its wilderness of trees and flowers. Immediately in the foreground, a large tract of unimproved land brought the wild grasses and plants to their very feet. Beyond these acres—upon which there were no trees—the orange groves were massed in dark green blocks and squares; with, here and there, thin rows of palms; clumps of peppers; or tall, plume-like eucalyptus; to mark the roads and the ranch homes. Beyond this—and rising, seemingly, out of the groves—the San Bernardinos heaved their mighty masses into the sky. It was almost dark. The city's lamps were lighted. The outlines of grove and garden were fast being lost in the deepening dusk. The foothills, with the lower spurs and ridges of the mountains, were softly modeled in dark blue against the deeper purple of the canyons

17

and gorges. Upon the cloudless sky that was lighted with clearest saffron, the lines of the higher crests were sharply drawn; while the lonely, snow-capped peaks,—ten thousand feet above the darkening valley below,—catching the last rays of the sun, glowed rose-pink— changing to salmon—deepening into mauve—as the light failed.

Aaron King broke the silence by drawing a long breath—as one who could find no words to express his emotions.

Conrad Lagrange spoke sadly; "And to think that there are,— in this city of ten thousand,—probably, nine thousand nine hundred and ninety people who never see it."

With a short laugh, the young man said, "It makes my fingers fairly itch for my palette and brushes—though it's not at all my sort of thing."

The other turned toward him quickly. "You are an artist?"

"I had just completed my three years study abroad when mother's illness brought me home. I was fortunate enough to get one on the line, and they say—over there—that I had a good chance. I don't know how it will go here at home." There was a note of anxiety in his voice.

"What do you do?"

"Portraits."

A curious expression of baffling quizzing half pathetic and wholly cynical interrogation

With his face again toward the mountains, the novelist said thoughtfully, "This West country will produce some mighty artists, Mr. King. By far the greater part of this land must remain, always, in its primitive naturalness. It will always be easier, here, than in the city crowded East, for a man to be himself. There is less of that spirit which is born of clubs and cliques and clans and schools—with their fine-spun theorizing, and their impudent assumption that they are divinely commissioned to sit in judgment. There is less of artistic tea-drinking, esthetic posing, and soulful talk; and more opportunity for that loneliness out of which great art comes. The atmosphere of these mountains and deserts and seas inspires to a self-assertion, rather than to a clinging fast to the traditions and culture of others—and what, after all, is a great artist, but one who greatly asserts himself?"

The younger man answered in a like vein; "Mr. Lagrange, your words recall to my mind a thought in one of mother's favorite books. She quoted from the volume so often that, as a youngster, I almost knew it by heart, and, in turn, it became my favorite. Indeed, I think that, with mother's aid as an interpreter, it has had more influence upon my life than any other one book. This is the thought: 'To understand the message of the mountains; to love them for what

18

they are; and, in terms of every-day life, to give expression to that understanding and love—is a mark of true greatness of soul.' I do not know the author. The book is anonymous."

"I am the author of that book, sir," the strange man answered with simple dignity, "—or, rather,—I should say,—I was the author," he added, with a burst of his bitter, sarcastic humor. "For God's sake don't betray me. I am, now, the famous Conrad Lagrange, you understand. I have a name to protect." His deep voice was shaken with feeling. His worn and rugged features twitched and worked with emotion.

Aaron King listened in amazement to the words that were spoken by the famous novelist with such pathetic regret and stinging self-accusation. Not knowing how to reply, he said casually, "You are working here, Mr. Lagrange?"

"Working! Me? I don't work anywhere. I am a literary scavenger. I haunt the intellectual slaughter pens, and live by the putrid offal that self-respecting writers reject. I glean the stinking materials for my stories from the sewers and cesspools of life. For the dollars they pay, I furnish my readers with those thrills that public decency forbids them to experience at first hand. I am a procurer for the purposes of mental prostitution. My books breed moral pestilence and spiritual disease. The unholy filth I write fouls the minds and pollutes the imaginations of my readers. I am an instigator of degrading immorality and unmentionable crimes. Work! No, young man, I don't work. Just now, I'm doing penance in this damned town. My rotten imaginings have proven too much— even for me—and the doctors sent me West to recuperate,"

The artist could find no words that would answer. In silence, the two men turned away from the mountains, and started back along the avenue by which they had come.

When they had walked some little distance, the young man said, "This is your first visit to Fairlands, Mr. Lagrange?"

"I was here last year"—answered the other—"here and in the hills yonder. Have you been much in the mountains?"

"Not in California. This is my first trip to the West. I have seen something of the mountains, though, at tourist resorts—abroad."

"Which means," commented the other, "that you have never seen them at all."

Aaron King laughed. "I dare say you are right."

"And you—?" asked the novelist, abruptly, eyeing his companion. "What brought you to this community that thinks so much more of its millionaires than it does of its mountains? Have you come to Fairlands to work?"

19

"I hope to," answered the artist. "There are—there are reasons why I do not care to work, for the present, in the East. I confess it was because I understood that Fairlands offered exceptional opportunities for a portrait painter that I came here. To succeed in my work, you know, one must come in touch with people of influence. It is sometimes easier to interest them when they are away from their homes—in some place like this—where their social duties and business cares are not so pressing."

"There is no question of the material that Fairlands has to offer, Mr. King," returned the novelist, in his grim, sarcastic humor. "God! how I envy you!" he added, with a flash of earnest passion. "You are young—You are beginning your life work—You are looking forward to success—You—"

"I must succeed"—the painter interrupted impetuously—"I must."

"Succeed in what? What do you mean by success?"

"Surely, you should understand what I mean by success," the younger man retorted. "You who have gained—"

"Oh, yes; I forgot"—came the quick interruption—"I am the famous Conrad Lagrange. Of course, you, too, must succeed. You must become the famous Aaron King. But perhaps you will tell me why you must, as you call it, succeed?"

The artist hesitated before answering; then said with anxious earnestness, "I don't think I can explain Mr. Lagrange. My mother—" he paused.

The older man stopped short, and, turning, stood for a little with his face towards the mountains where San Bernardino's pyramid-like peak was thrust among the stars. When he spoke, every bit of that bitter humor was gone from his deep voice. "I beg your pardon, Mr. King"—he said slowly—"I am as ugly and misshapen in spirit as in body."

But when they had walked some way—again in silence—and were drawing near the hotel, the momentary change in his mood passed. In a tone of stinging sarcasm he said. "You are on the right road, Mr. King. You did well to come to Fairlands. It is quite evident that you have mastered the modern technic of your art. To acquire fame, you have only to paint pictures of fast women who have no morals at all—making them appear as innocent maidens, because they have the price to pay, and, in the eyes of the world, are of social importance. Put upon your canvases what the world will call portraits of distinguished citizens—making low-browed money—thugs to look like noble patriots, and bloody butchers of humanity like benevolent saints. You need give yourself no uneasiness about your success. It is easy. Get in with the right people; use your family

20

name and your distinguished ancestors; pull a few judicious advertising wires; do a few artistic stunts; get yourself into the papers long and often, no matter how; make yourself a fad; become a pet of the social autocrats—and your fame is assured. And—you will be what I am."

The young man, quietly ignoring the humor of the novelist's words, said protestingly, "But, surely, to portray human nature is legitimate art, Mr. Lagrange. Your great artists that the West is to produce will not necessarily be landscape painters or write essays upon nature, will they?"

"To portray human nature is legitimate work for an artist, yes"—agreed the novelist—"but he must portray human nature plus. The forces that shape human nature are the forces that must be felt in the picture and in the story. That these determining forces are so seldom seen by the eyes of the world, is the reason for pictures and stories. The artist who fails to realize for his world the character-creating elements in the life which he essays to paint or write, fails, to just that degree, in being an artist; or is self-branded by his work as criminally careless, a charlatan or a liar. That one who, for a price, presents a picture or a story without regard for the influence of his production upon the characters of those who receive it, commits a crime for which human law provides no adequate punishment. Being the famous Conrad Lagrange, you understand, I have the right to say this. You will probably believe it, some day—if you do not now. That is, you will believe it if you have the soul and the intelligence of an artist—if you have not—it will not matter—and you will be happy in your success."

As the novelist finished speaking, the two men arrived at the hotel steps, where they halted, with that indecision of chance acquaintances who have no plans beyond the passing moment, yet who, in mutual interest, would extend the time of their brief companionship. While they stood there, each hesitating to make the advance, a big touring car rolled up the driveway, and stopped under the full light of the veranda. Aaron King recognized the lady of the observation car platform, with her two traveling companions and the heavy-faced man who had met them at the depot. As the party greeted the novelist and he returned their salutation, the artist turned away to find again the chair, where, an hour before, the strange character who was to play so large a part in his life and work had found him. The dog, Czar, as if preferring the companionship of the artist to the company of those who were engaging his master's attention, followed the young man.

From where he sat, the painter could see the tall, uncouth figure of the famous novelist standing beside the automobile, while the occupants of the car were, apparently, absorbingly interested in what he was saying. The beautiful face of the woman was brightly animated as she evidently took the lead in the conversation. The artist could see her laughing and shaking her head. Once, he even heard her speak the writer's name; whereupon, every lounger upon the veranda, within hearing, turned to observe the party with curious interest. Several times, the young man noted that she glanced in his direction, half inquiringly, with a suggestion of being pleased, as though she were glad to have seen him in company with her celebrated friend. Then the man who held so large a place in the eyes of the world drew back, lifting his hat; the automobile started forward; the party called, "Good night." The woman's voice rose clear—so that the spectators might easily understand—"Remember, Mr. Lagrange—I shall expect you Thursday—day after to-morrow."

As Conrad Lagrange came up the hotel steps, the eyes of all were upon him; but he—apparently unconscious of the company— went straight to the artist; where, without a word, he dropped into the vacant chair by the young man's side, and began thoughtfully refilling his brier pipe. Flipping the match over the veranda railing, and expelling a prodigious cloud of smoke, the novelist said grimly, "And there—my fellow artist—go your masters. I trust you observed them with proper reverence. I would have introduced you, but I do not like to take the initiative in such outrages. That will come soon enough. The young should be permitted to enjoy their freedom while they may."

Aaron King laughed. "Thank you for your consideration," he returned, "but I do not think I am in any immediate danger."

"Which"—the other retorted dryly—"betrays either innocence, caution, or an unusual understanding of life. I am not, now, prepared to say whether you know too much or too little."

"I confess to a degree of curiosity," said the artist. "I traveled in the same Pullman with three of the party. May I ask the names of your friends?"

The other answered in his bitterest vein; "I have no friends, Mr. King—I have only admirers. As for their names"—he continued—"there is no reason why I should withhold either who they are or what they are. Besides, I observed that the reigning 'Goddess' in the realm of 'Modern Art' has her eye upon you, already. As I shall very soon be commanded to drag you to her 'Court,' it is well for you to be prepared."

The young man laughed as the other paused to puff vigorously at his brier pipe.

"That red-faced, bull-necked brute, is James Rutlidge, the son and heir of old Jim Rutlidge," continued the novelist. "Jim inherited

22

a few odd millions from his father, and killed himself spending them in unmentionable ways. The son is most worthily carrying out his father's mission, with bright prospects of exceeding his distinguished parent's fondest dreams. But, unfortunately, he is hampered by lack of adequate capital—the bulk of the family wealth having gone with the old man."

"Do you mean James Rutlidge—the great critic?" exclaimed Aaron King, with increased interest.

"The same," answered the other, with his twisted smile. "I thought you would recognize his name. As an artist, you will undoubtedly have much to do with him. His friendship is one of the things that are vital to your success. Believe me, his power in modern art is a red-faced, bull-necked power that you will do well to recognize. Of his companions," he went on, "the horrible example is Edward J. Taine—friend and fellow martyr of James Rutlidge, Senior. Satan, perhaps, can explain how he has managed to outlive his partner. His home is in New York, but he has a big house on Fairlands Heights, with large orange groves in this district. He comes here winters for his health. He'll die before long. The effervescing young creature is his daughter, Louise—by his first wife. The 'Goddess'—who is not much older than his daughter—is the present Mrs. Taine."

"His wife!"

The artist's exclamation drew a sarcastic chuckle from the other. "I am prepared, now, to testify to your unworldly innocence of heart and mind," he gibed. "And, pray, why not his wife? You see, she was the ward of old Rutlidge—a niece, it is said. Mrs. Rutlidge—as you have no doubt heard—killed herself. It was shortly after her death that Jim took this little one into his home. She and young Jim grew up together. What was more natural or fitting than that her guardian—when he was about to depart from this sad world where human flesh is not able to endure an unlimited amount of dissipation—should give the girl as a lively souvenir to his bosom friend and companion of his unmentionable deviltries? The transaction also enabled him, you understand, to draw upon the Taine millions; and so permitted him to finish his distinguished career with credit. You, with your artist's extravagant fancy, have, no doubt, been thinking of her as fashioned for love. I assure you she knows better. The world in which she has been schooled has left her no hazy ideas as to what she was made for."

"I have heard of the Taines," said the younger man, thoughtfully. "I suppose this is the same family. They are very prominent in the social world, and quite generous patrons of the arts?"

23

"In the eyes of the world," said the novelist, "they are the noblest of our Nobility. They dwell in the rarefied atmosphere of millions. By the dollarless multitudes they are envied. They assume to be the cultured of the cultured. Patrons of the arts! Why, man, they have autographed copies of all my books! They and their kind feed me and my kind. They will feed you, sir, or by God you'll starve! But you need have no fear that the crust of genius will be your portion," he added meaningly. "As I remarked—the 'Goddess' has her eye upon you."

"And why do you so distinguish the lady?" asked the artist, quietly amused—with just a hint of well-bred condescension. "Has Mrs. Taine such powerful influence in the world of art?"

If Conrad Lagrange noticed his companion's manner he passed it by. "I perceive," he said, "that you are still somewhat lacking in the rudiments of your profession. The statement of faith adhered to by modern climbers on the ladder of fame—such as I have been, and you aspire to be—is that 'Pull' wins. Our creed is 'Graft.' By 'Influence' we stand, by 'Influence' we fall. It pleases Mrs. Taine to be, in the world of art, a lobbyist. She knows the insides of the inside rings and cliques and committees that say what is, and what is not, art; that declare who shall be, and who shall not be, artists. She has power with those who, in their might, grant position and place in the halls of fame; as their kinsmen in the political world pass the plums to those who court their favor. The great critics who thunder anathemas at the poor devils who are outside, eat out of her hand. Jim Rutlidge and his unholy crew are at her beck and call. Jim, you see, needing all he can get of the Taine millions, hopes to marry Louise. You can scarcely blame the young and beautiful Mrs. Taine for not being interested in her husband— who is going to die so soon. The poor girl must have some amusement, so she interests herself in art, don't you know. She gives more dinners to artists and critics; buys more pictures and causes more pictures to be bought; mothers more art-culture clubs; discovers more new and startling geniuses; in short, has a larger and better trained company of lions than any one else in the business. She deals in lions. It's her fad to collect them—same as others collect butterflies or postage stamps. She has one other fad that is less harmful and just as deceptive—a carefully nourished reputation for prudery. I sometimes think the Gods must laugh or choke. That woman would no more speak to you without a proper introduction than she would appear on the street without shoes or stockings. She has never been seen in an evening gown. Her beautiful shoulders have never been immodestly bared to the eyes of the world."

24

The artist thought of that moment on the observation car platform.

Presently, the novelist—refilling his pipe—said whimsically, "Some day, Mr. King, I shall write a true story. It shall be a novel of to-day, with characters drawn from life; and these characters, in my story, shall bear the names of the forces that have made them what they are and which they, in turn, have come to represent. I mean those forces that are so coloring and shaping the life and thought of this age."

"That ought to be interesting," said the other, "but I am not quite sure that I understand."

"Probably you don't. You have not been thinking much of these things. You have your eye upon Fame, and that old witch lives in another direction. To illustrate—our bull-necked friend and illustrious critic, James Rutledge, in my story, will be named 'Sensual.' His distinguished father was one 'Lust.' The horrible example, Mr. Edward Taine,—boon companion of 'Lust,'—is 'Materialism'."

"Good!" laughed the artist. "I see; go on. Who is the daughter of 'Materialism?'"

"'Ragtime'," promptly returned the novelist, with a grin. "Who else could she be?"

"And Mrs. Taine?" urged the other.

The novelist responded quickly; "Why, the reigning 'Goddess' in the realm of 'Modern Art,' is 'The Age,' of course. Do you see? 'The Age' given over to 'Materialism' for base purposes by his companion, 'Lust.' And you——" he paused.

"Go on," cried the young man, "who or what am I in your story?"

"You, sir,"—answered Conrad Lagrange, seriously,—"in my story of modern life, represent Art. It remains to be seen whether 'The Age' will add you to her collection, or whether some other influence will intervene."

"And you"—persisted the artist—"surely you are in the story."

"I am very much in the story," the other answered. "My name is 'Civilization.' My story will be published when I am dead. I have a reputation to sustain, you know."

Aaron King was not laughing, now. Something, that lay deep hidden beneath the rude exterior of the man, made itself felt in his deep voice. Some powerful force, underlying his whimsical words, gripped the artist's mind—compelling him to search for hidden meanings in the novelist's fanciful suggestions.

A few moments passed in silence before the young man said

slowly, "I met a character, yesterday, Mr. Lagrange, that might be added to your cast."

"There are several that will be added to my cast," the other answered dryly.

To which the painter returned, "Did you notice that woman with the disfigured face, at the depot?"

Conrad Lagrange looked at his companion, quickly. "Yes."

"Do you know her?" questioned the artist.

"No. Why do you ask?"

"Only because she interested me, and because she seemed to know your friends—Mr. Rutlidge and Mrs. Taine."

The novelist knocked the ashes from his pipe by tapping it on the veranda railing. The action seemed to express a peculiar mental effort; as though he were striving to recall something that had gone from his memory. "I saw what happened at the depot, of course," he said slowly. "I have seen the woman before. She lives here in Fairlands. Her name is Miss Willard. No one seems to know much about her. I can't get over the impression that I ought to know her— that I have met and known her somewhere years ago. Her manner, yesterday, at seeing Mrs. Taine, was certainly very strange." As if to free his mind from the unsuccessful effort to remember, he rose to his feet. "But why should she be added to the characters in my novel, Mr. King? What does she represent?"

"Her name,"—said the artist,—"in your study of life, is suggested by her face—so beautiful on the one side—so distorted on the other—her name should be 'Symbol'."

"There really is hope for you," returned the older man, with his quizzing smile. "Good night. Come, Czar." He passed into the hotel—the dog at his heels.

It was two days later—Thursday—that Conrad Lagrange made his memorable visit to the Taines—memorable, in my story, because, at that time, Mrs. Taine gave such unmistakable evidence of her interest in Aaron King and his future.

Chapter IV
At the House on Fairlands Heights

As my friend the social scientist would say; it is a phenomenon peculiar to urban life, that the social strata are more or less clearly defined geographically.

That is,—in the English of everyday,—people of different classes live in different parts of the city. As certain streets and blocks are given to the wholesale establishments, others to retail stores, and still others to the manufacturing plants; so there are the tenement districts, the slums, and the streets where may be found the homes of wealth and fashion.

In Fairlands, the social rating is largely marked by altitude. The city, lying in the lap of the hills and looking a little down upon the valley—plebeian business together with those who do the work of Fairlands occupies the lowest levels in the corporate limits. The heights are held by Fairlands' Pride. Between these two extremes, the Fairlanders are graded fairly by the levels they occupy. It is most gratifying to observe how generally the citizens of this fortunate community aspire to higher things; and to note that the peculiarly proud spirit of this people is undoubtedly explained by this happy arrangement which enables every one to look down upon his neighbor.

The view from the winter home of the Taines was magnificent.

From the window of the room where Mrs. Taine sat, that afternoon, one could have looked down upon all Fairlands. One might, indeed, have done better than that. Looking over the wealth of semi-tropical foliage that—save for the tower of the red-brick Y.M.C.A. building, the white, municipal flagstaff, and the steeples and belfries of the churches—hid the city, one might have looked up at the mountains. High, high, above the low levels occupied by the hill-climbing Fairlanders, the mountains lift their heads in solemn dignity; looking down upon the loftiest Fairlander of them all—looking down upon even the Taines themselves.

But the glory of Mrs. Taine's God was not declared by the mountains. She sat by the window, indeed, but her eyes were upon the open pages of a book—a popular novel that by some strange legal lapse of the governmental conscience was—and is still—permitted in print.

27

The author of the story that so engrossed Mrs. Taine was—in her opinion—almost as great in literature as Conrad Lagrange, himself. By those in authority who pronounce upon the worthiness or the unworthiness of writer folk, he is, to-day, said to be one of the greatest writers of his generation. He is a realist—a modern of the moderns. His pen has never been debased by an inartistic and antiquated idealism. His claim to genius rests securely upon the fact that he has no ideals. He writes for that select circle of leaders who, like the Taines and the Rutlidges, are capable of appreciating his art. All of which means that he tells filthy stories in good English. That his stories are identical in material and motive with the vile yarns that are permitted only in the lowest class barber shops and in disreputable bar-rooms, in no way detracts from the admiring praise of his critics, the generosity of his publishers, or the appreciation of those for whom he writes.

With tottering step and feeble, shaking limbs, Edward Taine entered the apartment. As he stood, silently looking at his young wife, his glazed, red-rimmed eyes fed upon her voluptuous beauty with a look of sullen, impotent lustfulness that was near insanity. A spasm of coughing seized him; he gasped and choked, his wasted body shaken and racked, his dissipated face hideously distorted by the violence of the paroxysm. Wrecked by the flesh he had lived to gratify, he was now the mocked and tortured slave of the very devils of unholy passion that he had so often invoked to serve him. Repulsive as he was, he was an object to awaken the deepest pity.

Mrs. Taine, looking up from her novel, watched him curiously—without moving or changing her attitude of luxurious repose—without speaking. Almost, one would have said, a shade of a smile was upon her too perfect features.

When the man—who had dropped weak and exhausted into a chair—could speak, he glared at her in a pitiful rage, and, in his throaty whisper, said with a curse, "You seem to be amused."

Still, she did not speak. A tantalizing smile broke over her face, and she stretched her beautiful body lazily in her chair, as a well-conditioned animal stirs in sleek, physical contentment.

Again, with curses, he said, "I'm glad you so enjoy my company. To be laughed at, even, is better than your damned indifference."

"You misjudge me," she answered in a voice that, low and soft, was still richly colored by the wealth of vitality that found expression in her splendid body. "I am not at all indifferent to your condition—quite the contrary. I am intensely interested. As for the

28

amusement you afford me—please consider—for three years I have amused you. Can you deny me my turn?"

He laughed with a hideously mirthless chuckle as he returned with ghastly humor, "I have had the worth of my money. I advise you to make the most of your opportunity. I shall make things as pleasant for you as I can, while I am with you, but, as you know, I am liable to leave you at any time, now."

"Pray don't hurry away," she replied sweetly. "I shall miss you so when you are gone."

He glared at her while she laughed mockingly.

"Where is everybody?" he asked. "The place is as lonely as a tomb."

"Louise is out riding with Jim."

"And what are you doing at home?" he demanded suspiciously.

"Me? Oh I remained to care for you—to keep you from being lonely."

"You lie. You are expecting some one."

She laughed.

"Who is it this time?" he persisted.

"Your insinuations are so unwarranted," she murmured.

"Whom are you expecting?"

"Dear me! how persistently you look for evil," she mocked. "You know perfectly well that, thanks to my tact, I am considered quite the model wife. You really should cultivate a more trusting disposition."

Another fit of coughing seized him, and while he suffered she again watched him with that curious air of interest. When he could command his voice, he gasped in a choking whisper, "You fiend! I know, and you know that I know. Am I so innocent that Jack Hanover, and Charlie Rodgers, and Black Whitman, and as many more of their kind, can make love to you under my very nose without my knowing it? You take damned good care—posing as a prude with your fad about immodest dress—that the world sees nothing; but you have never troubled to hide it from me."

Deliberately, she arose and stood before him. "And why should I trouble to hide anything from you?" she demanded. "Look at me"—she posed as if to exhibit for his critical inspection the charm of her physical beauty—"Look at me; am I to waste all this upon you? You tell me that you have had your money's worth—surely, the purchase price is mine to spend as I will. Even suppose that I were as evil as your foul mind sees me, what right have you to object? Are you so chaste that you dare cast a stone at me? Am I to

29

have no pleasure in this hell you have made for me but the horrible pleasure of watching you in the hell you have made for yourself? Be satisfied that the world does not see your shame—though it's from no consideration of you, but wholly for myself, that I am careful. As for my modesty—you know it is not a fad but a necessity."

"That is just it"—he retorted—"it is the way you make a fad of a necessity! Forced to hide your shoulders, you make a virtue of concealment. You make capital of the very thing of which you are ashamed."

"And is not that exactly what we all do?" she asked with brutal cynicism. "Do you not fear the eyes of the world as much as I? Be satisfied that I play the game of respectability with you—that I give the world no cause for talk. You may as well be," she finished with devilish frankness, "for you are past helping yourself in the matter."

As she finished, a servant appeared to announce Mr. Conrad Lagrange; and the tall, uncouth figure of the novelist stood framed in the doorway; his sharp eyes regarding them with that peculiar, quizzing, baffling look.

Edward Taine laughed with that horrid chuckle. "Howdy-do, Lagrange—glad to see you."

Mrs. Taine went forward to greet the caller; saying as she gave him her hand, "You arrived just in time, Mr. Lagrange; Edward and I were discussing your latest book. We think it a masterpiece of realistic fiction. I'm sure it will add immensely to your fame. I hear it talked of everywhere as the most popular novel of the year. You wonderful man! How do you do it?"

"I don't do it," answered Conrad Lagrange, looking straight into her eyes. "It does itself. My books are really true products of the age that reads them; and—to paraphrase a statesman who was himself a product of his age—for those who read my books they are just the kind of books that I would expect such people to read."

Mrs. Taine looked at him with a curious, half-doubtful half-wistful expression; as though she glimpsed a hint of a meaning that did not appear upon the surface of his words. "You do say such—such—twisty things," she murmured. "I don't think I always understand what you mean; but when you look at me that way, I feel as though my maid had neglected to finish hooking me up."

The novelist bowed in mock gallantry—a movement which made his ungainly form appear more grotesque than ever. "Indeed, madam, to my humble eyes, you are most beautifully and fittingly—ah—hooked up." He turned toward the invalid. "And how is the fortunate husband of the charming Mrs. Taine to-day?"

"Fine, Lagrange, fine," said the man—a cough interrupting his

30

words. "Really, I think that Gertrude is unduly alarmed about my condition. In this glorious climate, I feel like a three-year-old."

"You are looking quite like yourself," returned the novelist.

"There's nothing at all the matter with me but a slight bronchial trouble," continued the other, coughing again. Then, to his wife—"Dearest, won't you ring, please; I'm sure it's time for my toddy; perhaps Mr. Lagrange will join me in a drink. What'll it be, Lagrange?"

"Nothing, thanks, at this hour."

"No? But you'll pardon me, I'm sure—Doctor's orders you know."

A servant appeared. Mrs. Taine took the glass and carried it to her husband with her own hand, saying with tender solicitude, "Don't you think, dear, that you should lie down for a while? Mr. Lagrange will remain for dinner, you know. You must not tire yourself. I'm sure he will excuse you. I'll manage somehow to amuse him until Jim and Louise return."

"I believe I will rest a little, Gertrude." He turned to the guest—"While there is nothing really wrong, you know, Lagrange, still it's best to be on the safe side."

"By all means," said the novelist, heartily. "You should take care of yourself. Don't, I beg, permit me to detain you."

Mrs. Taine, with careful tenderness, accompanied her husband to the door. When he had passed from the room, she faced the novelist, with—"Don't you think Edward is really very much worse, Mr. Lagrange? I keep up appearances, you know, but—" she paused with a charming air of perplexed and worried anxiety.

"Your husband is certainly not a well man, madam—but you keep up appearances wonderfully. I really don't see how you manage it. But I suppose that for one of your nature it is natural."

Again, she received his words with that look of doubtful understanding—as though sensing some meaning beneath the polite, commonplace surface. Then, as if to lead away from the subject—"You must really tell me what you think of our California home. I told you in New York, you remember, that I should ask you, the first thing. We were so sorry to have missed you last year. Please be frank. Isn't it beautiful?"

"Very beautiful"—he answered—"exquisite taste—perfect harmony with modern art." His quizzing eyes twinkled, and a caricature of a smile distorted his face. "It fairly smells to heaven of the flesh pots."

She laughed merrily. "The odor should not be unfamiliar to you," she retorted. "By all accounts, your royalties are making you

31

immensely rich. How wonderful it must be to be famous—to know that the whole world is talking about you! And that reminds me—who is your distinguished looking friend at the hotel? I was dying to ask you, the other night, but didn't dare. I know he is somebody famous."

Conrad Lagrange, studying her face, answered reluctantly, "No, he is not famous; but I fear he is going to be."

"Another twisty saying," she retorted. "But I mean to have an answer, so you may as well speak plainly. Have you known him long? What is his name? And what is he—a writer?"

"His name is Aaron King. His mother and I grew up in the same neighborhood. He is an artist."

"How romantic! Do you mean that he belongs to that old family of New England Kings?"

"He is the last of them. His father was Aaron King—a prominent lawyer and politician in his state."

"Oh, yes! I remember! Wasn't there something whispered at the time of his death—some scandal that was hushed up—money stolen—or something? What was it? I can't think."

"Whatever it was, Mrs. Taine, the son had nothing to do with it. Don't you think we might let the dead man stay safely buried?" There was an ominous glint in Conrad Lagrange's eyes.

Mrs. Taine answered hurriedly, "Indeed, yes, Mr. Lagrange. You are right. And you shall bring Mr. King out to see me. If he is as nice as he looks, I promise you I will be very good to him. Perhaps I may even help him a little, through Jim, you know—bring him in touch with the right people and that sort of thing. What does he paint?"

"Portraits." The novelist's tone was curt.

"Then I am sure I could do a great deal for him."

"And I am sure you would do a great deal to him," said Conrad Lagrange, bluntly.

She laughed again. "And just what do you mean by that, Mr. Lagrange? I'm not sure whether it is complimentary or otherwise."

"That depends upon what you consider complimentary," retorted the other. "As I told you—Aaron King is an artist."

Again, she favored him with that look of doubtful understanding; shaking her head with mock sadness, and making a long sigh. "Another twister"—she said woefully—"just when we were getting along so beautifully, too. Won't you try again?"

"In words of one syllable then—let him alone. He is, to-day, exactly where I was twenty years ago. For God's sake, let him alone. Play your game with those who are no loss to the world; or with those who, like me, are already lost. Let this man do his work. Don't make him what I am."

"Oh dear, oh dear," she laughed, "and these are words of one syllable! You talk as though I were a dreadful dragon seeking a genius to devour!"

"You are," said the novelist, gruffly.

"How nice. I'm all shivery with delight, already. You really must bring him now, you see. You might as well, for, if you don't, I'll manage some other way when you are not around to protect him. You don't want to trust him to me unprotected, do you?"

"No, and I won't," retorted Conrad Lagrange—which, though Mrs. Taine did not remark it, was also a twister.

"But after all, perhaps he won't come," she said with mock anxiety.

"Don't worry madam—he's just as much a fool as the rest of us."

As the novelist spoke, they heard the voices of Miss Taine and her escort, James Rutlidge. Mrs. Taine had only time to shake a finger in playful warning at her companion, and to whisper, "Mind you bring your artist to me, or I'll get him when you're not looking; and listen, don't tell Jim about him; I must see what he is like, first."

At lunch, the next day, Conrad Lagrange greeted the artist in his bitterest humor. "And how is the famous Aaron King, to-day? I trust that the greatest portrait painter of the age is well; that the hotel people have been properly attentive to the comfort of their illustrious guest? The world of art can ill afford to have its rarest genius suffer from any lack of the service that is due his greatness."

The young man's face flushed at his companion's mocking tone; but he laughed. "I missed you at breakfast."

"I was sleeping off the effect of my intellectual debauch—it takes time to recover from a dinner with 'Materialism,' 'Sensual,' 'Ragtime' and 'The Age'," the other returned, the menu in his hand. "What slop are they offering to put in our troughs for this noon's feed?"

Again, Aaron King laughed. But as the novelist, with characteristic comments and instructions to the waitress, ordered his lunch, the artist watched him as though waiting with interest his further remarks on the subject of his evening with the Taines.

When the girl was gone, Conrad Lagrange turned again to his companion, and from under his scowling brows regarded him much as a withered scientist might regard an interesting insect under his glass. "Permit me to congratulate you," he said suggestively—as though the bug had succeeded in acting in some manner fully expected by the scientist but wholly disgusting to him.

The artist colored again as he returned curiously, "Upon what?"

"Upon the start you have made toward the goal you hope to reach."

"What do you mean?"

"Mrs. Taine wants you."

"You are pleased to be facetious." Under the eyes of his companion, Aaron King felt that his reply did not at all conceal his satisfaction.

"I am pleased to be exact. I repeat—Mrs. Taine wants you. I am ordered by the reigning 'Goddess' of 'Modern Art'—'The Age'—to bring you into her 'Court.' You have won favor in her sight. She finds you good to look at. She hopes to find you—as good as you look. If you do not disappoint her, your fame is assured."

"Nonsense," said the artist, somewhat sharply; nettled by the obvious meaning and by the sneering sarcasm of the novelist's words and tone.

To which the other returned suggestively, "It is precisely because you can say, 'nonsense,' when you know it is no nonsense at all, but the exact truth, that your chance for fame is so good, my friend."

"And did some reigning 'Goddess' insure your success and fame?"

The older man turned his peculiar, penetrating, baffling eyes full upon his companion's face, and in a voice full of cynical sadness answered, "Exactly so. I paid court to the powers that be. They gave me the reward I sought; and—they made me what I am."

So it came about that Conrad Lagrange, in due time, introduced Aaron King to the house on Fairlands Heights. Or,—as the novelist put it,—he, "Civilization",—in obedience to the commands of her "Royal Highness", "The Age",—presented the artist at her "Majesty's Court"; that the young man might sue for the royal favor.

It was, perhaps, a month after the presentation ceremony, that the painter made what—to him, at least—was an important announcement.

Chapter V
The Mystery of the Rose Garden

The acquaintance of Aaron King and Conrad Lagrange had developed rapidly into friendship.

The man whom the world had chosen to place upon one of the highest pinnacles of its literary favor, and who—through some queer twist in his nature—was so lonely and embittered by his exaltation, seemed to find in the younger man who stood with the crowd at the foot of the ladder, something that marked him as different from his fellows.

Whether it was the artist's mother; some sacredly hidden memories of Lagrange's past; or, perhaps, some fancied recognition of the artist's genius and its possibilities; the strange man gave no hint; but he constantly sought the company of Aaron King, with an openness that made his preference for the painter's society very evident. If he had said anything about it, at all, Conrad Lagrange, likely, would have accounted for his interest, upon the ground that his dog, Czar, found the companionship agreeable. Their friendship, meanwhile—in the eyes of the world—conferred a peculiar distinction upon the young man—a distinction not at all displeasing to the ambitious artist; and the value of which he, probably, overrated.

To Aaron King—aside from the subtle flattery of the famous novelist's attention—there was in the personality of the odd character a something that appealed to him with peculiar strength. Perhaps it was that the man's words, so often sharp and stinging with bitter sarcasm, seemed always to carry a hidden meaning that gave, as it were, glimpses of another nature buried deeply beneath a wreck of ruined dreams and disappointing achievements. Or, it may have been that, under all the cruel, world-hardness of the thoughts expressed, the young man sensed an undertone of pathetic sadness. Or, again, perhaps, it was those rare moments, when—on some walk that carried them beyond the outskirts of the town, and brought the mountains into unobstructed view—the clouds of bitterness were lifted; and the man spoke with poetic feeling of the realities of life, and of the true glory and mission of the arts; counseling his friend with an intelligence as true and delicate as it was rare and fine.

It was nearly two months after Conrad Lagrange had introduced the young man at the house on Fairlands Heights. The hour was late. The painter—returning from a dinner and an evening at the Taine home—found the novelist, with pipe and dog, in a deserted corner of the hotel veranda. Dropping into the chair that was placed as if it awaited his coming, the artist—with no word of greeting to the man—bent over the brown head that was thrust so insistently against his knee, as Czar, with gently waving tail, made him welcome. Looking affectionately into the brown eyes while he stroked the silky coat, the young man answered in the language that all dogs understand; while the novelist, from under his scowling brows, regarded the two intently.

"They were disappointed that you were not there," said the painter, presently. "Mrs. Taine, particularly, charged me to say that she will not forgive, until you do proper penance for your sin."

"I had better company," retorted the other. "Czar and I went for a look at the mountains. I suppose you have noticed that Czar does not care for the Fairlands Heights crowd. He is very peculiar in his friendships—for a dog. His instincts are remarkable."

At the sound of his name, Czar transferred his attentions, for a moment, to his master; then stretched himself in his accustomed place beside the novelist's chair.

The artist laughed. "I did my best to invent an acceptable excuse for you; but she said it was no use—nothing short of your own personal prayers for mercy would do."

"Humph; you should have reminded her that I purchased an indulgence some weeks ago."

Again, the other laughed shortly. Watching him closely, Conrad Lagrange said, in his most sneering tones, "I trust, young man, that you are not failing to make good use of your opportunities. Let's see—dinner and the evening five times—afternoon calls as many—with motor trips to points of interest—and one theater party to Los Angeles—believe me; it is not often that struggling genius is so rewarded—before it has accomplished anything bad enough to merit such attention."

"I have been idling most shamefully, haven't I?" said the artist.

"Idling!" rasped the other. "You have been the busiest hay-maker in the land. These scientific, intensive cultivation farmers of California are not in your class when it comes to utilizing the sunshine. Take my advice and continue your present activity without bothering yourself by any sentimental thoughts of your palette and brushes. The mere vulgar tools of your craft are of minor importance to one of your genius and opportunity."

Then, in a half embarrassed manner, Aaron King made his

announcement. "That may all be," he said, "but just the same, I am going to work."

"I knew it"—returned the other, in mocking triumph—"I knew it the moment you came up the steps there. I could tell it by your walk; by the air with which you carried yourself; by your manner, your voice, your laugh—you fairly reek of prosperity and achievement—you are going to paint her portrait."

"And why not?" retorted the young man, rather sharply, a trifle nettled by the other's tone.

"Why not, indeed!" murmured the novelist. "Indeed, yes—by all means! It is so exactly the right thing to do that it is startling. You scale the heights of fame with such confident certainty in every move that it is positively uncanny to watch you."

"If one's work is true, I fail to see why one should not take advantage of any influence that can contribute to his success," said the painter. "I assure you I am not so wealthy that I can afford to refuse such an attractive commission. You must admit that the beautiful Mrs. Taine is a subject worthy the brush of any artist; and I suppose it is conceivable that I might be ambitious to make a genuinely good job of it."

The older man, as though touched by the evident sincerity of the artist's words, dropped his sneering tone and spoke earnestly; "The beautiful Mrs. Taine is a subject worthy a master's brush, my friend. But take my word for it, if you paint her portrait as a master would paint it, you will sign your own death warrant—so far as your popularity and fame as an artist goes."

"I don't believe it," declared Aaron King, flatly.

"I know you don't. If you did, and still accepted the commission, you wouldn't be fit to associate with honest dogs like Czar, here."

"But why"—persisted the artist—"why do you insist that my portrait of Mrs. Taine will be disastrous to my success, just to the degree that it is a work of genuine merit?"

To which the novelist answered, cryptically, "If you have not the eyes to see the reason, it will matter little whether you know it or not. If you do see the reason, and, still, produce a portrait that pleases your sitter, then you will have paid the price; you will receive your reward; and"—the speaker's tone grew sad and bitter—"you will be what I am."

With this, he arose abruptly and, without another word, stalked into the hotel; the dog following with quiet dignity, at his heels.

From the beginning of their acquaintance, almost, the novelist and the artist had dropped into the habit of taking their meals together. At breakfast, the next morning, Conrad Lagrange reopened the conversation he had so abruptly closed the night before. "I suppose," he said, "that you will set up a studio, and do the thing in proper style?"

"Mrs. Taine told me of a place that is for rent, and that she thinks would be just the thing," returned the young man. "It is across the road from that big grove owned by Mr. Taine. I was wondering if you would care to walk out that way with me this morning and help me look it over."

The older man's hearty acceptance of the invitation assured the artist of his genuine interest, and, an hour later—after Aaron King had interviewed the agent and secured the keys, with the privilege of inspecting the premises—the two set out together.

They found the place on the eastern edge of the town; half-hidden by the orange groves that surrounded it on every side. The height of the palms that grew along the road in front, the pepper and eucalyptus trees that overshadowed the house, and the size of the orange-trees that shut in the little yard with walls of green, marked the place as having been established before the wealth of the far-away East discovered the peculiar charm of the Fairlands hills. The lawn, the walks, and the drive were unkempt and overgrown with weeds. The house itself,—a small cottage with a wide porch across the front and on the side to the west,—unpainted for many seasons, was tinted by the brush of the elements, a soft and restful gray.

But the artist and his friend, as they approached, exclaimed aloud at the beauty of the scene; for, as if rejoicing in their freedom from restraint, the roses had claimed the dwelling, so neglected by man, as their own. Up every post of the porch they had climbed; over the porch roof, they spread their wealth of color; over the gables, screening the windows with graceful lattice of vine and branch and leaf and bloom; up to the ridge and over the cornice, to the roof of the house itself—even to the top of the chimney they had won their way—and there, as if in an ecstasy of wanton loveliness, flung, a spray of glorious, perfumed beauty high into the air.

On the front porch, the men turned to look away over the gentle slope of the orange groves, on the other side of the road, to the towering peaks and high ridges of the mountains—gleaming cold and white in the winter of their altitude. To the northeast, San Bernardino reared his head in lonely majesty—looking directly down upon the foothills and the feeble dwellers in the valley below. Far beyond, and surrounded by the higher ridges and peaks and canyons of the range, San Gorgonio sat enthroned in the skies—the ruler of them all. From the northeast, westward, they viewed the mighty sweep of the main range to Cajon Pass and the San Gabriels, beyond, with San Antonio, Cucamonga, and their sister peaks lifting their heads above their fellows. In the immediate landscape, no house or building was to be seen. The dark-green mass of the orange groves hid every work of man's building between them and the tawny foothills save the gable and chimney of a neighboring cottage on the west.

"Listen"—said Conrad Lagrange, in a low tone, moved as always by the grandeur and beauty of the scene—"listen! Don't you hear them calling? Don't you feel the mountains sending their message to these poor insects who squirm and wriggle in this bit of muck men call their world? God, man! if only we, in our work, would heed the message of the hills!"

The novelist spoke with such intensity of feeling—with such bitter sadness and regret in his voice—that Aaron King could not reply.

Turning, the artist unlocked the door, and they entered the cottage.

They found the interior of the house well arranged, and not in bad repair. "Just the thing for a bachelor's housekeeping"—was the painter's verdict—"but for a studio—impossible," and there was a touch of regret in his voice.

"Let's continue our exploration," said the novelist, hopefully. "There's a barn out there." And they went out of the house, and down the drive on the eastern side of the yard.

Here, again, they saw the roses in full possession of the place—by man, deserted. From foundation to roof, the building—a small simple structure—was almost hidden under a mass of vines. There was one large room below; with a loft above. The stable was in the rear. Built, evidently, at a later date than the house, the building was in better repair. The walls, so hidden without by the roses, were well sided; the floors were well laid. The big, sliding, main door opened on the drive in front; between it and the corner, to the west, was a small door; and in the western end, a window.

Looking curiously from this window, Conrad Lagrange uttered an exclamation, and hurried abruptly from the building. The artist followed.

From the end of the barn, and extending, the full width of the building, to the west line of the yard, was a rose garden—such a garden as Aaron King had never seen. On three sides, the little plot was enclosed by a tall hedge of Ragged Robins; above the hedge, on the south and west, was the dark-green wall of the orange grove; on the north, the pepper and eucalyptus trees in the yard, and a view of the distant mountains; and on the east, the vine-hidden end of the

39

barn. Against the southern wall,—and, so, directly opposite the trellised, vine-covered arch of the entrance,—a small, lattice bower, with a rustic table and seats within, was completely covered, as was the barn, by the magically woven tapestry of the flowers. In the corner of the hedge farthest from the entrance they found a narrow gate. Unlike the rest of the premises, the garden was in perfect order—the roses trimmed and cared for; the walks neatly edged and clean; with no weed or sign of untidiness or neglect anywhere.

The two men had come upon the spot so suddenly—so unexpectedly—the contrast with the neglected grounds and buildings was so marked—that they looked at each other in silence. The little retreat—so lovely, so hidden by its own beauty from the world, so cared for by careful hands—seemed haunted by an invisible spirit. Very quietly,—almost reverently,—they moved about; talking in low tones, as though half expecting—they knew not what.

"Some one loves this place," said the novelist, softly, when they stood, again, in the entrance.

And the artist answered in the same hushed voice, "I wonder what it means?"

When they were again in the barn, Aaron King became eagerly enthusiastic over the possibilities of the big room. "Some rightly toned burlap on the walls and ceiling,"—he pointed out,—"with floor covering and rugs in harmony; there"—rolling back the big door as he spoke—"your north light; some hangings and screens to hide the stairway to the loft, and the stable door; your entrance over here in the corner, nicely out of the way; and the window looking into the garden—it's great man, great!"

"And," answered Conrad Lagrange, from where he stood in the big front door, "the mountains! Don't forget the mountains. The soft, steady, north light on your canvas, and a message from the mountains to your soul, through the same window, should make it a good place to work, Mr. Painter-man. I suppose over here"—he moved away from the window, and spoke in his mocking way—"over here, you will have a tea-table for the ladies of the circle elect—who will come to, 'oh', and, 'ah', their admiration of the newly discovered genius, and to chatter their misunderstandings of his art. Of course, there will be a page in velvet and gold. By all means, get hold of an oriental kid of some kind—oriental junk is quite the rage this year. You should take advantage of every influence that can contribute to your success, you know. And, whatever you do, don't fail to consult the 'Goddess' about these essentials of your craft. Many a promising genius has been lost to fame, through inviting the wrong people to take tea in his studio. But"—he finished whimsically, looking from

40

the window into the garden—"but what the devil do you suppose the spirit who lives out there will think about it all."

The days of the two following weeks were busy days for Aaron King. He leased the place in the orange groves, and set men to work making it habitable. The lawn and grounds were trimmed and put in order; the interior of the house was renovated by painter and paper-hanger; and the barn, under the artist's direction, was transformed into an ideal studio. There was a trip to Los Angeles—quite fortunately upon a day when Mrs. Taine must go to the city shopping—for rugs and hangings; and another trip to purchase the tools of the artist's craft. And, at last, there was a Chinese cook and housekeeper to find; with supplies for his kitchen. It was at Conrad Lagrange's suggestion, that, from the first, every one was given strict orders to keep out of the rose garden.

Every day, the novelist—accompanied, always, by Czar—walked out that way to see how things were progressing; and often,—if he had not been too busy to notice,—Aaron King might have seen a look of wistfulness in the keen, baffling eyes of the famous man—so world-weary and sad. And, while he did not cease to mock and jeer and offer sarcastic advice to his younger friend, the touch of pathos—that, like a minor chord, was so often heard in his most caustic and cruel speeches—was more pronounced. As for Czar—he always returned to the hotel with evident reluctance; and managed to express, in his dog way, the thoughts his distinguished master would not put in words.

Very often, too, the big touring car from the house on Fairlands Heights stopped in front of the cottage, while the occupants inspected the premises, and—with many exclamations of flattering praise, and a few suggestions—made manifest their interest.

In time, it was finished and ready—from the big easel by the great, north window in the studio, to the white-jacketed Yee Kee in the kitchen. When the last workman was gone with his tools; and the two men, after looking about the place for an hour, were standing on the front porch; Conrad Lagrange said, "And the stage is set. The scene shifters are off. The audience is waiting. Ring up the curtain for the next act. Even Czar has looked upon everything and calls it good—heh Czar?"

The dog went to him; and, for some minutes, the novelist looked down into the brown eyes of his four-footed companion who seemed so to understand. Still fondling the dog,—without looking at the artist,—the older man continued, "You will have your things moved over in the morning, I suppose? Or, will we lunch together, once more?"

41

Aaron King laughed—as a boy who has prepared a surprise, and has been struggling manfully to keep the secret until the proper moment should arrive. Placing his hand on the older man's shoulder, he answered meaningly, "I had planned that we would move in the morning." At the other's puzzled expression he laughed again.

"We?" said the novelist, facing his friend, quickly.

"Come here," returned the other. "I must show you something you haven't seen."

He led the way to a room that they had decided he would not need, and the door of which was locked. Taking a key from his pocket, he handed it to his friend.

"What's this?" said the older man, looking foolishly at the key in his hand.

"It's the key to that door," returned the other, with a gleeful chuckle. Then—"Unlock it."

"Unlock it?"

"Sure—that's what I gave you the key for."

Conrad Lagrange obeyed. Through the open door, he saw, not the bare and empty room he supposed was there, but a bedroom—charmingly furnished, complete in every detail. Turning, he faced his companion silently, inquiringly—with a look that Aaron King had never before seen in those strange, baffling eyes.

"It's yours"—said the artist, hastily—"if you care to come. You'll have a free hand here, you know; for I will be in the studio much of the time. Kee will cook the things you like. You and Czar can come and go as you will. There is the arbor in the rose garden, you know, and see here"—he stepped to the window—"I chose this room for you, because it looks out upon your mountains."

The strange man stood at the window for, what seemed to the artist, a long time. Suddenly, he turned to say sharply, "Young man, why did you do this?"

"Why"—stammered the other, disconcerted—"because I want you—because I thought you would like to come. I beg your pardon—if I have made a mistake—but surely, no harm has been done."

"And you think you could stand living with me—for any length of time?"

The' painter laughed with relief. "Oh, that's it! I didn't know you had such a tender conscience. You scared me for a minute, I should think you would know by this time that you can't phase me with your wicked tongue."

The novelist's face twisted into a grotesque smile. "I warn you—I will flay you and your friends just the same. You need it for the good of your soul."

42

"As often and as hard as you like"—returned the other, heartily—"just so it's for the good of my soul. You will come?"

"You will permit me to stand my share of the expense?"

"Anything you like—if you will only come."

The older man said gently,—for the first time calling the artist by his given name,—"Aaron, I believe that you are the only person in the world who would, really want me; and I know that you are the only person in the world to whom I would be grateful for such an invitation."

The artist was about to reply, when the big automobile stopped in front of the house. Czar, on the porch, gave a low growl of disapproval; and, through the open door, they saw Mr. Taine and his wife with James Rutlidge and Louise.

The novelist said something, under his breath, that had a vicious sound—quite unlike his words of the moment before. Czar, in disgust, retreated to the shelter of Yee Kee's domain. With a laugh, the younger man went out to meet his friends.

"Are you at home this afternoon, Sir Artist?" called Mrs. Taine, gaily, as he went down the walk.

"I will always be at home to the right people," he answered, greeting the other members of the party.

As they moved toward the house,—Mr. Taine choking and coughing, his daughter chattering and exclaiming, and James Rutlidge critically observing,—Mrs. Taine dropped a little back to Aaron King's side. "And are you really established, at last?" she asked eagerly; with a charming, confidential air.

"We move to-morrow morning," he answered.

"We?" she questioned.

"Conrad Lagrange and I. He is going to live with me, you know."

"Oh!"

It is remarkable how much meaning a woman can crowd into that one small syllable; particularly, when she draws a little away from you as she speaks it.

"Why," he murmured apologetically, "don't you approve?"

Mrs. Taine's beautiful eyebrows went up inquiringly—"And why should I either approve or disapprove?"

The young man was saved by the arrival of his guests at the porch steps, and by the appearance of Conrad Lagrange, in the doorway.

"How delightful!" exclaimed Mrs. Taine, heartily; as she, in turn, greeted the famous novelist. "Mr. King was just telling me that you were going to share this dear little place with him. I quite envy you both."

43

The others had passed into the house.

"You are sometimes guilty of saying twisty things yourself, aren't you?" returned the man; and, as he spoke, his remarkable eyes were fixed upon her as though reading her innermost thoughts.

She flushed under his meaning gaze, but carried it off gaily with—"Oh dear! I wonder if my maid has hooked me up properly, this time?"

They left Mr. Taine in an easy chair, with a bottle of his favorite whisky; and went over the place—from the arbor in the rose garden to Yee Kee's pantry—Mr. Rutlidge, critically and authoritatively approving; Louise, effervescing the same sugary nothings at every step; Mrs. Taine, with a pretty air of proprietorship; Conrad Lagrange, thoughtfully watching; and Aaron King, himself, irresponsibly gay and boyishly proud as he exhibited his achievements.

In the studio, Mrs. Taine—standing before the big easel—demanded to know of the artist, when he would begin her portrait—she was so interested, so eager to begin—how soon could she come? Louise assumed a worshipful attitude, and, gazing at the young man with reverent eyes, waited breathlessly. James Rutlidge drew near, condescendingly attentive, to the center of attraction. Conrad Lagrange turned his back.

"Really," murmured the painter, "I hope you will not be too impatient, Mrs. Taine, I fear I cannot be ready for some time yet. I suppose I must confess to being over-sensitive to my environment; for it is a fact that my working mood does not come upon me readily amid strange surroundings. When I have become acclimated, as it were, I will be ready for you."

"How wonderful!" breathed Louise.

"Quite right," agreed Mr. Rutlidge.

"Whenever you are ready," said Mrs. Taine, submissively.

When their friends from the Heights were gone, Conrad Lagrange looked the artist up and down, as he said with cutting sarcasm, "You did that very nicely. Over-sensitive to your environment, hell! If you are a bit fine strung, you have no business to make a show of it. It's a weakness, not a virtue. And the man who makes capital out of any man's weakness,—even of his own,—is either a criminal or a fool or both."

Then they went back to the hotel for dinner.

The next morning, the artist and the novelist moved from the hotel, to establish themselves in the little house in the orange groves—the little house with its unobstructed view of the mountains, and with its rose garden, so mysteriously tended.

Chapter VI
An Unknown Friend

When Yee Kee announced lunch, the artist, the novelist, and the dog were settled in their new home. In the afternoon, the painter spent an hour or two fussing over portfolios of old sketches, in his studio; while Conrad Lagrange and Czar lounged on the front porch.

Once, the dog rose quietly, and, walking sedately to the edge of the porch toward the west, stood for some minutes gazing intently into the dark green mass of the orange grave. At last, as if concluding that whatever it was it was all right, he went calmly back to his place beside the novelist's chair.

"Do you know,"—said the artist, as they sat on the porch that evening, with their after-dinner pipes,—"I believe this old place is haunted."

"If it isn't, it ought to be," answered the other, contentedly—playing with Czar's silky ears. "A good ghost would fit in nicely here, wouldn't it—or he, or she. Its spookship would travel far to find a more delightful place for spooking in, and—providing, of course, she were a perfectly respectable hant—what a charming addition to our family he would make. When it was weary of moping and mowing and sobbing and wailing and gibbering, she could curl up at the foot of your bed and sleep; as Czar, here, curls up and sleeps at the foot of mine. A good ghost, you know—if he becomes really attached to you—is as constant and faithful and affectionate and companionable as a good dog."

"B-r-r-r," said the artist. And Czar turned to look at him, questioningly.

"All the same"—the painter continued—"when I was out there in the studio, I could feel some one watching me—you know the feeling."

Conrad Lagrange returned mockingly, "I trust your over-sensitive, artistic temperament is not to be so influenced by our ghostly visitor that you will be unfitted for your work."

The other laughed. Then he said seriously, "Joking aside, Lagrange, I feel a presentiment—I can't put it into words—but—I feel that I am going to begin the real work of my life right here. I"—he hesitated—"it seems to me that I can sense some influence that I

45

can't define—it's the mystery of the rose garden, perhaps," he finished with another short laugh.

The man, who, in the eyes of the world, had won so large a measure of the success that his friend desired; and whose life was so embittered by the things for which he was envied by many; made no reply other than his slow, twisted smile.

Silently, they watched the purple shadows of the mountains deepen; and saw the outlines of the tawny foothills grow vague and dim, until they were lost in the dusky monotone of the evening. The last faint tint of sunset color went from the sky back of the San Gabriels; while, close to the mountain peaks and ridges, the stars came out. The rows and the contour of the orange groves could no longer be distinguished the forms of the nearby trees were lost—the rich, lustrous green of their foliage brushed out with the dull black of the night; while the twinkling lights of the distant towns and hamlets, in the valley below, shone as sparkling jewels on the inky, velvet robe that, fold on fold, lay over the landscape.

When the two had smoked in silence, for some time, the artist said slowly, "You knew my mother very well, did you not, Mr. Lagrange?"

"We were children together, Aaron." As he spoke, the man's deep voice was gentle, as always, when the young man's mother was mentioned.

Again, for a little, neither spoke. As they sat looking away to the mountains, each seemed occupied with his own thoughts. Yet each felt that the other, to a degree, understood what he, himself, was thinking.

Once more, the artist broke the silence,—facing his mother's friend with quiet resolution,—as though he felt himself forced to speak but knew not exactly how to begin. "Did you know her well—after—after my father's death—and while I was abroad?"

The other bowed his head—"Yes."

"Very well?"

"Very well."

As if at loss for words, Aaron King still hesitated. "Mr. Lagrange," he said, at last, "there are some things about—about mother—that I would like to tell you—that I think she would want me to tell you, under the circumstances."

"Yes," said Conrad Lagrange, gently.

"Well,—to begin,—you know, perhaps, how much mother and I have always been—" his fine voice broke and the older man bowed his head; but, with a slight lift of his determined chin, the painter

46

went on calmly—"to each other. After father's death, until I was seventeen, we were never separated. She was my only teacher. Then I went away to school, seeing her only during my vacations, which we always spent, together in the country. Three years ago, I went abroad to finish my study. I did not see her again until—until I was called home."

"I know," came in low tones from the other.

"But, sir, while it seemed necessary that I should be away from home,—that we should be separated,—all through this period, we exchanged almost daily letters; planning for the future, and looking forward to the time when we could, again, be together."

"I know, Aaron. It was very unusual—and very beautiful."

"When we were together, before I went away, I was a mere lad," continued the artist. "I knew in a general way that father had been a successful lawyer, and quite prominent in politics; and— because there was no change in our manner of living after his death, and there seemed to be always money for whatever we wanted, I suppose—I assumed, thoughtlessly, that there would always be plenty. During the years while I was at school, there was never, in any way, the slightest hint in mother's letters that would lead me to question the abundance of her resources. When they called me home,—" his voice broke, "—I found my mother dying—almost in poverty—our home stripped of the art treasures she loved—her own room, even, empty of everything save the barest necessities." In bitter sorrow and shame, the young man buried his face in his hands.

The novelist, his gaunt features twitching with the emotion that even his long schooling in the tragedies of life could not suppress, waited silently.

When the artist had regained, in a measure, his self-control, he continued,—and every word came from him in shame and humiliation,—"Before she died, she told me about—my father. In the settlement of his affairs, at the time of his death, it appeared that he had taken advantage of the confidence of certain clients and had betrayed his trust; appropriating large sums to his own interests. He had even taken advantage of mother's influence in certain circles, and, relying upon her unquestioning faith in his integrity, had made her an unconscious instrument in furthering his schemes."

Conrad Lagrange made as if to speak, but checked himself and waited for the other to continue.

Aaron King went on; "Out of regard for my mother, the matter

47

was kept as quiet as possible. The one who suffered the heaviest loss was able to protect her—in a measure. All the others were fully reimbursed. But mother—it would have been easier for her if she had died then. She withdrew from her friends and from the life she loved—she denied herself to all who sought her and devoted her life to me. Above all, she planned to keep me in ignorance of the truth until I should be equipped to win the place in the world that she coveted for me. It was for that, she sent me away, and kept me from home. As the demands for my educational expenses grew naturally heavier, she supplemented the slender resources, left in the final settlement of my father's estate, by sacrificing the treasures of her home, and by giving up the luxuries to which she had been accustomed from childhood. She even provided for me after her death—not wealth, but a comfortable amount, sufficient to support me in good circumstances until I can gain recognition and an income from my work."

Under the lash of his memories, the young man sprang to his feet.

"In God's name, Lagrange, why did not some one tell me? I did not know—I did not know—I thought—O mother, mother, mother—why did you do it? Why was I not told? All these years I have lived a selfish fool, and you—you—I would have given up everything—I would have worked in a ditch, rather than accept this."

The deep, quiet voice of Conrad Lagrange broke the stillness that followed the storm of the artist's passionate words. "And that is the answer, Aaron. She knew, too well, that you would not have accepted her sacrifice, if you had known. That is why she kept the secret until you had finished your education. She forbade her friends—she forbade me to interfere. And don't you see that she was right? Don't you see it? We would have done her the greatest injustice if we had, against her will, deprived her of this privilege. Her splendid pride, her high sense of honor, her nobility of spirit demanded the sacrifice. It was her right. God forgive me—I tried to make her see it otherwise—but she knew best. She always knew best, Aaron. Her only hope of regaining for you that self-respect and that position in life to which you—by right of birth and natural endowment—are entitled, was in you. The name which she had given to you could be restored to honor by you only. To train and equip you for your work, and to enable you, unhampered by need, to gain your footing, was the determined passion of her life. Her sacrifice, her suffering to that end, was the only restitution she could make to you for that which your father had squandered. Her proud spirit, her fine intelligence, her mother love for you, demanded it."

"I know," returned the artist. "She told me before she died. She made me understand. She said that it was my inheritance. She asked for my promise that I would be true to her purpose. Her last words were an expression of her confidence that I would not disappoint her—that I would win a place and name that would wipe out the shame of my father's dishonor. And I will, Lagrange, I must. Mother—mother shall not be disappointed—she shall not be disappointed."

"No,"—said the older man, so softly that the other, torn by the passion of his own thoughts, did not hear,—"No, Aaron, your mother will not be disappointed."

For a time longer they sat in silence. Then the young man said, "I wish I knew the name of my mother's friend—the one who suffered the heaviest loss through my father, and who so generously protected her in the crisis. I would like to thank him, at least. I begged her to tell me, but she would not. She said he would not want me to know—that for me to attempt to reimburse him would, to his mind, rob him of his real reward."

Conrad Lagrange, his head bowed, spoke quietly to the dog at his feet. Rising, Czar laid his soft muzzle on his master's knee and looked up into the homely, world-worn face. Gently, the strange man—so lonely and embittered in the fame that he had won—at a price—stroked the brown head. "Your mother knew best, Aaron," he said slowly, without looking at his companion. "You must believe that she knew best. Her beautiful spirit could not lead her astray. She was right in this, also. Your sentiment does you honor, but you must respect her wish. Whoever the man was—she had reasons, I am sure, for feeling as she did—that it would be better for you not to know. It was some one, perhaps, whose influence upon you, she had cause to fear."

"It was very strange," returned the artist, hesitatingly. "Perhaps I ought not to say it. But I felt that, as you suggest, she feared for me to know. She seemed to want to tell me, but did not, for my sake. It was very strange."

Conrad Lagrange made no reply.

"I wanted you to know about mother,"—continued the artist,—"because I would like you to understand why—why I must succeed in my work."

The older man smiled to himself, in the dusk. "I have always

49

known why you must succeed, Aaron," he returned. "I have never questioned your motives. I question only your understanding of success. I question—if you will pardon me—your understanding of your mother's wish for you."

Then, in one of those rare momentary moods, when he seemed to reveal to his young friend his real nature that lay so deeply hidden from the world, he added, "You are right, Aaron. This place is haunted—haunted by the spirit of the mountains, yonder—haunted by the spirit of the rose garden, out there. The silent strength of the hills, and the loveliness of the garden will attend you in your studio, as you work. I do not wonder that you feel a presentiment that your artistic future is to be shaped here; for between these influences and the other influences that will be brought to bear upon you, you will be forced to decide. May the God of all true art and artists help you to make no mistake. Listen!"

As though in answer to the solemn words of the man who spoke from the fullness of a life-long experience and from the depths of a life-old love, a strain of music came from out the fragrant darkness. Somewhere, hidden in the depths of the orange grove, the soul of a true musician was seeking expression in the tones of a violin.

Softly, sadly, with poignant clearness, the music lifted into the night—low and pleadingly at first; then stronger and more vibrant with feeling, as though sweetly insistent in its call; swelling next in volume and passion, as though in warning of some threatening evil; ringing with loving fear; sobbing, wailing, moaning, in anguish; clearly, gloriously, triumphant, at last; then sinking into solemn, reverent benediction—losing itself, finally, in the darkness, even as it had come.

The two men, so fashioned by nature to receive such music, listened with emotions they could not have put into words. For the moment, the music to them was the voice of the guarding, calling, warning spirit of the mountains that, in their calm, majestic strength, were so far removed from the petty passions and longings of the baser world at their feet—it was the voice of the loving intimacy, the sweet purity, and the sacred beauty of the spirit of the garden. It was as though the things of which Conrad Lagrange had just spoken so reverently had cried aloud to them, out of the night, in confirmation of his words.

Chapter VII
Mrs. Taine in Quaker Gray

Aaron King seemed loth to begin his work on the portrait of Mrs. Taine. Day after day, without apparent reason, he put it off—spending the hours in wandering aimlessly about the place, idling on the porch, or doing nothing in his studio. He would start from the house to the building at the end of the rose garden, as though moved by some clearly defined purpose—and then, for an hour or more, would dawdle among the things of his craft, with irresolute mind—turning over his sketches and drawings with uncertain hands, as though searching for something he knew was not there; toying with his paints and brushes; or sitting before his empty easel, looking away through the big window to the distant mountains. He seemed incapable of fixing his mind upon the task to which he attached so much importance. Several times, Mrs. Taine called, but he begged her to be patient; and she, with pretended awe of the moods of genius, waited.

Conrad Lagrange jeered and mocked, offered sneering advice or sarcastic compliment; and, under it all, was keenly watchful and sympathetic— understanding better than the artist himself, perhaps, the secret of the painter's hesitation. Every day,—sometimes in the morning, sometimes in the afternoon or evening unseen musician, in the orange grove wrought for them melodie that, whether grave or gay, always carried, somehow, the feeling that had so moved them in the mysterious darkness of that first evening.

They knew, now, of course, that the musician lived in the neighboring house—the gable and chimney of which was just visible above the orange-trees. But that was all. Obedient to some whimsical impulse that prompted them both, and was born, no doubt, of the circumstance and mood of that first evening, they did not seek to learn more. They feared—though they did not say it—that to learn the identity of the musician would rob them of the peculiar pleasure they found in the music, itself. So they spoke always of their unknown neighbor in a fanciful vein, as in like humor they spoke of the spirit that Aaron King still insisted haunted the place, or as they alluded to the mystery of the carefully tended rose garden.

When the artist could put it off no longer, a day was finally set when Mrs. Taine was to come for the beginning of her portrait. The appointed hour found the artist in his studio. A canvas stood ready upon the easel; palette, colors and brushes were at hand. The painter was standing at the big, north window, looking up away to the mountains—the mountains that the novelist said called so insistently. Suddenly, he turned his head to listen. Sweetly clear and low, through the green wall of the orange-trees, came the music of that hidden violin.

As he stood there,—with his eyes fixed upon the mountains, listening to the spirit that spoke in the tones of the unseen instrument,—Aaron King knew, all at once, that the passing moment was one of those rare moments—that come, all unexpectedly—when, with prophetic vision, one sees clearly the end of the course he pursues and the destiny that waits him at its completion. As clearly, too, he saw the other way, and knew the meaning of the vision. But seldom is the strength given to man, in such moments, to choose for himself. Though he may see the other way clearly, his feet cling to the path he has elected to follow; nor will he, unless some one takes him by the hand saying, "Come," turn aside.

A voice, not at all in harmony with the music, broke upon the artist's consciousness. He turned to see Mrs. Taine standing expectantly in the open door. "Hush!" said the painter, still under the spell of that moment so big with possibilities. "Listen,"—with a gesture, he checked her advance,—"listen."

A look of haughty surprise flashed over the woman's too perfect features. Then, as her ear caught the tones of the violin, she half turned—but only for a moment.

"Very clever, isn't it," she said as she came forward "It must be old Professor Becker. He lives somewhere around here, I understand. They say he is very good."

The artist looked at her for an instant, in amazement Then, as his normal mind asserted itself, he burst into an embarrassed laugh.

At her look of puzzled inquiry, he said, "I beg your pardon, Mrs. Taine. I did not realize how harshly I greeted you. The fact is I—I was dreaming"—he turned suggestively toward the canvas upon the easel. "You see I was expecting you—I was thinking—then the music came—and—well—when you actually appeared in the flesh, I did not for the moment realize that it was really you."

"How charming of you!" she returned. "To be made the subject of an artist's dream—really it is quite the nicest compliment

52

I have ever received. Tell me, do you like me in this?" she slipped the wrap she wore from her shoulders, and stood before him, gowned in the simple, gray dress of a Quaker Maid. Deliberately, she turned her beautiful self about for his critical inspection. Moving to and fro, sitting, half-reclining, standing—in various graceful poses she invited, challenged, dared, his closest attention—professional attention, of course—to every curve and detail.

In spite of its simplicity of color and line, the gown still bore the unmistakable stamp of the wearer's world. The severity of line was subtly made to emphasize the voluptuousness of the body that was covered but not hidden. The quiet color was made to accentuate the flesh the dress concealed only to reveal. The very lack of ornament but served to center the attention upon the charms that so loudly professed to scorn them. It was worldliness speaking in the quiet voice of religion. It was vulgarity advertising itself in terms of good taste. She had made modesty the handmaiden of blatant immodesty, and the daring impudence of it all fairly stunned the painter.

"Oh dear!" she said, watching his face, "I fear you don't like it, at all—and I thought it such a beautiful little gown. You told me to wear whatever I pleased, you know."

"It is a beautiful gown," he said—then added impulsively, "and you are beautiful in it. You would be beautiful in anything."

She shook her head; favoring him with an understanding smile. "You say that to please me. I can see that you don't like me this way."

"But I do," he insisted. "I like you that way, immensely. I was a bit surprised, that's all. You see, I thought, of course, that you would select an evening gown of some sort—something, you know, that would fit your social position—your place in the world. In this costume, the beauty of your shoulders—"

Lowering her eyes as if embarrassed, she said coldly, "The beauty of my shoulders is not for the public. I have never worn—I will not wear—one of those dreadful, immodest gowns."

Aaron King was bewildered. Suddenly, he remembered what Conrad Lagrange had said about her fad. But after so frankly exhibiting herself before him, dressed as she was in a gown that was deliberately planned to advertise her physical charms, to be particular about baring her shoulders in a conventional costume—! It was quite too much.

"Again, I beg your pardon, Mrs. Taine," he managed to say. "I did not know. Under the circumstances, this is exactly the thing.

Your portrait, in what is so frankly a costume assumed for the purpose, takes us out of the dilemma very nicely, indeed."

"Why, that's exactly what I thought," she returned eagerly. "And this is so in keeping with my real tastes—don't you see? A real portrait—I mean a serious work of art, you know—should always be something more than a mere likeness, should it not? Don't you think that to be genuinely good, a portrait must reveal the spirit and character—must portray the soul, as well as the features? I do so want this to be a truly great picture—for your sake." Her manner seemed to say that she was doing it all for him. "I have never permitted any one to paint my portrait before, you know," she added meaningly.

"You are very kind, Mrs. Taine," he returned gravely. "Believe me, I do appreciate this opportunity I shall do my best to express my appreciation here"—he indicated the canvas on the easel.

When his sitter was posed to his liking, and the artist, with a few bold, sweeping, strokes of the charcoal had roughed out his subject on the canvas, and was bending over his color-box—he said, casually, to put her at ease, "You came alone this afternoon, did you?"

"Oh, no, indeed! I brought Louise with me. I shall always bring her, or some one. One cannot be too careful, you know," she added with simulated artlessness.

The painter, studying her face, replied mechanically "No indeed."

As he turned back to his canvas, Mrs. Taine continued, "I left her in the house, with a box of chocolates and a novel. I felt that you would rather we were alone."

"Please don't look down," said the artist. "I want your eyes about here"—he indicated a picture on the wall, a little back and to the left of where he stood at the easel.

After this, there was silence in the studio, for a little while. Mrs. Taine obediently kept the pose; her eyes upon the point the artist had indicated; but—as the man, himself, was almost directly in her line of vision—it was easy for her to watch him at his work, when his eyes were on his canvas or palette. The arrangement was admirable in that it relieved the tedium of the hour for the sitter; and gave her face an expression of animated interest that, truthfully fixed upon the canvas, should insure the fame and future of any painter.

It would be quite too much to say that Aaron King became absorbed in his occupation. Thorough master of the tools of his craft, and of his own technic, as well; he was interested in the mere exercising of his skill, but he in no sense lost himself in his work. Two or three times, Mrs. Taine saw him glance quickly over his shoulder, as though expecting some one. Once, for quite a moment, he deliberately turned from his easel to stand at the window, looking up at the distant mountain peaks. Several times, he seemed to be listening.

"May I talk?" she said at last.

"Why, certainly," he returned. "I want you to feel perfectly at ease. You must be altogether at home here. Just let yourself go—say what you like, with no conventional restraints whatever—consider me a mechanical something that is no more than an article of furniture—be as thoroughly yourself as if alone in your own room."

"How funny," she said musingly.

"Not at all"—he returned—"just a matter of business."

"But it would be funny if I were to take you at your word," she replied; suddenly breaking the pose and meeting his gaze squarely. "Is it—is it quite necessary for the mechanical something to look at me like that?"

"I said that you were to consider me as an article of furniture. I didn't say that I felt like a table or chair."

"Oh!"

"Don't look down; keep the pose, please," came somewhat sharply from the man at the easel, as though he were mentally taking himself in hand.

After that, she watched him with increasing interest and, when he turned his head in that listening attitude, a curious, resentful light came into her eyes.

Presently, she asked abruptly, "What is it that you hear?"

"I thought I heard music," he answered, coloring slightly and turning to his work with suddenly absorbing interest.

"The violin that so enchanted you when I came to break the spell?" she persisted playfully—though the light in her eyes was not a playful light.

"Yes," he answered shortly; stepping back and shading his eyes with his hand for a careful look at his canvas.

"And don't you know who it is?"

"You said it was an old professor somebody."

"That was my first guess," she retorted. "Was I right?"

"I don't know."

"But it comes from that little box of a house, next door, doesn't it?"

"Evidently," the artist answered. Then, laying aside his palette and brushes he said abruptly, "That is all for to-day; thank you."

"Oh, so soon!" she exclaimed; and the regret in her voice was very pleasing to the man who was decidedly not a mechanical something.

She started eagerly forward toward the easel. But the artist, with a quick motion, drew a curtain across the canvas, to hide his work; while he checked her with—"Not yet, please. I don't want you to see it until I say you may."

"How mean of you," she protested; charmingly submissive. Then, eagerly—"And do you want me to-morrow? You do, don't you?"

"Yes, please—at the same hour."

When the Quaker Maiden's dress was safely hidden under her wrap, Mrs. Taine stood, for a moment, looking thoughtfully about the studio; while the artist waited at the door, ready to escort her to the automobile. "I am going to love this room," she said slowly; and, for the first time, her voice was genuinely sincere, with a hint of wistfulness in its tone that made him regard her wonderingly.

She went to him impulsively. "Will you, when you are famous—when you are a great artist and all the great and famous people go to you to have their portraits painted—will you remember poor me, I wonder?"

"Am I really going to be famous?" he returned doubtfully. "Are you so sure that this picture will mean success?"

"Of course I am sure—I know. You want to succeed don't you?"

Aaron King returned her look, for a moment, without answering. Then, with a quick, fierce determination that betrayed a depth of feeling she had never before seen in him, he exclaimed, "Do I want to succeed! I—I must succeed. I tell you I must."

And the woman answered very softly, with her hand upon his arm, "And you shall—you shall."

Conrad Lagrange and Czar found the artist on the front porch, pulling moodily at his pipe.

"Is it all over for to-day?" asked the novelist as he stood looking down upon the young man with that peculiarly piercing, baffling gaze.

"All over," replied the artist, answering the greeting thrust of Czar's muzzle against his knee, with caressing hand. "Where did you fly to?"

The other dropped into a chair. "I would fly anywhere to escape being entertained by that Ragtime' piece of human nonentity—Louise Taine. I saw them coming, just in time." He was filling his pipe as he spoke. "And how did the work go?"

56

"All right," replied the painter, indifferently.

The older man shot a curious sidewise glance at his moody companion; then, striking a match, he gave careful attention to his pipe. Watching the cloud of blue smoke, he said quizzingly, "I suppose 'Her Majesty' was royally apparelled for the occasion-properly arrayed in purple and fine linen; as befits the dignity of her state?"

The artist turned at the mocking, suggestive tone and answered savagely, "I suppose you have got to know, damn you! I'm painting her as a Quaker Maiden."

Conrad Lagrange's reply was as surprising in its way as was the outburst of the artist. Instead of the tirade of biting sarcasm and stinging abuse that the painter expected, the older man only gazed at him from under his scowling brows and, shaking his head, sadly, said with sincere regret and understanding "You poor fellow! It must be hell." Then, as his keen mind grasped the full significance of the artist's words, he murmured meditatively, "The personification of the age masquerading in Quaker gray—Shades of the giants who used to be! What an opportunity—if you only had the nerve to do it."

The artist flung out his hand in protest as he rose from his chair to pace up and down the porch. "Don't, Lagrange, don't! I can't stand it, just now."

"All right." said the other, heartily, "I won't." Rising, he put his hand on his friend's shoulder. "Come, let's go for a look at the roses, before Yee Kee calls us to dinner."

In the garden, the artist's eye caught sight of something white lying in the well-kept path. With an exclamation, he went quickly to pick it up. It was a dainty square of lace—a handkerchief—with an exquisitely embroidered "S" in the corner.

The two men looked at each other in silence; with smiling, questioning eyes.

Chapter VIII
The Portrait That Was Not a Portrait

Aaron King was putting the last touches to his portrait of the woman who—Conrad Lagrange said—was the personification of the age.

From that evening when the young man told his friend the story of his mother's sacrifice, their friendship had become like that friendship which passeth the love of women. While the novelist, true to his promise, did not cease to flay his younger companion— for the good of the artist's soul—those moments when his gentler moods ruled his speech were, perhaps, more frequent; and the artist was more and more learning to appreciate the rare imagination, the delicacy of feeling, the intellectual brilliancy, and the keenness of mental vision that distinguished the man whose life was so embittered by the use he had made of his own rich gifts.

The novelist steadily refused to look at the picture while the work was in progress. He said, bluntly, that he preferred to run no risk of interfering with the young man's chance for fame; and that it would be quite enough for him to look upon his friend's shame when it was accomplished; without witnessing the process in its various stages. The artist laughed to hide the embarrassing fact that he was rather pleased to be left to himself with this particular picture.

Conrad Lagrange did not, however, refuse to accompany his friend, occasionally, to the house on Fairlands Heights; where the painter continued to spend much of his time. When Mrs. Taine made mocking references to the novelist's promise not to leave the artist unprotected to her tender mercies, he always answered with some—as she said—twisty saying; to the effect that the present situation in no way lessened his determination to save the young man from the influences that would accomplish the ruin of his genius. "If"—he always added—"if he is worth saving; which remains to be seen." Always, at the Taine home, they met James Rutlidge. Frequently the celebrated critic dropped in at the cottage in the orange grove.

Under the skillful management of Rutlidge,—at the request of Mrs. Taine,—the newspapers were already busy with the name and work of Aaron King. True, the critic had never seen the artist's work; but, never-the-less, the papers and magazines throughout the country often mentioned the high order of the painter's genius. There were little stories of his study and success abroad; tactful references to his aristocratic family; entertaining accounts of his romantic life with the famous novelist in the orange groves of Fairlands, and of how, in his California studio among the roses, the distinguished painter was at work upon a portrait of the well-known social leader, Mrs. Taine—this being the first portrait ever painted of that famous beauty. That the picture would create a sensation at the exhibition, was the unanimous verdict of all who had been permitted to see the marvelous creation by this rare genius whose work was so little known in this country.

Said Conrad Lagrange—"It is all so easy."

Once or twice, the artist or his friend had seen the woman of the disfigured face; and the novelist still tried in vain to fix her in his memory. Every day, they heard, in the depths of the neighboring orange grove, the music of that unseen violin. They spoke, often, in playful mood, of the spirit that haunted the place; but they made no effort to solve the mystery of the carefully tended rose garden. They knew that whoever cared for the roses worked there only in the early morning hours; and they carefully avoided going into the yard back of the house until after breakfast. They felt that an investigation might rob them of the peculiar humor of their fancy—a fancy that was to them, both, such a pleasure; and gave to their home amid the orange-trees and roses such an added charm.

But the other member of the trio of friends was not so reticent. Czar had formed an—to his most proper dogship—unusual habit. Frequently, when the three were sitting on the porch in the evening, he would rise suddenly from his place beside his master's chair, and walking sedately to the side of the porch facing that neighboring gable and chimney, would stand listening attentively; then, without so much as a "by-your-leave," he would leap to the ground, and vanish somewhere around the corner of the house. Later, he would come sedately back; greeting each, in turn, with that insistent thrust his soft muzzle against a knee; and assuring them, in the wordless speech of his expressive, brown eyes, that his mission had been a most proper one, and that they might trust him to make no foolish mistakes that would mar the peace and harmony of their little household. The men never failed to agree with him that it was all right. In fact, so fully did they trust him that they never even stepped to the corner of the porch to see where he went; nor would they leave their chairs until he had returned.

Upon those days when Mrs. Taine came to the studio,—being always careful that Louise accompanied her as far as the house,—Conrad Lagrange vanished. The man swore by all the strange and

59

wonderful gods he knew—and they were many—that he feared to spend an hour with that effervescing young female devotee of the Arts—lest the mountains in their wrath should fall upon him.

But that day, when Mrs. Taine came for the last sitting, the novelist—engaged in interesting talk with the artist—forgot.

"You are caught," cried the painter, gleefully, as the big automobile stopped at the gate.

"I'll be damned if I am," retorted the novelist, with no profane intent but with meaning quite literal; and, seizing a book, he bolted through the kitchen—nearly upsetting the startled Yee Kee.

"What's matte'," inquired the Chinaman, putting his head in at the living-room door; his almond eyes as wide as they could go, with an expression of celestial consternation that convulsed the artist. Catching sight of the automobile, his oriental features wrinkled into a yellow grin of understanding; "Oh! see um come! Ha! I know. He all time go, she come. He say no like lagtime gal. Dog Cza', him all time gone, too; him no like lagtime—all same Miste' Laglange. Ha! I go, too," and he, in turn, vanished.

"You are early, to-day," said Aaron King, as he escorted Mrs. Taine to the studio.

Just inside the door, she turned impulsively to face him—standing close, her beautifully groomed and voluptuous body instinct with the lure of her sex, her too perfect features slightly flushed, and her eyes submissively downcast. "And have you forgotten that this is the last time I can come?" she asked in a low tone.

"Surely not"—he returned calmly—"you are coming to-morrow, with the others, aren't you?" Her husband with James Rutlidge and Louise Taine were invited for the next day, to view the portrait.

"Oh, but that will be so different!" She loosed the wrap she wore, and threw it aside with an indescribable familiar gesture. "You don't realize what these hours have meant to me—how could you? You do not live in my world. Your world is—is so different You do not know—you do not know." With a sudden burst of passion, she added, "The world that I live in is hell; and this—this—oh, it has been heavenly!"

Her words, her voice, the poise of her figure, the gesture with outstretched arms—it was all so nearly an invitation, so nearly a surrender of herself to him, that the man started forward impulsively. For the moment he forgot his work—he forgot everything—he was conscious only of the woman who stood before him. But even as the light of triumph blazed up in the woman's eyes, the man halted,—drew back; and his face was turned from her as he

60

listened to the sweetly appealing message of the gentle spirit that made itself felt in the music of that hidden violin. It was as though, in truth, the mountains, themselves,—from their calm heights so remote from the little world wherein men live their baser tragedies,—watched over him. "Don't you think we had better proceed with our work?" he said calmly.

The light in the woman's eyes changed to anger which she turned away to hide. Without replying, she went to her place and assumed the pose; and, as she had watched him day after day when his eyes were upon the canvas, she watched him now. Since that first day, when she had questioned him about the unseen musician, they had not mentioned the subject, although—as was inevitable under the circumstances—their intimacy had grown. But not once had he turned from his work in that listening attitude, or looked from the window as though half-expecting some one, without her noting it. And, always, her eyes had flashed with resentment, which she had promptly concealed when the painter, again turning to his easel, had looked from his canvas to her face.

Scarcely was the artist well started in his work, that afternoon, when the music ceased. Presently, Mrs. Taine broke her watchful silence, with the quite casual remark; "Your musical neighbor is still unknown to you, I suppose?"

"Yes,"—he answered smiling, as though more to himself than at her,—"we have never tried to make her acquaintance."

The woman caught him up quickly; "To make her acquaintance? Why do you say, 'her,' if you do not know who it is?"

The artist was confused. "Did I say, her?" he questioned, his face flushed with embarrassment. "It was a slip of the tongue. Neither Conrad Lagrange nor I know anything about our neighbor."

She laughed ironically. "And you could know so easily."

"I suppose so; but we have never cared to. We prefer to accept the music as it comes to us—impersonally—for what it is—not for whoever makes it." He spoke coldly, as though the subject was distasteful to him, under the circumstances of the moment.

But the woman persisted. "Well, I know who it is. Shall I tell you?"

"No. I do not care to know. I am not interested in the musician."

"Oh, but you might be, you know," she retorted.

"Please take the pose," returned Aaron King professionally. Mrs. Taine, wisely, for the time, dropped the subject; contenting herself with a meaning laugh.

The artist silently gave all his attention to the nearly finished portrait. He was not painting, now, with full brush and swift sure strokes,—as had been his way when building up his picture,—but worked with occasional deft touches here and there; drawing back from the canvas often, to study it intently, his eyes glancing swiftly from the picture to the sitter's face and back again to the portrait; then stepping forward quickly, ready brush in hand; to withdraw an instant later for another long and searching study. Presently, with an air of relief, he laid aside his palette and brushes; and turning to Mrs. Taine, with a smile, held out his hand. "Come," he said, "tell me if I have done well or ill."

"It is finished?" she cried. "I may see it?"

"It is all that I can do"—he answered—"come." He led her to the easel, where they stood side by side before his work.

The picture, still fresh from the painter's brush, was a portrait of Mrs. Taine—yet not a portrait. Exquisite in coloring and in its harmony of tone and line, it betrayed in every careful detail—in every mark of the brush—the thoughtful, painstaking care—the thorough knowledge and highly trained skill of an artist who was, at least, master of his own technic. But—if one might say so—the painting was more a picture than a portrait. The face upon the canvas was the face of Mrs. Taine, indeed, in that the features were her features; but it was also the face of a sweetly modest Quaker Maid. The too perfect, too well cared for face of the beautiful woman of the world was, on the canvas, given the charm of a natural unconscious loveliness. The eyes that had watched the artist with such certain knowledge of life and with the boldness born of that knowledge were, in the picture, beautiful with the charm of innocent maidenhood. The very coloring and the arrangement of the hair were changed subtly to express, not the skill of high-priced beauty-doctors and of fashionable hair-dressers, but the instinctive care of womanliness. The costume that, when worn by the woman, expressed so fully her true character; in the picture, became the emblem of a pure and deeply religious spirit.

Mrs. Taine turned impulsively to the artist, and, placing her hand upon his arm, exclaimed in delight, "Oh, is it true? Am I really so beautiful?"

The artist laughed. "You like it?"

"Like it? How could I help liking it? It is lovely."

"I am glad," he returned. "I hoped it would please you."

"And you"—she asked, with eager eyes—"are you satisfied with it? Does it seem good to you?"

"Oh, as for that," he answered, "I suppose one is never satisfied. I know the work is good—in a way. But it is very far from what it should be, I fear. I feel that, after all, I have not made the most of my opportunity." He spoke with a shade of sadness.

Again, she put out her hand impulsively to touch his arm, as she answered eagerly, "Ah, but no one else will say that. No one else will dare. It will be the sensation of the year—I tell you. Just you wait until Jim Rutlidge sees it. Wait until it is hung for exhibition, and he tells the world about it. Everybody worth while will be coming to you then. And I—I will remember these hours with you, and be glad that I could help—even so little. Will you remember them, too, I wonder. Are you glad the picture is finished?"

"And are you not glad?" he returned meaningly.

They had both forgotten the painting before them. They did not see it. They each saw only the other.

"No, I am not glad," she said in a low tone. "People would very soon be talking if I should come here, alone—now that the picture is finished."

"I suppose in any case you will be leaving Fairlands soon, for the summer," he returned slowly.

"O listen,"—she cried with quick eagerness—"we are going to Lake Silence. What's to hinder your coming too? Everybody goes there, you know. Won't you come?"

"But would it be altogether safe?" He reflected doubtfully.

"Why, of course,—Mr. Taine, Louise, and Jim,—we are all going together—don't you see? I don't believe you want to go," she pouted. "I believe you want to forget."

Her alluring manner, the invitation conveyed in her words and voice, the touch of her hand on his arm, and the nearness of her person, fairly swept the man off his feet. With quick passion, he caught her hand, and his words came with reckless heat. "You know that I will not forget you. You know that I could not, if I would. Do you think that I have been so engrossed with my brushes and canvas that I have been unconscious of you? What is that painted thing beside your own beautiful self? Do you think that because I must turn myself into a machine to make a photograph of your beauty, I am insensible to its charm? I am not a machine. I am a man; as you are a woman; and I—"

She checked him suddenly—stepping aside with a quick movement, and the words, "Hush, some one is coming."

The artist, too, heard voices, just without the door.

Mrs. Taine moved swiftly across the room toward her wrap. Aaron King, going to his easel, drew the velvet curtain to hide the picture.

Chapter IX
Conrad Lagrange's Adventure

Certainly, when Conrad Lagrange fled so precipitately from Louise Taine, that afternoon, he had no thought that the trivial incident was to mark the beginning of a new era in his life; or that it would work out in the life of his dearest friend such far reaching results. His only purpose was to escape an hour of the frothy vaporings of the poor, young creature who believed herself so interested in art and letters, and who succeeded so admirably in expressing the spirit of her environment and training.

With his pipe and book, the novelist hid himself in the rose garden; finding a seat on the ground, in an angle of the studio wall and the Ragged Robin hedge, where any one entering the enclosure would be least likely to observe him. Czar, heartily approving of his master's action, stretched himself comfortably under the nearest rose-bush, and waited further developments.

Presently, the novelist heard his friend, with Mrs. Taine, come from the house and enter the studio. For a moment, he entertained the uncomfortable fear that the artist, in a spirit of sheer boyish fun that so often moved him, would bring Mrs. Taine to the garden. But the moment passed, and the novelist,—mentally blessing the young man for his forbearance,—with a chuckle of satisfaction, lighted his pipe and opened his book. Scarcely had he found his place in the pages, however, when he was again interrupted—this time, by the welcome tones of their neighbor's violin. Putting his book aside, the man reclining in the shelter of the roses, with half-closed eyes, yielded himself to the fancy of the spirit that called from the depths of the fragrant orange grove.

The mass of roses in the hedge and on the wall of the studio above his head dropped their lovely petals down upon him. The warm, slanting rays of the afternoon sun, softened by the screen of shining leaves and branches, played over the bewildering riot of color. Here and there, golden-bodied bees and velvet-winged butterflies flitted about their fairy-like duties. Far above, in the deep blue, a hawk floated on motionless wings and a lonely crow laid his course toward the distant mountain peaks that gleamed, silvery white, above the blue and purple of the lower ridges and the tawny yellow of their foothills. The air was saturated with the fragrance of the rose and orange blossoms, of eucalyptus and pepper trees, and with the thousand other perfumes of a California spring.

The music ceased. The man waited—hoping that it would begin again. But it did not; and he was about to take up his book, once more, when Czar arose, stretched himself, stood for a moment in a picturesque, listening attitude, then trotted off among the roses; leaving the novelist with an odd feeling of uneasy expectancy—half resolved to stay, half determined to go. The thought of Louise in the house decided him, and he kept his place, hidden as he was, in the corner—a whimsical smile hovering over his world-lined features as though, after all, he felt himself entering upon some enjoyable adventure.

Presently, he heard indistinctly, somewhere in the other end of the garden, a low murmuring voice. As it came nearer, the man's smile grew more pronounced It was a wonderfully attractive voice, clear and full in its pure-toned sweetness. The unseen speaker was talking to the novelist's dog. The smile on the man's face was still more pronounced, as he whispered to himself, "The rascal! So this is what he has been up to!" Rising quietly to his knees, he peered through the flower-laden bushes.

A young woman of rare and exquisite beauty was moving about the garden—bending over the roses, and talking in low tones to Czar, who—to his hidden master—appeared to appreciate fully the favor of his gentle companion's intimacy. The novelist—old in the study of character and trained by his long years of observation and experience in the world of artificiality—was fascinated by the loveliness of the scene.

Dressed simply, in some soft clinging material of white, with a modestly low-cut square at the throat, and sleeves that ended in filmy lace just below the elbow—her lithe, softly rounded form, as she moved here and there, had all the charm of girlish grace with the fuller beauty of ripening womanhood. As she bent over the roses, or stooped to caress the dog, in gentle comradeship, her step, her poise, her every motion, was instinct with that strength and health that is seldom seen among those who wear the shackles of a too conventionalized society. Her face,—warmly tinted by the golden out-of-doors, firm fleshed and clear,—in its unconscious naturalness and in its winsome purity was like the flowers she stooped to kiss.

As he watched, the man noticed—with a smile of understanding—that she kept rather to the side of the garden toward the house; where the artist, at his easel by the big, north light, could not see her through the small window in the end of the room; and where, hidden by the tall hedge, she would not be noticed from Yee Kee's kitchen. Often, too, she paused to listen, as if for any chance approaching step—appearing, to the fancy of the man, as some creature from another world—poised lightly, ready to vanish if any rude observer came too near. Soon,—after a cautious, hesitating, listening look about,—she slipped, swift footed as a fawn, across the garden, and—followed by the dog—disappeared into the latticed rose-covered arbor against the southern wall.

With a chuckle to himself, Conrad Lagrange crept quietly along the hedge to the door of her retreat.

When she saw him there, she gave a little cry and started as though to escape. But the novelist, smiling barred her way; while Czar, joyfully greeting his master, turned from the man to the girl and back to the man again, as if, by dividing his attention equally between the two, he was bent upon assuring each that the other was a friend of the right sort. There was no mistaking the facts that the dog was introducing them, and that he was as proud of his new acquaintance as he was pleased to present his older and more intimate companion.

A sunny smile broke over the girl's winsome face, as she caught the meaning of Czar's behavior. "O," she said, "are you his master?" Her manner was as natural and unrestrained as a child's— her voice, musically sweet and low, as one unaccustomed to the speech of noisy, crowded cities or shrill chattering crowds.

"I am his most faithful and humble subject," returned the man, whimsically.

She was studying his face openly, while her own countenance—unschooled to hide emotions, untrained to deceive— frankly betrayed each passing thought and mood. The daintily turned chin, sensitive lips, delicate nostrils, and large, blue eyes,— with that wide, unafraid look of a child that has never been taught to fear,—revealed a spirit fine and rare; while the low, broad forehead, shaded by a wealth of soft brown hair,—that, arranged deftly in some simple fashion, seemed to invite the caress of every wayward breath of air,—gave the added charm of strength and purpose. The man, seeing these things and knowing—as few men ever know— their value, waited her verdict.

It came with a smile and a pretty fancy, as though she caught the mood of the novelist's reply. "He has told me so much about you—how kind you are to him, and how he loves you. I hope you don't mind that he and I have learned to be good friends. Won't you

66

tell me his name? I have tried everything, but nothing seems to fit. To call such a royal fellow, 'doggie', doesn't do at all, does it?"

Conrad Lagrange laughed—and it was the laugh of a Conrad Lagrange unknown to the world. "No," he said with mock seriousness, "'doggie,' doesn't do at all. He's not that kind of a dog. His name is Czar. That is"—he added, giving full rein to his droll humor—"I gave it to him for a name. He has made it his title. He did that, you know, so I would always remember that he is my superior."

She laughed—low, full-throated and clear—as a girl who has not sadly learned that she is a woman, laughs. Then she fell to caressing the dog and calling him by name; while Czar—in his efforts to express his delight and satisfaction—was as nearly undignified as it was possible for him to be.

As he watched them, the rugged, world-worn features of the famous novelist were lighted with an expression that transformed them.

"And I suppose," she said,—still responding to the novelist's playful mood,—"that Czar told you I was trespassing in your garden. Of course it was his duty to tell. I hope he told you, also, that I do not steal your roses."

The man shook his head, and his sharp, green-gray eyes were twinkling merrily, now—as a boy in the spirit of some amusing venture. "Oh, no! Czar said nothing at all about trespassers. He did tell me, though, about a wonderful creature that comes every day to visit the garden. A nymph, he thought it was—a beautiful Oread from away up there among the silver peaks and purple canyons—or, perhaps, a lovely Dryad from among the oaks and pines. I felt quite sure, though, that the nymph must be an Oread; because he said that she comes to gather colors from the roses, and that every morning and every evening she uses these colors to tint the highest peaks and crests of her mountains—making them so beautiful that mortals would always begin and end each day by looking up at them. Of course, the moment I saw, you I knew who you were."

Unaffectedly pleased as a child at his quaint fancy, she answered merrily, "And so you hid among the roses to trap me, I suppose."

"Indeed, I did not," he retorted indignantly. "I was forced to fly from a wicked Flibbertigibbet who seeks to torment me. I barely escaped with my life, and came into the garden to hide and recover from my fright. Then I heard the most wonderful music and guessed that you must be somewhere around. Then Czar, who had come

67

with me to hide from the Flibbertigibbet in the house, left me. I looked to see where he had gone, and so I saw, sure enough, that it was you. All my life, you know, I have wanted to catch a real nymph; but never could. So when you came into the arbor, I couldn't resist trying again. And, now, here we are—with Czar to say it is all right."

At his fanciful words, she laughed again, and her cheeks flushed with pleasure. Then, with grave sweetness, she said, "Won't you sit down, please, and let me explain seriously?"

"I suppose you must pretend to be like the rest of us," he returned with an air of resignation, "but all the same, Czar and I know you are not."

When they were seated, she said simply, "My name is Sibyl Andres. This place used to be my home. My mother planted this garden with her own hands. Many of these roses were brought from our home in the mountains, where I was born, and where I lived with father and mother until five years ago. I feel, still, as though the old place in the hills were my real home, and every summer, when nearly every one goes away from Fairlands and there is nothing for me to do, Myra Willard and I go up there, for as long as we can. You see, I teach music and play in the churches. Miss Willard taught me. She and mother are the only teachers I have ever had. After father's death, mother and Myra and I lived here for two years; then mother died, and Myra and I moved to that little house over there, because we could not afford to keep this place. But the man who bought it gave me permission to care for the garden; so I come almost every day—through that little gate in the corner of the hedge, there—to tend the roses. Since you men moved in, though, I come, mostly, in the morning—early—before you are up. I only slip in, sometimes, for a few minutes, in the afternoon—when I think it will be safe. You see, being strangers, I—I feared you would think me bold—if I—if I asked to come. So many people really wouldn't understand, you know."

Conrad Lagrange's deep voice was very gentle as he said, "Mr. King and I have known, all the time, that we had no real claim upon this garden, Miss Andrés." Then, with his whimsical smile, he added, "You see, we felt, from the very first, that it was haunted by a lovely spirit that would vanish utterly if we intruded. That is why we have been so careful. We did not want to frighten you away. And besides, you know, Czar told us that it was all right!"

The blue eyes shone through a bright mist as she answered the man's kindly words. "You are good, Mr. Lagrange. And all the time it was really you of whom I was so afraid."

"Why me, more than my friend?" he asked, regarding her thoughtfully.

She colored a little under his searching gaze, but answered with that childlike frankness that was so much a part of her winsome charm, "Why, because your friend is an artist—I thought he would be sure to understand. I knew, of course, that you were the famous author; everybody talks about your living here." She seemed to think that her words explained.

"You mean that you were afraid of me because I am famous?" he asked doubtfully.

"Oh no," she answered, "not because you are famous. I mean—I was not afraid of your fame," she smiled.

"And now," said the novelist decisively, "you must tell me at once—do you read my books?" He waited, as though much depended upon her answer.

The blue eyes were gazing at him with that wide, unafraid look as she answered sadly, "No, sir. I have tried, but I can't. They spoil my music. They hurt me, somehow, all over."

Conrad Lagrange received her words with mingled emotions—with pleased delight at her ingenuous frankness; with bitter shame, sorrow, and humiliation and, at the last, with genuine gladness and relief. "I knew it"—he said triumphantly—"I knew it. It was because of my books that you were so afraid of me?" He asked eagerly, as one would ask to have a deep conviction verified.

"You see," she said,—smiling at the manner of his words,—"I did not know that an author could be so different from the things he writes about." Then, with a puzzled air—"But why do you write the horrid things that spoil my music and make me afraid? Why don't you write as you talk—about—about the mountains? Why don't you make books like—like"—she seemed to be searching for a word, and smiled with pleasure when she found it—"like yourself?"

"Listen"—said the novelist impressively, taking refuge in his fanciful humor—"listen—I'll tell you a secret that must always be for just you and me—you like secrets don't you?"—anxiously.

She laughed with pleasure—responding instantly to his mood. "Of course I like secrets."

He nodded approval. "I was sure you did. Now listen—I am not really Conrad Lagrange, the man who wrote those books that hurt you so—not when I am here in your rose garden, or when I am listening to your music, or when I am away up there in your mountains, you know. It is only when I am in the unclean world that reads and likes my books that I am the man who wrote them."

Her eyes shone with quick understanding. "Of course," she agreed, "you couldn't be that kind of a man, and love the music, and like to be here among the roses or up in the mountains, could you?"

"No, and I'll tell you something else that goes with our secret. Your name is not really Sibyl Andrés, you know—any more than you really live over there in that little house. Your real home is in the mountains—just as you said—you really live among the glowing peaks, under the dark pines, on the ridges, and in the purple shadows of the canyons. You only come down here to the Fairlands folk with a message from your mountains—and we call your message music. Your name is—"

She was leaning forward, her face glowing with eagerness. "What is my name?"

"What can it be but 'Nature'," he said softly. "That's it, 'Nature'."

"And you? Who are you when you are not—when you are not in that other world?"

"Me? Oh, my real name is 'Civilization'. Can't you guess why?"

She shook her head. "Tell me."

"Because,—in spite of all that the world that reads my books can give,—poor old 'Civilization' cannot be happy without the message that 'Nature' brings from her mountains."

"And you, too, love the mountains and—and this garden, and my music?" she asked half doubtingly. "You are not pretending that too—just to amuse me?"

"No, I am not pretending that," he said.

"Then why—how can you do the—the other thing? I can't understand."

"Of course, you can't understand—how could you? You are 'Nature' and 'Nature' must often be puzzled by the things that 'Civilization' does."

"Yes. I think that is true," she agreed. "But I'm glad you like my music, anyway."

"And so am I glad—that I can like it. That's the only thing that saves me."

"And your friend, the artist,—does he like my mountain music, do you think?"

"Very much. He needs it too."

"I am glad," she answered simply. "I hoped he would like it, and that it would help him. It was really for him that I have played."

"You played for him?"

"Yes," she returned without confusion. "You see, I did not

know about you—then. I thought you were altogether the man who wrote those books—and so I could not play for you. That is—I mean—you understand—I could not play—" again she seemed to search for a word, and finding it, smiled—"I could not play myself for you. But I thought that because he was an artist he would understand; and that if I could make the music tell him of the mountains it would, perhaps, help him a little to make his work beautiful and right—do you see?"

"Yes," he answered smilingly, "I see. I might have known that it was for him that you brought your message from the hills. But poor old 'Civilization' is frightfully stupid sometimes, you know."

Laughingly, she turned to the lattice wall of the arbor, and parting the screen of vines a little, said to him, "Look here!"

Standing beside her, Conrad Lagrange, through the window in the end of the studio next the garden, saw Aaron King at his easel; the artist's position in the light of the big, north window being in a direct line between the two openings and the arbor. Mrs. Taine was sitting too far out of line to be seen.

The girl laughed gleefully. "Do you see him at his work? At first, I only hid here to find what kind of people were going to live in my old home. But when he was making our old barn into a studio, and I heard who you both were, I came because I love to watch him; as I try to make the music I think he would love to hear."

The novelist studied her intently. She was so artless—so unaffected by the conventions of the world—in a word, so natural in expressing her thoughts, that the man who had given the best years of his life to feed the vicious, grossly sensual and bestial imaginations of his readers was deeply moved. He was puzzled what to say. At last, he murmured haltingly, "You like the artist, then?"

Her eyes were full of curious laughter as she answered, "Why, what a funny question—when I have never even talked with him. How could I like any one I have never known?"

"But you make your music for him; and you come here to watch him?"

"Oh, but that is for the work he is doing; that is for his pictures." She turned to look through the tiny opening in the arbor. "How I wish I could see inside that beautiful room. I know it must be beautiful. Once, when you were all gone, I tried to steal in; but, of course, he keeps it locked."

"I'll tell you what we'll do," said the man, suddenly—prompted by her confession to resume his playful mood.

"What?" she asked eagerly, in a like spirit of fun.

71

"First," he answered, half teasingly, "I must know if you could, now, make your music for me as well as for him."

"For the you that loves the mountains and the garden I'm sure I could," she answered promptly.

"Well then, if you will promise to do that—if you will promise not to play yourself for just him alone but for me too—I'll fix it so that you can go into the studio yonder."

"Oh, I will always play for you, too, anyway—now that I know you."

"Of course," he said, "we could just walk up to the door, and I could introduce you; but that would not be proper for us would it?"

She shook her head positively, "I wouldn't like to do that. He would think I was intruding, I am sure."

"Well then, we will do it this way—the first day that Mr. King and I are both away, and Tee Kee is gone, too; I'll slip out here and leave a letter and a key on your gate. The letter will tell you just the time when we go, and when we will return—so you will know whether it is safe for you or not, and how long you can stay. Only"— he became very serious—"only, you must promise one thing."

"What?"

"That you won't look at the picture on the easel."

"But why must I promise that?"

"Because that picture will not be finished for a long time yet, and you must not look at it until I say it is ready. Mr. King wouldn't like you to see that picture, I am sure. In fact, he doesn't like for any one to see the picture he is working on just now."

"How funny," she said, with a puzzled look. "What is he painting it for? I like for people to hear my music."

The man answered before he thought—"But I don't like people to read my books."

She shrank back, with troubled eyes, "Oh! is he—is he that kind of an artist?"

"No, no, no!" exclaimed the novelist, hastily. "You must not think that. I did not mean you to think that. If he was that kind of an artist, I wouldn't let you go into the studio at all. Mr. King is a good man—the best man I have ever known. He is my friend because he knows the secret about me that you know. He does not read my books. He would not read one of them for anything. It is only that this picture is not finished. When it is finished, he will not care who sees it."

"I'm glad," she said. "You frightened me, for a minute—I understand, now."

"And you promise not to look at the picture on the easel?"

She nodded,—"Of course. And when I come out I'll lock the door and put the key back on the gate again; and no one but you and I will ever know."

"No one but you and I will know," he answered.

As he spoke, Czar, who had been lying quietly in the doorway of the arbor, rose quickly to his feet, with a low growl.

The girl, peering through the screen on the side toward the house, uttered an exclamation of fear and drew back, turning to her companion appealingly. "O please, please don't let that man find me here."

Conrad Lagrauge looked and saw James Rutlidge coming down the path toward the arched entrance to the garden, which was directly across from the arbor.

"Stop him, please stop him," whispered the girl, her hand upon his arm.

"Stay here until I get him out of sight," said the novelist quickly. "I won't let him come into the garden. When we are gone, you can make your escape. Don't forget the music for me, and the key at the gate."

He spoke to Czar, and with the dog obediently at heel went forward to meet Mr. Rutlidge, who had called for Mrs. Taine and Louise.

But all the while that Conrad Lagrange was talking to the man, and leading him toward the door of the studio, he was wondering—why that look of fear upon the face of the girl in the garden? What had Sibyl Andrés to do with James Rutlidge?

Chapter X
A Cry in the Night

As Conrad Lagrange and Mr. Rutlidge entered the studio, Aaron King turned from the easel, where he had drawn the velvet curtain to hide the finished portrait. Mrs. Taine was standing at the other side of the room, wrap in hand, calmly waiting, ready to go. The artist greeted Mr. Rutlidge cordially, while the woman triumphantly announced the completion of her portrait.

"Ah! permit me to congratulate you, old man," said Rutlidge, addressing the artist familiarly. "It is too much, I suppose, to expect a look at it this afternoon?"

"Thanks,"—returned the artist,—"you are all coming to-morrow, at three, you know. I would rather not show it to-day. It is a little late for the best light; and I would like for you to see it under the most favorable conditions possible."

The critic was visibly flattered by the painter's manner and by his well-chosen emphasis upon the personal pronoun. "Quite right"—he said approvingly—"quite right, old boy." He turned to the novelist—"These painter chaps, you know, Lagrange, like to have a few hours for a last touch or two before I come around." He laughed pompously at his own words—the others joining.

When Mrs. Taine and her companions were gone, the artist said hurriedly to his friend, "Come on, let's get it over." He led the way back to the studio.

"I thought the light was too bad," said the older man, quizzingly, as they entered the big room.

"It's good enough for your needs," retorted the painter savagely. "You could see all you want by candle-light." He jerked the curtain angrily aside, and—without a glance at the canvas—walked away to stand at the window looking out upon the rose garden—waiting for the flood of the novelist's scorn to overwhelm him. At last, when no sound broke the quiet of the room, he turned—to find himself alone.

Conrad Lagrange, after one look at the portrait on the easel, had slipped quietly out of the building.

The artist found his friend, a few minutes later, meditatively smoking his pipe on the front porch, with Czar lying at his feet.

"Well," said the painter, curiously,—anxious, as he had said, to have it over,—"why the deuce don't you say something?"

The novelist answered slowly, "My vocabulary is too limited, for one reason, and"—he looked thoughtfully down at Czar—"I prefer to wait until you have finished the portrait."

"It is finished," returned the artist desperately. "I swear I'll never touch a brush to the damned thing again."

The man with the pipe spoke to the dog at his feet; "Listen to him, Czar—listen to the poor devil of a painter-man."

The dog arose, and, placing his head upon his master's knee, looked up into the lined and rugged face, as the novelist continued, "If he was only a wee bit puffed up and cocky over the thing, now, we could exert ourselves, so we could, couldn't we?" Czar slowly waved a feathery tail in dignified approval. His master continued, "But when a fellow can do a crime like that, and still retain enough virtue in his heart to hear his work shrieking to heaven its curses upon him for calling it into existence, it's best for outsiders to keep quite still. Your poor old master knows whereof he speaks, doesn't he, dog? That he does!"

"And is that all you have to say on the subject?" demanded the artist, as though for some reason he was disappointed at his friend's reticence.

"I might add a word of advice," said the other.

"Well, what is it?"

"That you pray your gods—if you have any—to be merciful, and bestow upon you either less genius or more intelligence to appreciate it."

At three o'clock, the following afternoon, the little party from Fairlands Heights came to view, the portrait Or,—as Conrad Lagrange said, while the automobile was approaching the house, "Well, here they come—'The Age', accompanied by 'Materialism', 'Sensual', and 'Ragtime'—to look upon the prostitution of Art, and call it good." Escorted by the artist, and the novelist, they went at once to the studio.

The appreciation of the picture was instantaneous—so instantaneous, in fact, that Louise Taine's lips were shaped to deliver an expressive "oh" of admiration, even before the portrait was revealed. As though the painter, in drawing back the easel curtain, gave an appointed signal, that "oh" was set off with the suddenness of a sky-rocket's rush, and was accompanied in its flight by a great volume of sizzling, sputtering, glittering, adjectival sparks that—filling the air to no purpose whatever—winked out as they were born; the climax of the pyrotechnical display being reached in the explosive pop of another "oh" which released a brilliant shower of variegated sighs and moans and ecstatic looks and inarticulate exclamations—ending, of course, in total darkness.

Mrs. Taine hastened to turn the artist's embarrassed attention to an appreciation that had the appearance, at least, of a more enduring value. Drawing, with affectionate solicitude, close to her husband, she asked,—in a voice that was tremulous with loving care and anxiety to please,—"Do you like it, dear?"

"It is magnificent, splendid, perfect!" This effort to give his praise of the artist's work the appearance of substantial reality cost the wretched product of lust and luxury a fit of coughing that racked his burnt-out body almost to its last feeble hold upon the world of flesh and, with a force that shamed the strength of his words, drove home the truth that neither his praise nor his scorn could long endure. When he could again speak, he said, in his husky, rasping whisper,—while grasping the painter's hand in effusive cordiality,— "My dear fellow, I congratulate you. It is exquisite. It will create a sensation, sir, when it is exhibited. Your fame is assured. I must thank you for the honor you have done me in thus immortalizing the beauty and character of Mrs. Taine." And then, to his wife,— "Dearest, I am glad for you, and proud. It is as worthy of you as paint and canvas could be." He turned to Conrad Lagrange who was an interested observer of the scene—"Am I not right, Lagrange?"

"Quite right, Mr. Taine,—quite right. As you say, the portrait is most worthy the beauty and character of the charming subject."

Another paroxysm of coughing mercifully prevented the poor creature's reply.

With one accord, the little group turned, now, to James Rutlidge—the dreaded authority and arbiter of artistic destinies. That distinguished expert, while the others were speaking, had been listening intently; ostensibly, the while, he examined the picture with a show of trained skill that, it seemed, could not fail to detect unerringly those more subtle values and defects that are popularly supposed to be hidden from the common eye. Silently, in breathless awe, they watched the process by which professional criticism finds its verdict. That is, they thought they were watching the process. In reality, the method is more subtle than they knew.

While the great critic moved back and forth in front of the easel; drew away from or bent over to closely scrutinize the canvas; shifted the easel a hair breadth several times; sat down; stood erect; hummed and muttered to himself abstractedly; cleared his throat with an impressive "Ahem"; squinted through nearly closed eyes, with his head thrown back, or turned in every side angle his fat neck would permit: peered through his half-closed fist; peeped through funnels of paper; sighted over and under his open hand or a paper held to shut out portions of the painting;—the others thought they saw him expertly weighing the evidence for and against the merit of the work. In reality it was his ears and not his eyes that helped the critic to his final decision—a decision which was delivered, at last, with a convincing air of ponderous finality. Indeed it was a judgment from which there could be no appeal, for it expressed exactly the views of those for whose benefit it was rendered. Then, in a manner subtly insinuating himself into the fellowship of the famous, he, too, turned to Conrad Lagrange with a scholarly; "Do you not agree, sir?"

The novelist answered with slow impressiveness; "The picture, undoubtedly, fully merits the appreciation and praise you have given it. I have already congratulated Mr. King—who was kind enough to show me his work before you arrived."

After this, Yee Kee appeared upon the scene, and tea was served in the studio—a fitting ceremony to the launching of another genius.

"By the way, Mr. Lagrange," said Mrs. Taine, quite casually,—when, under the influence of the mildly stimulating beverage, the talk had assumed a more frivolous vein,—"Who is your talented neighbor that so charms Mr. King with the music of a violin?"

The novelist, as he turned toward the speaker, shot a quick glance at the Artist. Nor did those keen, baffling eyes fail to note that, at the question, James Rutlidge had paused in the middle of a sentence. "That is one of the mysteries of our romantic surroundings madam," said Conrad Lagrange, easily.

"And a very charming mystery it seems to be," returned the woman. "It has been quite affecting to watch its influence upon Mr. King."

The artist laughed. "I admit that I found the music, in combination with the beauty I have so feebly tried to out upon canvas, very stimulating."

A flash of angry color swept into the perfect cheeks of Mrs. Taine, as she retorted with meaning; "You are as flattering in your speech as you are with your brush. I assure you I do not consider myself in your unknown musician's class."

The small eyes of James Rutlidge were fixed inquiringly upon the speakers, while his heavy face betrayed—to the watchful novelist—an interest he could not hide. "Is this music of such exceptional merit?" he asked with an attempt at indifference.

Louise Taine—sensing that the performances of the unnamed violinist had been acceptable to Conrad Lagrange and Aaron King—the two representatives of the world to which she aspired—could not let the opportunity slip. She fairly deluged them with the spray of her admiring ejaculations in praise of the musician—employing, hit or miss, every musical term that popped into her vacuous head.

77

"Indeed,"—said the critic,—"I seem to have missed a treat." Then, directly to the artist,—"And you say the violinist is wholly unknown to you?"

"Wholly," returned the painter, shortly.

Conrad Lagrange saw a faint smile of understanding and disbelief flit for an instant over the heavy face of James Rutlidge.

When the automobile, at last, was departing with the artist's guests; the two friends stood for a moment watching it up the road to the west, toward town. As the big car moved away, they saw Mrs. Taine lean forward to speak to the chauffeur while James Rutlidge, who was in the front seat, turned and shook his head as though in protest. The woman appeared to insist. The machine slowed down, as though ihe chauffeur, in doubt, awaited the outcome of the discussion. Then, just in front of that neighboring house, Rutlidge seemed to yield abruptly, and the automobile turned suddenly in toward the curb and stopped. Mrs. Taine alighted, and disappeared in the depths of the orange grove.

Aaron King and Conrad Lagrange looked at each other, for a moment, in questioning silence. The artist laughed. "Our poor little mystery," he said.

But the novelist—as they went toward the house—cursed Mrs. Taine, James Rutlidge, and all their kin and kind, with a vehement earnestness that startled his companion—familiar as the latter was with his friend's peculiar talent in the art of vigorous expression.

After dinner, that evening, the painter and the novelist sat on the porch—as their custom was—to watch the day go out of the sky and the night come over valley and hill and mountain until, above the highest peaks, the stars of God looked down upon the twinkling lights of the towns of men. At that hour, too, it was the custom, now, for the violinist hidden in the orange grove, to make the music they both so loved.

In the music, that night, there was a feeling that, to them, was new—a vague, uncertain, halting undertone that was born, they felt, of fear. It stirred them to question and to wonder. Without apparent cause or reason, they each oddly connected the troubled tone in the music with the stopping of the automobile from Fairlands Heights, that afternoon, at the gate of the little house next door—the artist, because of Mrs. Taine's insistent inquiry about the, to him, unknown musician;—Conrad Lagrange, because of the manner of the girl in the garden when James Rutlidge appeared and because of the critic's interest when they had spoken of the violinist in the studio. But neither expressed his thought to the other.

Presently, the music ceased, and they sat for an hour, perhaps, in silence—as close friends may do—exchanging only now and then a word.

Suddenly, they were startled by a cry. In the still darkness of the night, from the mysterious depths of the orange grove, the sound came with such a shock that the two men, for the moment, held their places, motionless—questioning each other sharply— "What was that?" "Did you hear?"—as though they doubted, almost, their own ears.

The cry came again; this time, undoubtedly, from that neighboring house to the west. It was unmistakably the cry of a woman—a woman in fear and pain.

They leaped to their feet.

Again the cry came from the black depths of the orange grove—shuddering, horrible—in an agony of fear.

The two men sprang from the porch, and, through the darkness that in the orange grove was like a black wall, ran toward the spot from which the sound came—the dog at their heels.

Breathless, they broke into the little yard in front of the tiny box-like house. Lights shone in the windows. All seemed peaceful and still. Czar betrayed no uneasiness. Going to the front door, they knocked.

There was no answer save the sound of some one moving inside.

Again, the artist knocked vigorously.

The door opened, and a woman stood on the threshold.

Standing a little to one side, the men saw her features clearly, in the light from the room. It was the woman with the disfigured face.

Conrad Lagrange was first to command himself. "I beg your pardon, madam. We live in the house next door. We thought we heard a cry of distress. May we offer our assistance in any way? Is there anything we can do?"

"Thank you, sir, you are very kind,"—returned the woman, in a low voice,—"but it is nothing. There is nothing you can do."

And the voice of Sibyl Andrés, who stood farther back in the room, where the artist from his position could not see her, added, "It was good of you to come, Mr. Lagrange; but it is really nothing. We are so sorry you were disturbed."

"Not at all," returned the men, as the woman of the disfigured face drew back from the door. "Good night."

"Good night," came from within the house, and the door was shut.

Chapter XI
Go Look In Your Mirror, You Fool

As the Taine automobile left Aaron King and his friend, that afternoon, Mrs. Taine spoke to the chauffeur; "You may stop a moment, at the next house, Henry."

If she had fired a gun, James Rutlidge could not have turned with a more startled suddenness.

"What in thunder do you want there?" he demanded shortly.

"I want to stop," she returned calmly.

"But I must get down town, at once," he protested. "I have already lost the best part of the afternoon."

"Your business seems to have become important very suddenly," she observed, sarcastically.

"I have something to do besides making calls with you," he retorted. "Go on, Henry."

Mrs. Taine spoke sharply; "Really, Jim, you are going too far. Henry, turn in at the house." The machine moved toward the curb and stopped. As she stepped from the car, she added, "I will only be a minute, Jim."

Rutlidge growled an inarticulate curse.

"What deviltry do you suppose she is up to now," rasped Mr. Taine.

Which brought from his daughter the usual protest,—"O, papa, don't,"

As Mrs. Taine approached the house, Sibyl Andrés—busy among the flowers that bordered the walk—heard the woman's step, and stood quietly waiting her. Mrs. Taine's face was perfect in its expression of cordial interest, with just enough—but not too much—of a conscious, well-bred superiority. The girl's countenance was lighted by an expression of childlike surprise and wonder. What had brought this well-known leader in the social world from Fairlands Heights to the poor, little house in the orange grove, so far down the hill?

"Good afternoon," said the caller. "You are Miss Andrés, are you not?"

"Yes," returned the girl, with a smile. "Won't you come in? I will call Miss Willard."

"Oh, thank you, no. I have only a moment. My friends are waiting. I am Mrs. Taine."

"Yes, I know. I have often seen you passing."

The other turned abruptly. "What beautiful flowers."

"Aren't they lovely," agreed Sibyl, with frank pleasure at the visitor's appreciation. "Let me give you a bunch." Swiftly she gathered a generous armful.

Mrs. Taine protested, but the girl presented her offering with such grace and winsomeness that the other could not refuse. As she received the gift, the perfect features of the woman of the world were colored by a blush that even she could not control. "I understand, Miss Andrés," she said, "that you are an accomplished violinist."

"I teach and play in Park Church," was the simple answer.

"I have never happened to hear you, myself,"—said Mrs. Taine smoothly,—"but my friends who live next door—Mr. Lagrange and Mr. King—have told me about you."

"Oh!" The girl's voice was vaguely troubled, while the other, watching, saw the blush that colored her warmly tinted cheeks.

"It is good of you to play for them," continued the woman from Fairlands Heights, casually. "You must enjoy the society of such famous men, very much. There are a great many people, you know, who would envy you your friendship with them."

The girl replied quickly, "O, but you are mistaken. I am not acquainted with them, at all; that is—not with Mr. King—I have never spoken to him—and I only met Mr. Lagrange, for a few minutes, by accident."

"Indeed! But I am forgetting the purpose of my call, and my friends will become impatient. Do you ever play for private entertainments, Miss Andrés?—for—say a dinner, or a reception, you know?"

"I would be very glad for such an engagement, Mrs. Taine. I must earn what I can with my music, and there are not enough pupils to occupy all my time. But perhaps you should hear me play, first. I will get my violin."

Mrs. Taine checked her, "Oh, no, indeed. It is quite unnecessary, my dear. The opinion of your distinguished neighbors is quite enough. I shall keep you in mind for some future occasion. I just wished to learn if you would accept such an engagement. Good-by. Thanks—so much—for your flowers."

She was upon the point of turning away, when a low cry from the nearby porch startled them both. Turning, they saw the woman with the disfigured face, standing in the doorway; an expression of mingled wonder, love, and supplication upon her hideously marred

81

features. As they looked, she started toward them,—impulsively stretching out her arms, as though the gesture was an involuntary expression of some deep emotion,—then checked herself, suddenly as though in doubt.

Sibyl Andrés uttered an exclamation. "Why, Myra! what is it, dear?"

Mrs. Taine turned away with a gesture of horror, saying to the girl in a low, hurried voice, "Dear me, how dreadful! I really must be going."

As she went down the flower-bordered path towards the street, the woman on the porch, again, stretched out her arms appealingly. Then, as Sibyl reached her side, the poor creature clasped the girl in a close embrace, and burst into bitter tears.

Upon the return of the Taines and James Rutlidge to the house on Fairlands Heights, Mrs. Taine retired immediately to her own luxuriously appointed apartments.

At dinner, a maid brought to the household word that her mistress was suffering from a severe headache and would not be down and begged that she might not be disturbed during the evening.

Alone in her room, Mrs. Taine—her headache being wholly conventional—gave herself unreservedly to the thoughts that she could not, under the eyes of others, entertain without restraint. She was seated at a window that looked down upon the carefully graded levels of the envying Fairlanders and across the wide sweep of the valley below to the mountains which, from that lofty point of vantage, could be seen from the base of their lowest foothills to the crests of their highest peaks. But the woman who lived on the Heights of Fairlands saw neither the homes of their neighbors, the busy valley below, nor the mountains that lifted so far above them all. Her thoughts were centered upon what, to her, was more than these.

When night was gathering over the scene, her maid entered softly. Mrs. Taine dismissed the woman with a word, telling her not to return until she rang. Leaving the window, after drawing the shades close, she paced the now lighted room, in troubled uneasiness of mind. Here and there, she paused to touch or handle some familiar object—a photograph in a silver frame, a book on the carved table, the trifles on her open desk, or an ornamental vase on the mantle—then moved restlessly away to continue her aimless exercise. When the silence was rudely broken by the sound of a knock at her door, she stood still—a look of anger marring the well-schooled beauty of her features.

The knock was repeated.

With an exclamation of impatient annoyance, she crossed the room, and flung open the door.

Without leave or apology, her husband entered; and, as he did so, was seized by a paroxysm of coughing that sent him reeling, gasping and breathless, to the nearest chair.

Mrs. Taine stood watching her husband coldly, with a curious, speculative expression on her face that she made no attempt to hide. When his torture was abated—for the time—leaving him exhausted and trembling with weakness, she said coldly, "Well, what do you want? What are you doing here?"

The man lifted his pallid, haggard face and, with a yellow, claw-like hand wiped the beads of clammy sweat from his forehead; while his deep-sunken eyes leered at her with an insane light.

The woman was at no pains to conceal her disgust. In her voice there was no hint of pity. "Didn't Marie tell you that I wished to be alone?"

"Of course," he jeered in his rasping whisper, "that's why I came." He gave a hideous resemblance to a laugh, which ended in a cough—and, again, he drew his skinny, shaking hand across his damp forehead "That's the time that a man should visit his wife, isn't it? When she is alone. Or"—he grinned mockingly—"when she wishes to be?"

She regarded him with open scorn and loathing. "You unclean beast! Will you take yourself out of my room?"

He gazed at her, as a malevolent devil might gloat over a soul delivered up for torture. "Not until I choose to go, my dear."

Suddenly changing her manner, she smiled with deliberate, mocking humor. While he watched, she moved leisurely to a deep, many-cushioned couch; and, arranging the pillows, reclined among them in the careless abandonment of voluptuous ease and physical content. Openly, ostentatiously, she exhibited herself to his burning gaze in various graceful poses—lifting her arms above her head to adjust a cushion more to her liking; turning and stretching her beautiful body; moving her limbs with sinuous enjoyment—as disregardful of his presence as though she were alone. At last she spoke in cool, even, colorless tones; "Perhaps you will tell me what you want?"

The wretched victim of his own unbridled sensuality shook with inarticulate rage. Choking and coughing he writhed in his chair—his emaciated limbs twisted grotesquely; his sallow face bathed in perspiration his claw-like hands opening and closing; his

83

bloodless lips curled back from his yellow teeth, in a horrid grin of impotent fury. And all the while she lay watching him with that pitiless, mocking, smile. It was as though the malevolent devil and the tortured soul had suddenly changed places.

When the man could speak, he reviled her, in his rasping whisper, with curses that it seemed must blister his tongue. She received his effort with jeering laughter and taunting words; moving her body, now and then, among the cushions, with an air of purely physical enjoyment that, to the other, was maddening.

"If this is all you came for,"—she said, easily,—"might have spared yourself the effort—don't you think?"

Controlling himself, in a measure, he returned, "I came to tell you that your intimacy with that damned painter must stop."

Her eyes narrowed slightly. One hand, hidden in the cushions, clenched until her rings hurt. "Just what do you mean by my intimacy?" she asked evenly.

"You know what I mean," he replied coarsely. "I mean what intimacy with a man always means to a woman like you."

"The only meaning that a creature of your foul mind can understand," she retorted smoothly. "If it were worth while to tell you the truth, I would say that my conduct when alone with Mr. King has been as proper as—as when I am alone with you."

The taunt maddened him. Interrupted by spells of coughing— choking, gasping, fighting for breath, his eyes blazing with hatred and lust, mingling his words with oaths and curses—he raged at her. "And do you think—that, because I am so nearly dead,—I do not resent what—I saw, to-day? Do you think—I am so far gone that I cannot—understand—your interest in this man,—after—watching you, together, all—the afternoon? Has there been any one—in his studio, except you two, when—he was painting you in that dress— which you—designed for his benefit? Oh, no, indeed,—you and your—genius could not be interrupted,—for the sake—of his art. His art! Great God!—was there ever such a damnable farce—since hell was invented? Art!—you—you—you!—" crazed with jealous fury, he pointed at her with his yellow, shaking, skeleton fingers; and struggled to raise his voice above that rasping whisper until the cords of his scrawny neck stood out and his face was distorted with the strain of his effort—"You! painted as a—modest Quaker Maid,— with all the charm of innocence,—virtue, and religious piety in your face. You! And that picture will be exhibited—and written about—as a work of art! You'll pull all the strings,—and use all your influence,—and the thing—will be received as a—masterpiece."

"And," she added calmly, "you will write a check—and lie, as you did this afternoon."

Without heeding her remark, he went on,—"You know the picture is worthless. He knows it,—Conrad Lagrange knows it,—Jim Rutlidge knows it,—the whole damned clique and gang of you know it, He's like all his kind,—a pretender,—a poser,—playing into the hands—of such women as you; to win social position—and wealth. And we and our kind—we pretend to believe—in such damned parasites,—and exalt them and what we—call their art,—and keep them in luxury, and buy their pictures;—because they prostitute—their talents to gratify our vanity. We know it's all a damned sham—and a pretense that if they were real artists,—with an honest workman's respect for their work,—they wouldn't—recognize us."

"Don't forget to send him a check,"—she murmured—"you can't afford to neglect it, you know—think how people would talk."

"Don't worry," he replied. "There'll be no talk. I'll send the genius his check—for making love—to my wife in the sacred name of art,—and I'll lie—about his picture with—the rest of you. But there will be—no more of your intimacy with him. You're my wife,—in spite of hell,—and from now on—I'll see—that you are true—to me. Your sickening pose—of modesty in dress shall be something—more than a pose. For the little time I have left,—I'll have—you to—myself or I'll kill you."

His reference to her refusal to uncover her shoulders in public broke the woman's calm and aroused her to a cold fury. Springing to her feet, she stood over him as he sat huddled in his chair, exhausted by his effort.

"What is your silly, idle threat beside the fact," she said with stinging scorn. "To have killed me, instead of making me your wife, would have been a kindness greater than you are capable of. You know how unspeakably vile you were when you bought me. You know how every hour of my life with you has been a torment to me. You should be grateful that I have helped you to live your lie—that I have played the game of respectability with you—that I am willing to play it a little while longer, until you lay down your hand for good, and release us both.

"Suppose I were what you think me? What right have you to object to my pleasures? Have you—in all your life of idle, vicious, luxury—have you ever feared to do evil if it appealed to your bestial nature? You know you have not. You have feared only the appearance of evil. To be as evil as you like so long as you can avoid the appearance of evil; that's the game you have taught me to play.

85

That's the game we have played together. That's the game we and our kind insist the artists and writers shall help us play. That's the only game I know, and, by the rule of our game, so long as the world sees nothing, I shall do what pleases me.

"You have had your day with me. You have had what you paid for. What right have you to deny me, now, an hour's forgetfulness? When I think of what I might have been, but for you, I wonder that I have cared to live, and I would not—except for the poor sport of torturing you.

"You scoff at Mr. King's portrait of me because he has not painted me as I am! What would you have said if he had painted me as I am? What would you say if Conrad Lagrange should write the truth about us and our kind, for his millions of readers? You sneer at me because I cannot uncover my shoulders in the conventional dress of my class, and so make a virtue of a necessity and deceive the world by a pretense of modesty. Go look in your mirror, you fool! Your right to sneer at me for my poor little pretense is denied you by every line of your repulsive countenance Now get out. I'm going to retire."

And she rang for her maid.

Chapter XII
First Fruits of His Shame

When the postman, in his little cart, stopped at the home of Aaron King and his friend, that day, it was Conrad Lagrange who received the mail. The artist was in his studio, and the novelist, knowing that the painter was not at work, went to him there with a letter.

The portrait—still on the easel—was hidden by the velvet curtain. Sitting by a table that was littered with a confusion of sketches, books and papers, the young man was re-tying a package of old letters that he had, evidently, just been reading.

As the novelist went to him, the artist said quietly,—indicating the package in his hand,—"From my mother. She wrote them during the last year of my study abroad." When the other did not reply, he continued thoughtfully, "Do you know, Lagrange, since my acquaintance with you, I find many things in these old letters that—at the time I received them—I did not, at all, appreciate. You seem to be helping me, somehow, to a better understanding of my mother's spirit and mind." He smiled.

Presently, Conrad Lagrange, when he could trust himself to speak, said, "Your mother's mind and spirit, Aaron, were too fine and rare to be fully appreciated or understood except by one trained in the school of life, itself. When she wrote those letters, you were a student of mere craftsmanship. She, herself no doubt, recognized that you would not fully comprehend the things she wrote; but she put them down, out of the very fullness of her intellectual and spiritual wealth—trusting to your love to preserve the letters, and to the years to give you understanding."

"Why," cried the artist, "those are almost her exact words—as I have just been reading them!"

The other, smiling, continued quietly, "Your appreciation and understanding of your mother will continue to grow through all your life, Aaron. When you are old—as old as I am—you will still find in those letters hidden treasures of thought, and truths of greater value than you, now, can realize. But here—I have brought you your share of the afternoon's mail."

When Aaron King opened the envelope that his friend laid on the table before him, he sat regarding its contents with an air of thoughtful meditation—lost to his surroundings.

The novelist—who had gone to the window and was looking into the rose garden—turned to speak to his friend; but the other did not reply. Again, the man at the window addressed the painter; but still the younger man was silent. At this, Conrad Lagrange came back to the table; an expression of anxiety upon his face. "What is it, old man? What's the matter? No bad news, I hope?"

Aaron King, aroused from his fit of abstraction, laughed shortly, and held out to his friend the letter he had just received. It was from Mr. Taine. Enclosed was the millionaire's check. The letter was a formal business note; the check was for an amount that drew a low whistle from the novelist's lips.

"Rather higher pay than old brother Judas received for a somewhat similar service, isn't it," he commented, as he passed the letter and check back to the artist. Then, as he watched the younger man's face, he asked, "What's the matter, don't you like the flavor of these first fruits of your shame? I advise you to cultivate a taste for this sort of thing as quickly as possible—in your own defense."

"Don't you think you are a little bit too hard on us all, Lagrange?" asked the artist, with a faint smile. "These people are satisfied. The picture pleases them."

"Of course they are pleased," retorted the other. "You know your business. That's the trouble with you. That's the trouble with us all, these days—we painters and writers and musicians—we know our business too damned well. We have the mechanics of our crafts, the tricks of our trades, so well in hand that we make our books and pictures and music say what we please. We use our art to gain our own vain ends instead of being driven by our art to find adequate expression for some great truth that demands through us a hearing. You have said it all, my friend—you have summed up the whole situation in the present-day world of creative art—these people are satisfied. You have given them what they want, prostituting your art to do it. That's what I have been doing all these years—giving people what they want. For a price we cater to them—even as their tailors, and milliners, and barbers. And never again will the world have a truly great art or literature until men like us—in the divine selfishness of their, calling—demand, first and last, that they, themselves, be satisfied by the work of their hands."

Going to the easel, he rudely jerked aside the curtain. Involuntarily, the painter went to stand by his side before the picture.

"Look at it!" cried the novelist. "Look at it in the light of your own genius! Don't you see its power? Doesn't it tell you what you

88

could do, if you would? If you couldn't paint a picture, or if you couldn't feel a picture to be painted, it wouldn't matter. I'd let you ride to hell on your own palette, and be damned to you. But this thing shows a power that the world can ill afford to lose. It is so bad because it is so good. Come here!" he drew his friend to the big window, and pointed to the mountains. "There is an art like those mountains, my boy—lonely, apart from the world; remotely above the squalid ambitions of men; Godlike in its calm strength and peace—an art to which men may look for inspiration and courage and hope. And there is an art that is like Fairlands—petty and shallow and mean—with only the fictitious value that its devotees assume, but never, actually, realize. Listen, Aaron, don't continue to misread your mother's letters. Don't misunderstand her as thinking that the place she coveted for you is a place within the power of these people to give. Come with me into the mountains, yonder. Come, and let us see if, in those hills of God, you cannot find yourself."

When Conrad Lagrange finished, the artist stood, for a little, without reply—irresolute, before his picture—the check in his hand. At last, still without speaking, he went back to the table, where he wrote briefly his reply to Mr. Taine. When he had finished, he handed his letter to the older man, who read:

Dear Sir:

In reply to yours of the 13th, inst., enclosing your check in payment for the portrait of Mrs. Taine; I appreciate your generosity, but cannot, now, accept it.

I find, upon further consideration, that the portrait does not fully satisfy me. I shall, therefore, keep the canvas until I can, with the consent of my own mind, put my signature upon it.

Herewith, I am returning your check; for, of course, I cannot accept payment for an unfinished work.

In a day or two, Mr. Lagrange and I will start to the mountains, for an outing. Trusting that you and your family will enjoy the season at Lake Silence I am, with kind regards,

Yours sincerely, Aaron King.

That evening, the two men talked over their proposed trip, and laid their plans to start without delay As Conrad Lagrange put it—they would lose themselves in the hills; with no definite destination in view; and no set date for their return. Also, he stipulated that they should travel light—with only a pack burro to carry their supplies—and that they should avoid the haunts of the summer resorters, and keep to the more unfrequented trails. The novelist's acquaintance with the country into which they would go, and his experience in woodcraft—gained upon many like expeditions in the lonely wilds he loved—would make a guide unnecessary. It would be a new experience for Aaron King; and, as the novelist talked, he found himself eager as a schoolboy for the trip; while the distant mountains, themselves, seemed to call him— inviting him to learn the secret of their calm strength and the spirit of their lofty peace. The following day, they would spend in town; purchasing an outfit of the necessary equipment and supplies, securing a burro, and attending to numerous odds and ends of business preparatory to their indefinite absence.

It so happened, the next day, that Yee Kee,—who was to care for the place during their weeks of absence had matters of importance to himself, that demanded his attention in town. When his masters informed him that they would not be home for lunch, he took advantage of the opportunity and asked for the day.

Thus it came about that Conrad Lagrange—in the spirit of a boy bent upon some secret adventure—stole out into the rose garden, that morning, to leave the promised letter and key at the little gate in the corner of the Ragged Robin hedge.

Chapter XIII
Myra Willard's Challenge

Since her meeting with Conrad Lagrange in the rose garden, Sibyl Andrés had looked, every day, for that promised letter. She found it early in the afternoon. It was a quaint letter—written in the spirit of their meeting—telling her the probable time of her neighbor's return; warning her, in fear of some fanciful horror, to beware of the picture on the easel; and wishing her joy of the adventure. With the note, was a key.

A few minutes later, the girl unlocked the door of the studio, and entered the building that had once been so familiar to her, but was now, in its interior, so transformed. Slowly, she pushed the door to, behind her. As though half frightened at her own daring, she stood quite still, looking about. In the atmosphere of that somewhat richly furnished apartment; poised timidly as if for ready flight; she seemed, indeed, the spirit that the novelist—in playful fancy—insisted that she was. Her cheeks were glowing with color; her eyes were bright with the excitement of her innocent adventure, and with her genuine admiration and appreciation of the beautiful room.

Presently,—growing bolder,—she began moving about the studio—light-footed and graceful as a wild thing from her own mountain home, and, indeed, with much the air of a gentle creature of the woods that had strayed into the haunts of men. Intensely interested in the things she found, she gradually forgot her timidity, and gave herself to the enjoyment of her surroundings, with the freedom and abandon of a child. From picture to picture, she went, with wide, eager eyes. She turned over the sketches in the big portfolios that were so invitingly open; looked with awe upon the brushes stuck in the big Chinese jar—upon the palettes, and at the tubes of color; flitting to the window that looked out upon her garden, and back to the great, north light with its view of the distant mountains; and again and again, paused to stand with her hands clasped behind her, in front of the big easel with its canvas hidden under the velvet curtain. Then she must try the chairs, the oriental couch, and even the stool—where she had seen the artist sitting, sometimes, at his work, when she had watched him from the arbor; and last—in a pretty make believe—she tried the seat on the model throne, as though posing herself, for her portrait.

Suddenly, with a startled cry, she sprang to her feet; then shrank back, white and trembling—her big eyes fixed with pleading fear upon the man who stood in the open doorway, regarding her with a curious, triumphant smile. It was James Rutlidge.

Sibyl, occupied with her childlike delight, had failed to hear the automobile when it stopped in front of the house. Finding no one in the house the man had gone on to the studio, where—with the assurance of an intimate acquaintance—he had pushed open the door that was standing ajar.

At the girl's frightened manner, the man laughed. Closing the door, he said, with an insinuating sneer, "You were not expecting me, it seems."

His words aroused Sibyl from her momentary weakness. Rising, she said calmly, "I was not expecting any one, Mr. Rutlidge."

Again he laughed—with unpleasant meaning. "You certainly look to be very much at home." He moved confidently to the easel stool and, seating himself continued with a leering smile, "What's the matter with my taking the artist's place for a little while—at least, until he comes?"

The girl was too innocent to understand his assumption but her pure mind could not fail to sense the evil in his words.

"I had permission to come here this afternoon," she said—her voice trembling a little with the fear that she did not understand. "Won't you go, please? Neither Mr. King nor Mr. Lagrange are at home."

"I do not doubt your having permission to come here," he returned, with meaning stress upon the word, "permission". "I see you even carry a key to this really delightful room." He motioned with his head toward the door where he had seen the key in the lock, as she had left it.

At this, she grasped a hint of the man's thought and, for an instant, drew hack in shame. Then, suddenly with a burst of indignant anger, she took a step toward him, demanding clearly; "Are you saying that I am in the habit of coming here to meet Mr. King?"

He laughed mockingly. "Really, my dear, no one, seeing you, now, could blame the man for giving you a key to this place where he is popularly supposed to be undisturbed. Mr. King is neither such a virtuous saint, nor so engrossed in his art, as to resent the companionship of such a vision of loveliness—simply because it comes in the form of good flesh and blood. Why be angry with me?"

Her cheeks were crimson as she said, again, "Will you go?"

"Not until you have settled the terms of peace," he answered with that leering smile. "Fortune has favored me, this afternoon, and I mean to profit by it."

For an instant, she looked at him—frightened and dismayed. Suddenly, with the flash-like quickness that was a part of her physical inheritance from her mountain life, she darted past him; eluding his effort to detain her—and was out of the building.

With an oath, the man, acting upon the impulse of the moment, ran after her. Outside the door of the studio, he caught a glimpse of her white dress as she disappeared into the rose garden. In the garden, he saw her as she slipped through the little gate in the far corner of the hedge, into the orange grove. Recklessly he followed. Among the trees, he glimpsed, again, the white flash of her skirts, and dashed forward. At the farther edge of the grove that walled in the little yard where Sibyl lived, he saw her standing by the kitchen door. But between the girl and that last row of close-set trees, waiting his coming, stood the woman with the disfigured face.

Rutlidge paused—angry with himself for so foolishly yielding to the impulse of his passion.

Myra Willard went toward him fearlessly—her fine eyes blazing with righteous indignation. "What are you trying to do, James Rutlidge?" she demanded—and her words were bold and clear.

The man was silent.

"You are evidently a worthy son of your father," the woman continued—every clear-cut word biting into his consciousness with stinging scorn. "He, in his day, did all he knew to turn this world into a hell for those who were unfortunate enough to please his vile fancy. You, I see, are following faithfully his footsteps. I know you, and the creed of your kind—as I knew your father before you. No girl of innocent beauty is safe from you. Your unclean mind is as incapable of believing in virtue, as you are helpless in the grip of your own insane lust."

The man was stung to fury by her cutting words. "Take your ugly face out of my sight," he said brutally.

Fearlessly, she drew a step nearer. "It is because I am a woman that I have this ugly face, James Rutlidge." She touched her disfigured cheek—"These scars are the marks of the beast that rules you, sir, body and soul. Leave this place, or, as there is a God, I'll tell a tale that will forbid you ever showing your own evil countenance in public, again."

Something in her eyes and in her manner, as she spoke,

caused the man—beside himself with rage, as he was—to draw back. Some mysterious force that made itself felt in her bold words told him that hers was no idle threat. A moment they stood face to face, in the edge of the shadowy orange grove—the man of the world, prominent in circles of art and culture; and the woman whose natural loveliness was so distorted into a hideous mask of ugliness. With a short, derisive laugh, James Rutlidge turned and walked away.

Aaron King and Conrad Lagrange were returning from town. As they neared their home, they saw one of the Taine automobiles in front of the house. "Company," said the artist with a smile—thinking of his letter to the millionaire.

"It's Rutlidge," said the novelist—noting the absence of the chauffeur.

They were turning in at the entrance, when Czar—who had dashed ahead as if to investigate—halted, suddenly, with a low growl of disapproval.

"Huh!" ejaculated Conrad Lagrange, with his twisted grin. "It's Senior 'Sensual' all right. Look at Czar; he knows the beast is around. Go fetch him, Czar."

With an angry bark, the dog disappeared around the corner of the porch. The two men, following, were met by Rutlidge who had made his way back through the grove and the rose garden from the house next door. The dog, with muttering growls, was sniffing suspiciously at his heels.

"Czar," said his master, suggestively. With a meaning glance, the dog reluctantly ceased his embarrassing attentions and went to see if everything was all right about the premises.

In answer to their greeting and the quite natural question if he had been waiting long, Rutlidge answered with a laugh. "Oh, no—I have been amusing myself by prowling around your place. Snug quarters you have here; really, I never quite appreciated their charm, before."

They seated themselves on the porch. Conrad Lagrange—thinking of Sibyl Andrés and that letter which he had left on the gate—from under his brows, watched their caller closely; the while he filled with painstaking care his brier pipe.

"We like it," returned the artist.

"I should think so—I'd be sorry to leave it if I were you. Mr. Taine tells me you are going to the mountains."

"We're not giving up this place, though," replied Aaron King. "Yee Kee stays to take care of things until our return."

"Oh, I see. I generally go into the mountains, myself for a little hunt when the deer season opens. It may be that I will run across you somewhere. By the way—you haven't met your musical neighbor yet, have you?"

The novelist gave particular attention to his pipe which did not seem to be behaving properly.

The artist answered shortly, "No."

"I'd certainly make her acquaintance, if I were you," said Rutlidge, with his suggestive smile. "She is a dream. A delightful little retreat—that studio of yours."

The painter, puzzled by the man's words and by his insinuating air, returned coldly, "It does very well for a work-shop."

The other laughed meaningly; "Yes, oh yes—a great little work-shop. I suppose you—ah—do not fear to trust your art treasures to the Chinaman, during your absence?"

Conrad Lagrange—certain, now, that the man had seen Sibyl Andrés either entering or leaving the studio—said abruptly, "You need give yourself no concern for Mr. King's studio, Rutlidge. I can assure you that the treasures there will be well protected."

James Rutlidge understood the warning conveyed in the novelist's words that, to Aaron King, revealed nothing.

"Really," said the painter to their caller, "you are not uneasy for the safety of Mrs. Taine's portrait, are you, old man? If you are, of course—"

"Damn Mrs. Taine's portrait!" ejaculated the man, rising hurriedly. "You know what I mean. It's all right, of course. I must be going. Hope you have a good outing and come back to find all your art treasures safe." He laughed coarsely, as he went down the walk.

When the automobile was gone, the artist turned to his friend. "Now what in thunder did he mean by that? What's the matter with him? Do you suppose they imagine that there is anything wrong because I wouldn't turn over the picture?"

"He is an unclean beast, Aaron," the novelist answered shortly. "His father was the worst I ever knew, and he's like him. Forget him. Here comes the delivery boy with our stuff. Let's overhaul the outfit. I hope they'll get here with that burro, before dark. Where'll we put him, in the studio, heh?"

"Look here,"—said the artist a few minutes later, returning from a visit to the studio for something,—"this is what was the matter with Rutlidge. And you did it, old man. This is your key."

"What do you mean?" asked the other in confusion taking the key.

"Why, I found the studio door wide open, with your key in the lock. You must have been out there, just before we left this morning, and forgot to shut the door. Rutlidge probably noticed it when he was prowling about the place, and was trying to roast me for my carelessness."

Conrad Lagrange stared stupidly at the key in his hand. "Well I am damned," he muttered. Then added, in savage and—as it seemed to the artist—exaggerated wrath, "I'm a stupid, blundering, irresponsible old fool." Nor was he consoled when the painter innocently assured him that no harm had resulted from his carelessness.

That night, as the two men sat on the porch, watching the last of the light on the mountain tops, they heard again the cry of fear and pain that came from the little house hidden in the depths of the orange grove. Wonderingly they listened. Once more it came—filled with shuddering terror.

When the sound was not repeated, Conrad Lagrange thoughtfully knocked the ashes from his pipe. "Poor soul," he said. "Those scars did more than disfigure her beautiful face. I'll wager there's a sad story there, Aaron. It's strange how I am haunted by the impression that I ought to know her. But I can't make it come clear. Heigho,"—he added a moment later as if to free his mind from unpleasant thoughts,—"I'll be glad when we are safely up in the hills yonder. Do you know, old man, I feel as though we're getting away just in the nick of time. My back hair and the pricking of my thumbs warn me that your dearly beloved spooks are combining to put up some sort of a spooking job on us. I hope Yee Kee has a plentiful supply of joss-sticks to stand 'em off, if they get too busy while we are gone."

Aaron King laughed quietly in the dusk, as he returned "And I have a presentiment that those precious members of our household are preparing to accompany us to the hills. I feel in my bones that something is going to happen up there"—he pointed to the distant mountains, then added—"to me, at least. I feel as though I were about to bid myself good-by—if you know what I mean. I hope that donkey of ours isn't a psychic donkey, or, if he is, that he'll listen to reason and be content with his escorts of flesh and blood."

As he finished speaking, the quiet of the evening was broken by a lusty, "Hee-haw, hee-haw," in front of the house.

"There, I told you so!" ejaculated the painter.

Laughing, the two men followed Czar down the walk, in the dark, to receive the shaggy, long-eared companion for their wanderings.

As many a man has done—Aaron King had spoken, in jest, more truth than he knew.

Chapter XIV
In The Mountains

In the gray of the early morning, hours before the dwellers on Fairlands Heights thought of leaving their beds, Aaron King and Conrad Lagrange made ready for their going.

The burro, Croesus—so named by the novelist because, as the famous writer explained, "that ancient multi-millionaire, you know, really was an ass"—was to be entrusted with all the available worldly possessions of the little party. An arrangement—the more experienced man carefully pointed out—that, considering the chief characteristics of Croesus, was quite in accord with the customs of modern pilgrimages. Conrad Lagrange, himself, skillfully fixed the pack in place—adjusting the saddle with careful hand; accurately dividing the weight, with the blankets on top, and, over all, the canvas tarpaulin folded the proper size and neatly tucked in around the ends; and finally securing the whole with the, to the uninitiated, intricate and complicated diamond hitch. The order of their march, also, would place Croesus first; which position—the novelist, again, gravely explained, as he drew the cinches tight—is held by all who value good form, to be the donkey's proper place in the procession. As he watched his friend, the artist felt that, indeed, he was about to go far from the ways of life that he had always known.

When all was ready, the two men—dressed in flannels, corduroys, and high-laced, mountain boots—called good-by to Yee Kee, respectfully invited Croesus to proceed, and set out—with Czar, the fourth member of the party, flying here and there in such a whirlwind of good spirits that not a shred of his usual dignity was left. The sun was still below the mountain's crest, though the higher points were gilded with its light, when they turned their backs upon the city made by men, and set their faces toward the hills that bore in every ridge and peak and cliff and crag and canyon the signature of God.

As Conrad Lagrange said—they might have hired a wagon, or even an automobile, to take them and their goods to some mountain ranch where they would have had no trouble in securing a burro for their wanderings A team would have made the trip by noon. A machine would have set them down in Clear Creek Canyon before the sun could climb high enough to look over the canyon walls. "But that"—explained the novelist, as they trudged leisurely along between rows of palms that bordered the orange groves on either side of their road, and sensed the mystery that marks the birth of a new day—"but that is not a proper way to go to the mountains.

"The mountains"—he continued, with his eyes upon the distant heights—"are not seen by those who would visit them with a rattle and clatter and rush and roar—as one would visit the cities of men. They are to be seen only by those who have the grace to go quietly; who have the understanding to go thoughtfully; the heart to go lovingly; and the spirit to go worshipfully. They are to be approached, not in the manner of one going to a horse-race, or a circus, but in the mood of one about to enter a great cathedral; or, indeed, of one seeking admittance to the very throne-room of God. When going to the mountains, one should take time to feel them drawing near. They are never intimate with those who hurry. Mere sight-seers seldom see much of anything. If possible,"—insisted the speaker, smiling gravely upon his companion,—"one should always spend, at least, a full day in the approach. Before entering the immediate presence of the hills, one should first view them from a distance, seeing them from base to peak—in the glory of the day's beginning, as they watch the world awake; in the majesty of full noon, as they maintain their calm above the turmoil of the day's doing; and in the glory of the sun's departure, as it lights last their crests and peaks. And then, after such a day, one should sleep, one night, at their feet."

The artist listened with delight, as he always did when his friend spoke in those rare moods that revealed a nature so unknown to the world that had made him famous. When the novelist finished, the young man said gently, "And your words, my friend, are almost a direct quotation from that anonymous book which my mother so loved."

"Perhaps they are, Aaron"—admitted Conrad Lagrange—"perhaps they are."

So it was that they spent that day—in leisure approach—the patient Croesus, with his burden, always in the lead, and Czar, like a merry sprite, playing here and there. Several times they stopped to rest beside the road, while provident Croesus gathered a few mouthfuls of grass or weeds. Many times they halted to enjoy the scene that changed with every step.

Their road led always upward, with a gradual, easy grade; and by noon they had left the cultivated section of the lower valley for the higher, untilled lands. The dark, glossy-green of the orange and the lighter shining tints of the lemon groves, with the rich, satiny-gray tones of the olive-trees, were replaced now by the softer grays, greens, yellows, and browns of the chaparral. The air was no longer heavy with the perfume of roses and orange-blossoms, but came to their nostrils laden with the pungent odors of yerba santa and greasewood and sage. Looking back, they could see the valley—marked off by its roads into many squares of green, and dotted here and there by small towns and cities—stretching away toward the western ocean until it was lost in a gray-blue haze out of which the distant San Gabriels, beyond Cajon Pass, lifted into the clear sky above, like the shore-line of dreamland rising out of a dream sea. Before them, the San Bernardinos drew ever nearer and more intimate—silently inviting them; patiently, with a world old patience, bidding them come; in the majestic humbleness of their lofty spirit, offering themselves and the wealth of their teaching.

So they came, in the late afternoon, to that spot where the road for the first time crosses the alder and cottonwood bordered stream that, before it reaches the valley, is drawn from its natural course by the irrigation flumes and pipes.

The sound of the mountain waters leaping down their granite-bouldered way reached the men while they were yet some distance. Croesus pointed his long ears forward in burro anticipation—his experience telling him that the day's work was about to end. Czar was already ranging along the side of the creek—sending a colony of squirrels scampering to the tree tops, and a bevy of quail whirring to the chaparral in frightened flight. The artist greeted the waters with a schoolboy shout of gladness. Conrad Lagrange, with the smile and the voice of a man miraculously recreated, said quietly, "This is the place where we stop for the night."

Their camp was a simple matter. Croesus asked nothing but to be released from his burden—being quite capable of caring for himself. A wash in the clear, cold water of the brook; a simple meal, prepared by Conrad Lagrange over a small fire made of sticks gathered by the artist; their tarpaulin and blankets spread within sound of the music of the stream; a watching of the sun's glorious going down; a quiet pipe in the hush of the mysterious twilight; a "good night" in the soft darkness, when the myriad stars looked down upon the dull red glow of their camp-fire embers; with the guarding spirit of the mighty hills to give them peace—and they lay down to sleep at the mountain's feet.

There is no sleeping late in the morning when one sleeps in the open, under the stars. After breakfast, the artist received another lesson in packing, and they moved on toward the world that already seemed to dwarf that other world which they had left, by

99

one day's walking, so far below. A heavy fog, rolling in from the ocean in the night, submerged the valley in its dull, gray depths—leaving to the eye no view but the view of the mountains before them, and forcing upon the artist's mind the weird impression that the life he had always known was a fantastically unreal dream.

And now,—as they approached,—the frowning entrance of Clear Creek Canyon grew more and more clearly defined. The higher peaks appeared to draw back and hide themselves behind the foothills, which—as the men came closer under their immediate slopes and walls—seemed to grow magically in height and bulk. A little before noon, they were in the rocky vestibule of the canyon. On either hand, the walls rose almost sheer, while their road, now, was but a narrow shelf under the overhanging cliffs, below which the white waters of the stream—cold from the snows so far above—tumbled impetuously over the boulders that obstructed their way—filling the hall-like gorge with tumultuous melody. Soon, the canyon narrowed to less than a stone's throw in width. The walls grew more grim and forbidding in their rocky nearness. And then they came to that point where, on either side, great cliffs, projecting, form the massive, rugged portals of the mountain's gate.

First seen, from a point where the road rounds a jutting corner on the extreme right, the projecting cliffs ahead appear as a blank wall of rock that forbids further progress. But, as the men moved forward,—the road swinging more toward the center of the gorge,—the cliffs seemed to draw apart, and, through the way thus opened, they saw the great canyon and the mountains beyond. It was as though a mighty, invisible hand rolled silently back those awful doors to give them entrance.

Abruptly, upon the inner side of the narrow passage the canyon widens to many times the width of the outer vestibule; and the road, crossing the creek, curves to the left; so that, looking back as they went, the two men saw the mighty doors closing again, behind them—as they had opened to let them in. It was as though that spirit sentinel, guarding the treasures of the hills, had jealously barred the way, that no one else from the world of men might follow.

Aaron King stopped. Drawing a deep breath, and removing his hat, he turned his face from that mountain wall, upward to the encircling pine-fringed ridges and towering peaks. He had, indeed, come far from the world that he had always known.

Conrad Lagrange, smiling, watched his friend, but spoke no word.

Clear Creek Canyon is a deep, narrow valley, some fifteen

100

miles in length, and approaching a mile in its greatest width; lying between the main range of the San Bernardinos and the lower ridge of the Galenas. The lower end of the canyon is shut in by the sheer cliff walls, and by the rugged portals of the narrow entrance; the upper end is formed by the dividing ridge that separates the Clear Creek from the Cold Water country which opens out onto the Colorado Desert below San Gorgonio Pass and the peaks of the San Jacintos. Perhaps two miles above the entrance the canyon widens to its greatest width; and in this portion of the little valley,—which extends some five miles to where the walls again draw close,— located on the benches above the boulder-strewn wash of Clear Creek, are the homes of several mountain ranchers, and the Government Forest Ranger Station.

At the Ranger Station, they stopped—Conrad Lagrange wishing to greet the mountaineer official, whom he had learned to know on his former trip. But the Ranger was away somewhere, riding his lonely trails, and they did not tarry.

Just above the Station, they left the main road to follow the way that leads to the Morton Ranch in the mouth of Alder Canyon— a small side canyon leading steeply up to a low gap in the main range. Beyond Morton's, there is only a narrow trail. Three hundred yards above the ranch corral, where the road ends and the trail begins, the buildings of the mountaineer's home were lost to view. Except for the narrow winding path that they must follow single file, there was no sign of human life.

For three weeks, they knew no roads other than those lonely, mountain trails. At times, they walked under dark pines where the ground was thickly carpeted with the dead, brown needles and the air was redolent with the odor of the majestic trees; or made their camps at night, feeding their blazing fires with the pitchy knots and cones. At other times, they found their way through thickets of manzanita and buckthorn, along the mountain's flank; or, winding zigzag down some narrow canyon wall, made themselves at home under the slender, small-trunked alders; and added to the stores that Croesus packed, many a lusty trout from the tumbling, icy torrent. Again, high up on some wind-swept granite ridge or peak, where the pines were twisted and battered and torn by the warring elements, they looked far down upon the rolling sea of clouds that hid the world below; or, in the shelter of some mighty cliff, built their fires; and, when the night was clear, saw, miles away and below, the thousands of twinkling star-like lights of the world they had left behind. Or, again, they halted in some forest and hill encircled glen; where the lush grass in the cienaga grew almost as

101

high as Croesus' back, and the lilies even higher; and where, through the dark green brakes, the timid deer come down to drink at the beginning of some mountain stream. At last, their wanderings carried them close under the snowy heights of San Gorgonio—the loftiest of all the peaks. That night, they camped at timber-line and in the morning,—leaving Croesus and the outfit, while it was still dark,—made their way to the top, in time to see the sun come up from under the edge of the world.

So they were received into the inner life of the mountains; so the spirit that dwells in that unmarred world whispered to them the secrets of its enduring strength and lofty peace.

From San Gorgonio, they followed the trail that leads down to upper Clear Creek—halting, one night, at Burnt Pine Camp on Laurel Creek, above the falls. Then—leaving the Laurel trail—they climbed over a spur of the main range, and so down the steep wall of the gorge to Lone Cabin on Fern Creek. The next day, they made their way on down to the floor of the main canyon—five miles above the point where they had left it at the beginning of their wanderings.

Crossing the canyon at the Clear Creek Power Company's intake, they took the company trail that follows the pipe-line along the southern wall. From the headwork to the reservoir two thousand feet above the power-house at the mouth of Clear Creek Canyon, this trail is cut in the steep side of the Galena range—overhanging the narrow valley below—nine beautiful miles of it. At Oak Knoll,—where a Government trail for the Forest Ranger zigzags down from the pipe-line to the wagon road below,—they halted.

Conrad Lagrange explained that there were three ways back to the world they had left, nearly a month before—the pipe-line trail to the reservoir and so down to the power-house and the Fairlands road; the Government trail from the pipe-line, over the Galenas to the valley on the other side; or, the Oak Knoll trail down to Clear Creek and out through the canyon gates—the way they had come.

"But," objected Aaron King, lazily,—from where he lay under a live-oak on the mountainside, a few feet above the trail,—"either route presupposes our wish to return to Fairlands."

The novelist laughed. "Listen to him, Czar,"—he said to the dog lying at his feet,—"listen to that painter-man. He doesn't want to go back to Fairlands any more than we do, does he?"

Rising, Czar looked at his master a moment, with slow waving tail, then turned inquiringly toward the artist.

"Well," said the young man, "what about it, old boy? Which trail shall we take? Or shall we take any of them?"

With a prodigious yawn,—as though to indicate that he

wearied of their foolish indecision,—Czar turned, with a low "woof," toward the fourth member of the company, who was browsing along the edge of the trail. Whenever Czar was in doubt as to the wants of his human companions he always barked at the burro.

"He says, 'ask Croesus'," commented the artist.

"Good!" cried the older man, with another laugh. "Let's put it up to the financier and let him choose."

"Wait,"—said the artist, as the other turned toward the burro,—"don't be hasty—the occasion calls for solemn meditation and lofty discourse."

"Your pardon,"—returned the novelist,—"'tis so. I will orate." Carefully selecting a pebble in readiness to emphasize his remarks, he addressed the shaggy arbiter of their fate. "Sir Croesus, thy pack is lighter by many meals than when first thou didst set out from that land where we did rescue thee from the hands of thy tormenting trader; but thy responsibilities are weightier, many fold. Upon the wisdom of thy choice, now, great issue rests. Thou hast thy chance, O illustrious ass, to recompense the world, this day, for the many evils wrought by thy odious ancestor and by all his long-eared kin. Choose, now, the way thy benefactors' feet shall go; and see to it, Croesus, that thou dost choose wisely; or, by thy ears, we'll flay thy woolly hide and hang it on the mountainside—a warning to thy kind."

The well-thrown pebble struck that part of the burro's anatomy at which it was aimed; the dog barked; and Croesus—with an indignant jerk of his head, and a flirt of his tail—started forward. At the fork of the trail, he paused. The two men waited with breathless interest. With an air of accepting the responsibility placed upon him, the burro whirled and trotted down the narrow path that led to the floor of the canyon below. Laughing, the men followed—but far enough in the rear to permit their leader to choose his own way when they should reach the wagon road at the foot of the mountain wall. Without an instant's hesitation, Croesus turned down the road—quickening his pace, almost, into a trot.

"By George!" ejaculated the novelist, "he acts like he knew where he was going."

"He's taking you at your word," returned the artist. "Look at him go! Evidently, he's still under the inspiration of your oratory."

The burro had broken into a ridiculous, little gallop that caused the frying-pan and coffee-pot, lashed on the outside of the pack, to rattle merrily. Splashing through the creek, he disappeared in the dark shadow of a thicket of alders and willows, where the road crosses a tiny rivulet that flows from a spring a hundred yards

103

above. Climbing out of this gloomy hollow, the road turns sharply to the left, and the men hurried on to overtake their four-footed guide before he should be too long out of their sight. Just at the top of the little rise, before rounding the turn, they stopped. A few feet to the right of the road, with his nose at an old gate, stood Croesus. Nor would he heed Czar's bark commanding him to go on.

On the other side of the fence, an old and long neglected apple orchard, a tumble-down log barn, and the wreck of a house with the fireplace and chimney standing stark and alone, told the story. The place was one of those old ranches, purchased by the Power Company for the water rights, and deserted by those who once had called it home. From the gate, ancient wagon tracks, overgrown with weeds, led somewhere around the edge of the orchard and were lost in the tangle of trees and brush on its lower side.

The two men looked at each other in laughing surprise. The burro, turning his head, gazed at them over his shoulder, inquiringly, as much as to say, "Well, what's the matter now? Why don't you come along?"

"When in doubt, ask Croesus," said the artist, gravely.

Conrad Lagrange calmly opened the gate.

Promptly, the burro trotted ahead. Following the ancient weed-grown tracks, he led them around the lower end of the orchard; crossed a little stream; and, turning again, climbed a gentle rise of open, grassy land behind the orchard; stopping at last, with an air of having accomplished his purpose, in a beautiful little grove of sycamore trees that bordered a small cienaga.

Completely hidden by the old orchard from the road in front, and backed by the foot of the mountain spur that here forms the northern wall of the little valley, the spot commanded a magnificent view of the encircling peaks and ridges. San Bernardino was almost above their heads. To the east, were the more rugged walls of the upper and narrower end of the canyon; in their front, the beautiful Oak Knoll, with the dark steeps and pine-fringed crest of the Galenas against the sky; while to the west, the blue peaks of the far San Gabriels showed above the lower spurs and foothills of the more immediate range. The foreground was filled in by the gentle slope leading down to the tiny stream at the edge of the old orchard and, a little to the left, by the cienaga—rich in the color of its tall marsh grass and reeds, gemmed with brilliant flowers of gold and scarlet, bordered by graceful willows, and screened from the eye of the chance traveler by the lattice of tangled orchard boughs.

Seated in the shade of the sycamores on the little knoll, the two friends enjoyed the beauty of the scene, and the charming seclusion of the lovely retreat; while Croesus stood patiently, as though waiting to be rewarded for his virtue, by the removal of his pack. Even Czar refrained from charging here and there, and lay down contentedly at their feet, with an air of having reached at last the place they had been seeking.

A few days later found them established in a comfortable camp; with tents and furniture and hammocks and books and the delighted Yee Kee to take care of them. It had been easy to secure permission from the neighboring rancher who leased the orchard from the Company. Conrad Lagrange, with the man and his big mountain wagon, had made a trip to town—returning the next day with Yee Kee and the outfit. He brought, also, things from the studio; for the artist declared that he would no longer be without the materials of his art.

The first day after the camp was built, the artist—declaring that he would settle the question, at once, as to whether Yee Kee could cook a trout as skillfully as the novelist—took rod and flies, and—leaving the famous author in a hammock, with Czar lying near—set out up the canyon. For perhaps two miles, the painter followed the creek—taking here and there from clear pool or swirling eddy a fish for his creel, and pausing often, as he went, to enjoy—in artist fashion—the beauties of the ever changing landscape.

The afternoon was almost gone when he finally turned back toward camp. He had been away, already longer than he intended; but still—as all fishermen will understand—he could not, on his way back down the stream, refrain from casting here and there over the pools that tempted him.

The sun was touching the crest of the mountains when he had made but little more than half the distance of his return. He had just sent his fly skillfully over a deep pool in the shadow of a granite boulder, for what he determined must be his last cast, when, startlingly clear and sweet, came the tones of a violin.

A master trout leaped. The hand of the unheeding fisherman felt the tug as the leader broke. Giving the victorious fish no thought, Aaron King slowly reeled in his line.

There was no mistaking the pure, vibrant tones of the music to which the man listened with amazed delight. It was the music of the, to him, unknown violinist who lived hidden in the orange grove next door to his studio home in Fairlands.

Chapter XV
The Forest Ranger's Story

Perhaps the motive that, in Fairlands, had restrained the artist from seeking to know his neighbor was without force in the mountains. Perhaps it was that, in the unconventional freedom of the hills, the man obeyed more readily his impulse. Aaron King did not stop to question. As though in answer to the call of that spirit which spoke in the tones of the violin, he moved in the direction from which the music came.

Climbing out of the bed of the stream to the bench that slopes hack—a quarter of a mile, perhaps—to the foot of the canyon wall, he found himself in an old road that, where it once crossed the creek, had been destroyed by the mountain floods. Wonderingly he followed the dimly marked track that led through the chaparral toward a thicket of cedars, from beyond which the music seemed to come. Where the road curved to find its way through the green barrier he paused—the musician, undoubtedly, now, was just beyond. Still acting upon the impulse of the moment, he cautiously parted the boughs and peered through into a little, open glade that was closed in on every side by the rank growth of the mountain vegetation, by the thicket of dark cedars and by tangled masses of wild rose-bushes. Opposite the spot where he stood, and half concealed by great sycamore trees, was a small, log house with a thread of blue smoke curling lazily from the chimney. The place was another of those old ranches that had been purchased by the Power Company and permitted to go back to the wilderness from which it had been won by some hardy settler. The little plot of open ground—well sodded with firm turf and short-cropped by roving cattle and deer—had evidently been, at one time, the front yard of the mountaineer's home. A little out from the porch, and in full view of the artist,—her graceful form outlined against the background of wild roses,—stood Sibyl Andrés with her violin.

As the girl played,—her winsome face upturned to the mountain heights and her body, lightly poised, swaying with the movement of her arm as easily as a willow bough,—she appeared, to the man hidden in the cedars, as some beautiful spirit of the woods and hills—a spirit that would vanish instantly if he should step from his hiding place. He was so close that he could see her blue eyes, wide and unmindful of her surroundings; her lips, curved in an unconscious smile; and her cheeks, flushed with emotion under their warm brown tint—as she appeared to listen for the music that she, in turn,—seemingly with no effort of her will,—gave forth again in the tones of the instrument under her chin.

Aaron King was moved by the beauty of the picture as he had never been stirred before. The peculiar charm of the music; the loveliness of the girl herself; the setting of the scene in the little glade with its wild roses, giant sycamores, dark cedars, and encircling mountain walls, all in the soft mystery of the twilight's beginning; and, withal, the unexpectedness of the vision—combined to make an impression upon the artist's mind that would endure for many years.

Suddenly, as he watched, the music ceased. The girl lowered her violin, and, with a low laugh, said to some one on the porch— concealed from the painter by the trunk of a sycamore—"O Myra, I want to dance. I can't keep still. I'm so glad, glad to be home again— to see old 'San Berdo' and 'Gray Back' and all the rest of them up there!" She stretched out her arms as if in answer to a welcome from the hills. Then, whirling quickly, she gave the violin to her companion on the porch. "Play, Myra; please, dear, play."

At her word, the music of the violin began again—coming now, from behind the trunk of the sycamore. In the hands of the unseen musician, the instrument laughed and sang a song of joyous abandonment—of freedom and rejoicing—of happiness and love— while in perfect harmony with the spirit and the rhythm of the melody, the girl danced upon the firm, green carpet of grass. Here and there, to and fro, about the little glade shut in from the world by its walls of living green, she tripped and whirled in unstudied grace—lightly as if winged—unconscious as the wild creatures that play in the depths of the woods—wayward as the zephyr that trips along the mountainside.

It was a spontaneous expression of her spiritual and physical exaltation and was as natural as the laughter in her voice or the flush upon her cheeks. It was a dance that was like no dance that Aaron King had ever seen.

The artist—watching through the screen of cedar boughs beside the old wagon road and scarcely daring to breathe lest the beautiful vision should vanish—forgot his position—forgot what he was doing. Fascinated by the scene to which he had been led, so unexpectedly by the music he had so often heard while at work in his studio, he was unmindful of the rude part he was playing. He

107

was brought suddenly to himself by a heavy hand upon his shoulder. As he straightened, the hand whirled him half around and he found himself looking into a face that was tanned and seamed by many years in the open.

The man who had so unceremoniously commanded the artist's attention stood a little above six feet in height, and was of that deep-chested, lean, but full-muscled build that so often marks the mountain bred. He wore no coat. At his hip, a heavy Colt revolver hung in its worn holster from a full, loosely buckled, cartridge belt. Upon his unbuttoned vest was the shield of the United States Forest Service. From under the brim of his slouch hat, he gazed at Aaron King questioningly—in angry disapproval.

Instinctively, neither of the men spoke. A word would have been heard the other side of the cedars. With a gesture commanding the artist to follow, the Ranger quietly, withdrew along the wagon road toward the creek.

When they were at a distance where their voices would not reach the girl in the glade, the Ranger said with angry abruptness, "Now, sir, perhaps you will tell me who you are and what you mean by spying upon a couple of women, like that."

The other could not conceal his embarrassment. "I don't blame you for calling me to account," he said. "If it were me—if our positions were reversed I mean—I should kick you down into the creek there."

The cold, blue eyes—that had been measuring the painter so shrewdly—twinkled with a hint of humor. "You do look like a gentleman, you know," the officer said,—as if excusing himself for not following the artist's suggestion. "But, all the same, you must explain. Who are you?"

"That part is easy, at least," returned the other. "Though the circumstance of our meeting is a temptation to lie."

"Which would do you no good, and might lead to unpleasant complications," retorted the Ranger, sharply.

The man under question, still embarrassed, laughed shortly, as he returned, "I really was not thinking of it seriously. My name is Aaron King. I am an artist. You are Mr. Oakley, I suppose."

The officer nodded—beginning to smile. "Yes, I am Brian Oakley."

The artist continued, "A month ago, Conrad Lagrange and I came into the mountains for an outing. We stopped at the Station, but there was no one at home. Most of the time, we have been just roaming around. Now, we are camped down there, back of that old apple orchard."

108

The Ranger broke into a laugh. "Mrs. Oakley was visiting friends up the canyon, the day you came in; but Morton told me. I've crossed your trail a dozen times, and sighted you nearly as many; but I was always too busy to go to you. I knew Lagrange didn't need any attention, you see; so I just figured on meeting up with you somewhere by accident like—about meal time, mebbe." He laughed again. "The accident part worked out all right." He paused, still laughing—enjoying the artist's discomfiture; then ended with a curious—"What in thunder were you sneaking around in the brush like that for, anyway? Those women won't bite."

Aaron King explained how he had heard the music while fishing; and how, following the sound, he had acted upon an impulse to catch a glimpse of the unknown musician before revealing himself; and then, in his interest, had forgotten that he was playing the part of a spy—until so rudely aroused by the hand of the Ranger.

Brian Oakley chuckled; "If I'd acted upon impulse when I first saw you peeking through those cedars, you would have been more surprised than you were. But while I was sneaking up on you I noticed your get-up—with your creel and rod—and figured how you might have come there. So I thought I would go a little slow."

"And you wear rather heavy boots too," said the artist suggestively. Then, more at ease, he joined in the laugh at himself.

"Catch any fish?" asked the Ranger—lifting the cover of the creel. "Whee!" as he saw the contents. "That's bully! And I'm hungry as a she wolf too! Been in the saddle since sunup without a bite. What do you say if I make that long deferred social call upon you and Lagrange this evening?"

"I say, good! Mr. Oakley," returned the artist, heartily. "I guess you know what Lagrange will say."

"You bet I do." He whistled—a low, birdlike note. In answer, a beautiful, chestnut saddle-horse came out of the chaparral, where it had not been seen by the painter. "We're going, Max," said the officer, in a matter-of-fact way. And, as the two men set out, the horse followed, with a business-like air that brought a word of admiring comment from the artist.

That Aaron King had won the approval of the Ranger was evidenced by the mountaineer's inviting himself to supper the camp in the sycamores. The fact that the officer considerately told Conrad Lagrange only that he had met the artist with his creel full of trout, and so had been tempted to accompany him, won the enduring gratitude of the young man. Thus the circumstances of their

109

meeting introduced each to the other, with recommendations of peculiar value, and marked the beginning of a genuine and lasting friendship. But, while, out of delicate regard for the artist's feelings, he refrained from relating the—to the young man—embarrassing incident, Brian Oakley could not resist making, at every opportunity, sly references to their meeting—for the painter's benefit and his own amusement. Thus it happened that, after supper, as they sat with their pipes, the talk turned upon Sibyl Andrés and the woman with the disfigured face.

The Ranger, to tease the artist, had remarked casually,—after complimenting them upon the location of their camp,—"And you've got some mighty nice neighbors, less than a mile above too."

"Neighbors!" ejaculated Conrad Lagrange—in a tone that left no doubt as to his sentiment in the matter.

The others laughed; while the officer said, "Oh, I know how you feel! You think you don't want anybody poaching on your preserves. You're up here in the hills to get away from people, and all that. But you don't need to be uneasy. You won't even see these folks—unless you sneak up on them." He stole a look at the artist, and chuckled maliciously as the painter covertly shook his fist at him. "You may hear them though."

"Which would probably be as bad," retorted the novelist, gruffly.

"Oh, I don't know!" returned the other. "You might be able to stand it. I don't reckon you would object to a little music now and then, would you?—real music, I mean."

"So our neighbors are musical, are they?" The novelist seemed slightly interested.

"Sibyl Andrés is the most accomplished violinist I have ever heard," said the Ranger. "And I haven't always lived in these mountains, you know. As for Myra Willard—well—she taught Sibyl—though she doesn't pretend to equal her now."

Conrad Lagrange was interested, now, in earnest He turned to the artist, eagerly—but with caution—"Do you suppose it could be our neighbors in the orange grove, Aaron?"

Brian Oakley watched them with quiet amusement.

"I know it is," returned the artist.

"You know it is!" ejaculated the other.

"Sure—I heard the violin this afternoon. While I was fishing," he added hastily, when the Ranger laughed.

The novelist commented savagely, "Seems to me you're mighty careful about keeping your news to yourself!"

This brought another burst of merriment from the mountaineer.

When the two men had explained to the Ranger about the music in the orange grove, Conrad Lagrange related how they had first heard that cry in the night; and how, when they had gone to the neighboring house, they had seen the woman of the disfigured face standing in the doorway.

"It was Miss Willard who cried out," said Brian Oakley, quietly. "She dreams, sometimes, of the accident—or whatever it was—that left her with those scars—at least, that's what I think it is. Certainly it's no ordinary dream that would make a woman cry like that. The first time I heard her—the first time that she ever did it, in fact—she and Sibyl were stopping over night at my house. It was three years ago. Jim Rutlidge had just come West, on his first trip, and was up in the hills on a hunt. He happened along about sundown, and when he stepped into the room and Myra saw him, I thought she would faint. He looked like some one she had known—she said. And that night she gave that horrible cry. Lord! but it threw a fright into me. My wife didn't get over being nervous, for a week. Myra explained that she had dreamed—but that's all she would say. I figured that being upset by Rutlidge's reminding her of some one she had known started her mind to going on the past—and then she dreamed of whatever it was that gave her those scars."

"You have known Miss Willard a long time, haven't you, Brian?" asked Conrad Lagrange, with the freedom of an old comrade—for men may grow closer together in one short season in the mountains than in years of meeting daily in the city.

"I've known her ever since she came into the hills. That was the year Sibyl was born. All that anybody knows is what has happened since. Sibyl's mother, even—a month before she died—told me that Myra's history, before she came to them, was as unknown to her as it was the day she stopped at their door."

"I can't get over the feeling that I ought to know her—that I have seen her somewhere, years ago," said the novelist, by way of explaining his interest.

"Then it was before she got those scars," returned the Ranger. "No one could ever forget her face as it is now."

"At the same time," commented the artist, "the scars would prevent your identifying her if she received them after you had known her."

"All the same," said Conrad Lagrange,—as though his mind was bothered by his inability to establish some incident in his

111

memory,—"I'll place her yet. Do you mind, Brian, telling us what you do know of her?"

"Why, not at all," returned the officer. "The story is anybody's property. Its being so well known is probably the reason you didn't hear it when you were up here before.

"Sibyl's father and mother were here in the mountains when I came. They lived up there at the old place where Myra and Sibyl are camping now, and I never expect to meet finer people—either in this world or the next. For twenty years I knew them intimately. Will Andrés was as true and square and white a man as ever lived and Nelly was just as good a woman as he was a man. They and my wife and I were more like brothers and sisters than most folks who are actually blood kin.

"One day, along toward sundown, about a month before Sibyl was born, Nelly heard the dogs barking and went to see what was up. There stood Myra Willard at the gate—like she'd dropped out of the sky. Where she came from God only knows—except that she'd walked from some station on the railroad over toward the pass. She was just about all in; and, of course, Nelly had her into the house and was fixing her up in no time. She wanted to work, but admitted that she had never done much housework. She said, straight out, that they should never know more about her than they knew, then; but insisted that she was not a bad woman. At first, Will and I were against it for, of course, it was easy to see that she was trying to get away from something. But the women—Nelly and my wife— somehow, believed in her, and—with the baby due to arrive in a month and any kind of help hard to get—they carried the day. Well, sir, she made good. If twenty years acquaintance goes for anything, she's one of God's own kind, and I don't care a damn what her history is.

"We soon saw that she was educated and refined, and—as you can see for yourself—she must have been remarkably beautiful before she got so disfigured. When the baby was born, she just took the little one into her poor, broken heart like it had been her own, until Sibyl hardly knew which was her own mother. When the girl was old enough for school, Myra begged Will and Nelly to let her teach the child. She was always sending for books and it was about that time that she sent for a violin. The girl took to music like a bird. And—well—that's the way Sibyl was raised. She's got all the education that the best of them have—even to French and Italian and German—and she's missed some things that the schools teach outside of their text-books. She has a library—given to her mostly by

Myra, a book at a time—that represents the best of the world's best writers. You know what her music is. But, hell!"—the Ranger interrupted himself with an apologetic laugh—"I'm supposed to be talking about Myra Willard. I don't know as I'm so far off, either, because what Sibyl is—aside from her natural inheritance from Will and Nelly—Myra has made her.

"When Will was killed by those Mexican outlaws,—which is a story in itself,—Nelly sold the ranch to the Power Company, and bought an orange grove in Fairlands—which was the thing for her to do, as she and Myra could handle that sort of property, and the ranch had to go, anyway. Before Nelly died, she and I talked things over, and she put everything in Myra's hands, in trust for the girl. Later, Myra sold the grove and the house where you men live, now, and bought the little place next door—putting the rest of the money into gilt-edged securities in Sibyl's name; which insures the girl against want, for years to come. Sibyl helps out their income with her music. And that's the story, boys, except that they come up here into the mountains, every summer, to spend a month or so in the old home place."

The Ranger rose to go.

"But do you think it is safe for those women to stay up there alone?" asked Aaron King.

Brian Oakley laughed. "Safe! You don't know Myra Willard! Sibyl, herself, can pick a squirrel out of the tallest pine in the mountains with her six-shooter. Will and I taught her all we knew, as she grew up. Besides, you see, I drop in every day or so, to see that they're all right." He laughed meaningly as he added,—to Conrad Lagrange for the artist's benefit,—"I'm going to tell them, though, that Sibyl must be careful how she goes dancing around these hills—now that she has such distinguished but irresponsible neighbors."

He whistled—and the chestnut horse was at his side before the echo of their laughter died away.

With a "so-long," the Ranger rode away into the night.

Chapter XVI
When the Canyon Gates Are Shut

If Aaron King had questioned what it was that had held him in the cedar thicket until Brian Oakley's heavy hand broke the spell, he would probably have answered that it was his artistic appreciation of the beautiful scene. But—deep down in the man's inner consciousness—there was a still, small voice—declaring, with an insistency not to be denied, that—for him—there was a something in that picture that was not to be put into the vernacular of his profession.

Had he acted without his habitual self-control, the day following the Ranger's visit, he would, again, have gone fishing—up Clear Creek—at least, to the pool where that master trout had broken his leader. But he did not. Instead, he roamed aimlessly about the vicinity of the camp—explored the sycamore grove; climbed a little way up the mountain spur, and down again; circled the cienaga; and so came, finally, to the ruins of the house and barn on the creek side of the orchard.

Not far from the lonely fireplace with its naked chimney, a little, old gate of split palings, in an ancient tumble-down fence, under a great mistletoe-hung oak, at the top of a bank—attracted his careless attention. From the gate, he saw what once had been a path leading down the bank to a spring, where the tiny streamlet that crossed the road a hundred yards away, on its course to Clear Creek, began. Pushing open the gate that sagged dejectedly from its leaning post, the artist went down the path, and found himself in a charming nook—shut in on every side by the forest vegetation that, watered by the spring, grew rank and dense.

For a space on the gate side of the spring, the sod was firm and smooth—with a gray granite boulder in the center of the little glade, and, here and there, wild rose-bushes and the slender, gray trunks of alder trees breaking through. From the higher branches of the alders that shut out the sky with their dainty, silvery-green leaves, hung—with many a graceful loop and knot—ropes of wild grape-vine and curtains of virgin's-bower. Along the bank below the old fence, the wild blackberries disputed possession with the roses; while the little stream was mottled with the tender green of watercress and bordered with moss and fragrant mint. Above the

114

arroyo willows, on the farther side of the glade, Oak Knoll, with bits of the pine-clad Galenas, could be glimpsed; but on the orchard side, the vine-dressed bank with the old gate under the mistletoe oak shut out the view. Through the screen of alder and grape and willow and virgin's-bower the sunlight fell, as through the delicate traceries of a cathedral window. The bright waters of the spring, softly held by the green sod, crept away under the living wall, without a sound; but the deep murmur of the distant, larger stream, reached the place like the low tones of some great organ. A few regularly placed stones, where once had stood the family spring-house; with the names, initials, hearts and dates carved upon the smooth bark of the alders—now grown over and almost obliterated—seemed to fill the spot with ghostly memories.

All that afternoon, the artist remained in the little retreat. The next day, equipped with easel, canvas and paint-box, he went again to the glade—determined to make a picture of the charming scene.

For a month, now, uninterrupted by the distractions of social obligations or the like, Aaron King had been subjected to influences that had aroused the creative passion of his artist soul to its highest pitch. With his genius clamoring for expression, he had denied himself the medium that was his natural language. Forbidding his friend to accompany him, he worked now in the spring glade with a delight—with an ecstasy—that he had seldom, before, felt. And Conrad Lagrange, wisely, was content to let him go uninterrupted.

As the hours of each day passed, the artist became more and more engrossed with his art. His spirit sang with the joy of receiving the loveliness of the scene before him, of making it his own, and of giving it forth again—a literal part of himself. The memories suggested by the stones of the spring-house foundation and the old carvings on the trees; the sunlight, falling so softly into the hushed seclusion of the glade, as through the traceried windows of a church; and the deep organ-tones of the distant creek; all served to give to the spot the religious atmosphere of a sanctuary; while the artist's abandonment in his work was little short of devotion.

It was the third afternoon, when the painter became conscious that he had been hearing for some time—he could not have said how long—a low-sung melody—so blending with the organ-tones of the mountain stream that it seemed to come out of the music of the tumbling waters.

With his brush poised between palette and canvas, the artist paused,—turning his head to listen,—half inclined to the belief that his fancy was tricking him. But no; the singer was coming nearer; the melody was growing more distinct; but still the voice was in

115

perfect harmony with the deep-toned accompaniment of the distant creek.

Then he saw her. Dressed in soft brown that blended subtly with the green of the willows, the gray of the alder trunks, the russet of rose and blackberry-bush, and the umber of the swinging grape-vines—in the flickering sunshine, the soft changing half-lights, and deep shadows—she appeared to grow out of the scene itself; even as her low-sung melody grew out of the organ-sound of the waters.

To get the effect that satisfied him best, the painter had placed his easel a little back from the grassy, open spot. Seated as he was, on a low camp-stool, among the bushes, he would not have been easily observed—even by eyes trained to the quickness of vision that belongs to those reared in the woods and hills. As the girl drew closer, he saw that she carried a basket on her arm, and that she was picking the wild blackberries that grew in such luscious profusion in the rich, well watered ground at the foot of the sheltering bank. Unconscious of any listener, as she gathered the fruit of Nature's offering, she sang to the accompaniment of Nature's music, with the artless freedom of a wild thing unafraid in its native haunts.

The man kept very still. Presently, when the girl had moved so that he could not see her, he turned to his canvas as if, again, absorbed in his work—but hearing still, behind him, the low-voiced melody of her song.

Then the music ceased; not abruptly, but dying away softly—losing itself, again, in the organ-tones of the distant waters, as it had come. For a while, the artist worked on; not daring to take his eyes from his picture; but feeling, in every tingling nerve of him, that she was there. At last, as if compelled, he abruptly turned his head—and looked straight into her face.

The man had been, apparently, so absorbed in his work, when first the girl caught sight of him, that she had scarcely been startled. When she had ceased her song, and he, still, had not looked around; drawn by her interest in the picture, she had softly approached until she was standing quite close. Her lips were slightly parted, her face was flushed, and her eyes were shining with delight and excited pleasure, as she stood leaning forward, her basket on her arm. So interested was she in the painting, that she seemed to have quite forgotten the painter, and was not in the least embarrassed when he so suddenly looked directly into her face.

"It is beautiful," she said, as though in answer to his question. And no one—hearing her, and watching her face as she spoke—could have doubted her sincerity. "It is so true, so—so"—she searched for a word, and smiled in triumph when she found it—"so

116

right—so beautifully right. It—it makes me feel as—as I feel when I am at church—and the organ plays soft and low, and the light comes slanting through the window, and some one reads those beautiful words, 'The Lord is in his holy temple; let all the earth keep silence before him'."

"Why!" exclaimed the artist, "that is exactly what I wanted it to say. When I saw this place, and heard the waters over there, like a great organ; and saw how the sunshine falls through the trees; I felt as you say, and I am trying to paint the picture so that those who see it will feel that way too."

Her face was aglow with enthusiastic understanding as she cried eagerly, "Oh, I know! I know! I'm like that with my music! When I look at the mountains sometimes—or at the trees and flowers, or hear the waters sing, or the winds call—I—I get so full and so—so kind of choked up inside that it hurts; and I feel as though I must try to tell it—and then I take my violin and try and try to make the music say what I feel. I never can though—not altogether. But you have made your picture say what you feel. That's what makes it so right, isn't it? They said in Fairlands that you were a great artist, and I understand why, now. It must be wonderful to put what you see and feel into a picture like that—where nothing can ever change or spoil it."

Aaron King laughed with boyish embarrassment. "Oh, but I'm not a great artist, you know. I am scarcely known at all."

She looked at him with her great, blue eyes sincerely troubled. "And must one be known—to be great?" she asked. "Might not an artist be great and still be unknown? Or, might not one who was really very, very"—again she seemed to search for a word and as she found it, smiled—"very small, be known all over the world? The newspapers make some really bad people famous, sometimes, don't they? No, no, you are joking. You do not really think that being known to the world and greatness are the same."

The man, studying her closely, saw that she was speaking her thoughts as openly as a child. Experimentally, he said, "If putting what you feel into your work is greatness, then you are a great artist, for your music does make one feel as though it came from the mountains, themselves."

She was frankly pleased, and cried intimately, "Oh! do you like my music? I so wanted you to."

It did not occur to her to ask when he had heard her music. It did not occur to him to explain. They, neither of them, thought to remember that they had not been introduced. They really should have pretended that they did not know each other.

117

"Sometimes," she continued with winsome confidence, "I think, myself, that I am really a great violinist—and then, again,"—she added wistfully,—"I know that I am not. But I am sure that I wouldn't like to be famous, at all."

He laughed. "Fame doesn't seem to matter so much, does it; when one is up here in the hills and the canyon gates are closed."

She echoed his laughter with quick delight. "Did you see that? Did you see those great doors open to let you in, and then close again behind you as if to shut the world outside? But of course you would. Any one who could do that"—she pointed to the canvas—"would not fail to see the canyon gates." With her eyes again upon the picture, she seemed once more to forget the presence of the painter.

Watching her face,—that betrayed her every passing thought and emotion as an untroubled pool mirrors the flowers that grow on its banks or the song-bird that pauses to drink,—the artist—to change her mood—said, "You love the mountains, don't you?"

She turned her face toward him, again, as she answered simply, "Yes, I love the mountains."

"If you were a painter,"—he smiled,—"you would paint them, wouldn't you?"

"I don't know that I would,"—she answered thoughtfully,—"but I would try to get the mountains into my picture, whatever it was. I wonder if you know what I mean?"

"Yes," he answered, "I think I know what you mean; and it is a beautiful thought. You wouldn't paint portraits, would you?"

"I don't think I could," she answered. "It seems to me it would be so hard to get the mountains into a portrait of just anybody. An artist—a great artist, I mean—must make his picture right, mustn't he? And if his picture was a portrait of some one who wasn't very good, and he made it right; he wouldn't be liked very well, would he? No, I don't think I would paint portraits—unless I could paint just the people who would want me to make my picture right."

Aaron King's face flushed at the words that were spoken so artlessly; and he looked at her keenly. But the girl was wholly innocent of any purpose other than to express her thoughts. She did not dream of the force with which her simple words had gone home.

"You love the mountains, too, don't you?" she asked suddenly.

"Yes," he answered, "I love the mountains. I am learning to love them more and more. But I fear I don't know them as well as you do."

"I was born up here," she said, "and lived here until a few years ago. I think, sometimes, that the mountains almost talk to me."

"I wonder if you would help me to know the mountains as you know them," he asked eagerly.

She drew a little back from him, but did not answer.

"We are neighbors, you see," he continued smiling. "I heard your violin, the other evening, when I was fishing up the creek, near where you live; and so I know it is you who live next door to us in the orange grove. Mr. Lagrange and I are camped just over there back of the orchard. May we not be friends? Won't you help me to know your mountains?"

"I know about you," she said. "Brian Oakley told us that you and Mr. Lagrange were camped down here. Mr. Lagrange said that you are a good man; Brian Oakley says that you are too—are you?"

The artist flushed. In his embarrassment, he did not note the significance of her reference to the novelist. "At least," he said gently, "I am not a very bad man."

A smile broke over her face—her mood changing as quickly as the sunlight breaks through a cloud. "I know you are not"—she said—"a bad man wouldn't have wanted to paint this place as you have painted it."

She turned to go.

"But wait!" he cried, "you haven't told me—will you teach me to know your mountains as you know them?"

"I'm sure I cannot say," she answered smiling, as she moved away.

"But at least, we will meet again," he urged.

She laughed gaily, "Why not? The mountains are for you as well as for me; and though the hills are so big, the trails are narrow, and the passes very few."

With another laugh, she slipped away—her brown dress, that, in the shifty lights under the thick foliage, so harmonized with the colors of bush and vine and tree and rock, being so quickly lost to the artist's eye that she seemed almost to vanish into the scene before him.

But presently, from beyond the willow wall, he heard her voice again—singing to the accompaniment of the mountain stream. Softly, the melody died away in the distance—losing itself, at last, in the deeper organ-tones of the mountain waters.

For some minutes, the artist stood listening—thinking he heard it still.

Aaron King did not, that night, tell Conrad Lagrange of his adventure in the spring glade.

119

Chapter XVII
Confessions in the Spring Glade

All the next day, while he worked upon his picture in the glade, Aaron King listened for that voice in the organ-like music of the distant waters. Many times, he turned to search the flickering light and shade of the undergrowth, behind him, for a glimpse of the girl's brown dress and winsome face.

The next day she came.

The artist had been looking long at a splash of sunlight that fell upon the gray granite boulder which was set in the green turf, and had turned to his canvas for—it seemed to him—only an instant. When he looked again at the boulder, she was standing there—had, apparently, been standing there for some time, waiting with smiling lips and laughing eyes for him to see her.

A light creel hung by its webbed strap from her shoulder; in her hand, she carried a slender fly rod of good workmanship. Dressed in soft brown, with short skirts and high laced boots, and her wavy hair tucked under a wide, felt hat; with her blue eyes shining with fun, and her warmly tinted skin glowing with healthful exercise; she appeared—to the artist—more as some mythical spirit of the mountains, than as a maiden of flesh and blood. The manner of her coming, too, heightened the impression. He had heard no sound of her approach—no step, no rustle of the underbrush. He had seen no movement among the bushes—no parting of the willows in the wall of green. There had been no hint of her nearness. He could not even guess the direction from which she had come.

At first, he could scarce believe his eyes, and sat motionless in his surprise. Then her merry laugh rang out—breaking the spell.

Springing from his seat, he went forward. "Are you a spirit?" he cried. "You must be something unreal, you know—the way you appear and disappear. The last time, you came out of the music of the waters, and went again the same way. To-day, you come out of the air, or the trees, or, perhaps, that gray boulder that is giving me such trouble."

Laughing, she answered, "My father and Brian Oakley taught me. If you will watch the wild things in the woods, you can learn to do it too. I am no more a spirit than the cougar, when it stalks a rabbit in the chaparral; or a mink, as it slips among the rocks along the creek; or a fawn, when it crouches to hide in the underbrush."

"You have been fishing?" he asked.

She laughed mockingly, "You are so observing! I think you might have taken that for granted, and asked what luck."

"I believe I might almost take that for granted too," he returned.

"I took a few," she said carelessly. Then, with a charming air of authority—"And now, you must go back to your work. I shall vanish instantly, if you waste another moment's time because I am here."

"But I want to talk," he protested. "I have been working hard since noon."

"Of course you have," she retorted. "But presently the light will change again, and you won't be able to do any more to-day; so you must keep busy while you can."

"And you won't vanish—if I go on with my work?" he asked doubtfully. She was smiling at him with such a mischievous air, that he feared, if he turned away, she would disappear.

She laughed aloud; "Not if you work," she said. "But if you stop—I'm gone."

As she spoke, she went toward his easel, and, resting her fly rod carefully against the trunk of a near-by alder, slipped the creel from her shoulder, placing the basket on the ground with her hat. Then, while the painter watched her, she stood silently looking at the picture. Presently, she faced him, and, with an impulsive stamp of her foot, said, "Why don't you work? How can you waste your time and this light, looking at me? I shall go, if you don't come back to your picture, this minute."

With a laugh, he obeyed.

For a moment, she watched him; then turned away; and he heard her moving about, down by the tiny stream, where it disappeared under the willows.

Once, he paused and turned to look in her direction "What are you up to, now?" he said.

"I shall be up to leaving you,"—she retorted,—"if you look around, again."

He promptly turned once more to his picture.

Soon, she came back, and seated herself beside her creel and rod, where she could see the picture under the artist's brush. "Does it bother, if I watch?" she asked softly.

"No, indeed," he answered. "It helps—that is, it helps when it is you who watch." Which—to the painter's secret amazement—was a literal truth. The gray rock with the splash of sunshine that would not come right, ceased to trouble him, now. Stimulated by her presence, he worked with a freedom and a sureness that was a delight.

When he could not refrain from looking in her direction, he saw that she was bending, with busy hands, over some willow twigs in her lap. "What in the world are you doing?" he asked curiously.

"You are not supposed to know that I am doing anything," she retorted. "You have been peeking again."

"You were so still—I feared you had vanished," he laughed. "If you'll keep talking to me, I'll know you are there, and will be good."

"Sure it won't bother?"

"Sure," he answered.

"Well, then, you talk to me, and I'll answer."

"I have a confession to make," he said, carefully studying the gray tones of the alder trunk beyond the gray boulder.

"A confession?"

"Yes, I want to get it over—so it won't bother me."

"Something about me?"

"Yes."

"Why, that's what I am trying so hard to make you keep your eyes on your work for—because I have to make a confession to you."

"To me?"

"Yes—don't look around, please."

"But what under the sun can you have to confess to me?"

"You started yours first," she answered. "Go on. Maybe it will make it easier for me."

Studiously keeping his eyes upon his canvas, he told her how he had watched her from the cedar thicket. When he had finished,—and she was silent,—he thought that she was angry, and turned about—expecting to see her gathering up her things to go.

She was struggling to suppress her laughter. At the look of surprise on his face, she burst forth in such a gale of merriment that the little glade was filled with the music of her glee; while, in spite of himself, the painter joined.

"Oh!" she cried, "but that is funny! I am glad, glad!"

"Now, what do you mean by that?" he demanded.

"Why—why—that's exactly what I was trying to get courage enough to confess to you!" she gasped. And then she told him how she had spied upon him from the arbor in the rose garden; and how, in his absence, she had visited his studio.

"But how in the world did you get in? The place was always locked, when I was away."

"Oh," she said quaintly, "there was a good genie who let me in through the keyhole. I didn't meddle with anything, you know—I just looked at the beautiful room where you work. And I didn't glance, even, at the picture on the easel. The genie told me you wouldn't like that. I would not have drawn the curtain anyway, even if I hadn't been told. At least, I don't think I would—but perhaps I might—I can't always tell what I'm going to do, you know."

Suddenly, the artist remembered finding the studio door open with Conrad Lagrange's key in the lock, and how the novelist had berated himself with such exaggerated vehemence; and, in a flash, came the thought of James Rutlidge's visit, that afternoon, and of his strange manner and insinuating remarks.

"I think I know the name of your good genie," said the painter, facing the girl, seriously. "But tell me, did no one disturb you while you were in the studio?"

Her cheeks colored painfully, and all the laughter was gone from her voice as she replied, "I didn't want you to know that part."

"But I must know," he insisted gravely.

"Yes," she said, "Mr. Rutlidge found me there; and I ran away through the garden. I don't like him. He frightens me. Please, is it necessary for us to talk about it any more? I had to make my confession of course, but must we talk about that part?"

"No," he answered, "we need not talk about it. It was necessary for me to know; but we will never mention that part, again. When we are back in the orange groves, you shall come to the rose garden and to the studio, as often as you like; your good genie and I will see to it that you are not disturbed—by any one."

Her face brightened at his words. "And do you really like for me to make music for you—as Mr. Lagrange says you do?"

"I can't begin to tell you how much I like it," he answered smiling.

"And it doesn't bother you in your work?"

"It helps me," he declared—thinking of that portrait of Mrs. Taine.

"Oh, I am glad, glad!" she cried. "I wanted it to help. It was for that I played."

"You played to help me?" he asked wonderingly.

She nodded. "I thought it might—if I could get enough of the mountains into my music, you know."

"And will you dance for me, sometimes too?" he asked.

She shook her head. "I cannot tell about that. You see, I only dance when I must—when the music, somehow, doesn't seem quite enough. When I—when I"—she searched for a word, then finished abruptly—"oh, I can't tell you about it—it's just something you feel—

there are no words for it. When I first come to the mountains,—after living in Fairlands all winter,—I always dance—the mountains feel so big and strong. And sometimes I dance in the moonlight—when it feels so soft and light and clean; or in the twilight—when it's so still, and the air is so—so full of the day that has come home to rest and sleep; and sometimes when I am away up under the big pines and the wind, from off the mountain tops, under the sky, sings through the dark branches."

"But don't you ever dance to please your friends?"

"Oh, no—I don't dance to please any one—only just when it's for myself—when nothing else will do—when I must. Of course, sometimes, Myra or Brian Oakley or Mrs. Oakley are with me—but they don't matter, you know. They are so much a part of me that I don't mind."

"I wonder if you will ever dance for me?"

Again, she shook her head. "I don't think so. How could I? You see, you are not like anybody that I have ever known."

"But I saw you the other evening, you remember."

"Yes, but I didn't know you were there. If I had known, I wouldn't have danced."

All the while—as she talked—her fingers had been busy with the slender, willow branches. "And now"—she said, abruptly changing the subject, and smiling as she spoke—"and now, you must turn back to your work."

"But the light is not right," he protested.

"Never mind, you must pretend that it is," she retorted. "Can't you pretend?"

To humor her, he obeyed, laughing.

"You may look, now," she said, a minute later.

He turned to see her standing close beside him, holding out a charming little basket that she had woven of the green willows and decorated with moss and watercress. In the basket, on the cool, damp moss, and lightly covered with the cress, lay a half dozen fine rainbow trout.

"How pretty!" he exclaimed. "So that is what you have been doing!"

"They are for you," she said simply.

"For me?" he cried.

She nodded brightly; "For you and Mr. Lagrange. I know you like them because you said you were fishing when you heard my violin. And I thought that you wouldn't want to leave your picture, to fish for yourself, so I took them for you."

The artist concealed his embarrassment with difficulty; and,

124

while expressing his thanks and appreciation in rather formal words, studied her face keenly. But she had tendered her gift with a spontaneous naturalness, an unaffected kindliness, and an innocent disregard of conventionalities, that would have disarmed a man with much less native gentleness than Aaron King.

Leaving the basket of trout in his hand, she turned, and swung the empty creel over her shoulder. Then, putting on her hat, she picked up her rod.

"Oh—are you going?" he said.

"You have finished your work for to-day," she answered

"But let me go with you, a little way."

She shook her head. "No, I don't want you."

"But you will come again?"

"Perhaps—if you won't stop work—but I can't promise—you see I never know what I am going to do up here in the mountains," she answered whimsically. "I might go to the top of old 'Berdo' in the morning; or I might be here, waiting for you, when you come to paint."

He was putting his things in the box—thinking he would persuade her to let him accompany her a little way; if she saw that he really would paint no more. When he bent over the box, she was speaking. "I hope you will," he answered.

There was no reply.

He straightened up and looked around.

She was gone.

For some time, he stood searching the glade with his eyes, carefully; listening to catch a sound—a puzzled, baffled look upon his face. Taking his things, at last, he started up the little path. But before he reached the old gate, a low laugh caused him to whirl quickly about.

There she stood, beside the spring—a teasing smile on her face. Before he could command himself, she danced a step or two, with an elfish air, and slipped away through the green willow wall. Another merry laugh came back to him and then—the silence of the little glade, and the sound of the distant waters.

With the basket of fish in his hand, Aaron King went slowly to camp; where, when Conrad Lagrange saw what the artist carried so carefully, explanations were in order.

Chapter XVIII
Sibyl Andrés and the Butterflies

On the following day, the artist was putting away his things, at the close of the afternoon's work, when the girl appeared.

The long, slanting bars of sunshine and the deepening shadows marked the lateness of the hour. As he bent over his paint-box, the man was thinking with regret that she would not come—that, perhaps, she would never come. And at the thought that he might not see her again, an odd fear gripped his heart. His thoughts were interrupted by a low, musical laugh; and he sprang to his feet, to search the glade with careful eyes.

"Come out," he cried, as though adjuring an invisible spirit. "I know you are here; come out."

With another laugh, she stepped from behind the trunk of one of the largest trees, within a few feet of where he stood. As she went toward him, she carried in her outstretched hands a graceful basket, woven of sycamore leaves and ferns, and filled with the ripest sweetest blackberries. She did not speak as she held out her offering; but the man, looking into her laughing eyes, fancied that there was a meaning and a purpose in the gift that did not appear upon the surface of her simple action.

Expressing his pleasure, as he received the dainty basket, he could not refrain from adding, "But why do you bring me things?"

She answered with that wayward, mocking humor that so often seized her; "Because I like to. I told you that I always do what I like—up here in the mountains."

"I hope you always will," he returned, "if your likes are all as delicious as this one."

With the manner of a child playfully making a mystery yet anxious to have the secret discussed, she said, "I have one more gift to bring you, yet."

"I knew you meant something by your presents," he cried. "It isn't just because you want me to have the things you bring."

"Oh, yes it is," she retorted, laughing mischievously at his triumphant and expectant tone. "If I didn't want you to have the things I bring—why—I wouldn't bring them, would I?"

"But that isn't all," he insisted. "Tell me—why do you say you have one more gift to bring?"

She shook her head with a delightful air of mystery "Not until I come again. When I come again, I will tell you."

"And you will come to-morrow?"

She laughed teasingly at his eagerness. "How can I tell?" she answered. "I do not know, myself, what I will do to-morrow—when I am up here in the mountains—when the canyon gates are shut and the world is left outside." Even as she spoke, her mood changed and the last words were uttered wistfully, as a captive spirit—that, by nature wild and free, was permitted, for a brief time only, to go beyond its prison walls—might have spoken.

The artist—puzzled by her flash-like change of moods, and by her manner as she spoke of the world beyond the canyon gates—had no words to reply. As he stood there,—in that little glade where the light fell as in a quiet cathedral and the air trembled with the deep organ-tones of the distant waters—holding in his hands the basket of leaves and ferns with its wild fruit, and looking at the beautiful girl who had brought her offering with the naturalness of a child of the mountains and the air of a woodland spirit,—he again felt that the world he had always known was very far away.

The girl, too, was silent—as though, by some subtle power, she knew his thoughts and did not wish to interrupt.

So still were they, that a wild bird—darting through the screen of alder boughs—stopped to swing on a limb above their heads, with a burst of wild-wood melody. In the arroyo beyond the willow wall, a quail called his evening call, and was answered by his mate from the top of the bank under the mistletoe oak. A pair of gray squirrels crept down the gray trunks of the trees and slipped around the granite boulder to drink at the spring; then scampered away again— half in frolic, half in fright—as they caught sight of the man and the maid. As the squirrels disappeared, the girl laughed—a low laugh of fellowship with the creatures of the wilderness—in complete understanding of their humor. Then—as though following the path of a sunbeam—two gorgeously brown and yellow winged butterflies came flitting through the draperies of virgin's-bower, and floated in zigzag flight about the glade—now high among the alder boughs; now low over the tops of the roses and berry-bushes; down to the fragrant mint at the water's edge; and up again to the tops of the willows, as if to leave the glade; but only to return again to the vines that covered the bank, and to the flowers that, here and there, starred the grassy sward.

"Oh!"—cried the girl impulsively, as the beautiful winged creatures disappeared at last,—"if people could only be like that! It's

127

so hard to be yourself in the world. Everybody, there, seems trying to be something they are not. No one dares to be just themselves. Everything, up here, is so right—so true—so just what it is—and down there, everything tries so hard to be just what it is not. The world even sees so crooked that it can't believe when a thing is just what it is."

While watching the butterflies, she had turned away from the artist and, in following their flight with her eyes, had taken a few light steps that brought her into the open, grassy center of the glade. With her face upturned to the opening in the foliage through which the butterflies had disappeared, she had spoken as if thinking aloud, rather than as addressing her companion.

Before the artist could reply, the beautiful creatures came floating back as they had gone. With a low exclamation of delight, the girl watched them as they circled, now, above her head, in their aerial waltz among the sunbeams and leafy boughs. Then the man, watching, saw her—unheeding his presence—stretch her arms upward. For a moment she stood, lightly poised, and then, with her wide, shining eyes fixed upon those gorgeously winged spirits whirling in the fragrant air, with her lips parted in smiling delight, she danced upon the smooth turf of the glade—every step and movement in perfect harmony with the spirit of care-free abandonment that marked the movements of the butterflies that danced above her head. Unmindful of the watching man, as her dainty companions themselves,—forgetful of his presence,—she yielded to the impulse to express her emotions in free, rhythmic movement.

Instinctively, Aaron King was silent—standing motionless, as if he feared to startle her into flight.

Suddenly, as the girl danced—her eyes always upon her winged companions—the insects floated above the artist's head, and she became conscious of his presence. Her cheeks flushed and, laughing low,—as she danced, lightly as a spirit,—she impulsively stretched out her arms to him, in merry invitation—as though challenging him to join her.

The gesture was as spontaneous and as innocent, in its freedom, as had been her offering of the gifts from mountain stream and bush. But the man—lured into forgetfulness of everything save the wild loveliness of the scene—started toward her. At his movement, a look of bewildered fear came into her face; but—too startled to control her movements on the instant, and as though impelled by some hidden power—she moved toward him—blindly,

128

unconsciously—her eyes wide with that look of questioning fright. He had almost reached her when, as though by an effort of her will, she stopped and stood still—gazing into his face—trembling in every limb. Then, with a low cry, she sank down in a frightened, cowering, pleading attitude, and buried her crimson face in her hands.

As though some unseen hand checked him, the man halted, and the girl's cheeks were not more crimson than his own.

A moment he stood, then a step brought him to her side. Putting out his hand, he touched her upon the shoulder, and was about to speak. But at his touch, with another cry, she sprang to her feet and, whirling with the flash-like quickness of a wild thing, vanished into the undergrowth that walled in the glade.

With a startled exclamation, the man tried to follow calling to her, reassuring her, begging her to come back. But there was no answer to his words; nor did he catch a glimpse of her; though once or twice he thought he heard her in swift flight up the canyon.

All the way to the place where he had first seen her, he followed; but at the cedar thicket he stopped. For a long time, he stood there; while the twilight failed and the night came. Slowly,—in the soft darkness with bowed head, as one humbled and ashamed,— he went back down the canyon to the little glade, and to the camp.

Chapter XIX
The Three Gifts and Their Meanings

The next day, Aaron King—too distracted to paint—idled all the afternoon in the glade. But the girl did not come. When it was dark, he returned to camp; telling himself that she would never come again; that his rude yielding to the lure of her wild beauty had rightly broken forever the charm of their intimacy—and he cursed himself—as many a man has cursed—for that momentary lack of self-control.

But the following afternoon, as the artist worked,—bent upon quickly finishing his picture of the place that seemed now to reproach him with its sweet atmosphere of sacred purity,—he heard, as he had heard that first day, the low music of her voice blending with the music of the mountain stream. Scarce daring to move, he sat as though absorbed in his work—listening with all his heart, for some sound of her approach, other than the melody of her song that grew more and more distinct. At last, he knew that she was standing just the other side of the willows, beyond the little spring. He felt her hidden eyes upon him, but dared not look that way—feeling sure that if he betrayed himself in too eager haste she would vanish. Bending forward toward his canvas, he made show of giving close attention to his work and waited.

For some minutes, she remained concealed; singing low, as though to try him with temptation. Then, all at once,—as the painter, with poised brush, glanced from his canvas to the scene,— she stood in full view beside the spring; her graceful, brown-clad figure framed by the willow's green. Her arms were filled with wild flowers that she had gathered from the mountainside—from nook and glade and glen.

"If you will not seek me, there is no use to hide," she called, still holding her place on the other side of the spring, and regarding him seriously; and the man felt under her words, and saw in her wide, blue eyes a troubled question.

"I sought you all the way to your home," he said, gently, "but you would not let me come near."

"I was frightened," she returned, not lowering her eyes but regarding him steadily with that questioning appeal.

"I am sorry,"—he said,—"won't you forgive me? I will never frighten you so again. I did not mean to do it."

"Why," she answered, "I have to forgive myself as well as you. You see, I frightened myself quite as much as you frightened me. I can't feel that you were really to blame—any more than I. I have tried, but I can't—so I came back. Only, I—I must never dance for you again, must I?"

The man could not answer.

As though fully reassured, and quite satisfied to take his answer for granted, she sprang over the tiny stream at her feet, and came to him across the glade, holding out her arms full of blossoms. "See," she said with a smile, "I have brought you the last one of the three gifts." Gracefully, she knelt and placed the flowers on the ground, beside his box of colors.

Deeply moved by her honesty and by her simple trust in him; and charmed by the air of quiet, natural dignity with which she spoke of her gifts; the artist tried to thank her.

"And now," he added, "the meaning—tell me the meaning of your gifts. You promised—you remember—that you would read the pretty riddle, when you came again."

She laughed merrily. "And haven't you guessed the meaning?" she said in her teasing mood.

"How could I?" he retorted. "I was not schooled in your mountains, you know. Your world up here is still a strange world to me."

Still smiling with the pleasure of her fancy, she replied, "But didn't you ask me again and again to help you to know the mountains as I know them?"

"Yes," he said, "but you would not promise."

"I did better than promise"—she returned—"I brought you, from the mountains themselves, their three greatest gifts."

He shook his head, with the air of a backward schoolboy— "Won't you read the lesson?"

"If you will work while I talk, I will," she answered—amused by the hopelessness of his manner and tone.

Obediently, he took up his brushes, and turned toward his picture.

Removing her hat, she seated herself on the ground, where she had woven the willow basket for the fish.

After a moment's silence, she began—timidly, at first, then with increasing confidence as she found words to express her charming fancy. "First, you must know, that in all the wild life of the mountains there is no creature so strong—in proportion to its size and weight, I mean—as the trout that lives in the mountain streams. Its home is in the icy torrents that are fed by the snows of the

131

highest peaks and canyons. It lives, literally, in the innermost heart and life of the hills. It seeks its food at the foot of the falls, where the water boils in fierce fury; where the current swirls and leaps among the boulders; and where the stream rushes with all its might down the rocky channels. With its muscles, fine as tempered steel, it forces its way against the strength of the stream—conquering even the fifty-foot downward pour of a cataract. Its strength is a silent strength. It has no voice other than the voice of its own beautiful self. And all its gleaming colors you may see, in the morning and in the evening, tinting the mighty heads and shoulders and sides of the hills themselves. And so, the first gift that I brought you—fresh from the mountain's heart—was the gift of the mountain's strength.

"The second gift was gathered from bushes that were never planted by the hand of man. They grow as free and untamed as the rains that water them, and the earth that feeds them, and the sunshine that sweetens hem. In them is the flavor of mountain mists, and low hung clouds, and shining dew; the odor of moist leaf-mould, and unimpoverished soil; the pleasant tang of the sunshine; and the softer sweetness of the shady nooks where they grow. In the second gift, I brought you the purity, and the flavor of the mountains."

"And to-day"—she finished simply—"to-day I have brought you the beauty of the hills."

"You have brought me more than the strength and purity and beauty of the mountains," exclaimed the painter. "You have brought me their mystery."

She looked at him questioningly.

"In your own beautiful self," he continued sincerely "you have brought me the mystery of these hills. You are wonderful! I have never known any one like you."

She was wholly unconscious of the compliment—if indeed, he meant it as such. "I suppose I must be different," she returned with just a touch, of sadness in her voice. "You see I have never been taught like other girls. I know nothing at all of the world where you live—except what Myra has told me." Then, as if to change the subject, she asked shyly, "Would you care for my music to-day?"

He assented eagerly—thinking she meant to sing. But, rising, she crossed the glade, and disappeared behind the willows—returning, a moment later, with her violin.

In answer to his exclamation of pleased surprise, she said smiling, "I brought my violin because I thought, if you would let me play, the music would perhaps help us both to forget what—what happened when I danced."

132

Standing by the gray boulder, with her face up turned to the mountains, she placed the instrument under her chin and drew the bow softly across the strings.

For an hour or more she played. Then, as Czar trotted sedately into the glade, she lowered her instrument and, with a smile, called merrily to Conrad Lagrange who, attracted by the music, was standing at the gate on the bank—from the artist's position invisible; "Come down, good genie,—come down! You have been watching there quite long enough. Come, instantly; or with my magic I'll turn you into a fantastic, dancing bug, such as those that straddle there upon the waters of the spring, or else into a fat pollywog that wiggles in the black ooze among the dead leaves and rotting bits of wood."

With a quick movement, she tucked her violin under her chin and played a few measures of the worst sort of ragtime, in perfect imitation of a popular performer. The effect, following the music she had just been making, was grotesque and horrible.

"Mercy, mercy!" cried the man at the gate. "I beg! I beg! Do not, I pray, good nymph, torture me with thy dreadful power. I swear that I will obey thy every wish and whim."

Pointing with her bow—as with a wand—to the boulder, she sternly commanded, "Come, then, and sit here upon this rock; and give to me an account of all that thou hast done since I left thee in the rose garden or I will split thy ears and stretch thy soul upon a torture rack of hideous noise."

She lifted her violin again, threateningly. The novelist came down the path, on a run, to seat himself upon the gray boulder.

The artist shouted with laughter. But the novelist and the girl paid no heed to his unseemly merriment.

"Speak,"—she commanded, waving her wand,—"what hast thou done?"

"Did I not obey thy will and, under such terms as I could procure, open for thee the treasure room of thy desire?" growled the man on the rock.

"And still," she retorted, "when I made myself subject to those terms, and obediently looked not upon the hidden mystery—still the room of my desires became a trap betraying me into rude hands from which I narrowly escaped. And you—you fled the scene of your wrong-doing, without so much as by-your-leave, and for these long weeks have wandered, irresponsible, among my hills. Did you not say that my home was under these glowing peaks, and in the purple shadows of these canyons? Did you think that I would not find you here, and charm you again within reach of my power?"

133

"And what is thy will, good spirit?"—he asked, humbly—"tell me thy will and it shall be done—if thou wilt but make music only upon the instrument that is in thy hand."

With a laugh, she ended the play, saying, "My will is that you and Mr. King come, to-morrow evening, for supper with Miss Willard and me. Brian Oakley and Mrs. Oakley will be there. I want you too."

The men looked at each other in doubt.

"Really, Miss Andrés," said the artist, "we—"

The girl interrupted with one of her flash-like changes. "I have invited you. You must come. I shall expect you." And before either of the men could speak again, she sprang lightly across the little stream, and disappeared through the willow wall.

"Well, I'll be—" The novelist checked himself, solemnly—staring blankly at the spot where she had disappeared.

The artist laughed.

"What do you think of it?" demanded Conrad Lagrange, turning to his friend.

Aaron King, packing up his things, answered, "I think we'd better go."

Which opinion was concurred in by Brian Oakley who dropped in on them that evening.

Chapter XX
Myra's Prayer and the Ranger's Warning

That same afternoon, while Sibyl Andrés was making music for Aaron King in the spring glade, Brian Oakley, on his way down the canyon, stopped at the old place where Myra Willard and the girl were living. Riding into the yard that was fenced only by the wild growth, he was greeted cordially by the woman with the disfigured face, who was seated on the porch.

"Howdy, Myra," he called in return, as he swung from the saddle; and leaving the chestnut to roam at will, he went to the porch, his spurs clinking softly over the short, thick grass.

"Where's Sibyl?" he asked, seating himself on the top step.

"I'm sure I don't know, Mr. Oakley," the woman answered, smiling. "You really didn't expect me to, did you?"

The Ranger laughed. "Did she take gun, basket, rod or violin? If I know whether she's gone shooting berrying, fishing or fiddling, it may give me a clue—or did she take all four?"

The woman watched him closely. "She took only her violin. She went sometime after lunch—down the canyon, I think. Do you wish particularly to see her, Mr. Oakley?"

It was evident to the woman that the officer was relieved. "Oh, no; she wouldn't be going far with her violin. If she went down the canyon, it's all right anyway. But I stopped in to tell the girl that she must be careful, for a while. There's an escaped convict ranging somewhere in my district. I received the word this morning, and have been up around Lone Cabin and Burnt Pine and the head of Clear Creek to see if I could start anything. I didn't find any signs, but the information is reliable. Tell Sibyl that I say she must not go out without her gun—that if I catch her wandering around unarmed, I'll pack her off back to civilization, pronto."

"I'll tell her," said Myra Willard, "and I'll help her to remember. It would be better, I suppose, if she stayed at home; but that seems so impossible."

"She'll be all right if she has her gun," asserted the Ranger, confidently. "I'd back the girl against anything I ever met up with—when she has her artillery. By the way, Myra, have your neighbors below called yet?"

"No—at least, not while I have been at home. I have been berrying, two or three times. They might have come while I was out."

"Has Sibyl met them yet?" came the next question.

"She has not mentioned it, if she has."

"H-m-m," mused Brian Oakley.

The woman's love for the girl prompted her to quick suspicion of the Ranger's manner.

"What is it, Mr. Oakley?" she asked. "Has the child been indiscreet? Has she done anything wrong? Has she been with those men?"

"She has called upon one of them several times," returned Brian, smiling. "Mr. King is painting that little glade by the old spring at the foot of the bank, you know, and I guess she stumbled onto him. The place is one of her favorite spots. But bless your heart, Myra, there's no harm in it. It would be natural for her to get interested in any one making a picture of a place she loves as she does that old spring glade. She has spent days at a time there—ever since she was big enough to go that far from home."

"It's strange that she has not mentioned it to me," said the woman—troubled in spite of the Ranger's reassuring words.

The man directed his attention suddenly to his horse; "Max! You let Sibyl's roses alone." The animal turned his head questioningly toward his master. "Back!" said the Ranger, "back!" At his word, the chestnut promptly backed across the yard until the officer called, "That will do," when he halted, and, with an impatient toss of his head, again looked toward the porch, inquiringly. "You are all right now," said the man. Whereupon the horse began contentedly cropping the grass.

"I met Mr. King, accidentally, once, at the depot in Fairlands," continued the woman with the disfigured face. "He impressed me, then, as being a genuinely good man—a true gentleman. But, judging from his books, Conrad Lagrange is not a man I would wish Sibyl to meet. I have wondered at the artist's friendship with him."

"I tell you, Myra, Lagrange is all right," said Brian Oakley, stoutly. "He's odd and eccentric and rough spoken sometimes; but he's not at all what you would think him from the stuff he writes. He's a true man at heart, and you needn't worry about Sibyl getting anything but good from an acquaintance with him. As for King— well—Conrad Lagrange vouches for him. If you knew Lagrange, you'd understand what that means. He and the young fellow's mother grew up together. He swears the lad is right; and, from what I've seen of him, I believe it. It doesn't follow, though, that you don't need to keep your eyes open. The girl is as innocent as a child— though she is a woman—and—well—accidents have happened, you know." As he spoke he glanced unconsciously at the scars that disfigured the naturally beautiful face of the woman.

Myra Willard blushed as she answered sadly, "Yes, I know that accidents have happened. I will talk with Sibyl; and will you not speak to her too? She loves you so, and is always guided by your wishes. A little word or two from you would be an added safeguard."

"Sure I'll talk to her," said the Ranger, heartily—rising and whistling to the chestnut. "But look here, Myra,"—he said, pausing with his foot in the stirrup,—"the girl must have her head, you know. We don't want to put her in the notion that every man in the world is a villain laying for a chance to do her harm. There are clean fellows—a few—and it will do Sibyl good to meet that kind." He swung himself lightly into the saddle.

The woman smiled; "Sibyl could not think that all men are evil, after knowing her father and you, Mr. Oakley."

The Ranger laughed as he turned Max toward the opening in the cedar thicket. "Will was what God and Nelly made him, Myra; and I—if I'm fairly decent it's because Mary took me in hand in time. Men are mostly what you women make 'em, anyway, I reckon."

"Don't forget that you and Mrs. Oakley are coming for supper to-morrow," she called after him.

"No danger of our forgetting that," he answered. "Adios!" And the chestnut loped easily out of the yard.

Myra Willard kept her place on the porch until the sound of the horse's galloping feet died away down the canyon. But, as she listened to the vanishing sound of the Ranger's going, her eyes were looking far away—as though his words had aroused in her heart memories of days long past. When the last echo had lost itself in the thin mountain air, she went into the house.

Standing before the small mirror that served—in the rude, almost camp-like furnishings of the house—for both herself and Sibyl, she studied the face reflected there—turning her head slowly, as if comparing the beautiful unmarked side with the other that was so hideously disfigured. For some time she stood there, unflinchingly giving herself to the torture of this contemplation of her ruined loveliness; drinking to its bitter dregs the sorrowful cup of her secret memories; until, as though she could bear no more, she drew back—her eyes wide with pain and horror, her marred features twisted grotesquely in an agony of mental suffering. With a pitiful moan she sank upon her knees in prayer.

In the earnestness of her spirit—out of the deep devotion of her love—as she prayed God for wisdom to guide the girl entrusted to her care, she spoke aloud. "Let me not rob her, dear Christ, of love; but help me to help her love aright. Help me, that in my fear for her I do not turn her heart against her mate when he shall come.

Help me, that I do not so fill her pure mind with doubt and distrust of all men that she will look for evil, only. Help me, that I do not teach her to associate love wholly with that which is base and untrue. Grant, O God, that her beautiful life may not be marred by a love that is unworthy."

As the woman with the disfigured face rose from her knees, she heard the voice of Sibyl, who was coming up the old road toward the cedars—singing as she came.

When Sibyl entered the house, a moment later, Myra Willard, still agitated, was bathing her face. The girl, seeing, checked the song upon her lips; and going to the woman who in everything but the ties of blood was mother to her, sought to discover the reason for her troubled manner, and tried to soothe her with loving words.

The woman held the girl close in her arms and looked into the lovely, winsome face that was so unmarred by vicious thoughts of the world's teaching.

"Dear child, do you not sometimes hate the sight of my ugliness?" she said. "It seems to me, you must."

With her arms about her companion's neck, Sibyl pressed her pure, young lips to those disfiguring scars, in an impulsive kiss. "Foolish Myra," she cried, "you know I love you too well to see anything but your own beautiful self behind the scars. To me, your face is all like this"—and she softly kissed, in turn, the woman's unmarred cheek. "Whatever made the marks, I know that they are not dishonorable. So I never think of them at all, but see only the beautiful side—which is really you, you know."

"No,"—answered Myra Willard, gently,—"my scars are not dishonorable. But the world does not see with your pure eyes, dear child. The world sees only the ugly, disfigured side of my face. It never looks at the other side. And listen, dear heart, so the world often sees dishonor where there is no dishonor It sees evil in many things where there is only good."

"Yes," returned the girl, "but you have never taught me to see with the eyes of the world. So, to me, what the world sees, does not matter."

"Pray that it may never matter, child," answered the woman with the disfigured face, earnestly.

Then, as they went out to the porch, she asked, "Did you meet Mr. Oakley as you were coming home?"

Sibyl laughed and colored with a confusion that was new to her, as she answered, "Yes, I did—and he scolded me."

"About your going unarmed?"

"No,—but he told me about that too. I don't see why, whenever a poor criminal escapes, he always comes into our mountains. I don't like to 'pack a gun'—unless I'm hunting. But Brian Oakley didn't scold me for that, though—he knows I always do as he says. He scolded because I hadn't told you about my going to see Mr. King, in the spring glade." She laughed, conscious of the color that was in her cheeks. "I told him it didn't matter whether I told you or not, because he always knows every single move I make, anyway."

"Why didn't you tell me, dear?" asked the woman. "You never kept anything from me, before—I'm sure."

"Why dearest," the girl answered frankly, "I don't know, myself, why I didn't tell you"—which, Myra Willard knew, was the exact truth.

Then Sibyl told her foster-mother everything about her acquaintance with the artist and Conrad Lagrange—from the time she first watched the painter, from the arbor in the rose garden, where she met the novelist; until that afternoon, when she had invited them to supper, the next day. Only of her dancing before the artist, the girl did not tell.

Later in the evening, Sibyl—saying that she would sing Myra to sleep—took her violin to the porch, outside the window; and in the dusk made soft music until the woman's troubled heart was calmed. When the moon came up from behind the Galenas, across the canyon, the girl tiptoed into the house, to bend over the sleeping woman, in tender solicitude. With that mother tenderness belonging to all true women, she stooped and softly kissed the disfigured face upon the pillow. At the touch, Myra Willard stirred uneasily; and the girl—careful to make no sound—withdrew.

On the porch, she again took up her violin as if to play; but, instead, sat motionless—her face turned down the canyon—her eyes looking far away. Then, quickly, she put aside the instrument, and— as though with sudden yielding to some inner impulse—slipped out into the grassy yard. And there, in the moon's white light,—with only the mountains, the trees, and the flowers to see,—she danced, again, as she had danced before the artist in the glade—with her face turned down the canyon, and her arms outstretched, longingly, toward the camp in the sycamores back of the old orchard.

Suddenly, from the room where Myra Willard slept, came that shuddering, terror-stricken cry.

The girl, fleet-footed as a deer, ran into the house. Kneeling, she put her strong young arms about the cowering, trembling form on the bed. "There, there, dear, it's all right."

The woman of the disfigured face caught Sibyl's hand, impulsively. "I—I—was dreaming again," she whispered, "and—and this time—O Sibyl—this time, I dreamed that it was you."

Chapter XXI
The Last Climb

That first visit of Aaron King and Conrad Lagrange to the old home of Sibyl Andrés was the beginning of a delightful comradeship.

Often, in the evening, the two men, with Czar, went to spend an hour in friendly intercourse with their neighbors up the canyon. Always, they were welcomed by Myra Willard with a quiet dignity; while Sibyl was frankly delighted to have them come. Always, they were invited with genuine hospitality to "come again." Frequently, Brian Oakley and perhaps Mrs. Oakley would be there when they arrived; or the Ranger would come riding into the yard before they left. At times, the canyon's mountain wall echoed the laughter of the little company as Sibyl and the novelist played their fantastical game of words; or again, the older people would listen to the blending voices of the artist and the girl as, in the quiet hush of the evening, they sang together to Myra Willard's accompaniment on the violin; or, perhaps, Sibyl, with her face upturned to the mountain tops, would make for her chosen friends the music of the hills.

Not infrequently, too, the girl would call at the camp in the sycamore grove—sometimes riding with the Ranger, sometimes alone; or they would hear her merry hail from the gate the other side of the orchard as she passed by. And sometimes, in the morning, she would appear—equipped with rod or gun or basket—to frankly challenge Aaron King to some long ramble in the hills.

So the days for the young man at the beginning of his life work, and for the young woman at the beginning of her womanhood, passed. Up and down the canyon, along the boulder-strewn bed of the roaring Clear Creek, from the Ranger Station to the falls; in the quiet glades under the alders hung with virgin's-bower and wild grape; beneath the live-oaks on the mountains' flanks or shoulders; in dimly lighted, cedar-sheltered gulches, among tall brakes and lilies; or high up on the canyon walls under the dark and fragrant pines—over all the paths and trails familiar to her girlhood she led him—showing him every nook and glade and glen—teaching him to know, as he had asked, the mountains that she herself so loved.

The time came, at last, when the two men must return to Fairlands. With Mr. and Mrs. Oakley they were spending the evening at Sibyl's home when Conrad Lagrange announced that they would leave the mountains, two days later.

"Then,"—said the girl, impulsively,—"Mr. King and I are going for one last good-by climb to-morrow. Aren't we?" she concluded—turning to the artist.

Aaron King laughed as he answered, "We certainly seem to be headed that way. Where are we going?"

"We will start early and come back late"—she returned—"which really is all that any one ought to know about a climb that is just for the climb. And listen—no rod, no gun, no sketch-book. I'll fix a lunch."

"Watch out for my convict," warned the Ranger. "He must be getting mighty hungry, by now."

Early in the morning, they set out. Crossing the canyon, they climbed the Oak Knoll trail—down which the artist and Conrad Lagrange had been led by the uncanny wisdom of Croesus, a few weeks before—to the pipe-line. Where the path from below leads into the pipe-line trail, under the live-oaks, on a shelf cut in the comparatively easy slope of the mountain's shoulder, they paused for a look over the narrow valley that lay a thousand feet below. Across the wide, gray, boulder-strewn wash of the mountain torrent's way, with the gleaming thread of tumbling Clear Creek in its center, they could see the white dots that marked the camp back of the old orchard; and, farther up the stream, could distinguish the little opening with the cedar thicket and the giant sycamores that marked the spot where Sibyl was born.

Aaron King, looking at the girl, recalled that day when he and Conrad Lagrange, in a spirit of venturesome fun, had left the choice of trails to the burro. "Good, old Croesus!" he said smiling.

She knew the story of how they had been guided to their camping place, and laughed in return, as she answered, "He's a dear old burro, is Croesus, and worthy of a better name."

"Plutus would be better," suggested the artist.

"Because a Greek God is better than a Lydian King?" she asked curiously.

"Wasn't Plutus the giver of wealth?" he returned.

"Yes."

"Well, and wasn't he forced by Zeus to distribute his gifts without regard to the characters of the recipients?"

She laughed merrily. "Plutus or Croesus—I'm glad he chose the Oak Knoll trail."

"And so am I," answered the man, earnestly.

Leisurely, they followed the trail that is hung—narrow thread-like path—high upon the mountain wall, invisible from the floor of the canyon below. At a point where the trail turns to round the inward curve of one of the small side canyons—where the pines grow dark and tall—some thoughtful hand had laid a small pipe from the large conduit tunnel, under the trail, to a barrel fixed on the mountainside below the little path. Here they stopped again and, while they loitered, filled a small canteen with the cold, clear water from the mountain's heart. Farther on, where the pipe-line again rounds the inward curve of the wall between two mountain spurs, they turned aside to follow the Government trail that leads to the fire-break on the summit of the Galenas and then down into the valley on the other side. At the gap where the Galena trail crosses the fire-break, they again turned aside to make their leisure way along the broad, brush-cleared break that lies in many a fold and curve and kink like a great ribbon on the thin top of the ridge. With every step, now, they were climbing. Midday found them standing by a huge rock at the edge of a clump of pines on one of the higher points of the western end of the range. Here they would have their lunch.

As they sat in the lee of the great rock, with the wind that sweeps the mountain tops singing in the pines above their heads, they looked directly down upon the wide Galena Valley and far across to the spurs and slopes of the San Jacintos beyond. Sibyl's keen eyes—mountain-trained from childhood—marked a railway train crawling down the grade from San Gorgonio Pass toward the distant ocean. She tried in vain to point it out to her companion. But the city eyes of the man could not find the tiny speck in the vast landscape that lay within the range of their vision. The artist looked at his watch. The train was the Golden State Limited that had brought him from the far away East, a few months before.

Aaron King remembered how, from the platform of the observation car, he had looked up at the mountains from which he now looked down. He remembered too, the woman into whose eyes he had, for the first time, looked that day. Turning his face to the west, he could distinguish under the haze of the distance the dark squares of the orange groves of Fairlands. Before three days had passed he would be in his studio home again. And the woman of the observation car platform—From distant Fairlands, the man turned his eyes to the winsome face of his girl comrade on the mountain top.

142

"Please"—she said, meeting his serious gaze with a smile of frank fellowship—"please, what have I done?"

Smiling, he answered gravely, "I don't exactly know—but you have done something."

"You look so serious. I'm sure it must be pretty bad. Can't you think what it is?"

He laughed. "I was thinking about down there"—he pointed into the haze of the distant valley to the west.

"Don't," she returned, "let's think about up here"—she waved her hand toward the high crest of the San Bernardinos, and the mountain peaks about them.

"Will you let me paint your portrait—when we get back to the orange groves?" he asked.

"I'm sure I don't know," she returned. "Why do you want to paint me? I'm nobody, you know—but just me."

"That's the reason I want to paint you," he answered.

"What's the reason?"

"Because you are you."

"But a portrait of me would not help you on your road to fame," she retorted.

He flinched. "Perhaps," he said, "that's partly why I want to do it."

"Because it won't help you?"

"Because it won't help me on the road to fame. You will pose for me, won't you?"

"I'm sure I cannot say"—she answered—"perhaps—please don't let's talk about it."

"Why not?" he asked curiously.

"Because"—she answered seriously—"we have been such good friends up here in the mountains; such—such comrades. Up here in the hills, with the canyon gates shut against the world that I don't know, you are like—like Brian Oakley—and like my father used to be—and down there"—she hesitated.

"Yes," he said, "and down there I will be what?"

"I don't know," she answered wistfully, "but sometimes I can see you going on and on and on toward fame and the rewards it will bring you and you seem to get farther and farther and farther away from—from the mountains and our friendship; until you are so far away that I can't see you any more at all. I don't like to lose my mountain friends, you know."

He smiled. "But no matter how famous I might become—no matter what fame might bring me—I could not forget you and your mountains."

143

"I would not want you to remember me," she answered "if you were famous. That is—I mean"—she added hesitatingly—"if you were famous just because you wanted to be. But I know you could never forget the mountains. And that would be the trouble; don't you see? If you could forget, it would not matter. Ask Mr. Lagrange, he knows."

For some time Aaron King sat, without speaking, looking about at the world that was so far from that other world—the world he had always known. The girl, too,—seeming to understand the thoughts that he himself, perhaps, could not have expressed,—was silent.

Then he said slowly, "I don't think that I care for fame as I did before you taught me to know the mountains. It doesn't, somehow, now, seem to matter so much. It's the work that really matters—after all—isn't it?"

And Sibyl Andrés, smiling, answered, "Yes, it's the work that really matters. I'm sure that must be so."

In the afternoon, they went on, still following the fire-break, down to where it is intersected by the pipe-line a mile from the reservoir on the hill above the power-house; then back to Oak Knoll, again on the pipe-line trail all the way—a beautiful and never-to-be-forgotten walk.

The sun was just touching the tops of the western mountains when they started down Oak Knoll. The canyon below, already, lay in the shadow. When they reached the foot of the trail, it was twilight. Across the road, by a small streamlet—a tributary to Clear Creek—a party of huntsmen were making ready to spend the night. The voices of the men came clearly through the gathering gloom. Under the trees, they could see the camp-fire's ruddy gleam. They did not notice the man who was standing, half hidden, in the bushes beside the road, near the spot where the trail opens into it. Silently, the man watched them as they turned up the road which they would follow a little way before crossing the canyon to Sibyl's home. Fifty yards farther on, they met Brian Oakley.

"Howdy, you two," called the Ranger, cheerily—without stopping his horse. "Rather late to-night, ain't you?"

"We'll be there by dark," called the artist And the Ranger passed on.

At sound of the mountaineer's voice, the man in the bushes drew quickly back. The officer's trained eyes caught the movement in the brush, and he leaned forward in the saddle.

A moment later, the man reappeared in the road, farther

down, around the bend. As the Ranger approached, he was hailed by a boisterous, "Hello, Brian! better stop and have a bite."

"How do you do, Mr. Rutlidge?" came the officer's greeting, as he reined in his horse. "When did you land in the hills?"'

"This afternoon," answered the other. "We're just making camp. Come and meet the fellows. You know some of them."

"Thanks, not to-night,"—returned Brian Oakley,—"deer hunt, I suppose."

"Yes—thought we would be in good time for the opening of the season. By the way, do you happen to know where Lagrange and that artist friend of his are camped?"

"In that bunch of sycamores back of the old orchard down there," answered the Ranger, watching the man's face keenly. "I just passed Mr. King, up the road a piece."

"That so? I didn't see him go by," returned the other. "I think I'll run over and say 'hello' to Lagrange in the morning. We are only going as far as Burnt Pine to-morrow, anyway."

"Keep your eyes open for an escaped convict," said the officer, casually. "There's one ranging somewhere in here—came in about a month ago. He's likely to clean out your camp. So long."

"Perhaps we'll take him in for you," laughed the other. "Good night." He turned toward the camp-fire under the trees, as the officer rode away.

"Now what in hell did that fellow want to lie to me like that for," said Brian Oakley to himself. "He must have seen King and Sibyl as they came down the trail. Max, old boy, when a man lies deliberately, without any apparent reason, you want to watch him."

145

Chapter XXII
Shadows of Coming Events

Aaron King and Conrad Lagrange were idling in their camp, after breakfast the next morning, when Czar turned his head, quickly, in a listening attitude. With a low growl that signified disapproval, he moved forward a step or two and stood stiffly erect, gazing toward the lower end of the orchard.

"Some one coming, Czar?" asked the artist.

The dog answered with another growl, while the hair on his neck bristled in anger.

"Some one we don't like, heh!" commented the novelist. "Or"—he added as if musing upon the animal's instinct—"some one we ought not to like."

A bark from Czar greeted James Rutlidge who at that moment appeared at the foot of the slope leading up to their camp.

The two men—remembering the occasion of their visitor's last call at their home in Fairlands, when he had seen Sibyl in the studio—received the man with courtesy, but with little warmth. Czar continued to manifest his sentiments until rebuked by his master. The coolness of the reception, however, in no way disconcerted James Rutlidge; who, on his part, rather overdid his assumption of pleasure at meeting them again.

Explaining that he had come with a party of friends on a hunting trip, he told them how he had met Brian Oakley, and so had learned of their camp hidden behind the old orchard. The rest of his party, he said, had gone on up the canyon. They would stop at Burnt Pine on Laurel Creek, where he could easily join them before night. He could not think, he declared, of passing so near without greeting his friends.

"You two certainly are expert when it comes to finding snug, out-of-the-way quarters," he commented, searching the camp and the immediate surroundings with a careful and, ostensibly, an appreciative eye. "A thousand people might pass this old, deserted place without ever dreaming that you were so ideally hidden back here."

As he finished speaking, his roving eye came to rest upon a pair of gloves that Sibyl—the last time she had called—had carelessly left lying upon a stump close by a giant sycamore where, in camp fashion, the rods and creels and guns were kept. The artist

146

had intended to return the gloves the day before, together with a book of trout-flies which the girl had also forgotten; but, in his eagerness for the day's outing, he had gone off without them.

The observing Conrad Lagrange did not fail to note that James Rutlidge had seen the telltale gloves. Fixing his peculiar eyes upon the visitor, he asked abruptly, with polite but purposeful interest, after the health of Mr. and Mrs. Taine and Louise.

The faint shadow of a suggestive smile that crossed the heavy features of James Rutlidge, as he turned his gaze from the gloves to meet the look of the novelist was maddening.

"The old boy is steadily going down," he said without feeling. "The doctors tell me that he can't last through the winter. It'll be a relief to everybody when he goes. Mrs. Taine is well and beautiful, as always—remarkable how she keeps up appearances, considering her husband's serious condition. Louise is quite as usual. They will all be back in Fairlands in another month. They sent regards to you both—in case I should run across you.'"

The two men made the usual conventional replies, adding that they were returning to Fairlands the next day.

"So soon?" exclaimed their visitor, with another meaning smile. "I don't see how you can think of leaving your really delightful retreat. I understand you have such charming neighbors too. Perhaps though, they are also returning to the orange groves and roses."

Aaron King's face flushed hotly, and he was about to reply with vigor to the sneering words, when Conrad Lagrange silenced him with a quick look. Ignoring the reference to their neighbors, the novelist replied suavely that they felt they must return to civilization as some matters in connection with the new edition of his last novel demanded his attention, and the artist wished to get back to his studio and to his work.

"Really," urged Rutlidge, mockingly, "you ought not to go down now. The deer season opens in two days. Why not join our party for a hunt? We would be delighted to have you."

They were coolly thanking him for the invitation,—that, from the tone in which it was given, was so evidently not meant,—when Czar, with a joyful bark, dashed away through the grove. A moment, and a clear, girlish voice called from among the trees that bordered the cienaga, "Whoo-ee." It was the signal that Sibyl always gave when she approached their camp.

James Rutlidge broke into a low laugh while Sibyl's friends looked at each other in angry consternation as the girl, following her hail and accompanied by the delighted dog, appeared in full view; her fishing-rod in hand, her creel swung over her shoulder.

147

The girl's embarrassment, when, too late, she saw and recognized their visitor, was pitiful. As she came slowly forward, too confused to retreat, Rutlidge started to laugh again, but Aaron King, with an emphasis that checked the man's mirth, said in a low tone, "Stop that! Be careful!"

As he spoke, the artist arose and with Conrad Lagrange went forward to greet Sibyl in—as nearly as they could—their customary manner.

Formally, Rutlidge was presented to the girl; and, under the threatening eyes of the painter, greeted her with no hint of rudeness in his voice or manner; saying courteously, with a smile, "I have had the pleasure of Miss Andrés' acquaintance for—let me see—three years now, is it not?" he appealed to her directly.

"It was three years ago that I first saw you, sir," she returned coolly.

"It was my first trip into the mountains, I remember," said Rutlidge, easily. "I met you at Brian Oakley's home."

Without replying, she turned to Aaron King appealingly. "I—I left my gloves and fly-book. I was going fishing and called to get them."

The artist gave her the articles with a word of regret for having so carelessly forgotten to return them to her. With a simple "good-by" to her two friends but without even a glance toward their caller, she went back up the canyon, in the direction from which she had come.

When the girl had disappeared among the trees, James Rutlidge said, with his meaning smile, "Really, I owe you an apology for dropping in so unexpectedly. I—"

Conrad Lagrange interrupted him, curtly. "No apology is due, sir."

"No?" returned Rutlidge, with a rising inflection and a drawling note in his voice that was almost too much for the others. "I really must be going, anyway," he continued. "My party will be some distance ahead. Sure you wouldn't care to join us?"

"Thanks! Sorry! but we cannot this time. Good of you to ask us," came from Aaron King and the novelist.

"Can't say that I blame you," their caller returned. "The fishing used to be fine in this neighborhood. You must have had some delightful sport. Don't blame you in the least for not joining our stag party. Delightful young woman, that Miss Andrés. Charming companion—either in the mountains or in civilization Good-by—see you in Fairlands, later."

When he was out of hearing the two men relieved their
148

feelings in language that perhaps it would be better not to put in print.

"And the worst of it is," remarked the novelist, "it's so damned dangerous to deny something that does not exist or make explanations in answer to charges that are not put into words."

"I could scarcely refrain from kicking the beast down the hill," said Aaron King, savagely.

"Which"—the other returned—"would have complicated matters exceedingly, and would have accomplished nothing at all. For the girl's sake, store your wrath against the day of judgment which, if I read the signs aright, is sure to come."

When Sibyl Andrés went down the canyon to the camp in the sycamores, that morning, the world, to her, was very bright. Her heart sang with joyous freedom amid the scenes that she so loved. Care-free and happy, as when, in the days of her girlhood, she had gone to visit the spring glade, she still was conscious of a deeper joy than in her girlhood she had ever known.

When she returned again up the canyon, all the brightness of her day was gone. Her heart was heavy with foreboding fear. She was oppressed with a dread of some impending evil which she could not understand. At every sound in the mountain wild-wood, she started. Time and again, as if expecting pursuit, she looked over her shoulder—poised like a creature of the woods ready for instant panic-stricken flight. So, without pausing to cast for trout, or even to go down to the stream, she returned home; where Myra Willard, seeing her come so early and empty handed, wondered. But to the woman's question, the girl only answered that she had changed her mind—that, after recovering her gloves and fly-book at the camp of their friends, she had decided to come home. The woman with the disfigured face, knowing that Aaron King was leaving the hills the next day, thought that she understood the girl's mood, and wisely made no comment.

The artist and Conrad Lagrange went to spend their last evening in the hills with their friends. Brian Oakley, too, dropped in. But neither of the three men mentioned the name of James Rutlidge in the presence of the women; while Sibyl was, apparently, again her own bright and happy self—carrying on a fanciful play of words with the novelist, singing with the artist, and making music for them all with her violin. But before the evening was over, Conrad Lagrange found an opportunity to tell the Ranger of the incident of the morning, and of the construction that James Rutlidge had evidently put upon Sibyl's call at the camp. Brian Oakley,—thinking of the night before, and how the man must have seen the artist and the girl coming down the Oak Knoll trail in the twilight,—swore softly under his breath.

149

Chapter XXIII
Outside the Canyon Gates Again

Aaron King and Conrad Lagrange determined to go back from the mountains, the way they had come. Said the novelist, "It is as unseemly to rush pell-mell from an audience with the gods as it is to enter their presence irreverently."

To which the artist answered, laughing, "Even criminals under sentence have, at least, the privilege of going to their prisons reluctantly."

So they went down from the mountains, reverently and reluctantly.

Yee Kee, with the more elaborate equipment of the camp, was sent on ahead by wagon. The two men, with Croesus packed for a one night halt, and Czar, would follow. When all was ready, and they could neither of them invent any more excuses for lingering, Conrad Lagrange gave the word to the burro and they set out—down the little slope of grassy land; across the tiny stream from the cienaga; around the lower end of the old orchard, by the ancient weed-grown road—even Czar went slowly, with low-hung head, as if regretful at leaving the mountains that he, too, in his dog way, loved.

At the gate, Aaron King asked the novelist to go on, saying that he would soon overtake him. It was possible, he said, that he might have left something in the spring glade. He thought he had better make sure. Conrad Lagrange, assenting, went through the gate and down the road, with the four-footed members of the party; and Czar must have thought that there was something very funny about old Croesus that morning, from the way his master laughed; when they were safely around the first turn.

There was, of course, no material thing in the spring glade that the artist wanted. He knew that—quite as well as his laughing friend. Under the mistletoe oak, at the top of the bank, he paused, hesitating—as one will often pause when about to enter a sacred building. Softly, he pushed open the old gate, as he might have pushed open the door of a church. Slowly, reverently, he went down the path; baring his head as he went. He did not search for anything that he might have left. He simply stood for a few minutes under the gray-trunked alders that were so marked by the loving hands of long ago men and maidens—beside the mint bordered spring with the scattered stones of that old foundation—where, through the screen

150

of boughs and vines and virgin's-bower the sunlight fell as through the traceries of a cathedral window, and the low, deep tones of the mountain waters came like the music of a great organ.

It is likely that Aaron King, himself, could not, at that time, have told why, as he was leaving the hills, he had paused to visit once more the spot where Sibyl Andrés had brought to him her three gifts from the mountains—where, in her pure innocence, she had danced before him the dance of the mating butterflies—and where, with the music of her violin, she had saved their friendship from the perils that threatened it—lifting their intimate comradeship into the pure atmosphere of the higher levels, even as she had shown him the trails that lead from the lower canyon to the summits and peaks of the encircling mountain walls. But when he rejoined his friend there was something in his face that prevented the novelist from making any comment in a laughing vein.

As the two men passed outward through the canyon gates and, looking backward as they went, saw those mighty doors close silently behind them, the artist was moved by emotions that were strange and new to the man who, two months before, had watched those gates open to receive him. This, too, is true; as that man, then, knew, but did not know, the mountains; so this man, now, knew, yet still did not know, himself.

Where the road crosses, for the last time, the tumbling stream from the heart of the hills, they halted; and for one night slept again at the foot of the mountains. The next day they arrived at their little home in the orange grove. To Aaron King, it seemed that they had been away for years.

When the traces of their days upon the road had been removed, and they were garbed again in the conventional costume of the world; when their outfit had been put away, and a home found for patient Croesus; the artist went to his studio. The afternoon passed and Yee Kee called dinner; but Aaron King did not come. Then Conrad Lagrange went to find him. Softly, the older man pushed open the studio door to see the painter sitting before the portrait of Mrs. Taine, with the package of his mother's letters in his hand.

Without a sound, the novelist withdrew, leaving the door ajar. Going to the corner of the house, he whistled low, and in answer, Czar come bounding to him from the porch. "Go find Aaron, Czar," said the man, pointing toward the studio. "Go find Aaron."

Obediently, with waving tail, the dog trotted off, and pushing open the door entered the room; followed a few moments later by his master.

Conrad Lagrange smiled as he saw that the easel was without a canvas. The portrait of Mrs. Taine was turned to the wall.

Chapter XXIV
James Rutlidge Makes a Mistake

When Aaron King and Conrad Lagrange had said, "good-by," to their friends, at Sibyl Andrés' home, that evening; and had returned to spend their last night at the camp in the sycamores; the girl's mood was again the mood of one oppressed by a haunting, foreboding fear.

Sibyl could not have expressed, or even to herself defined, her fear. She only knew that in the presence of James Rutlidge she was frightened. She had tried many times to overcome her strange antipathy; for Rutlidge, until that day in the studio, had never been other than kind and courteous in his persistent efforts to win her friendship. Perhaps it was the impression left by the memory of Myra Willard's manner at the time of their first meeting with him, three years before, in Brian Oakley's home; perhaps it was because the woman with the disfigured face had so often warned her against permitting her slight acquaintance with Rutlidge to develop; perhaps it was something else—some instinct, possible, only, to one of her pure, unspoiled nature—whatever it was, the mountain girl who was so naturally unafraid, feared this man who, in his own world, was an acknowledged authority upon matters of the highest spiritual and moral significance.

That night, she slept but little. With the morning, every nerve demanded action, action. She felt as though if she could not spend herself in physical exertion she would go mad. Taking her lunch, and telling her companion that she was going for a good, full day with the trout; she was starting off, when the woman called her back.

"You have forgotten Mr. Oakley's warning, dear. You are not to go unarmed, you know."

"Oh, bother that old convict, Brian Oakley is so worried about," cried the girl. "I don't like to carry a gun when I am fishing. It's only an extra load." But, never-the-less, as she spoke, she went back to the porch; where Myra Willard handed her a belt of cartridges, with a serviceable Colt revolver in the holster. There was no hint of awkwardness when the girl buckled the belt about her waist and settled the holster in its place at her hip.

"You will be careful, won't you, dear," said the woman, earnestly.

Lifting her face for another good-by kiss, the girl answered, "Of course, dear mother heart." Then, with a laugh—"I'll agree to shoot the first man I meet, and identify him afterwards—if it will make you easier in your mind. You won't worry, will you?"

Myra Willard smiled. "Not a bit, child. I know how Brian Oakley loves you, and he says that he has no fear for you if you are armed. He takes great chances himself, that man, but he would send us back to Fairlands, in a minute, if he thought you were in any danger in your rambles."

Beside the roaring Clear Creek, Sibyl seated self upon a great boulder—her rod and flies neglected—apparently unmindful of the purpose that had brought her to the stream. Her eyes were not upon the swirling pool at her feet, but were lifted to a spot, a thousand feet up on Oak Knoll, where she knew the pipe-line trail lay, and where Croesus had made the momentous decision that had resulted in her comradeship with Aaron King. Following the canyon wall with her eyes—as though in her mind she walked the thread-like path—from Oak Knoll to the fire-break a mile from the reservoir; her gaze then traced the crest of the Galenas, resting finally upon that clump of pines high up on the point that was so clearly marked against the sky. Once, she laid aside her rod, and slipped the creel from her shoulder. But even as she set out, she hesitated and turned back; resolutely taking up her fishing-tackle again, as though, angry with herself for her state of mind, she was determined to indulge no longer her mood of indecision.

But the fishing did not go well. To properly cast a trout-fly, one's thoughts must be upon the art. A preoccupied mind and wandering attention tends to a tangled line, a snarled leader, and all sorts of aggravating complications. Sibyl—usually so skillful at this most delicate of sports—was as inaccurate and awkward, this day, as the merest tyro. The many pools and falls and swirling eddies of Clear Creek held for her, now, memories more attractive, by far, than the wary trout they sheltered. The familiar spots she had known since childhood were haunted by a something that made them seem new and strange.

At last,—thoroughly angry with her inability to control her mood, and half ashamed of the thoughts that forced themselves so insistently upon her; with her nerves and muscles craving the action that would bring the relief of physical weariness,—she determined to leave the more familiar ground, for the higher and less frequented waters of Fern Creek. Climbing out of the canyon, by the steep, almost stair-like trail on the San Bernardino side, she walked hard and fast to reach Lone Cabin by noon. But, before she had finished her lunch, she decided not to fish there, after all; but to go

153

on, over the still harder trail to Burnt Pine on Laurel Creek, and, returning to the lower canyon by the Laurel trail, to work down Clear Creek on the way to her home, in the late afternoon and twilight.

The trail up the almost precipitous wall of the gorge at Lone Cabin, and over the mountain spur to Laurel Creek, is one that calls for a clear head and a sure foot. It is not a path for the city bred to essay, save with the ready arm of a guide. But the hill-trained muscles and nerves of Sibyl Andrés gloried in the task. The cool-headed, mountain girl enjoyed the climb from which her city sisters would have drawn back in trembling fear.

Once, at a point perhaps two-thirds of the height to the top, she halted. Her ear had caught a slight noise above her head, as a few pebbles rolled down the almost perpendicular face of the wall and bounded from the trail where she stood, into the depths below. For a few minutes, the girl, on the little, shelf-like path that was scarcely wider than the span of her two hands, was as motionless and as silent as the cliff itself; while, with her face turned upward, she searched with keen eyes the rim of the gorge; her free, right hand resting upon the butt of the revolver at her hip. Then she went on—not timidly, but neither carelessly; not in the least frightened, but still,—knowing that the spot was far from the more frequented paths,—with experienced care.

As her head and shoulders came above the rim, she paused again, to search with careful eyes the vicinity of the trail that from this point leads for a little way down the knife-like ridge of the spur, and then, by easier stages, around the shoulder and the flank of the mountain, to Burnt Pine Camp. When no living object met her eye, and she could hear no sound save the lonely wind in the pines and the faint murmur of the stream in the gorge below, she took the few steps that yet remained of the climb, and seated herself for a moment's well-earned rest. Some small animal, she told herself,—a squirrel or a wood-rat, perhaps,—frightened at her approach, and scurrying hastily to cover, had dislodged the pebbles with the slight noise that she had heard.

From where she sat with her back against the trunk of a great pine, she could see—far below, and beyond the immediate spurs and shoulders of the range, on the farther side of the gorge out of which she had just come—the lower end of Clear Creek canyon, and, miles away, under the blue haze of the distance, the dark squares of the orange groves of Fairlands.

Somewhere between those canyon gates and the little city in the orange groves, the girl knew that Aaron King and his friend were making their way back to the world of men. With her eyes fixed

154

upon the distant scene, as if striving for a wholly impossible strength of vision to mark the tiny, moving spots that she knew were there, the girl upon the high rim of the wild and lonely mountain gorge was lost to her surroundings, in an effort, as vain, to see her comrade of the weeks just past, in the years that were to come. Would the friendship born in the hills endure in the world beyond the canyon gates? Could it endure away from those scenes that had given it birth? Was it possible for a fellowship, established in the free atmosphere of the mountains, to live in the lower altitude of Fairlands? Sibyl Andrés,—as she sat there, alone in the hills she loved,—in her heart of hearts, answered her own questions, "No." But still she searched the years to come—even as her eyes so futilely searched the distant landscape beyond the mighty gates that seemed, now, to shut her in from that world to which Aaron King was returning.

The girl was aroused from her abstraction by a sound behind her and a little to the left of the tree against which she was leaning. In a flash, she was on her feet.

James Rutlidge stood a few steps away. He had been approaching her as she sat under the tree; but when she sprang to her feet and faced him, he halted. Lifting his hat, he greeted her with easy assurance; a confident, triumphant smile upon his heavy features.

White-faced and trembling, the mountain girl—who a few moments before, had been so unafraid—stood shrinking before this cultured representative of the arts. Returning his salutation, she was starting hurriedly away down the trail, when he said, "Wait. Why be in such a hurry?"

As if against her will, she paused. "It is growing late," she faltered; "I must go."

He laughed. "I will go with you presently. Don't be afraid." Coming forward, with an air of making himself very much at home, he placed his rifle against the tree where she had been sitting. Then, as if to calm her fears, he continued, "I am camped at Burnt Pine, with a party of friends. I was up here looking for deer sign when I noticed you below, at the cabin there. I was just starting down to you, when I saw that you were going to come up; so I waited. Beautiful spot—this—don't you think?—so out of the way, too. Just the place for a quiet little visit."

As the man spoke, he was eyeing her in a way that only served to confuse and frighten her the more. Murmuring some inaudible reply, she again started to go. But again he said, peremptorily, "Wait." And again, as if against her will, she paused. "If you have no scruples about wandering over the mountains alone with that artist fellow, I do not see why you should hesitate to favor me."

The man's words were, undoubtedly, prompted by what he firmly believed to be the nature of the relation between the girl and Aaron King—a belief for which he had, to his mind, sufficient evidence. But Sibyl had no understanding of his meaning. In the innocence of her pure mind, the purport of his words was utterly lost. Her very fear of the man was not a reasoning fear, but the instinctive shrinking of a nature that had never felt the unclean touch of the world in which James Rutlidge habitually moved. It was this very unreasoning element in her emotions that made her always so embarrassed in the man's presence. It was because she did not understand her fear of him, that the girl, usually so capable of taking her own part, was, in his presence, so helpless.

James Rutlidge, by the intellectual, moral, and physical atmosphere in which he lived, was made wholly incapable of understanding the nature of Sibyl Andrés. Secure in the convictions of his own debased mind, as to her relation to the artist; and misconstruing her very manner in his presence; he was not long in putting his proposal into words that she could not fail to understand.

When she did grasp his meaning, her fears and her trembling nervousness gave place to courageous indignation and righteous anger that found expression in scathing words of denunciation.

The man, still, could not understand the truth of the situation. To him, there was nothing more in her refusal than her preference for the artist. That this young woman—to him, an unschooled girl of the hills—whom he had so long marked as his own, should give herself to another, and so scornfully turn from him, was an affront that he could not brook. The very vigor of her wrath, as she stood before him,—her eyes bright, her cheeks flushed, and her beautiful body quivering with the vehemence of her passionate outburst,— only served to fan the flame of his desire; while her stinging words provoked his bestial mind to an animal-like rage. With a muttered oath and a threat, he started toward her.

But the woman who faced him now, with full understanding, was very different from the timid, frightened girl who had not at first understood. With a business-like movement that was the result of Brian Oakley's careful training, her hand dropped to her hip and was raised again.

James Rutlidge stopped, as though against an iron bar. In the blue eyes that looked at him, now, over the dark barrel of the revolver, he read no uncertainty of purpose. The small hand that had drawn the weapon with such ready swiftness, was as steady as though at target practice. Instinctively, the man half turned, throwing up his arm as if to shield his face from a menacing blow. "For God's sake," he gasped, "put that down."

In truth, James Rutlidge was nearer death, at that instant, than he had ever been before.

Drawing back a few fearful paces, his hands still uplifted, he said again, "Put it down, I tell you. Don't you see I'm not going to touch you? You are crazy. You might kill me."

Her words came cold and collected, expressing, together with her calm manner, perfect self-possession "If you can give any good reason why I should not kill you, I will let you go."

The man was carefully drawing backward toward the tree against which he had placed his rifle.

She watched him, with a disconcerting smile. "You may as well stop now," she said, in those even, composed tones. "I shall fire, the moment you are within reach of your gun."

He halted with a gesture of despair; his face livid with fear at her apparent indecision as to his fate.

Presently, she spoke again. "Don't worry. I'm not going to kill you—unless you force me to—which I assure you will not be at all difficult for you to do. Move down the trail until I tell you to stop." She indicated the direction, along the ridge of the mountain spur.

He obeyed.

"That will do," she said, when he was some twenty paces away.

He stopped, turning to face her again.

Picking up his Winchester, she skillfully and rapidly threw all of the shells out of the magazine. Then, covering him again with her own weapon, she went a few steps closer and threw the empty rifle at his feet. "Now," she said, "put that gun over your left shoulder, and go on ahead of me down the trail. If you try to dodge or run, or if you change the position of your rifle, I'll kill you."

"What are you going to do?" he asked.

"I'm going to take you down to your camp at Burnt Pine."

James Rutlidge, pale with rage and shame, stood still. "You may as well kill me," he said. "I will never go into camp, this way."

"Don't be uneasy," she returned. "I am no more anxious for the world to know of this, than you are. Do as I say. When we come within sight of your camp, or if we meet any one, I will put up my gun and we will go on together. That's why I am permitting you to carry your rifle."

So they went down the mountainside—the man with his empty rifle over his shoulder; the girl following, a few paces in the rear, with ready weapon.

157

When they had come within sight of the camp, James Rutlidge said, "There's some one there."

"I see," returned Sibyl, slipping her gun in its holster and stepping forward beside her companion. And there was a note of glad relief in her voice, for it was Brian Oakley who was bending over the camp-fire "Come," she continued to her companion, "and act as though nothing had happened."

The Ranger, on his way down from somewhere in the vicinity of San Gorgonio, had stopped at the hunters' camp for a belated dinner. Finding no one at home, he had started a fire, and had helped himself to coffee and bacon. He was just concluding his appropriated meal, when Sibyl and James Rutlidge arrived.

In a few words, the girl explained to her friend, that she was on her way over the trail from Lone Cabin, and had accidentally met Mr. Rutlidge who had accompanied her as far as the camp. James Rutlidge had little to say beyond assuring the Ranger of his welcome; and very soon, the officer and the girl set out on their way down the Laurel trail to Clear Creek canyon. As they went, Sibyl's old friend asked not a few questions about her meeting with James Rutlidge; but the girl, walking ahead in the narrow trail, evaded him, and was glad that he could not see her face.

Sibyl had spoken the literal truth when she said to Rutlidge, that she did not want any one to know of the incident. She felt ashamed and humiliated at the thought of telling even her father's old comrade and friend. She knew Brian Oakley too well to have any doubts as to what would happen if he knew how the man had approached her, and she shrank from the inevitable outcome. She wished only to forget the whole affair, and, as quickly as possible, turned the conversation into other and safer channels.

The Ranger could not stop at the house with her, but must go on down the canyon, to the Station. So the girl returned to Myra Willard, alone; and, to the woman's surprise, for the second time, with an empty creel.

Sibyl explained her failure to bring home a catch of trout, with the simple statement that she had not fished; and then—to her companion's amazement—burst into tears; begging to return at once to their little home in Fairlands.

Myra Willard thought that she understood, better than the girl herself, why, for the first time in her life, Sibyl wished to leave the mountains. Perhaps the woman with the disfigured face was right.

Chapter XXV
On the Pipe-Line Trail

James Rutlidge spent the day following his experience with Sibyl Andrés, in camp. His companions very quickly felt his sullen, ugly mood, and left him to his own thoughts.

The manner in which Sibyl received his advances had in no way changed the man's mind as to the nature of her relation to Aaron King. To one of James Rutlidge's type,—schooled in the intellectual moral and esthetic tenets of his class,—it was impossible to think of the companionship of the artist and the girl in any other light. If he had even considered the possibility of a clean, pure comradeship existing between them—under all the circumstances of their friendship as he had seen them in the studio, on the trail at dusk, and in the artist's camp—he would have answered himself that Aaron King was not such a fool as to fail to take advantage of his opportunities. The humiliation of his pride, and his rage at being so ignominiously checked by the girl whom he had so long endeavored to win, served only to increase his desire for her. Sibyl's resolute spirit, and vigorous beauty, when aroused by him, together with her unexpected opposition to his advances, were as fuel to the flame of his passion.

His day of sullen brooding over the matter did not improve his temper; and the next morning his friends were relieved to see him setting out alone, with rifle and field-glass and lunch. Ostensibly starting in the direction of the upper Laurel Creek country he doubled back, as soon as he was out of sight of camp, and took the trail leading down to Clear Creek canyon.

It could not be said that the man had any definite purpose in mind. He was simply yielding in a purposeless way to his mood, which, for the time being, could find no other expression. The remote chance that some opportunity looking toward his desire might present itself, led him to seek the scenes where such an opportunity would be most likely to occur.

Crossing the canyon above the Company Headwork he came into the pipe-line trail at a point a little back from the main wagon road and, an hour later, reached the place on Oak Knoll where the Government trail leads down into the canyon below, and where Aaron King and Conrad Lagrange had committed themselves to the

159

judgment of Croesus. Here he left the trail, and climbed to a point on a spur of the mountain, from which he could see the path for some distance on either side and below, and from which his view of the narrow valley was unobstructed. Comfortably seated, with his back against a rock, he adjusted his field-glass and trained it upon the little spot of open green—marked by the giant sycamores, the dark line of cedars, and the half hidden house—where he knew that Sibyl Andrés and Myra Willard were living.

No sooner had he focused the powerful glass upon the scene that so interested him, than he uttered a low exclamation. The two women, surrounded by their luggage and camp equipment, were sitting on the porch with Brian Oakley; waiting, evidently, for the wagon that was crossing the creek toward the house. It was clear to the man on the mountainside, that Sibyl Andrés and the woman with the disfigured face were returning to Fairlands.

For some time, James Rutlidge sat watching, with absorbing interest, the unconscious people in the canyon below. Once, he turned for a brief glance at the grove of sycamores behind the old orchard, farther down the creek. The camp of Conrad Lagrange and Aaron King was no longer there. Quickly he fixed his gaze again upon Sibyl and her friends. Presently,—as one will when looking long through a field-glass or telescope,—he lowered his hands, to rest his eyes by looking, unaided, at the immediate objects in the landscape before him. At that moment, the figure of a man appeared on the near-by trail below. It was a pitiful figure—ill-kempt ragged, half-starved, haggard-faced.

Creeping feebly along the lonely little path—without seeing the man on the mountainside above—crouching as he walked with a hunted, fearful air—the poor creature moved toward the point of the spur around which the trail led beneath the spot where Rutlidge sat.

As the man on the trail drew nearer, the watcher on the rocks above involuntarily glanced toward the distant Forest Ranger; then back to the—as he rightly guessed—escaped convict.

There are, no doubt, many moments in the life of a man like James Rutlidge when, however bad or dominated by evil influences he may be, he feels strongly the impulse of pity and the kindly desire to help. Undoubtedly, James Rutlidge inherited from his father those tendencies that made him easily ruled by his baser passions. His character was as truly the legitimate product of the age, of the social environment, and of the thought that accepts such characters. What he might have been if better born, or if schooled in an atmosphere of moral and intellectual integrity, is an idle speculation. He was what his inheritance and his life had made him.

160

He was not without impulses for good. The pitiful, hunted creature, creeping so wearily along the trail, awoke in this man of the accepted culture of his day a feeling of compassion, and aroused in him a desire to offer assistance. For the legal aspect of the case, James Rutlidge had all the indifference of his kind, who imbibe contempt for law with their mother's milk. For the moment he hesitated. Then, as the figure below passed from his sight, under the point of the spur, he slipped quietly down the mountainside, and, a few minutes later, met the convict face to face.

At the leveled rifle and the sharp command, "Hands up," the poor fellow halted with a gesture of tragic despair. An instant they stood; then the hunted one turned impulsively toward the canyon that, here, lies almost a sheer thousand feet below.

James Rutlidge spoke sharply. "Don't do that. I'm not an officer. I want to help you."

The convict turned his hunted, fearful, starving face in doubtful bewilderment toward the speaker.

The man with the gun continued, "I got the drop on you to prevent accidents—until I could explain—that's all." He lowered the rifle.

The other went a staggering step forward. "You mean that?" he said in a harsh, incredulous whisper. "You—you're not playing with me?"

"Why should I want to play with you?" returned the other, kindly. "Come, let's get off the trail. I have something to eat, up there." He led the way back to the place where he had left his lunch.

Dropping down upon the ground, the starving man seized the offered food with an animal-like cry; feeding noisily, with the manner of a famished beast. The other watched with mingled pity and disgust.

Presently, in stammering, halting phrases, but in words that showed no lack of education, the wretched creature attempted to apologize for his unseemly eagerness, and endeavored to thank his benefactor. "I suppose, sir, there is no use trying to deny my identity," he said, when James Rutlidge had again assured him of his kindly interest.

"Not at all," agreed the other, "and, so far as I am concerned, there is no reason why you should."

"Just what do you mean by that, sir?" questioned the convict.

"I mean that I am not an officer and have no reason in the world for turning you over to them. I saw you coming along the trail down there and, of course, could not help noticing your condition and guessing who you were. To me, you are simply a poor devil who

161

has gotten into a tight hole, and I want to help you out a bit, that's all."

The convict turned his eyes despairingly toward the canyon below, as he answered, "I thank you, sir, but it would have been better if you had not. Your help has only put the end off for a few hours. They've got me shut in. I can keep away from them, up here in the mountains, but I can't get out. I won't go back to that hell they call prison though—I won't." There was no mistaking his desperate purpose.

James Rutlidge thought of that quick movement toward the edge of the trail and the rocky depth below. "You don't seem such a bad sort, at heart," he said invitingly.

"I'm not," returned the other, "I've been a fool—miserably weak fool—but I've had my lesson—only—I have had it too late."

While the man was speaking, James Rutlidge was thinking quickly. As he had been moved, at first, by a spirit of compassion to give temporary assistance to the poor hunted creature, he was now prompted to offer more lasting help—providing, of course, that he could do so without too great a risk to his own convenience. The convict's hopeless condition, his despairing purpose, and his evident wish to live free from the past, all combined to arouse in the other a desire to aid him. But while that truly benevolent inclination was, in his consciousness, unmarred with sinister motive of any sort; still, deeper than the impulse for good in James Rutlidge's nature lay those dominant instincts and passions that were his by inheritance and training. The brutal desire, the mood and purpose that had brought him to that spot where with the aid of his glass he could watch Sibyl Andrés, were not denied by his impulse to kindly service. Under all his thinking, as he considered how he could help the convict to a better life, there was the shadowy suggestion of a possible situation where a man like the one before him—wholly in his power as this man would be—might be of use to him in furthering his own purpose—the purpose that had brought about their meeting.

Studying the object of his pity, he said slowly, "I suppose the most of us are as deserving of punishment as the majority of those who actually get it. One way or another, we are all trying to escape the penalty for our wrong-doing. What if I should help you out— make it possible for you to live like other men who are safe from the law? What would you do if I were to help you to your freedom?"

The hunted man became incoherent in his pleading for a chance to prove the sincerity of his wish to live an orderly, respectable, and honest life.

162

"You have a safe hiding place here in the mountains?" asked Rutlidge.

"Yes; a little hut, hidden in a deep gorge, over on the Cold Water. I could live there a year if I had supplies."

James Rutlidge considered. "I've got it!" he said at last. "Listen! There must be some peak, at the Cold Water end of this range, from which you can see Fairlands as well as the Galena Valley."

"Yes," the other answered eagerly.

"And," continued Rutlidge, "there is a good 'auto' road up the Galena Valley. One could get, I should think, to a point within—say nine hours of your camp. Do you know anything about the heliograph?"

"Yes," said the man, his face brightening. "That is, I understand the general principle—that it's a method of signaling by mirror flashes."

"Good! This is my plan. I will meet you to-morrow on the Laurel Creek trail, where it turns off from the creek toward San Gorgonio. You know the spot?"

"Yes."

"We will go around the head of Clear Creek, on the divide between this canyon and the Cold Water, to some peak in the Galenas from which we can see Fairlands; and where, with the field-glass, we can pick out some point at the upper end of Galena Valley, that we can both find later."

"I understand."

"When I get back to Fairlands, I will make a night trip in the 'auto' to that point, with supplies. You will meet me there. The day before I make the trip, I'll signal you by mirror flashes that I am coming; and you will answer from the peak. We'll agree on the time of day and the signals to-morrow. When you have kept close, long enough for your beard and hair to grow out well, everybody will have given you up for dead or gone. Then I will take you down and give you a job in an orange grove. There's a little house there where you can live. You won't need to show yourself down-town and, in time, you will be forgotten. I'll bring you enough food to-morrow to last you until I can return to town and can get back on the first night trip."

The man who left James Rutlidge a few minutes later, after trying brokenly to express his gratitude, was a creature very different from the poor, frightened hunted, starving, despairing, wretch that Rutlidge had halted an hour before. What that man was to become, would depend almost wholly upon his benefactor.

When the man was gone, James Rutlidge again took up his field-glass. The old home of Sibyl Andrés was deserted. While he had been talking with the convict, the girl and Myra Willard had started on their way back to Fairlands.

With a peculiar smile upon his heavy features, the man slipped the glass into its case, and, with a long, slow look over the scene, set out on his way to rejoin his friends.

Chapter XXVI
I Want You Just as You Are

The evening of that day after their return from the mountains, when Conrad Lagrange had found Aaron King so absorbed in his mother's letters, the artist continued in his silent, preoccupied, mood. The next morning, it was the same. Refusing every attempt of his friend to engage him in conversation, he answered only with absent-minded mono-syllables; until the novelist, declaring that the painter was fit company for neither beast nor man, left him alone; and went off somewhere with Czar.

The artist spent the greater part of the forenoon in his studio, doing nothing of importance. That is, to a casual observer he would have seemed to be doing nothing of importance. He did, however, place his picture of the spring glade beside the portrait of Mrs. Taine, and then, for an hour or more, sat considering the two paintings. Then he turned the "Quaker Maid" again to the wall and fixed a fresh canvas in place on the easel. That was all.

Immediately after their midday lunch, he returned to the studio—hurriedly, as if to work. He arranged his palette, paints, and brushes ready to his hand, indeed—but he, then, did nothing with them. Listlessly, without interest, he turned through his portfolios of sketches. Often, he looked away through the big, north window to the distant mountain tops. Often, he seemed to be listening. He was sitting before the easel, staring at the blank canvas, when, clear and sweet, from the depths of the orange grove, came the pure tones of Sibyl Andrés' violin.

So soft and low was the music, at first, that the artist almost doubted that it was real, thinking—as he had thought that day when Sibyl came singing to the glade—that it was his fancy tricking him. When he and Conrad Lagrange left the mountains three days before, the girl and her companion had not expected to return to Fairlands for at least two weeks. But there was no mistaking that music of the hills. As the tones grew louder and more insistent, with a ringing note of gladness, he knew that the mountain girl was announcing her arrival and, in the language she loved best, was greeting her friends.

But so strangely selfish is the heart of man, that Aaron King gave the novelist no share in their neighbor's musical greeting. He received the message as if it were to himself alone. As he listened, his eyes brightened; he stood erect, his face turned upward toward the mountain peaks in the distance; his lips curved in a slow smile. He fancied that he could see the girl's winsome face lighted with merriment as she played, knowing his surprise. Once, he started impulsively toward the door, but paused, hesitating, and turned back. When the music ceased, he went to the open window that looked out into the rose garden, and watched expectantly.

Presently, he heard her low-voiced song as she came through the orange grove beyond the Ragged Robin hedge. Then he glimpsed her white dress at the little gate in the corner. Then she stood in full view.

The artist had, so far, seen Sibyl only in her mountain costume of soft brown,—made for rough contact with rocks and underbrush,—with felt hat to match, and high, laced boots, fit for climbing. She was dressed, now, as Conrad Lagrange had seen her that first time in the garden, when he was hiding from Louise Taine. The man at the window drew a little back, with a low exclamation of pleased surprise and wonder. Was that lovely creature there among the roses his girl comrade of the hills? The Sibyl Andrés he had known—in the short skirt and high boots of her mountain garb—was a winsome, fanciful, sometimes serious, sometimes wayward, maiden. This Sibyl Andrés, gowned in clinging white, was a slender, gracefully tall, and beautifully developed woman.

Slowly, she came toward the studio end of the garden; pausing here and there to bend over the flowers as though in loving, tender greeting; singing, the while, her low-voiced melody; unafraid of the sunshine that enveloped her in a golden flood, undisturbed by the careless fingers of the wind that caressed her hair. A girl of the clean out-of-doors, she belonged among the roses, even as she had been at home among the pines and oaks of the mountains. The artist, fascinated by the lovely scene, stood as though fearing to move, lest the vision vanish.

Then, looking up, she saw him, and stretched out her hands in a gesture of greeting, with a laugh of pleasure.

"Don't move, don't move!" he called impulsively. "Hold the pose—please hold it! I want you just as you are!"

The girl, amused at his tragic earnestness, and at the manner of his welcome, understood that the zeal of the artist had brushed aside the polite formalities of the man; and, as unaffectedly natural as she did everything, gave herself to his mood.

Dragging his easel with the blank canvas upon it across the studio, he cried out, again, "Don't move, please don't move!" and

166

began working. He was as one beside himself, so wholly absorbed was he in translating into the terms of color and line, the loveliness purity and truth that was expressed by the personality of the girl as she stood among the flowers. "If I can get it! If I can only get it!" he exclaimed again and again, with a kind of savage earnestness, as he worked.

All his years of careful training, all his studiously acquired skill, all his mastery of the mechanics of his craft, came to him, now, without conscious effort—obedient to his purpose. Here was no thoughtful straining to remember the laws of composition, and perspective, and harmony. Here was no skillful evading of the truth he saw. So freely, so surely, he worked, he scarcely knew he painted. Forgetting self, as he was unconscious of his technic, he worked as the birds sing, as the bees toil, as the deer runs. Under his hand, his picture grew and blossomed as the roses, themselves, among which the beautiful girl stood.

Day after day, at that same hour, Sibyl Andrés came singing through the orange grove, to stand in the golden sunlight among the roses, with hands outstretched in greeting. Every day, Aaron King waited her coming—sitting before his easel, palette and brush in hand. Each day, he worked as he had worked that first day—with no thought for anything save for his picture.

In the mornings, he walked with Conrad Lagrange or, sometimes, worked with Sibyl in the garden. Often, in the evening, the two men would visit the little house next door. Occasionally, the girl and the woman with the disfigured face would come to sit for a while on the front porch with their friends. Thus the neighborly friendship that began in the hills was continued in the orange groves. The comradeship between the two young people grew stronger, hour by hour, as the painter worked at his easel to express with canvas and color and brush the spirit of the girl whose character and life was so unmarred by the world.

A11 through those days, when he was so absorbed in his work that he often failed to reply when she spoke to him, the girl manifested a helpful understanding of his mood that caused the painter to marvel. She seemed to know, instinctively, when he was baffled or perplexed by the annoying devils of "can't-get-at-it," that so delight to torment artist folk; just as she knew and rejoiced when the imps were routed and the soul of the man exulted with the sureness and freedom of his hand. He asked her, once, when they had finished for the day, how it was that she knew so well how the work was progressing, when she could not see the picture.

She laughed merrily. "But I can see you; and I"—she hesitated with that trick, that he was learning to know so well, of searching for a word—"I just feel what you are feeling. I suppose it's because my music is that way. Sometimes, it simply won't come right, at all, and I feel as though I never could do it. Then, again, it seems to do itself; and I listen and wonder—just as if I had nothing to do with it."

So that day came when the artist, drawing slowly back from his easel, stood so long gazing at his picture without touching it that the girl called to him, "What's the matter? Won't it come right?"

Slowly he laid aside his palette and brushes. Standing at the open window, he looked at her—smiling but silent—as she held the pose.

For an instant, she did not understand. "Am I not right?" she asked anxiously. Then, before he could answer—"Oh, have you finished? Is it all done?"

Still smiling, he answered almost sadly, "I have done all that I can do. Come."

A moment later, she stood in the studio door.

Seeing her hesitate, he said again, "Come."

"I—I am afraid to look," she faltered.

He laughed. "Really I don't think it's quite so bad as that."

"Oh, but I don't mean that I'm afraid it's bad—it isn't."

The painter watched her,—a queer expression on his face,—as he returned curiously, "And how, pray tell, do you know it isn't bad—when you have never seen it? It's quite the thing, I'll admit, for critics to praise or condemn without much knowledge of the work; but I didn't expect you to be so modern."

"You are making fun of me," she laughed. "But I don't care. I know your work is good, because I know how and why you did it. You painted it just as you painted the spring glade, didn't you?"

"Yes," he said soberly, "I did. But why are you afraid?"

"Why, that's the reason. I—I'm afraid to see myself as you see me."

The man's voice was gentle with feeling as he answered seriously, "Miss Andrés, you, of all the people I have ever known, have the least cause to fear to look at your portrait for that reason. Come."

Slowly, she went forward to stand by his side before the picture.

For some time, she looked at the beautiful work into which Aaron King had put the best of himself and of his genius. At last, turning full upon him, her eyes blue and shining, she said in a low tone, "O Mr. King, it is too—too—beautiful! It is so beautiful it—it—

hurts. She seems to, to"—she searched for the word—"to belong to the roses, doesn't she? It makes you feel just as the rose garden makes you feel."

He laughed with pleasure, "What a child of nature you are! You have forgotten that it is a portrait of yourself, haven't you?"

She laughed with him. "I had forgotten. It's so lovely!" Then she added wistfully, "Am I—am I really like that?—just a little?"

"No," he answered. "But that is just a little, a very little, like you."

She looked at him half doubtfully—sincerely unmindful of the compliment, in her consideration of its truth. Shaking her head, with a serious smile, she returned slowly, "I wish that I could be sure you are not mistaken."

"You will permit me to exhibit the picture, will you?" he asked.

"Why, yes! of course! You made it for people to see, didn't you? I don't believe any one could look at it seriously without having good thoughts, could they?"

"I'm sure they could not," he answered. "But, you see, it's a portrait of you; and I thought you might not care for the—ah—" he finished with a smile—"shall I say fame?"

"Oh! I did not think that you would tell any one that I had anything to do with it. Is it necessary that my name should be mentioned?"

"Not exactly necessary"—he admitted—"but few women, these days, would miss the opportunity."

She shook her head, with a positive air. "No, no; you must exhibit it as a picture; not as a portrait of me. The portrait part is of no importance. It is what you have made your picture say, that will do good."

"And what have I made it say?" he asked, curiously pleased.

"Why it says that—that a woman should be beautiful as the roses are beautiful—without thinking too much about it, you know— just as a man should be strong without thinking too much about his strength, I mean."

"Yes," he agreed, "it says that. But I want you to know that, whatever title it is exhibited under, it will always be, to me, a portrait—the truest I have ever painted."

She flushed with genuine pleasure as she said brightly, "I like you for that. And now let's try it on Conrad Lagrange and Myra Willard. You get him, and I'll run and bring her. Mind you don't let Mr. Lagrange in until I get back! I want to watch him when he first sees it."

When the artist found Conrad Lagrange and told him that the

169

picture was finished, the novelist, without comment, turned his attention to Czar.

The painter, with an amused smile, asked, "Won't you come for a look at it, old man?"

The other returned gruffly, "Thanks; but I don't think I care to risk it."

The artist laughed. "But Miss Andrés wants you to come. She sent me to fetch you."

Conrad Lagrange turned his peculiar, baffling eyes upon the young man. "Does she like it?"

"She seems to."

"If she seems to, she does," retorted the other, rising. "And that's different."

When the novelist, with his three friends, stood before the easel, he was silent for so long that the girl said anxiously, "I—I thought you would like it, Mr. Lagrange."

They saw the strange man's eyes fill with tears as he answered, in the gentle tones that always marked his words to her, "Like it? My dear child, how could I help liking it? It is you—you!" To the artist, he added, "It is great work, my boy, great! I—I wish your mother could have seen it. It is like her—as I knew her. You have done well." He turned, with gentle courtesy, to Myra Willard; "And you? What is your verdict, Miss Willard?"

With her arm around the beautiful original of the portrait, the woman with the disfigured face answered, "I think, sir, that I, better than any one in all the world, know how good, how true, it is."

Conrad Lagrange spoke again to the artist, inquiringly; "You will exhibit it?"

"Miss Andrés says that I may—but not as a portrait."

The novelist could not conceal his pleasure at the answer. Presently, he said, "If it is not to be shown as a portrait, may I suggest a title?"

"I was hoping you would!" exclaimed the painter.

"And so was I," cried Sibyl, with delight. "What is it, Mr. Lagrange?"

"Let it be exhibited as 'The Spirit of Nature—A Portrait'," answered Conrad Lagrange.

As the novelist finished speaking, Yee Kee appeared in the doorway. "They come—big automobile. Whole lot people. Misse Taine, Miste' Lutlidge, sick man, whole lot—I come tell you."

The artist spoke quickly,—"Stop them in the house, Kee; I'll be right in,"—and the Chinaman vanished.

170

At Yee Kee's announcement, Myra Willard's face went white, and she gave a low cry.

"Never mind, dear," said the girl, soothingly. "We can slip away through the garden—come."

When Sibyl and the woman with the disfigured face were gone, Conrad Lagrange and Aaron King looked at each other, questioningly.

Then the novelist said harshly,—pointing to the picture on the easel,—"You're not going to let that flock of buzzards feed on this, are you? I'll murder some one, sure as hell, if you do."

"I don't think I could stand it, myself," said the artist, laughing grimly, as he drew the velvet curtain to hide the portrait.

Chapter XXVII
The Answer

When Aaron King and Conrad Lagrange entered the house to meet their callers from Fairlands Heights, the artist felt, oddly, that he was meeting a company of strangers.

The carefully hidden, yet—to him—subtly revealed, warmth of Mrs. Taine's greeting embarrassed him with a momentary sense of shame. The frothing gush of Louise's inane ejaculations, and the coughing, choking, cursing of Mr. Taine,—whose feeble grip upon the flesh that had so betrayed him was, by now, so far loosed that he could scarcely walk alone,—set the painter struggling for words that would mean nothing—the only words that, under the circumstances, could serve. Aaron King was somewhat out of practise in the use of meaningless words, and the art of talking without saying anything is an art that requires constant exercise if one would not commit serious technical blunders. James Rutlidge's greeting was insolently familiar; as a man of certain mind greets—in public—a boon companion of his private and unmentionable adventures. Toward the great critic, the painter exercised a cool self-restraint that was at least commendable.

While Aaron King, with James Rutlidge and Mr. Taine, with carefully assumed interest, was listening to Louise's effort to make a jumble of "ohs" and "ahs" and artistic sighs sound like a description of a sunset in the mountains, Mrs. Taine said quietly to Conrad Lagrange, "You certainly have taken excellent care of your protege, this summer. He looks splendidly fit."

The novelist, watching the woman whose eyes, as she spoke, were upon the artist, answered, "You are pleased to flatter me, Mrs. Taine."

She turned to him, with a knowing smile. "Perhaps I am giving you more credit than is due. I understand Mr. King has not been in your care altogether. Shame on you, Mr. Lagrange! for a man of your age and experience to permit your charge to roam all over the country, alone and unprotected, with a picturesque mountain girl!—and that, after your warning to poor me!"

Conrad Lagrange smiled grimly. "I confess I thought of you in that connection several times."

She eyed him doubtfully. "Oh, well," she said easily, "I

suppose artists must amuse themselves, occasionally—the same as the rest of us."

"I don't think that, 'amuse' is exactly the word, Mrs. Taine," the other returned coldly.

"No? Surely you don't meant to tell me that it is anything serious?"

"I don't mean to tell you anything about it," he retorted rather sharply.

She laughed. "You don't need to. Jim has already told me quite enough. Mr. King, himself, will tell me more."

"Not unless he's a bigger fool than I think," growled the novelist.

Again, she laughed into his face, mockingly. "You men are all more or less foolish when there's a woman in the case, aren't you?"

To which, the other answered tartly, "If we were not, there would be no woman in the case."

As Conrad Lagrange spoke, Louise, exhausted by her efforts to achieve that sunset in the mountains with her limited supply of adjectives, floundered hopelessly into the expressive silence of clasped hands and heaving breast and ecstatically upturned eyes. The artist, seizing the opportunity with the cunning of desperation, turned to Mrs. Taine, with some inane remark about the summers in California.

Whatever it was that he said, Mrs. Taine agreed with him, heartily, adding, "And you, I suppose, have been making good use of your time? Or have you been simply storing up material and energy for this winter?"

This brought Louise out of the depths of that sunset, with a flop. She was so sure that Mr. King had some inexpressibly wonderful work to show them. Couldn't they go at once to the equally inexpressibly beautiful studio, to see the inexpressibly lovely pictures that she was so inexpressibly sure he had been painting in the inexpressibly grand and beautiful and wonderfully lovely mountains?

The painter assured them that he had no work for them to see; and Louise floundered again into the depths of inexpressible disappointment and despair.

Nevertheless, a few minutes later, Aaron King found himself in his studio, alone with Mrs. Taine. He could not have told exactly how she managed it, or why. Perhaps, in sheer pity, she had rescued him from the floods of Louise's appreciation. Perhaps—she had some other reasons. There had been something said about her right

173

to see her own picture, and then—there they were—with the others safely barred from intruding upon the premises sacred to art.

When there was no longer need to fear the eyes of the world, Mrs. Taine was at no pains to hide the warmth of her feeling. With little reserve, she confessed herself in every look and tone and movement.

"Are you really glad to see me, I wonder," she said invitingly. "All this summer, while I have been forced to endure the company of all sorts of stupid people, I have been thinking of you and your work. And, you see, I have come to you, the first possible moment after my return home."

The man—being a man—could not remain wholly insensible to the alluring physical beauty of the splendid creature who stood so temptingly before him; but, to the honor of his kind, he could and did remain master of himself.

The woman, true to her life training,—as James Rutlidge had been true to his schooling when he approached Sibyl Andrés in the mountains,—construed the artist's manner, not as a splendid self-control but as a careful policy. To her, and to her kind, the great issues of life are governed, not at all by principle, but by policy. It is not at all what one is, or what one may accomplish that matters; it is wholly what one may skillfully appear to be, and what one may skillfully provoke the world to say, that is of vital importance. Turning from the painter to the easel, as if to find in his portrait of her the fuller expression of that which she believed he dared not yet put into words, she was about to draw aside the curtain; when Aaron King checked her quickly, with a smile that robbed his words of any rudeness.

"Please don't touch that, Mrs. Taine. I am not yet ready to show it."

As she turned from the easel to face him, he took her portrait from where it rested, face to the wall; and placed it upon another easel, saying, "Here is your picture."

With the painting before her, she talked eagerly of her plans for the artist's future; how the picture was to be exhibited, and how, because it was her portrait, it would be praised and talked about by her friends who were leaders in the art circles. Frankly, she spoke of "pull" and "influence" and "scheme"; of "working" this and that "paper" for "write-ups"; of "handling" this or that "critic" and "writer"; of "reaching the committees"; of introducing the painter into the proper inside cliques, and clans; and of clever "advertising stunts" that would make him the most popular portrait painter of his day; insuring thus his—as she called it—fame.

174

The man who had painted the picture of the spring glade, and who had so faithfully portrayed the truth and beauty of Sibyl Andrés as she stood among the roses, listened to this woman's plans for making his portrait of herself famous, with a feeling of embarrassment and shame.

"Do you really think that the work merits such prominence as you say will be given it?" he asked doubtfully.

She laughed knowingly, "Just wait until Jim Rutlidge's 'write-up' appears, and all the others follow his lead, and you'll see! The picture is clever enough—you know it as well as I. It is beautiful. It has everything that we women want in a portrait. I really don't know much about what you painters call art; but I know that when Jim and our friends get through with it, your picture will have every mark of a great masterpiece, and that you will be on the topmost wave of success."

"And then what?" he asked.

Again, she interpreted his words in the light of her own thoughts, and with little attempt to veil the fire that burned in her eyes, answered, "And then—I hope that you will not forget me."

For a moment he returned her look; then a feeling of disgust and shame for her swept over him, and he again turned away, to stand gazing moodily out of the window that looked into the rose garden.

"You seem to be disturbed and worried," she said, in a tone that implied a complete understanding of his mood, and a tacit acceptance of the things that he would say if it were not for the world.

He laughed shortly—"I fear you will think me ungrateful for your kindness. Believe me, I am not."

"I know you are not," she returned. "But don't think that you had better confess, just the same?"

He answered wonderingly, "Confess?"

"Yes." She shook her finger at him, in playful severity. "Oh, I know what you have been up to all summer—running wild with your mountain girl! Really, you ought to be more discreet."

Aaron King's face burned as he stammered something about not knowing what she meant.

She laughed gaily. "There, there, never mind—I forgive you— now that you are safely back in civilization again. I know you artists, and how you must have your periods of ah—relaxation—with rather more liberties than the common herd. Just so you are careful that the world doesn't know too much."

At this frank revelation of her mind, the man stood amazed. For the construction she put upon his relation with the girl whose pure and gentle comradeship had led him to greater heights in his art than he had ever before attained, he could have driven this woman from the studio he felt that she profaned. But what could he say? He remembered Conrad Lagrange's counsel when James Rutlidge had seen the girl at their camp. What could he say that would not injure Sibyl Andrés? To cover his embarrassment, he forced a laugh and answered lightly, "Really, I am not good at confessions."

"Nor I at playing the part of confessor," she laughed with him. "But, just the same, you might tell me what you think of yourself. Aren't you just a little ashamed?"

The artist had moved to a position in front of her portrait; and, as he looked upon the painted lie, his answer came. "Rather let me tell you what I think of you, Mrs. Taine. And let me tell you in the language I know best. Let me put my answer to your charges here," he touched her portrait.

Almost, his reply was worthy of Conrad Lagrange, himself.

"I don't quite understand," she said, a trifle put out by the turn his answer had taken.

"I mean," he explained eagerly, "that I want to repaint your portrait. You remember, I wrote, when I returned Mr. Taine's generous check, that I was not altogether satisfied with it. Give me another chance."

"You mean for me to come here again, to pose for you?—as I did before?"

"Yes," he answered, "just as you did before. I want to make a portrait worthy of you, as this is not. Let me tell you, on the canvas, what I cannot—" he hesitated then said deliberately—"what I dare not put into words."

The woman received his words as a veiled declaration of a passion he dared not, yet, openly express. She thought his request a clever ruse to renew their meetings in the privacy of his studio, and was, accordingly delighted.

"Oh, that will be wonderful!—heavenly!" she cried, springing to her feet. "Can we begin at once? May I come to-morrow?"

"Yes," he answered, "come to-morrow."

"And may I wear the Quaker gown?"

"Yes, indeed! I want you just as you were before—the same dress, the same pose. It is to be the same picture, you understand, only a better one—one more worthy of us, both. And now," he continued hurriedly "don't you think that we should return to the house?"

"I suppose so," she answered regretfully—lingering.

The artist was already opening the door.

As they passed out, she placed her hand on his arm, and looked up into his face admiringly. "What a clever, clever man you are, to think of it! And what a story it will make for the papers— when my picture is shown—how you were not satisfied with the portrait and refused to let it go—and how, after keeping it in your studio for months, you repainted it, to satisfy your artistic conscience!"

Aaron King smiled.

The announcement in the house that the artist was to repaint Mrs. Taine's picture, provoked characteristic comment. Louise effervesced a frothy stream of bubbling exclamations. James Rutlidge gave a hearty, "By Jove, old man, you have nerve! If you can really improve on that canvas, you are a wonder." And Mr. Taine, under the watchful eye of his beautiful wife, responded with a husky whisper, "Quite right—my boy—quite right! Certainly—by all means—if you feel that way about it—" his consent and approval ending in a paroxysm of coughing that left him weak and breathless, and nearly eliminated him from the question, altogether.

When the Fairlands Heights party had departed, Conrad Lagrange looked the artist up and down.

"Well,"—he growled harshly, in his most brutal tones,—"what is it? Is the dog returning to his vomit?—or is the prodigal turning his back on his hogs and his husks?"

Aaron King smiled as he answered, "I think, rather, it's the case of the blind beggar who sat by the roadside, helpless, until a certain Great Physician passed that way."

And Conrad Lagrange understood.

Chapter XXVIII
You're Ruined, My Boy

It was no light task to which Aaron King had set his hand. He did not doubt what it would cost him. Nor did Conrad Lagrange, as they talked together that evening, fail to point out clearly what it would mean to the artist, at the very beginning of his career, to fly thus rudely in the face of the providence that had chosen to serve him. The world's history of art and letters affords too many examples of men who, because they refused to pay court to the ruling cliques and circles of their little day, had seen the doors of recognition slammed in their faces; and who, even as they wrought their great works, had been forced to hear, as they toiled, the discordant yelpings of the self-appointed watchdogs of the halls of fame. Nor did the artist question the final outcome,—if only his work should be found worthy to endure,—for the world's history establishes, also, the truth—that he who labors for a higher wage than an approving paragraph in the daily paper, may, in spite of the condemnation of the pretending rulers, live in the life of his race, long after the names to which he refused to bow are lost in the dust of their self-raised thrones.

The painter was driven to his course by that self-respect, without which, no man can sanely endure his own company; together with that reverence—I say it deliberately—that reverence for his art, without which, no worthy work is possible. He had come to understand that one may not prostitute his genius to the immoral purposes of a diseased age, without reaping a prostitute's reward. The hideous ruin that Mr. Taine had, in himself, wrought by the criminal dissipation of his manhood's strength, and by the debasing of his physical appetites and passions, was to Aaron King, now, a token of the intellectual, spiritual, and moral ruin that alone can result from a debased and depraved dissipation of an artist's creative power. He saw clearly, now, that the influence his work must wield upon the lives of those who came within its reach, must be identical with the influence of Sibyl Andrés, who had so unconsciously opened his eyes to the true mission and glory of the arts, and thus had made his decision possible. In that hour when Mrs. Taine had revealed herself to him so clearly, following as it did so closely his days of work and the final completion of his portrait of the girl among the roses, he saw and felt the woman, not as one who could help him to the poor rewards of a temporary popularity, but as the spirit of an age that threatens the very life of art by seeking to destroy the vital truth and purpose of its existence. He felt that in painting the portrait of Mrs. Taine—as he had painted it—he had betrayed a trust; as truly as had his father who, for purely personal aggrandizement, had stolen the material wealth intrusted to him by his fellows. The young man understood, now, that, instead of fulfilling the purpose of his mother's sacrifice, and realizing for her her dying wish, as he had promised; the course he had entered upon would have thwarted the one and denied the other.

The young man had answered the novelist truly, that it was a case of the blind beggar by the wayside. He might have carried the figure farther; for that same blind beggar, when his eyes had been opened, was persecuted by the very ones who had fed him in his infirmity. It is easier, sometimes, to receive blindly, than to give with eyes that see too clearly.

When Mrs. Taine went to the artist, in the studio, the next day, she found him in the act of re-tying the package of his mother's letters. For nearly an hour, he had been reading them. For nearly an hour before that, he had been seated, motionless, before the picture that Conrad Lagrange had said was a portrait of the Spirit of Nature.

When Mrs. Taine had slipped off her wrap, and stood before him gowned in the dress that so revealed the fleshly charms it pretended to hide, she indicated the letters in the artist's hands, with an insinuating laugh; while there was a glint of more than passing curiosity in her eyes. "Dear me," she said, "I hope I am not intruding upon the claims of some absent affinity."

Aaron King gravely held out his hand with the package of letters, saying quietly, "They are from my mother."

And the woman had sufficient grace to blush, for once, with unfeigned shame.

When he had received her apologies, and, putting aside the letters, had succeeded in making her forget the incident, he said, "And now, if you are ready, shall we begin?"

For some time the painter stood before the picture on his easel, without touching palette or brush, studying the face of the woman who posed for him. By a slight movement of her eyes, without turning her head, she could look him fairly in the face. Presently as he continued to gaze at her so intently, she laughed; and, with a little shrug of her shoulders and a pretense as of being cold, said, "When you look at me that way, I feel as though you had surprised me at my bath."

The artist turned his attention instantly to his color-box. While setting his palette, with his eyes upon his task, he said deliberately, "'Venus Surprised at the Bath.' Do you know that you would make a lovely Venus?"

With a low laugh, she returned, daringly. "Would you care to paint me as the Goddess of Love?"

He, still, did not look at her; but answered, while, with deliberate care, he selected a few brushes from the Chinese jar near the easel, "Venus is always a very popular subject, you know."

She did not speak for a moment or two; and the painter felt her watching him. As he turned to his canvas—still careful not to look in her direction—she said, suggestively, "I suppose you could change the face so that no one would know it was I who posed."

The man remembered her carefully acquired reputation for modesty, but held to his purpose, saying, as if considering the question seriously, "Oh, as for that part; it could be managed with perfect safety." Then, suddenly, he turned his eyes upon her face, with a gaze so sharp and piercing that the blood slowly colored neck and cheek.

But the painter did not wait for the blush. He had seen what he wanted and was at work—with the almost savage intensity that had marked his manner while he had worked upon the portrait of Sibyl Andrés.

And so, day after day, as he painted, again, the portrait of the woman who Conrad Lagrange fancifully called "The Age," the artist permitted her to betray her real self—the self that was so commonly hidden from the world, under the mask of a pretended culture, and the cloak of a fraudulent refinement. He led her to talk of the world in which she lived—of the scandals and intrigues among those of her class who hold such enviable positions in life. He drew from her the philosophies and beliefs and religions of her kind. He encouraged her to talk of art—to give her understanding of the world of artists as she knew it, and to express her real opinions and tastes in pictures and books. He persuaded her to throw boldly aside the glittering, tinsel garb in which she walked before the world, and so to stand before him in all the hideous vulgarity, the intellectual poverty and the moral depravity of her naked self.

At times, when, under his intense gaze, she drew the cloak of her pretenses hurriedly about her, he sat before his picture without touching the canvas, waiting; or, perhaps, he paced the floor; until, with skillful words, her fears were banished and she was again herself. Then, with quick eye and sure, ready hand, he wrought into

180

the portrait upon the easel—so far as the power was given him—all that he saw in the face of the woman who—posing for him, secure in the belief that he was painting a lie—revealed her true nature, warped and distorted as it was by an age that, demanding realism in art, knows not what it demands. Always, when the sitting was finished, he drew the curtain to hide the picture; forbidding her to look at it until he said that it was finished.

Much of the time, when he was not in the studio at work, the painter spent with Mrs. Taine and her friends, in the big touring car, and at the house on Fairlands Heights. But the artist did not, now, enter into the life of Fairlands' Pride for gain or for pleasure—he went for study—as a physician goes into the dissecting room. He justified himself by the old and familiar argument that it was for his art's sake.

Sibyl Andrés, he seldom saw, except occasionally, in the early morning, in the rose garden. The girl knew what he was doing—that is, she knew that he was painting a portrait of Mrs. Taine—and so, with Myra Willard, avoided the place. But Conrad Lagrange now, made the neighboring house in the orange grove his place of refuge from Louise Taine, who always accompanied Mrs. Taine,—lest the world should talk,—but who never went as far as the studio.

But often, as he worked, the artist heard the music of the mountain girl's violin; and he knew that she, in her own beautiful way, was trying to help him—as she would have said—to put the mountains into his work. Many times, he was conscious of the feeling that some one was watching him. Once, pausing at the garden end of the studio as he paced to and fro, he caught a glimpse of her as she slipped through the gate in the Ragged Robin hedge. And once, in the morning, after one of those afternoons when he had gone away with Mrs. Taine at the conclusion of the sitting, he found a note pinned to the velvet curtain that hid the canvas on his working easel. It was a quaint little missive; written in one of the girl's fanciful moods, with a reference to "Blue Beard," and the assurance that she had been strong and had not looked at the forbidden picture.

As the work progressed, Mrs. Taine remarked, often, how the artist was changed. When painting that first picture, he had been so sure of himself. Working with careless ease, he had been suave and pleasant in his manner, with ready smile or laugh. Why, she questioned, was he, now, so grave and serious? Why did he pause so often, to sit staring at his canvas, or to pace the floor? Why did he seem to be so uncertain—to be questioning, searching, hesitating?

The woman thought that she knew. Rejoicing in her fancied victory—all but won—she looked forward to the triumphant moment when this splendid man should be swept from his feet by the force of the passion she thought she saw him struggling to conceal. Meanwhile she tempted him by all the wiles she knew—inviting him with eyes and lips and graceful pose and meaning gesture.

And Aaron King, with clear, untroubled eye seeing all; with cool brain understanding all; with steady, skillful hand, ruled supremely by his purpose, painted that which he saw and understood into his portrait of her.

So they came to the last sitting. On the following evening, Mrs. Taine was giving a dinner at the house on Fairlands Heights, at which the artist was to meet some people who would be—as she said—useful to him. Eastern people they were; from the accredited center of art and literature; members of the inner circle of the elect. They happened to be spending the season on the Coast, and she had taken advantage of the opportunity to advance the painter's interests. It was very fortunate that her portrait was to be finished in time for them to see it.

The artist was sorry, he said, but, while it would not be necessary for her to come to the studio again, the picture was not yet finished, and he could not permit its being exhibited until he was ready to sign the canvas.

"But I may see it?" she asked, as he laid aside his palette and brushes, and announced that he was through.

With a quick hand, he drew the curtain. "Not yet; please—not until I am ready."

"Oh!" she cried with a charming air of submitting to one whose wish is law, "How mean of you! I know it is splendid! Are you satisfied? Is it better than the other? Is it like me?"

"I am sure that it is much better than the other," he replied. "It is as like you as I can make it."

"And is it as beautiful as the other?"

"It is beautiful—as you are beautiful," he answered.

"I shall tell them all about it, to-morrow night—even if I haven't seen it. And so will Jim Rutlidge."

Aaron King and Conrad Lagrange spent that evening at the little house next door. The next morning, the artist shut himself up in his studio. At lunch time, he would not come out. Late in the afternoon, the novelist went, again, to knock at the door.

The artist called in a voice that rang with triumph, "Come in, old man, come in and help me celebrate."

Entering, Conrad Lagrange found him; sitting, pale and worn, before his picture—his palette and brushes still in his hand.

And such a picture!

A moment, the novelist who knew—as few men know—the world that was revealed with such fidelity in that face upon the canvas, looked; then, with weird and wonderful oaths of delight, he caught the tired artist and whirled him around the studio, in a triumphant dance.

"You've done it! man—you've done it! It's all there; every rotten, stinking shred of it! Wow! but it's good—so damned good that it's almost inhuman. I knew you had it in you. I knew it was in you, all the time—if only you could come alive. God, man! if that could only be exhibited alongside the other! Look here!"

He dragged the easel that held Sibyl Andrés' portrait to a place beside the one upon which the canvas just finished rested, and drew back the curtain. The effect was startling.

"'The Spirit of Nature' and 'The Spirit of the Age'," said Conrad Lagrange, in a low tone.

"But you're ruined, my boy," he added gleefully. "You're ruined. These canvases will never be exhibited Her own, she'll smash when she sees it; and you'll be artistically damned by the very gods she has invoked to bless you with fame and wealth. Lord, but I envy you! You have your chance now—a real chance to be worthy your mother's sacrifice.

"Come on, let's get ready for the feast."

Chapter XXIX
The Hand Writing on the Wall

It was November. Nearly a year had passed since that day when the young man on the Golden State Limited—with the inheritance he had received from his mother's dying lips, and with his solemn promise to her still fresh in his mind—looked into the eyes of the woman on the platform of the observation car. That same day, too, he first saw the woman with the disfigured face, and, for the first time, met the famous Conrad Lagrange.

Aaron King was thinking of these things as he set out, that evening, with his friend, for the home of Mrs. Taine. He remarked to the novelist that the time seemed, to him, many years.

"To me, Aaron," answered the strange man, "it has been the happiest and—if you would not misunderstand me—the most satisfying year of my life. And this"—he added, his deep voice betraying his emotion—"this has been the happiest day of the year. It is your independence day. I shall always celebrate it as such—I—I have no independence day of my own to celebrate, you know."

Aaron King did not misunderstand.

As the two men approached the big house on Fairlands Heights, they saw that modern palace, from concrete foundation to red-tiled roof, ablaze with many lights. Situated upon the very topmost of the socially graded levels of Fairlands, it outshone them all; and, quite likely, the glittering display was mistaken by many dwellers in the valley below for a new constellation of the heavenly bodies. Quite likely, too, some lonely dweller, high up among the distant mountain peaks, looked down upon the sparkling bauble that lay for the moment, as it were, on the wide lap of the night, and smiled in quiet amusement that the earth children should attach such value to so fragile a toy.

As they passed the massive, stone pillars of the entrance to the grounds, Conrad Lagrange said, "Really, Aaron, don't you feel a little ashamed of yourself?—coming here to-night, after the outrageous return you have made for the generous hospitality of these people? You know that if Mrs. Taine had seen what you have done to her portrait, you could force the pearly gates easier than you could break in here."

The artist laughed. "To tell the truth, I don't feel exactly at home. But what the deuce can I do? After my intimacy with them, all these months, I can't assume that they are going to make my picture a reason for refusing to recognize me, can I? As I see it, they, not I, must take the initiative. I can't say: 'Well, I've told the truth about you, so throw me out'."

The novelist grinned. "Thus it is when 'Art' becomes entangled with the family of 'Materialism.' It's hard to break away from the flesh-pots—even when you know you are on the road to the Promised Land. But don't worry—'The Age' will take the initiative fast enough when she sees your portrait of her. Wow! In the meantime, let's play their game to-night, and take what spoils the gods may send. There will be material here for pictures and stories a plenty." As they went up the wide steps and under the portal into the glare of the lights, and caught the sound of the voices within, he added under his breath, "Lord, man, but 'tis a pretty show!—if only things were called by their right names. That old Babylonian, Belshazzar, had nothing on us moderns after all, did he? Watch out for the writing upon the wall."

When Aaron King and his companion entered the spacious rooms where the pride of Fairlands Heights and the eastern lions were assembled, a buzz of comment went round the glittering company. Aside from the fact that Mrs. Taine, with practised skill, had prepared the way for her protege, by subtly stimulating the curiosity of her guests—the appearance of the two men, alone, would have attracted their attention The artist, with his strong, splendidly proportioned, athletic body, and his handsome, clean-cut intellectual face—calmly sure of himself—with the air of one who knows that his veins are rich with the wealth of many generations of true culture and refinement; and the novelist—easily the most famous of his day—tall, emaciated, grotesquely stooped—with his homely face seamed and lined, world-worn and old, and his sharp eyes peering from under his craggy brows with that analyzing, cynical, half-pathetic half-humorous expression—certainly presented a contrast too striking to escape notice.

For an instant, as comrades side by side upon a battle-field might do, they glanced over the scene. To the painter's eye, the assembled guests appeared as a glittering, shimmering, scintillating, cloud-like mass that, never still, stirred within itself, in slow, graceful restless motions—forming always, without purpose new combinations and groupings that were broken up, even as they were shaped, to be reformed; with the black spots and splashes of the men's conventional dress ever changing amid the brighter colors and textures of the women's gowns; the warm flesh tints of bare white arms and shoulders, gleaming here and there; and the flash and sparkle of jewels, threading the sheen of silks and the filmy softness of laces. Into the artist's mind—fresh from the tragic earnestness of his day's work, and still under the enduring spell of his weeks in the mountains—flashed a sentence from a good old book; "For what is your life? It is even a vapor, that appeareth for a little time, and then vanisheth away."

Then they were greeting, with conventional nothings their beautiful hostess; who, with a charming air of triumphant—but not too triumphant—proprietorship received them and passed them on, with a low spoken word to Aaron King; "I will take charge of you later."

Conrad Lagrange, before they drifted apart, found opportunity to growl in his companion's ear; "A near-great musician—an actress of divorce court fame—an art critic, boon companion of our friend Rutlidge—two free-lance yellow journalists—a poet—with leading culture-club women of various brands, and a mob of mere fashion and wealth. The pickings should be good. Look at 'Materialism', over there."

In a wheeled chair, attended by a servant in livery, a little apart from the center of the scene,—as though the pageant of life was about to move on without him,—but still, with desperate grip, holding his place in the picture, sat the genius of it all—the millionaire. The creature's wasted, skeleton-like limbs, were clothed grotesquely in conventional evening dress. His haggard, bestial face—repulsive with every mark of his wicked, licentious years— grinned with an insane determination to take the place that was his by right of his money bags; while his glazed and sunken eyes shone with fitful gleams, as he rallied the last of his vital forces, with a devilish defiance of the end that was so inevitably near.

As Aaron King, in the splendid strength of his inheritance, went to pay his respects to the master of the house, that poor product of our age was seized by a paroxysm of coughing, that shook him—gasping and choking—almost into unconsciousness. The ready attendant held out a glass of whisky, and he clutched the goblet with skinny hands that, in their trembling eagerness, rattled the crystal against his teeth. In the momentary respite afforded by the powerful stimulant, he lifted his yellow, claw-like hand to wipe the clammy beads of sweat that gathered upon his wrinkled, ape- like brow; and the painter saw, on one bony, talon-like finger, the gleaming flash of a magnificent diamond.

Mr. Taine greeted the artist with his husky whisper "Hello, old chap—glad to see you!" Peering into the laughing, chattering, glittering, throng he added, "Some beauties here to-night, heh? Gad! my boy, but I've seen the day I'd be out there among them! Ha, ha! Mrs. Taine, Louise, and Jim tried to shelve me—but I fooled 'em. Damn me, but I'm game for a good time yet! A little off my feed, and under the weather; but game, you understand, game as hell!" Then to the attendant—"Where's that whisky?" And, again, his yellow, claw-like hand—with that beautiful diamond, a gleaming point of pure, white light—lifted the glass to his grinning lips.

When Mrs. Taine appeared to claim the artist, her husband—huddled in his chair, an unclean heap of all but decaying flesh—watched them go, with hidden, impotent rage.

A few moments later, as Mrs. Taine and her charge were leaving one group of celebrities in search of another they encountered Conrad Lagrange. "What's this I see?" gibed the novelist, mockingly. "Is it 'Art being led by Beauty to the Judges and Executioners'? or, is it 'Beauty presenting an Artist to the Gods of Modern Art'?"

"You had better be helping a good cause instead of making fun, Mr. Lagrange," the woman retorted. "You weren't always so famous yourself that you could afford to be indifferent, you know."

Aaron King laughed as his friend replied, "Never fear, madam, never fear—I shall be on hand to assist at the obsequies."

In the shifting of the groups and figures, when dinner was announced, the young man found himself, again, within reach of Conrad Lagrange; and the novelist whispered, with a grin, "Now for the flesh-pots in earnest. You will be really out of place in the next act, Aaron. Only we artists who have sold our souls have a right to the price of our shame. You should dine upon a crust, you know. A genius without his crust, huh! A devil without his tail, or an ass without his long ears!"

Most conspicuous in the brilliant throng assembled in that banquet hall, was the horrid figure of Mr. Taine who sat in his wheeled chair at the head of the table; his liveried attendant by his side. Frequently—as though compelled—eyes were turned toward that master of the feast, who was, himself, so far past feasting; and toward his beautiful young wife—the only woman in the room, whose shoulders and arms were not bare.

At first, the talk moved somewhat heavily. Neighbor chattered nothings to neighbor in low tones. It was as though the foreboding presence of some grim, unbidden guest overshadowed the spirits of the company But gradually the scene became more animated The glitter of silver and crystal on the board; the sparkle of jewels and the wealth of shimmering colors that costumed the diners; with the strains of music that came from somewhere behind a floral screen that filled the air with fragrance; concealed, as it were, the hideous image of immorality which was the presiding genius of the feast. As the glare of a too bright light blinds the eyes to the ditch across one's path, so the brilliancy of their surroundings blinded the eyes of his guests to the meaning of that horrid figure in the seat of highest honor. But rich foods and rare wines soon loose the tongues that chatter the thoughts of those who do not think. As the glasses were filled and refilled again, the scene took color from the sparkling goblets. Voices were raised to a higher pitch. Shrill or boisterous laughter rang out, as jest and story went the rounds. It was Mrs. Taine, now, rather than her husband, who dominated the scene. With cheeks flushed and eyes bright she set the pace, nor permitted any laggards.

Conrad Lagrange watched, cool and cynical—his worn face twisted into a mocking smile; his keen, baffling eyes, from under their scowling brows, seeing all, understanding all. Aaron King, weary with the work of the past days, endured—wishing it was over.

The evening was well under way when Mrs. Taine held up her hand. In the silence, she said, "Listen! I have a real treat for you, to-night, friends. Listen!" As she spoke the last word, her eyes met the eyes of the artist, in mocking, challenging humor. He was wondering what she meant, when,—from behind that screen of flowers,—soft and low, poignantly sweet and thrilling in its purity of tone, came the music of the violin that he had learned to know so well.

Instantly, the painter understood. Mrs. Taine had employed Sibyl Andrés to play for her guests that evening; thinking to tease the artist by presenting his mountain comrade in the guise of a hired servant. Why the girl had not told him, he did not know. Perhaps she had thought to enjoy his surprise. The effect of the girl's presence—or rather of her music, for she, herself, could not be seen—upon the artist was quite other than Mrs. Taine intended.

Under the spell of the spirit that spoke in the violin, Aaron King was carried far from his glittering surroundings. Again, he stood where the bright waters of Clear Creek tumbled among the granite boulders, and where he had first moved to answer the call of that music of the hills. Again, he followed the old wagon road to the cedar thicket; and, in the little, grassy opening with its wild roses, its encircling wilderness growth, and its old log house under the sheltering sycamores, saw a beautiful girl dancing with the unconscious grace of a woodland sprite, her arms upheld in greeting to the mountains. Once again, he was painting in the sacred quiet of the spring glade where she had come to him with her three gifts; where, in maidenly innocence, she had danced the dance of the butterflies; and, later, with her music, had lifted their friendship to heights of purity as far above the comprehension of the company that listened to her now, as the mountain peaks among the stars that night were high above the house on Fairlands Heights.

The music ceased. It was followed by the loud clapping of hands—with exclamations in high-pitched voices. "Who is it?" "Where did you find him?" "What's his name?"—for they judged, from Mrs. Taine's introductory words, that she expected them to show their appreciation.

Mrs. Taine laughed, and, with her eyes mockingly upon the artist's face answered lightly, "Oh, she is a discovery of mine. She teaches music, and plays in one of the Fairlands churches."

"You are a wonder," said one of the illustrious critics, admiringly. And lifting his glass, he cried, "Here's to our beautiful and talented hostess—the patron saint of all the arts—the friend of all true artists."

In the quiet that followed the enthusiastic endorsement of the distinguished gentleman's words, another voice said, "If it's a girl, can't we see her?" "Yes, yes," came from several. "Please, Mrs. Taine, bring her out." "Have her play again." "Will she?"

Mrs. Taine laughed. "Certainly, she will. That's what she's here for—to amuse you." And, again, as she spoke, her eyes met the eyes of Aaron King.

At her signal, a servant left the room. A moment later, the mountain girl, dressed in simple white, with no jewel or ornament other than a rose in her soft, brown hair, stood before that company. Unconscious of the eyes that fed upon her loveliness; there was the faintest shadow of a smile upon her face as she met, in one swift glance, the artist's look; then, raising her violin, she made music for the revelers, at the will of Mrs. Taine. As she stood there in the modest naturalness of her winsome beauty—innocent and pure as the flowers that formed the screen behind her; hired to amuse the worthy friends and guests of that hideously repulsive devotee of lust and licentiousness who, from his wheeled chair, was glaring at her with eyes that burned insanely—she seemed, as indeed she was, a spirit from another world.

James Rutlidge, his heavy features flushed with drink, was gazing at the girl with a look that betrayed his sensual passion. The face of Conrad Lagrange was dark and grim with scowling appreciation of the situation. Mrs. Taine was looking at the artist. And Aaron King, watching his girl comrade of the hills as she seemed to listen for the music which she in turn drew from the instrument, felt,—by the very force of the contrast between her and her surroundings he had never felt before, the power and charm of her personality—felt—and knew that Sibyl Andrés had come into his life to stay.

In the flood of emotions that swept over him, and in the mental and spiritual exultation caused by her music and by her presence amid such scenes; it was given the painter to understand that she had, in truth, brought to him the strength, the purity, and the beauty of the hills; that she had, in truth, shown him the paths that lead to the mountain heights; that it was her unconscious influence and teaching that had made it impossible for him to prostitute his genius to win favor in the eyes of the world. He knew, now, that in those days when he had painted her portrait, as she stood with outstretched hands in the golden light among the roses, he had mixed his colors with the best love that a man may offer a woman. And he knew that the repainting of that false portrait of Mrs. Taine, with all that it would cost him, was his first offering to that love.

The girl musician finished playing and slipped away. When they would have recalled her, Mrs. Taine—too well schooled to betray a hint of the emotions aroused by what she had just seen as she watched Aaron King—shook her head.

At that instant, Mr. Taine rose to his feet, supporting himself by holding with shaking hands to the table. A hush, sudden as the hush of death, fell upon the company. The millionaire's attendant put out his hand to steady his master, and another servant stepped quickly forward. But the man who clung so tenaciously to his last bit of life, with a drunken strength in his dying limbs, shook them off, saying in a hoarse whisper, "Never mind! Never mind—you fools—can't you see I'm game!"

In the quiet of the room, that a moment before rang with excited voices and shrill laughter, the man's husky, straining, whispered boast sounded like the mocking of some invisible, fiendish presence at the feast.

Lifting a glass of whisky with that yellow, claw-like hand upon which the great diamond gleamed—a spot of flawless purity; with

190

his repulsive features twisted into a grewsome ugliness by his straining effort to force his diseased vocal chords to make his words heard; the wretched creature said: "Here's to our girl musician. The prettiest—lassie that I—have seen for many a day—and I think I know a pretty girl—when I see one too. Who comes bright and fresh—from her mountains, to amuse us—and to add, to the beauty—and grace and wit and genius—that so distinguishes this company—the flavor and the freedom of her wild-wood home. Her music—is good, you'll all agree—" he paused to cough and to look inquiringly around, while every one nodded approval and smiled encouragingly. "Her music is good—but I—maintain that she, herself, is better. To me—her beauty is more pleasing to the eye—than—her fiddling can possibly—be to the ear!" Again he was forced to pause, while his guests, with hand and voice, applauded the clever words. Lifting the glass of whisky toward his lips that, by his effort to speak, were drawn back in a repulsive grin, he leered at the celebrities sitting nearest. "I suppose to-morrow—if we desire the company of these distinguished artists—we will have to follow—them to the mountains. I don't blame you, gentlemen—if I was not—ah—temporarily incapacitated—I would certainly—go for a little trip to the inspiring hills—myself. Even if I don't know—as much about music and art as some of you." Again his words were interrupted by that racking cough, the sound of which was lost in the applause that greeted his witticism. Lifting the glass once more, he continued, "So here's to our girl musician—who is her own—lovely self so much more attractive than any music—she can ever make." He drained the glass, and sank back into his chair, exhausted by his effort.

Aaron King was on the point of springing to his feet, when Conrad Lagrange caught his eye with a warning look. Instantly, he remembered what the result would be if he should yield to his impulse. Wild with indignation, rage, and burning shame, he knew that to betray himself would be to invite a thousand sneering questions and insinuations to besmirch the name of the girl he loved.

In the continued applause and laughter that followed the drinking of the millionaire's toast, the artist caught the admiring words, "Bully old sport." "Isn't he game?" "He has certainly traveled some pace in his day." "The girl is a beauty." "Let's have her in again." This last expression was so insistently echoed that Mrs. Taine—who, through it all, had been covertly watching Aaron King's face, and whose eyes were blazing now with something more than the effect of the wine she had been drinking—was forced to yield. A servant left the room, and, a moment later, reappeared, followed by Sibyl.

The girl was greeted, now, by hearty applause which she, accepting as an expression of the company's appreciation of her music, received with smiling pleasure. The artist, his heart and soul aflame with his awakening love, fought for self-control. Conrad Lagrange, catching his eye, again, silently bade him wait.

Sibyl lifted her violin and the noisy company was stilled. Slowly, under the spell of the music that, to him, was a message from the mountain heights, Aaron King grew calm. His tense muscles relaxed. His twitching nerves became steady. He felt himself as it were, lifted out of and above the scene that a moment before had so stirred him to indignant anger. His brain worked with that clearness and precision which he had known while repainting Mrs. Taine's portrait. Wrath gave way to pity; indignation to contempt. In confidence, he smiled to think how little the girl he loved needed his poor defense against the animalism that dominated the company she was hired to amuse. With every eye in the room fixed upon her as she played, she was as far removed from those who had applauded the suggestive words of the dying sensualist as her music was beyond their true comprehension.

Then it was that the genius of the artist awoke. As the flash of a search-light in the darkness of night brings out with startling clearness the details of the scene upon which it is turned, the painter saw before him his picture. With trained eye and carefully acquired skill, he studied the scene; impressing upon his memory every detail—the rich appointments of the room; the glittering lights; the gleaming silver and crystal; the sparkling jewels and shimmering laces; the bare shoulders; the wine-flushed faces and feverish eyes; and, in the seat of honor, the disease-wasted form and repulsive, sin-marked countenance of Mr. Taine who—almost unconscious with his exertion—was still feeding the last flickering flame of his lustful life with the vision of the girl whose beauty his toast had profaned: and in the midst of that company—expressing as it did the spirit of an age that is ruled by material wealth and dominated by the passions of the flesh—the center of every eye, yet, still, in her purity and innocence, removed and apart from them all; standing in her simple dress of white against the background of flowers—the mountain girl with her violin—offering to them the highest, holiest, gift of the gods—her music. Upon the girl's lovely, winsome face, was a look, now, of troubled doubt. Her wide, blue eyes, as she played, were pleading, questioning, half fearful—as though she sensed, instinctively the presence of the spirit she could not understand; and felt, in spite of the pretense of the applause that had greeted her, the rejection of her offering.

Not only did the artist, in that moment of conception see his picture and feel the forces that were expressed by every character in the composition, but the title, even, came to him as clearly as if Conrad Lagrange had uttered it aloud, "The Feast of Materialism."

Sibyl Andrés finished her music, and quickly withdrew as if to escape the noisy applause. Amid the sound of the clapping hands and boisterous voices, Mr. Taine, summoning the last of his wasted strength, again struggled to his feet. With those claw-like hands he held to the table for support; while—shaking in every limb, his features twisted into a horrid, leering grin—he looked from face to face of the hushed and silent company; with glazed eyes in which the light that flickered so feebly was still the light of an impotent lust.

Twice, the man essayed to speak, but could not. The room grew still as death. Then, suddenly—as they looked—he lifted that yellow, skinny hand, to his wrinkled, ape-like brow, and—partially loosing, thus, his supporting grip upon the table—fell back, in a ghastly heap of diseased flesh and fine raiment; in the midst of which blazed the great diamond—as though the cold, pure beauty of the inanimate stone triumphed in a life more vital than that of its wearer.

His servants carried the unconscious master of the house from the room. Mrs. Taine, excusing herself, followed.

In the confusion that ensued, the musicians, hidden behind the floral screen, struck up a lively air. Some of the guests made quiet preparations for leaving. A group of those men—famous in the world of art and letters—under the influence of the wine they had taken so freely, laughed loudly at some coarse jest. Others, thinking, perhaps,—if they could be said to think at all,—that their host's attack was not serious, renewed conversations and bravely attempted to restore a semblance of animation to the interrupted revelries.

Aaron King worked his way to the side of Conrad Lagrange, "For God's sake, old man, let's get out of here."

"I'll find Rutlidge or Louise or some one," returned the other, and disappeared.

As the artist waited, through the open door of an adjoining room, he caught sight of Sibyl Andrés; who, with her violin-case in her hand, was about to leave. Obeying his impulse, he went to her.

"What in the world are you doing here?" he said almost roughly—extending his hand to take the instrument she carried.

She seemed a little bewildered by his manner, but smiled as she retained her violin. "I am here to earn my bread and butter, sir. What are you doing here?"

"I beg your pardon," he said. "I did not mean to be rude."

She laughed, then, with a troubled air—"But is it not right for me to be here? It is all right for me to play for these people, isn't it? Myra didn't want me to come, but we needed the money, and Mrs. Taine was so generous. I didn't tell you and Mr. Lagrange because I wanted the fun of surprising you." As he stood looking at her so gravely, she put out her hand impulsively to his arm. "What is it, oh, what is it? How have I done wrong?"

"You have done no wrong, my dear girl," he answered "It is only that—"

He was interrupted by the cold, clear voice of Mrs. Taine, who had entered the room, unnoticed by them. "I see you are going, Miss Andrés. Good-night. I will mail you a check to-morrow. Your music was very satisfactory. An automobile is waiting to take you home. Good night."

Before Aaron King could speak, the girl was gone.

"Mr. Lagrange and I were just about to go," said the artist, as the woman faced him. "I hope Mr. Taine has not suffered severely from the excitement of the evening?"

The woman's cheeks were flushed, and her eyes were bright with feverish excitement. Going close to him, she said in a low, hurried tone, "No, no, you must not go. Mr. Taine is all right in his room. Every one else is having a good time. You must not go. Come, I have had no opportunity, at all, to have you to myself for a single moment. Come, I—"

As she had interrupted Aaron King's reply to Sibyl Andrés, the cool, sarcastic tones of Conrad Lagrange's deep voice interrupted her. "Mrs. Taine, they are hunting for you all over the house. Your husband is calling for you. I'm sure that Mr. King will excuse you, under the circumstances."

Chapter XXX
In the Same Hour

In a splendid chamber, surrounded by every comfort and luxury that dollars could buy, and attended by liveried servants, Mr. Taine was dying.

The physician who met Mrs. Taine at the door, answered her look of inquiry with; "Your husband is very near the end, madam." Beside the bed, sat Louise, wringing her hands and moaning. James Rutlidge stood near. Without speaking, Mrs. Taine went forward.

The doctor, bending over his patient, with his fingers upon the skeleton-like wrist, said, "Mr. Taine, Mr. Taine, your wife is here."

In response, the eyes, deep sunken under the wrinkled brow, opened; the loosely hanging, sensual lips quivered.

The physician spoke again; "Your wife is here, Mr. Taine."

A sudden gleam of light flared up in the glazed eyes. The doctor could have sworn that the lips were twisted into a shadow of a ghastly, mocking smile. As if summoning, by a supreme effort of his will, from some unguessed depths of his being, the last remnant of his remaining strength, the man looked about the room and, in a hoarse whisper, said, "Send the others away—everybody—but her."

"O papa, papa!" exclaimed poor Louise, protestingly.

"Never mind, daughter," came the whispered answer from the bed. "Try to be game, girl—game as your father. Take her away, Jim."

As the physician passed Mrs. Taine, who had thus far stood like a statue, seemingly incapable of thought or feeling or movement, he said in a low tone, "I will be just outside the door, madam; easily within call."

When only the woman was left in the room with her husband, the dying man spoke again; "Come here. Stand where I can see you."

Mechanically, she obeyed; moving to a position near the foot of the bed.

After a moment's silence, during which he seemed to be rallying the very last of his vital forces for the effort, he said, "Well—the game is played—out. You think—you're the winner. You're—wrong—damn you—you're wrong. I wasn't—so drunk to-night that—I couldn't see." His face twisted in a hideous, malicious grin. "You—love—that artist fellow. Your—interest in his art is—all rot. It's him you want—and you—you have been thinking—you'd get him—with my money—the same as I got you. But you won't. You've—lost him already. I'm glad—you love him—damn glad—because—I know that after—what he's seen of me—even if he didn't love—that mountain—girl, he wouldn't wipe—his feet on you. You've tortured me—you've mocked—and sneered and laughed—at me—in my suffering—you fiend—and I've—tried my damnedest—to pay you back. What I couldn't do—the man you love—will—do for me. You'll suffer—now in earnest. You thought you'd be a—sure winner—as soon—as I was out of—the game. But you've lost—you've lost—you've lost! I saw your love for him—in your—face to-night—as I have seen—it every time—you two were together. I saw his love—for the girl—too—and I—saw—that you—saw it. I—I—wouldn't—wouldn't die—until I'd told you—that I knew." He paused to gather his strength for the last evil effort of his evil life.

The woman—who had stood, frozen with horror, her eyes fixed upon the face of the dying man, as though under a dreadful spell—cowered before him, livid with fear. Cringing, helpless—as though before some infernal monster—she hid her face; while her husband, struggling for breath to make her hear, called her every foul name he could master—derided her with fiendish glee—mocked her, taunted her, cursed her—with words too vile to print. With an oath and a profane wish for her future upon his lips, the end came. The sensual mouth opened—the diseased wasted limbs shuddered— the insane light in the lust-worn eyes went out.

With a scream, Mrs. Taine sank unconscious upon the floor beside the bed.

From the lower part of the house came the faint sounds of the few remaining revelers.

When Aaron King and Conrad Lagrange left the house on Fairlands Heights that night, they walked quickly, as though eager to escape from the brilliantly lighted vicinity. Neither spoke until they were some distance away. Then the novelist, checking his quick stride, pointed toward the shadowy bulk of the mountains that heaved their mighty crests and peaks in solemn grandeur high into the midnight sky.

"Well, boy," he said, "the mountains are still there. It's good to see them again, isn't it?"

Reaching home, the older man bade his friend good night. But the artist, declaring that he was not yet ready to turn in, went, with pipe and Czar for company, to sit for a while on the porch.

Looking away over the dark mass of the orange groves to the distant peaks, he lived over again, in his thoughts, those weeks of comradeship with Sibyl Andrés in the hills. Every incident of their friendship he recalled—every hour they had spent together amid the scenes she loved—reviewing every conversation—questioning searching, wondering, hoping, fearing.

Later, he went out into the rose garden—her garden—where the air was fragrant with the perfume of the flowers she tended with such loving care. In the soft, still darkness of the night, the place seemed haunted by her presence. Quietly, he moved here and there among the roses—to the little gate in the Ragged Robin hedge, through which she came and went; to the vine-covered arbor where she had watched him at his work; and to the spot where she had stood, day after day, with hands outstretched in greeting, while he worked to make the colors and lines upon his canvas tell the secret of her loveliness. He remembered how he had felt her presence in those days when he had laughingly insisted to Conrad Lagrange that the place was haunted. He remembered how, even when she was unknown to him, her music had always moved him—how her message from the hills had seemed to call to the best that was in him.

So it was, that, as he recalled these things,—as he lived again the days of his companionship with her and realized how she had come into his life, how she had appealed always to the best of him, and satisfied always his best needs,—he came to know the answer to his questions—to his doubts and fears and hopes. There, in the rose garden, with its dark walls of hedge and vine and grove, in the still night under the stars, with his face to the distant mountains, he knew that the mountain girl would not deny him—that, when she was ready, she would come to him.

In the hour when Mr. Taine, with the last strength of his evil life, profanely cursed the woman that his gold had bought to serve his licentious will—and cursing—died; Aaron King—inspired by the character and purity of the woman he loved, and by whom he knew he was loved, and dreaming of their comradeship that was to be— dedicated himself anew to the ministry of his art and so entered into that more abundant life which belongs by divine right to all who will claim it.

But it was not given Aaron King to know that before Sibyl Andrés could come to him he must be tested by a trial that would tax his manhood's best strength to the uttermost. In that night of his awakened love, as he dreamed of the days of its realization, the man did not know that the days of his testing were so near at hand.

Chapter XXXI
As the World Sees

It was three days after the incidents just related when an automobile from Fairlands Heights stopped at the home of Aaron King and the novelist.

Mrs. Taine, dressed in black and heavily veiled, went, alone, to the house, where Yee Kee appeared in answer to her ring.

There was no one at home, the Chinaman said. He did not know where the artist was. He had gone off somewhere with Mr. Lagrange and the dog. Perhaps they would return in a few minutes; perhaps not until dinner time.

Mrs. Taine was exceedingly anxious to see Mr. King. She was going away, and must see him, if possible, before she left. She would come in, and, if Yee Kee would get her pen and paper, would write a little note, explaining—in case she should miss him. The Chinaman silently placed the writing material before her, and disappeared.

Before sitting down to her letter, the woman paced the floor restlessly, in nervous agitation. Her face, when she had thrown back the veil, appeared old and worn, with dark circles under the eyes, and a drawn look to the weary, downward droop of the lips. As she moved about the room, nervously fingering the books and trifles upon the table or the mantle, she seemed beside herself with anxiety. She went to the window to stand looking out as if hoping for the return of the artist. She went to the open door of his bedroom, her hands clenched, her limbs trembling, her face betraying the agony of her mind.

With Louise, she was leaving that evening, at four o'clock, for the East—with the body of her husband. She could not go without seeing again the man whom, as Mr. Taine had rightly said, she loved—loved with the only love of which—because of her environment and life—she was capable. She still believed in her power over him whose passion she had besieged with all the lure of her physical beauty, but that which she had seen in his face as he had watched the girl musician the night of the dinner, filled her with fear. Presently, in her desperation, when the artist did not return, she seated herself at the table to put upon paper, as best she could, the things she had come to say.

Her letter finished, she looked at her watch. Calling the

Chinaman, she asked for a key to the studio, explaining that she wished to see her picture. She still hoped for the artist's return and that her letter would not be necessary. She hoped, too, that in her portrait, which she had not yet seen, she might find some evidence of the painter's passion for her. She had not forgotten his saying that he would put upon the canvas what he thought of her, nor could she fail to recall his manner and her interpretation of it as he had worked upon the picture.

In the studio, she stood before the easel, scarce daring to draw the curtain. But, calling up in her mind the emotions and thoughts of the hours she had spent in that room alone with the artist, she was made bold by her reestablished belief in his passion and by her convictions that were founded upon her own desires. Under the stimulating influence of her thoughts, a flush of color stole into her cheeks, her eyes grew bright with the light of triumphant anticipation. With an eager hand she boldly drew aside the curtain.

The picture upon the easel was the artist's portrait of Sibyl Andrés.

With an exclamation that was not unlike fear, Mrs. Taine drew back from the canvas. Looking at the beautiful painting,—in which the artist had pictured, with unconscious love and an almost religious fidelity, the spirit of the girl who was so like the flowers among which she stood,—the woman was moved by many conflicting emotions. Surprise, disappointment admiration, envy, jealousy, sadness, regret, and anger swept over her. Blinded by bitter tears, with a choking sob, in an agony of remorse and shame, she turned away her face from the gaze of those pure eyes. Then, as the flame of her passion withered her shame, hot rage dried her tears, and she sprang forward with an animal-like fierceness, to destroy the picture. But, even as she put forth her hand, she hesitated and drew back, afraid. As she stood thus in doubt—halting between her impulse and her fear—a sound at the door behind her drew her attention. She turned to face the beautiful original of the portrait Instantly the woman of the world had herself perfectly in hand.

Sibyl Andrés drew back with an embarrassed, "I beg your pardon. I thought—" and would have fled.

But Mrs. Taine, with perfect cordiality, said quickly, "O how do you do, Miss Andrés; come in."

She seemed so sincere in the welcome that was implied in her voice and manner; while her face, together with her somber garb of mourning, was so expressive of sadness and grief that the girl's gentle heart was touched. Going forward, with that natural, dignity that belongs to those whose minds and hearts are unsullied by habitual pretense of feeling and sham emotions, Sibyl spoke a few well chosen words of sympathy.

Mrs. Taine received the girl's expression of condolence with a manner that was perfect in its semblance of carefully controlled sorrow and grief, yet managed, skillfully, to suggest the wide social distance that separated the widow of Mr. Taine from the unknown, mountain girl. Then, as if courageously determined not to dwell upon her bereavement, she said, "I was just looking, again, at Mr. King's picture—for which you posed. It is beautiful, isn't it? He told me that you were an exceptionally clever model—quite the best he has ever had."

The girl—disarmed by her own genuine feeling of sympathy for the speaker—was troubled at something that seemed to lie beneath the kindly words of the experienced woman. "To me, it is beautiful," she returned doubtfully. "But, of course, I don't know. Mr. Lagrange thinks, though, that it is really a splendid portrait."

Mrs. Taine smiled with a confident air, as one might smile at a child. "Mr. Lagrange, my dear, is a famous novelist—but he really knows very little of pictures."

"Perhaps you are right," returned Sibyl, simply. "But the picture is not to be shown as a portrait of me, at all."

Again, that knowing smile. "So I understand, of course. Under the circumstances, you would scarcely expect it, would you?"

Sibyl, not in the least understanding what the woman meant, answered doubtfully, "No. I—I did not wish it shown as my portrait."

Mrs. Taine, studying the girl's face, became very earnest in her kindly interest; as if, moved out of the goodness of her heart, she stooped from her high place to advise and counsel one of her own sex, who was so wholly ignorant of the world. "I fear, my dear, that you know very little of artists and their methods."

To which the girl replied, "I never knew an artist before I met Mr. King, this summer, in the mountains."

Still watching her face closely, Mrs. Taine said, with gentle solicitude, "May I tell you something for your own good, Miss Andrés?"

"Certainly, if you please, Mrs. Taine."

"An artist," said the older woman, carefully, with an air of positive knowledge, "must find the subjects for his pictures in life. As he goes about, he is constantly on the look-out for new faces or

200

figures that are of interest to him—or, that may be used by him to make pictures of interest. The subjects—or, I should say, the people who pose for him—are nothing at all to the artist—aside from his picture, you see—no more than his paints and brushes and canvas. Often, they are professional models, whom he hires as one hires any sort of service, you know. Sometimes—" she paused as if hesitating, then continued gently—"sometimes they are people like yourself, who happen to appeal to his artistic fancy, and whom he can persuade to pose for him."

The girl's face was white. She stared at the woman with pleading, frightened dismay. She made a pitiful attempt to speak, but could not.

The older woman, watching her, continued, "Forgive me, dear child. I do not wish to hurt you. But Mr. King is so careless. I told him he should be careful that you did not misunderstand his interest in you. But he laughed at me. He said that it was your innocence that he wanted to paint, and cautioned me not to warn you until his picture was finished." She turned to look at the picture on the easel with the air of a critic. "He really has caught it very well. Aaron—Mr. King is so good at that sort of thing. He never permits his models to know exactly what he is after, you see, but leads them, cleverly, to exhibit, unconsciously, the particular thing that he wishes to get into his picture."

When the tortured girl had been given time to grasp the full import of her words, the woman said again,—turning toward Sibyl, as she spoke, with a smiling air that was intended to show the intimacy between herself and the artist,—"Have you seen his portrait of me?"

"No," faltered Sibyl. "Mr. King told me not to look at it. It has always been covered when I have been in the studio."

Again, Mrs. Taine smiled, as though there was some reason, known only to herself and the painter, why he did not wish the girl to see the portrait. "And do you come to the studio often—alone as you came to-day?" she asked, still kindly, as though from her experience she was seeking to counsel the girl. "I mean—have you been coming since the picture for which you posed was finished?"

The girl's white cheeks grew red with embarrassment and shame as she answered, falteringly, "Yes."

"You poor child! Really, I must scold Aaron for this. After my warning him, too, that people were talking about his intimacy with you in the mountains It is quite too bad of him! He will ruin himself, if he is not more careful." She seemed sincerely troubled over the situation.

201

"I—I do not understand, Mrs. Taine," faltered Sibyl. "Do you mean that my—that Mr. King's friendship for me has harmed him? That I—that it is wrong for me to come here?"

"Surely, Miss Andrés, you must understand what I mean."

"No, I—I do not know. Tell me, please."

Mrs. Taine hesitated as though reluctant. Then, as if forced by her sense of duty, she spoke. "The truth is, my dear, that your being with Mr. King in the mountains—going to his camp as familiarly as you did, and spending so much time alone with him in the hills— and then your coming here so often, has led people to say unpleasant things."

"But what do people say?" persisted Sibyl.

The answer came with cruel deliberateness; "That you are not only Mr. King's model, but that you are his mistress as well."

Sibyl Andrés shrank back from the woman as though she had received a blow in the face. Her cheeks and brow and neck were crimson. With a little cry, she buried her face in her hands.

The kind voice of the older woman continued, "You see, dear, whether it is true or not, the effect is exactly the same. If in the eyes of the world your relations to Mr. King are—are wrong, it is as bad as though it were actually true. I felt that I must tell you, child, not alone for your own good but for the sake of Mr. King and his work— for the sake of his position in the world. Frankly, if you continue to compromise him and his good name by coming like this to his studio, it will ruin him. The world may not care particularly whether Mr. King keeps a mistress or not, but people will not countenance his open association with her, even under the pretext that she is a model."

As she finished, Mrs. Taine looked at her watch. "Dear me, I really must be going. I have already spent more time than I intended. Good-by, Miss Andrés. I know you will forgive me if I have hurt you."

The girl looked at her with the pain and terror filled eyes of some gentle wild creature that can not understand the cruelty of the trap that holds it fast. "Yes—yes, I—I suppose you know best. You must know more than I. I—thank you, Mrs. Taine. I—"

When Mrs. Taine was gone, Sibyl Andrés sat for a little while before her portrait; wondering, dumbly, at the happiness of that face upon the canvas. There were no tears. She could not cry. Her eyes burned hot and dry. Her lips were parched. Rising, she drew the curtain carefully to hide the picture, and started toward the door. She paused. Going to the easel that held the other picture, she laid her hand upon the curtain. Again, she paused. Aaron King had said that she must not look at that picture—Conrad Lagrange had said that she must not—why? She did not know why.

Perhaps—if the mountain girl had drawn aside the curtain and had looked upon the face of Mrs. Taine as Aaron King had painted it—perhaps the rest of my story would not have happened.

But, true to the wish of her friends, even in her misery, Sibyl Andrés held her hand. At the door of the studio, she turned again, to look long and lingeringly about the room. Then she went out, closing and locking the door, and leaving the key on a hidden nail, as her custom was.

Going slowly, lingeringly, through the rose garden to the little gate in the hedge, she disappeared in the orange grove.

Aaron King and Conrad Lagrange, returning from a long walk, overtook Myra Willard, who was returning from town, just as the woman of the disfigured face arrived at the gate of the little house in the orange grove. For a moment, the three stood chatting—as neighbors will,—then the two men went on to their own home. Czar, racing ahead, announced their coming to Yee Kee and the Chinaman met them as they entered the living-room. Telling them of Mrs. Taine's visit, he gave Aaron King the letter that she had left for him.

As the artist, conscious of the scrutinizing gaze of his friend, read the closely written pages, his cheeks flushed with embarrassment and shame. When he had finished, he faced the novelist's eyes steadily and, without speaking, deliberately and methodically tore Mrs. Taine's letter into tiny fragments. Dropping the scraps of paper into the waste basket, he dusted his hands together with a significant gesture and looked at his watch. "Her train left at four o'clock. It is now four-thirty."

"For which," returned Conrad Lagrange, solemnly, "let us give thanks."

As the novelist spoke, Czar, on the porch outside, gave a low "woof" that signalized the approach of a friend.

Looking through the open door, they saw Myra Willard coming hurriedly up the walk. They could see that the woman was greatly agitated, and went quickly forward to meet her.

Women of Myra Willard's strength of character—particularly those who have passed through the furnace of some terrible experience as she so evidently had—are not given to loud, uncontrolled expression of emotion. That she was alarmed and troubled was evident. Her face was white, her eyes were frightened and she trembled so that Aaron King helped her to a seat; but she told them clearly, with no unnecessary, hysterical exclamations, what had happened. Upon entering the house, after parting from the two men at the gate, a few minutes before, she had found a letter from Sibyl. The girl was gone.

As she spoke, she handed the letter to Conrad Lagrange who read it and gave it to the artist. It was a pitiful little note—rather vague—saying only that she must go away at once; assuring Myra that she had not meant to do wrong; asking her to tell Mr. King and the novelist good-by; and begging the artist's forgiveness that she had not understood.

Aaron King looked from the letter in his hand to the faces of his two friends, in consternation. "Do you understand this, Miss Willard?" he asked, when he could speak.

The woman shook her head. "Only that something has happened to make the child think that her friendship with you has injured you; and that she has gone away for your sake. She—she thought so much of you, Mr. King."

"And I—I love her, Miss Willard. I should have told you soon. I tell you now to reassure you. I love her."

Aaron King made his declaration to his two friends with a simple dignity, but with a feeling that thrilled them with the force of his earnestness and the purity and strength of his passion.

Conrad Lagrange—world-worn, scarred by his years of contact with the unclean, the vicious, and debasing passions of mankind—grasped the young man's hand, while his eyes shone with an emotion his habitual reserve could not conceal. "I'm glad for you, Aaron"—he said, adding reverently—"as your mother would be glad."

"I have known that you would tell me this, sometime Mr. King," said Myra Willard. "I knew it, I think, before you, yourself, realized; and I, too, am glad—glad for my girl, because I know what such a love will mean to her. But why—why has she gone like this? Where has she gone? Oh, my girl, my girl!" For a moment, the distracted woman was on the point of breaking down; but with an effort of her will, she controlled herself.

"It's clear enough what has sent her away," growled Conrad Lagrange, with a warning glance to the artist. "Some one has filled her mind with the notion that her friendship with Aaron has been causing talk. I think there's no doubt as to where she's gone."

"You mean the mountains?" asked Myra Willard, quickly.

"Yes. I'd stake my life that she has gone straight to Brian Oakley. Think! Where else would she go?"

204

"She has sometimes borrowed a saddle-horse from your neighbor up the road, hasn't she, Miss Willard?" asked Aaron King.

"Yes. I'll run over there at once."

Conrad Lagrange spoke quickly; "Don't let them think anything unusual has happened. We'll go over to your house and wait for you there."

Fifteen minutes later, Myra Willard returned. Sibyl had borrowed the horse; asking them if she might keep it until the next day. She did not say where she was going. She had left about four o'clock.

"That will put her at Brian's by nine," said the novelist.

"And I will arrive there about the same time," added Aaron King, eagerly. "It's now five-thirty. She has an hour's start; but I'll ride an hour harder."

"With an automobile you could overtake her," said Myra Willard.

"I know," returned the artist, "but if I take a horse, we can ride back together."

He started through the grove, toward the other house, on a run.

Chapter XXXII
The Mysterious Disappearance

By the time Aaron King had found a saddle-horse and was ready to start on his ride, it was six o'clock.

Granting that Conrad Lagrange was right in his supposition that the girl had left with the intention of going to Brian Oakley's, the artist could scarcely, now, hope to arrive at the Ranger Station until some time after Sibyl had reached the home of her friends—unless she should stop somewhere on the way, which he did not think likely. Once, as he realized how the minutes were slipping away, he was on the point of reconsidering his reply to Myra Willard's suggestion that he take an automobile. Then, telling himself that he would surely find Sibyl at the Station and thinking of the return trip with her, he determined to carry out his first plan.

But when he was finally on the road, he did not ride with less haste because he no longer expected to overtake Sibyl. In spite of his reassuring himself, again and again, that the girl he loved was safe, his mind was too disturbed by the situation to permit of his riding leisurely. Beyond the outskirts of the city, with his horse warmed to its work, the artist pushed his mount harder and harder until the animal reached the limit of a pace that its rider felt it could endure for the distance they had to go. Over the way that he and Conrad Lagrange had walked with Czar and Croesus so leisurely, he went, now, with such hot haste that the people in the homes in the orange groves, sitting down to their evening meal, paused to listen to the sharp, ringing beat of the galloping hoofs. Two or three travelers, as he passed, watched him out of sight, with wondering gaze. Those he met, turned their heads to look after him.

Aaron King's thoughts, as he rode, kept pace with his horse's flying feet. The points along the way, where he and the famous novelist had stopped to rest, and to enjoy the beauty of the scene, recalled vividly to his mind all that those weeks in the mountains had brought to him. Backward from that day when he had for the first time set his face toward the hills, his mind traveled—almost from day to day—until he stood, again, in that impoverished home of his boyhood to which he had been summoned from his studies abroad. As he urged his laboring horse forward, in the eagerness and anxiety of his love for Sibyl Andrés, he lived again that hour

206

when his dying mother told her faltering story of his father's dishonor; when he knew, for the first time, her life of devotion to him, and learned of her sacrifice—even unto poverty—that he might, unhampered, be fitted for his life work; and when, receiving his inheritance, he had made his solemn promise that the purpose and passion of his mother's years of sacrifice should, in him and in his work, be fulfilled. One by one, he retraced the steps that had led to his understanding that only a true and noble art could ever make good that promise. Not by winning the poor notice of the little passing day, alone; not by gaining the applause of the thoughtless crowd; not by winning the rewards bestowed by the self-appointed judges and patrons of the arts; but by a true, honest, and fearless giving of himself in his work, regardless alike of praise or blame—by saying the thing that was given him to say, because it was given him to say—would he keep that which his mother had committed to him. As mile after mile of the distance that lay between him and the girl he loved was put behind him in his race to her side, it was given him to understand—as never before—how, first the friendship of the world-wearied man who had, himself, profaned his art; and then, the comradeship of that one whose life was so unspotted by the world; had helped him to a true and vital conception of his ministry of color and line and brush and canvas.

It was twilight when the artist reached the spot where the road crosses the tumbling stream—the spot where he and Conrad Lagrange had slept at the foot of the mountains. Where the road curves toward the creek, the man, without checking his pace, turned his head to look back upon the valley that, far below, was fast being lost in the gathering dusk. In its weird and gloomy mystery,—with its hidden life revealed only by the sparkling, twinkling lights of the towns and cities,—it was suggestive, now, to his artist mind, of the life that had so nearly caught him in its glittering sensual snare. A moment later, he lifted his eyes to the mountain peaks ahead that, still in the light of the western sun, glowed as though brushed with living fire. Against the sky, he could distinguish that peak in the Galena range, with the clump of pines, where he had sat with Sibyl Andrés that day when she had tried to make him see the train that had brought him to Fairlands.

He wondered now, as he rode, why he had not realized his love for the girl, before they left the hills. It seemed to him, now, that his love was born that evening when he had first heard her violin, as he was fishing; when he had watched her from the cedar thicket, as she made her music of the mountains and as she danced in the grassy yard. Why, he asked himself, had he not been conscious of his love in those days when she came to him in the spring glade, and in the days that followed? Why had he not known, when he painted her portrait in the rose garden? Why had the awakening not come until that night when he saw her in the company of revelers at the big house on Fairlands Heights—the night that Mr. Taine died?

It was dark before he reached the canyon gates. In the blackness of the gorge, with only the light of a narrow strip of stars overhead, he was forced to ride more slowly. But his confidence that he would find her at the Ranger Station had increased as he approached the scenes of her girlhood home. To go to her friends, seemed so inevitably the thing that she would do. A few miles farther, now, and he would see her. He would tell her why he had come. He would claim the love that he knew was his. And so, with a better heart, he permitted his tired horse to slacken the pace. He even smiled to think of her surprise when she should see him.

It was a little past nine o'clock when the artist saw, through the trees, the lights in the windows at the Station, and dismounted to open the gate. Hiding up to the house, he gave the old familiar hail, "Whoo-e-e." The door opened, and with the flood of light that streamed out came the tall form of Brian Oakley.

"Hello! Seems to me I ought to know that voice."

The artist laughed nervously. "It's me, all right, Brian—what there is left of me."

"Aaron King, by all that's holy!" cried the Ranger, coming quickly down the steps and toward the shadowy horseman. "What's the matter? Anything wrong with Sibyl or Myra Willard? What brings you up here, this time of night?"

Aaron King heard the questions with sinking heart. But so certain had he come to feel that the girl would be at the Station, that he said mechanically, as he dropped wearily from his horse to grasp his friend's hand, "I followed Sibyl. How long has she been here?"

Brian Oakley spoke quickly; "Sibyl is not here, Aaron."

The artist caught the Ranger's arm. "Do you mean, Brian, that she has not been here to-day?"

"She has not been here," returned the officer, coolly.

"Good God!" exclaimed the other, stunned and bewildered by the positive words. Blindly, he turned toward his horse.

Brian Oakley, stepping forward, put his hand on the artist's shoulder. "Come, old man, pull yourself together and let a little light in on this matter," he said calmly. "Tell me what has happened. Why did you expect to find Sibyl here?"

When Aaron King had finished his story, the other said, still without excitement, "Come into the house. You're about all in. I heard Doctor Gordan's 'auto' going up the canyon to Morton's about an hour ago. Their baby's sick. If Sibyl was on the road, he would have passed her. I'll throw the saddle on Max, and we'll run over there and see what he knows. But first, you've got to have a bite to eat."

The young man protested but the Ranger said firmly, "You can eat while I saddle; come. I wish Mary was home," he added, as he set out some cold meat and bread. "She is in Los Angeles with her sister. I'll call you when I'm ready." He spoke the last word from the door as he went out.

The artist tried to eat; but with little success. He was again mounted and ready to go when the Ranger rode up from the barn on the chestnut.

When they reached the point where the road to Morton's ranch leaves the main canyon road, Brian Oakley said, "It's barely possible that she went on up to Carleton's. But I think we better go to Morton's and see the Doctor first. We don't want to miss him. Did you meet any one as you came up? I mean after you got within two or three miles of the mouth of the canyon?"

"No," replied the other. "Why?"

"A man on a horse passed the Station about seven o'clock, going down. Where did the Doctor pass you?"

"He didn't pass me."

"What?" said the Ranger, sharply.

"No one passed me after I left Fairlands."

"Hu-m-m. If Doc left town before you, he must have had a puncture or something, or he would have passed the Station before he did."

It was ten o'clock when the two men arrived at the Morton ranch.

"We don't want to start any excitement," said the officer, as they drew rein at the corral gate. "You stay here and I'll drop in— casual like."

It seemed to Aaron King, waiting in the darkness, that his companion was gone for hours. In reality, it was only a few minutes until the Ranger returned. He was walking quickly, and, springing into the saddle he started the chestnut off at a sharp lope.

"The baby is better," he said. "Doctor was here this afternoon—started home about two o'clock. That 'auto' must have gone on up the canyon. Morton knew nothing of the man on horseback who went down. We'll cut across to Carleton's."

209

Presently, the Ranger swung the chestnut aside from the wagon road, to follow a narrow trail through the chaparral. To the artist, the little path in the darkness was invisible, but he gave his horse the rein and followed the shadowy form ahead. Three-quarters of an hour later, they came out into the main road, again; near the Carleton ranch corral, a mile and a half below the old camp in the sycamores behind the orchard of the deserted place.

It was now eleven o'clock and the ranch-house was dark. Without dismounting, Brian Oakley called, "Hello, Henry!" There was no answer. Moving his horse close to the window of the room where he knew the rancher slept, the Ranger tapped on the sash. "Henry, turn out; I want to see you; it's Oakley."

A moment later the sash was raised and Carleton asked, "What is it, Brian? What's up?"

"Is Sibyl stopping with you folks, to-night?"

"Sibyl! Haven't seen her since they went down from their summer camp. What's the matter?"

Briefly, the Ranger explained the situation. The rancher interrupted only to greet the artist with a "howdy, Mr. King," as the officer's words made known the identity of his companion.

When Brian Oakley had concluded, the rancher said, "I heard that 'auto' going up, and then heard it going back down, again, about an hour ago. You missed it by turning off to Morton's. If you'd come on straight up here you'd a met it."

"Did you see the man on horseback, going down, just before dusk?" asked the officer.

"Yes, but not near enough to know him. You don't suppose Sibyl would go up to her old home do you, Brian?"

"She might, under the circumstances. Aaron and I will ride up there, on the chance."

"You'll stop in on your way back?" called the rancher, as the two horsemen moved away.

"Sure," answered the Ranger.

An hour later, they were back. They had found the old home under the giant sycamores, on the edge of the little clearing, dark and untenanted.

Lights were shining, now, from the windows of the Carleton ranch-house. Down at the corral, the twinkling gleam of a lantern bobbed here and there. As the Ranger and his companion drew near, the lantern came rapidly up the hill. At the porch, they were met by Henry Carleton, his two sons, and a ranch hand. As the four stood in the light of the window, and of the lantern on the porch, listening to Brian Oakley's report, each held the bridle-reins of a saddle-horse.

"I figured that the chance of her being up there was so mighty slim that we'd better be ready to ride when you got back," said the mountain ranchman. "What's your program, Brian?" Thus simply he put himself and his household in command of the Ranger.

The officer turned to the eldest son, "Jack, you've got the fastest horse in the outfit. I want you to go down to the Power-House and find out if any one there saw Sibyl anywhere on the road. You see," he explained to the group, "we don't know for sure, yet, that she came into the mountains. While I haven't a doubt but she did, we've got to know."

Jack Carleton was in the saddle as the Ranger finished The officer turned to him again. "Find out what you can about that automobile and the man on horseback. We'll be at the Station when you get back." There was a sharp clatter of iron-shod hoofs, and the rider disappeared in the darkness of the night.

The other members of the little party rode more leisurely down the canyon road to the Ranger Station. When they arrived at the house, Brian Oakley said, "Make yourselves easy, boys. I'm going to write a little note." He went into the house where, as they sat on the porch, they saw him through the window, his desk.

The Ranger had finished his letter and with the sealed official envelope in his hand, appeared in the doorway when his messenger to the Power-House returned. Without dismounting, the rider reined his horse up to the porch. "Good time, Jack," said the officer, quietly.

The young man answered, "One of the company men saw Sibyl. He was coming up with a load of supplies and she passed him a mile below the Power-House just before dark. When he was opening the gate, the automobile went by. It was too dark to see how many were in the machine. They heard the 'auto' go down the canyon, again, later. No one noticed the man on horseback. Three Company men will be up here at daybreak."

"Good boy," said Brian Oakley, again. And then, for a little, no sound save the soft clinking of bit or bridle-chain in the darkness broke the hush that fell over the little group. With faces turned toward their leader, they waited his word. The Ranger stood still, the long official envelope in his hand. When he spoke, there was a ring in his voice that left in the minds of his companions no doubt as to his view of the seriousness of the situation. "Milt," he said sharply.

The youngest of the Carleton sons stepped forward. "Yes, sir."

211

"You will ride to Fairlands. It's half past one, now. You should be back between eight and nine in the morning. Give this letter to the Sheriff and bring me his answer. Stop at Miss Willard's and tell her what you know. You'll get something to eat there, while you're talking. If I'm not at your house when you get back, feed your horse and wait."

"Yes, sir," came the answer, and an instant later the boy rider vanished into the night.

While the sound of the messenger's going still came to them, the Ranger spoke again. "Henry, you'll ride to Morton's. Tell him to be at your place, with his crowd, by daylight. Then go home and be ready with breakfast for the riders when they come in. We'll have to make your place the center. It'll be hard on your wife and the girls, but Mrs. Morton will likely go over to lend them a hand. I wish to God Mary was here."

"Never mind about my folks, Brian," returned the rancher as he mounted. "You know they'll be on the job."

"You bet I know, Henry," came the answer as the mountaineer rode away. Then—"Bill, you'll take every one between here and the head of the canyon. If there's a man shows up at Carleton's later than an hour after sunup, we'll run him out of the country. Tom, you take the trail over into the Santa Ana, circle around to the mouth of the canyon, and back up Clear Creek. Turn out everybody. Jack, you'll take the Galena Valley neighborhood. Send in your men but don't come back yourself until you've found that man who went down the canyon on horseback."

When the last rider was gone in the darkness, the Ranger said to the artist, "Come, Aaron, you must get some rest. There's not a thing more that can be done, until daylight."

Aaron King protested. But, strong as he was, the unusual exertion of his hours in the saddle, together with his racking anxiety, had told upon muscles and nerves. His face, pale and drawn, gave the lie to his words that he was not tired.

"You must rest, man," said Brian Oakley, shortly. "There may be days of this ahead of us. You've got to snatch every minute, when it's possible, to conserve your strength. You've already had more than the rest of us. Jerk off your boots and lie down until I call you, even if you can't sleep. Do as I say—I'm boss here."

As the artist obeyed, the Ranger continued, "I wrote the Sheriff all I knew—and some things that I suspect. It's that automobile that sticks in my mind—that and some other things. The machine must have left Fairlands before you did, unless it came over through the Galena Valley, from some town on the railroad, up

212

San Gorgonio Pass way—which isn't likely. If it did come from Fairlands, it must have waited somewhere along the road, to enter the canyon after dark. Do you think that any one else besides Myra Willard and Lagrange and you know that Sibyl started up here?"

"I don't think so. The neighbor where she borrowed the horse didn't know where she was going."

"Who saw her last?"

"I think Mrs. Taine did."

The artist had already told the Ranger about the possible meeting of Mrs. Taine and Sibyl in his studio.

"Hu-m-m," said the other.

"Mrs. Taine left for the East at four o'clock, you know," said the artist.

"Jim Rutlidge didn't go, you said." The Ranger spoke casually. Then, as if dismissing the matter, he continued, "You get some rest now, Aaron. I'll take care of your horse and saddle a fresh one for you. As soon as it's light, we'll ride. I'm going to find out where that automobile went—and what for."

Chapter XXXIII
Beginning the Search

Aaron King lay with closed eyes, but not asleep. He was thinking, thinking, thinking In a weary circle, his tired brain went round and round, finding no place to stop. The man on horseback, the automobile, some accident that might have befallen the girl in her distraught state of mind—he could find no place in the weary treadmill of conjecture to rest. While it was still too dark to see, Brian Oakley called him. And the call was a relief.

As the artist pulled on his boots, the Ranger said, "It'll be light enough to see, by the time we get above Carleton's. We know the automobile went that far anyway."

At the Carleton ranch, as they passed, they saw, by the lights, that the mountaineer's family were already making ready for the gathering of the riders. A little beyond, they met two men from the Company Head-Work, on their way to the meeting place. Soon, in the gray, early morning light, the tracks of the automobile were clearly seen. Eagerly, they followed to the foot of the Oak Knoll trail, where the machine had stopped and, turning around, had started back down the canyon. With experienced care, Brian Oakley searched every inch of the ground in the vicinity.

Shaking his head, at last, as though forced to give up hope of finding any positive signs pointing to the solution of the puzzle, the officer remounted, slowly. "I can't make it out," he said. "The road is so dry and cut up with tracks, and the trail is so gravelly, that there are no clear signs at all. Come, we better get back to Carleton's, and start the boys out. When Milt returns from Fairlands he may know something."

With the rising of the sun, the mountain folk, summoned in the night by the Ranger's messengers, assembled at the ranch; every man armed and mounted with the best his possessions afforded. Tied to the trees in the yard, and along the fence in front, or standing with bridle-reins over their heads, the horses waited. Lying on the porch, or squatting on their heels, in unconscious picturesque attitudes, the mountain riders who had arrived first and had finished their breakfast were ready for the Ranger's word. In the ranch kitchen, the table was filled with the later ones; and these, as fast as they finished their meal, made way for the new arrivals.

There was no loud talk; no boisterous laughter; no uneasy restlessness. Calm-eyed, soft-voiced, deliberate in movement, these hardy mountaineers had answered Brian Oakley's call; and they placed themselves, now, under his command, with no idle comment, no wasteful excitement but with a purpose and spirit that would, if need be, hold them in their saddles until their horses dropped under them, and would, then, send them on, afoot, as long as their iron nerves and muscles could be made to respond to their wills.

There was scarce a man in that company, who did not know and love Sibyl Andrés, and who had not known and loved her parents. Many of them had ridden with the Ranger at the time of Will Andrés' death. When the officer and his companion appeared, they gathered round their leader with simple words of greeting, and stood silently ready for his word.

Briefly, Brian Oakley divided them into parties, and assigned the territory to be covered by each. Three shots in quick succession, at intervals of two minutes, would signal that the search was finished. Two men, he held to go with him up Oak Knoll trail, after his messenger to the Sheriff had returned. At sunset, they were all to reassemble at the ranch for further orders. When the officer finished speaking, the little group of men turned to the horses, and, without the loss of a moment, were out of sight in the mountain wilderness.

A half hour before he was due, young Carleton appeared with the Sheriff's answer to the Ranger's letter. "Well done, boy," said Brian Oakley, heartily. "Take care of your horse, now, and then get some rest yourself, and be ready for whatever comes next."

He turned to those he had held to go with him; "All right, boys, let's ride. Sheriff will take care of the Fairlands end. Come, Aaron."

All the way up the Oak Knoll trail the Ranger rode in the lead, bending low from his saddle, his gaze fixed on the little path. Twice he dismounted and walked ahead, leaving the chestnut to follow or to wait, at his word. When they came out on the pipe-line trail, he halted the party, and, on foot, went carefully over the ground either way from the point where they stood.

"Boys," he said at last, "I have a hunch that there was a horse on this trail last night. It's been so blamed dry, and for so long, though, that I can't be sure. I held you two men because I know you are good trailers. Follow the pipe-line up the canyon, and see what you can find. It isn't necessary to say stay with it if you strike

215

anything that even looks like it might be a lead. Aaron and I will take the other way, and up the Galena trail to the fire-break."

While Brian Oakley had been searching for signs in the little path, and the artist, with the others, was waiting, Aaron King's mind went back to that day when he and Conrad Lagrange had sat there under the oaks and, in a spirit of irresponsible fun, had committed themselves to the leadership of Croesus. To the young man, now, that day, with its care-free leisure, seemed long ago. Remembering the novelist's fanciful oration to the burro, he thought grimly how unconscious they had been, in their merriment, of the great issues that did actually rest upon the seemingly trivial incident. He recalled, too, with startling vividness, the times that he had climbed to that spot with Sibyl, or, reaching it from either way on the pipe-line, had gone with her down the zigzag path to the road in the canyon below. Had she, last night, alone, or with some unwelcome companions, paused a moment under those oaks? Had she remembered the hours that she had spent there with him?

As he followed the Ranger over the ground that he had walked with her, that day of their last climb together, it seemed to him that every step of the way was haunted by her sweet personality. The objects along the trail—a point of rock, a pine, the barrel where they had filled their canteen, a broken section of the concrete pipe left by the workmen, the very rocks and cliffs, the flowers—dry and withered now—that grew along the little path—a thousand things that met his eyes—recalled her to his mind until he felt her presence so vividly that he almost expected to find her waiting, with smiling, winsome face, just around the next turn. The officer, who, moving ahead, scanned with careful eyes every foot of the way, seemed to the artist, now, to be playing some fantastic game. He could not, for the moment, believe that the girl he loved was—God! where was she? Why did Brian Oakley move so slowly, on foot, while his horse, leisurely cropping the grass, followed? He should be in the saddle! They should be riding, riding riding—as he had ridden last night. Last night! Was it only last night?

Where the Government trail crosses the fire-break on the crest of the Galenas, Brian Oakley paused. "I don't think there's been anything over this way," he said. "We'll follow the fire-break to that point up there, for a look around."

At noon, they stood by the big rock, under the clump of pines, where Aaron King and Sibyl Andrés had eaten their lunch.

"We'll be here some time," said the Ranger. "Make yourself comfortable. I want to see if there's anything stirring down yonder."

With his back to the rock, he searched the Galena Valley side of the range, through his powerful glass; commenting, now and then, when some object came in the field of his vision, to his companion who sat beside him.

They had risen to go and the officer was returning his glass to its case on his saddle, when Aaron King—pointing toward Fairlands, lying dim and hazy in the distant valley—said, "Look there!"

The other turned his head to see a flash of light that winked through the dull, smoky veil, with startling clearness. He smiled and turned again to his saddle. "You'll often see that," he said. "It's the sun striking some bright object that happens to be at just the right angle to hit you with the reflection. A bit of new tin on a roof, a window, an automobile shield, anything bright enough, will do the trick. Come, we'll go back to the trail and follow the break the other way."

In the dusk of the evening, at the close of the long, hard day, as Brian Oakley and Aaron King were starting down the Oak Knoll trail on their return to the ranch, the Ranger uttered an exclamation. His quick eyes had caught the twinkling gleam of a light at Sibyl's old home, far below, across the canyon. The next instant, the chestnut, followed by his four-footed companion, was going down the steep trail at a pace that sent the gravel flying and forced the artist, unaccustomed to such riding, to cling desperately to the saddle. Up the canyon road, the Ranger sent the chestnut at a run, nor did he draw rein as they crossed the rough boulder-strewn wash. Plunging through the tumbling water of the creek, the horses scrambled up the farther bank, and dashed along the old, weed-grown road, into the little clearing They were met by Czar with a bark of welcome. A moment later, they were greeted by Conrad Lagrange and Myra Willard.

"But why don't you stay down at the ranch, Myra?" asked the Ranger, when he had told them that his day's work was without results.

"Listen, Mr. Oakley," returned the woman with the disfigured face. "I know Sibyl too well not to understand the possibilities of her temperament. Natures, fine and sensitive as hers, though brave and cool and strong under ordinary circumstances, under peculiar mental stress such as I believe caused her to leave us, are easily thrown out of balance. We know nothing. The child may be wandering, alone—dazed and helpless under the shock of a cruel and malicious attempt to wreck her happiness. Only some terrible stress of emotion could have caused her to leave me as she did. If

217

she is alone, out here in the hills, there is a chance that—even in her distracted state of mind—she will find her way to her old home." The woman paused, and then, in the silence, added hesitatingly, "I—I may say that I know from experience the possibilities of which I speak."

The three men bowed their heads. Brian Oakley said softly, "Myra, you've got more heart and more sense than all of us put together." To Conrad Lagrange, he added, "You will stay here with Miss Willard?"

"Yes," answered the novelist, "I would be little good in the hills, at such work as you are doing, Brian. I will do what I can, here."

When the Ranger and the artist were riding down the canyon to the ranch, the officer said, "There's a big chance that Myra is right, Aaron. After all, she knows Sibyl better than any of us, and I can see that she's got a fairly clear idea of what sent the child off like this. As it stands now, the girl may be just wandering around. If she is, the boys will pick her up before many hours. She may have met with some accident. If that's it, we'll know before long. She may have been—I tell you, Aaron, it's that automobile acting the way it did that I can't get around."

The searchers were all at the ranch when the two men arrived. No one had a word of encouragement to report. A messenger from the Sheriff brought no light on the mystery of the automobile. The two men who had followed the pipe-line trail had found nothing. A few times, they thought they had signs that a horse had been over the trail the night before, but there was no certainty; and after the pipe-line reached the floor of the canyon there was absolutely nothing. Jack Carleton was back from the Galena Valley neighborhood, and, with him, was the horseman who had gone down the canyon the evening before. The man was known to all. He had been hunting, and was on his way home when Henry Carleton and the Ranger had seen him. He had come, now, to help in the search.

Picking a half dozen men from the party, Brian Oakley sent them to spend the night riding the higher trails and fire-breaks, watching for camp-fire lights. The others, he ordered to rest, in readiness to take up the search at daylight, should the night riders come in without results.

Aaron King, exhausted, physically and mentally, sank into a stupor that could scarcely be called sleep.

At daybreak, the riders who had been all night on the higher trails and fire-breaks, searching the darkness for the possible gleam of a camp-fire's light, came in.

All that day—Wednesday—the mountain horsemen rode, widening the area of their search under the direction of the Ranger. From sundown until long after dark, they came straggling wearily back; their horses nearly exhausted, the riders beginning to fear that Sibyl would never be found alive. There was no further word from the Sheriff at Fairlands.

Then suddenly, out of the blackness of the night, a rider from the other side of the Galenas arrived with the word that the girl's horse had been found. The animal was grazing in the neighborhood of Pine Glen. The saddle and the horse's sides were stained with dirt, as if the animal had fallen. The bridle-reins had been broken. The horse might have rolled on the saddle; he might have stepped on the bridle-reins; he might have fallen and left his rider lying senseless. In any case, they reasoned, the animal would scarcely have found his way over the Galena range after he had been left to wander at will.

Brian Oakley decided to send the main company of riders over into the Pine Glen country, to continue the search there. He knew that the men who found the horse would follow the animal's track back as far as possible. He knew, also, that if the animal had been wandering several hours, as was likely, it would be impossible to back-track far. Late as it was, Aaron King rode up the canyon to tell Myra Willard and Conrad Lagrange the result of the day's work.

The artist's voice trembled as he told the general opinion of the mountaineers; but Myra Willard said, "Mr. King, they are wrong. My baby will come back. There's harm come to her no doubt; but she is not dead or—I would know it."

In spite of the fact that Aaron King's reason told him the woman of the disfigured face had no ground for her belief, he was somehow helped, by her words, to hope.

Chapter XXXIV
The Tracks on Granite Peak

The searching party was already on the way over to Pine Glen, when Brian Oakley stopped at Sibyl's old home for Aaron King. The Ranger, himself, had waited to receive the morning message from the Sheriff.

When the two men, following the Government trail that leads to the neighborhood where the girl's horse had been found, reached the fire-break on the summit of the Galenas, the officer said, "Aaron, you'll be of little use over there in that Pine Glen country, where you have never been." He had pulled up his horse and was looking at his companion, steadily.

"Is there nothing that I can do, Brian?" returned the young man, hopelessly. "God, man! I must do something! I must, I tell you!"

"Steady, old boy, steady," returned the mountaineer's calm voice. "The first thing you must do, you know, is to keep a firm grip on yourself. If you lose your nerve I'll have you on my hands too."

Under his companion's eye, the artist controlled himself. "You're right, Brian," he said calmly. "What do you want me to do? You know best, of course."

The officer, still watching him, said slowly, "I want you to spend the day on that point, up there,"—he pointed to the clump of pines,—"with this glass." He turned to take an extra field-glass from his saddle. Handing the glass to the other, he continued "You can see all over the country, on the Galena Valley side of this range, from there." Again he paused, as though reluctant to give the final word of his instructions.

The young man looked at him, questioningly. "Yes?"

The Ranger answered in a low tone, "You are to watch for buzzards, Aaron."

Aaron King went white. "Brian! You think—"

The answer came sharply, "I am not thinking. I don't dare think. I am only recognizing every possibility and letting nothing, nothing, get away from me. I don't want you to think. I want you to do the thing that will be of greatest service. It's because I am afraid you will think, that I hesitate to assign you to the position."

The sharp words acted like a dash of cold water in the young man's face. Unconsciously, he straightened in his saddle. "Thank you, Brian. I understand. You can depend upon me."

"Good boy!" came the hearty and instant approval. "If you see anything, go to it; leaving a note here, under a stone on top of this rock; I'll find it to-night, when I come back. If nothing shows up, stay until dark, and then go down to Carleton's. I'll be in late. The rest of the party will stay over at Pine Glen."

Alone on the peak where he had sat with Sibyl the day of their last climb, Aaron King watched for the buzzards' telltale, circling flight—and tried not to think.

It was one o'clock when the artist—resting his eyes for a moment, after a long, searching look through the glass—caught, again, that flash of light in the blue haze that lay over Fairlands in the distant valley. Brian Oakley had said,—when they had seen it that first day of the search,—that it was a common sight; but the artist, his mind preoccupied, watched the point of light with momentary, idle interest.

Suddenly, he awoke to the fact that there seemed to be a timed regularity in the flashes. Into his mind came the memory of something he had read of the heliograph, and of methods of signalling with mirrors Closely, now, he watched—three flashes in quick succession—pause—two flashes—pause—one flash—pause— one flash—pause—two flashes—pause—three flashes—pause. For several minutes the artist waited, his eyes fixed on the distant spot under the haze. Then the flashes began again, repeating the same order: —- — - - — —-.

At the last flash, the man sprang to his feet, and searched the mountain peaks and spurs behind him. On lonely Granite Peak, at the far end of the Galena Range, a flash of light caught his eye—then another and another. With an exclamation, he lifted his glass. He could distinguish nothing but the peak from which had come the flashes. He turned toward the valley to see a long flash and then— only the haze and the dark spot that he knew to be the orange groves about Fairlands.

Aaron King sank, weak and trembling, against the rock. What should he do? What could he do? The signals might mean much. They might mean nothing. Brian Oakley's words that morning, came to him; "I am recognizing every possibility, and letting nothing nothing, get away from me." Instantly, he was galvanized into life. Idle thinking, wondering, conjecturing could accomplish nothing.

Riding as fast as possible down to the boulder beside the trail, where he was to leave his message, he wrote a note and placed it under the rock. Then he set out, to ride the fire-break along the top of the range, toward the distant Granite Peak. An hour's riding took him to the end of the fire-break, and he saw that from there on he must go afoot.

Tying the bridle-reins over the saddle-horn, and fastening a note to the saddle, in case any one should find the horse, he turned the animal's head back the way he had come, and, with a sharp blow, started it forward. He knew that the horse—one of Carleton's—would probably make its way home. Turning, he set his face toward the lonely peak; carrying his canteen and what was left of his lunch.

There was no trail for his feet now. At times, he forced his way through and over bushes of buckthorn and manzanita that seemed, with their sharp thorns and tangled branches, to be stubbornly fighting him back. At times, he made his way along some steep slope, from pine to pine, where the ground was slippery with the brown needles, and where to lose his footing meant a fall of a thousand feet. Again, he scaled some rocky cliff, clinging with his fingers to jutting points of rock, finding niches and projections for his feet; or, with the help of vine and root and bush, found a way down some seemingly impossible precipice. Now and then, from some higher point, he sighted Granite Peak. Often, he saw, far below, on one hand the great canyon, and on the other the wide Galena Valley. Always he pushed forward. His face was scratched and stained; his clothing was torn by the bushes; his hands were bloody from the sharp rocks; his body reeked with sweat; his breath came in struggling gasps; but he would not stop. He felt himself driven, as it were, by some inner power that made him insensible to hardship or death. Far behind him, the sun dropped below the sky-line of the distant San Gabriels, but he did not notice. Only when the dusk of the coming night was upon him, did he realize that the day was gone.

On a narrow shelf, in the lee of a great cliff, he hastily gathered material for a fire, and, with his back to the rock, ate a little of the food he carried. Far up on that wind-swept, mountain ridge, the night was bitter cold. Again and again he aroused himself from the weary stupor that numbed his senses, and replenished the fire, or forced himself to pace to and fro upon the ledge. Overhead, he saw the stars glittering with a strange brilliancy. In the canyon, far below, there were a few twinkling lights to mark the Carleton ranch, and the old home of Sibyl, where Conrad Lagrange and Myra

Willard waited. Miles away, the lights of the towns among the orange groves, twinkled like feeble stars in another feeble world. The cold wind moaned and wailed in the dark pines and swirled about the cliff in sudden gusts. A cougar screamed somewhere on the mountainside below. An answering scream came from the ledge above his head. The artist threw more fuel upon his fire, and grimly walked his beat.

In the cold, gray dawn of that Friday morning, he ate a few mouthfuls of his scanty store of food and, as soon as it was light,— even while the canyon below was still in the gloom,—started on his way.

It was eleven o'clock when, almost exhausted, he reached what he knew must be the peak that he had seen through his glass the day before. There was little or no vegetation upon that high, wind-swept point. The side toward the distant peak from which the artist had seen the signals, was an abrupt cliff—hundreds of feet of sheer, granite rock. From the rim of this precipice, the peak sloped gradually down and back to the edge of the pines that grew about its base. The ground in the open space was bare and hard.

Carefully, Aaron King searched—as he had seen the Ranger do—for signs. Beginning at a spot near the edge of the cliff, he worked gradually, back and forth, in ever widening arcs, toward the pines below. He was almost ready to give up in despair, cursing himself for being such a fool as to think that he could pick up a trail, when, clearly marked in a bit of softer soil, he saw the print of a hob-nailed boot.

Instantly the man's weariness was gone. The long, hard way he had come was forgotten. Insensible, now, to hunger and fatigue, he moved eagerly in the direction the boot-track pointed. He was rewarded by another track. Then, as he moved nearer the softer ground, toward the trees, another and another and then—

The man—worn by his physical exertion, and by his days of mental anguish—for a moment, lost control of himself. Clearly marked, beside the broad track of the heavier, man's boot, was the unmistakable print of a smaller, lighter foot.

For a moment he stood with clenched fists and heaving breast; then, with grim eagerness, with every sense supernaturally alert, with nerves tense, quick eyes and ready muscles, he went forward on the trail.

It was after dark, that night, when Brian Oakley, on his way back to Clear Creek, stopped at the rock where the artist had left his note.

Reaching the floor of the canyon, he crossed to tell Myra

Willard and the novelist the result of the day's search. The men riding in the vicinity of Pine Glen had found nothing. It had been—as the Ranger expected—impossible to follow back for any distance on the track of the roaming horse, for the animal had been grazing about the Pine Glen neighborhood for at least a day. Over the note left by Aaron King, the mountaineer shook his head doubtfully. Aaron had done right to go. But for one of his inexperience, the way along the crest of the Galenas was practically impossible. If the young man had known, he could have made the trip much easier by returning to Clear Creek and following up to the head of that canyon, then climbing to the crest of the divide, and so around to Granite Peak. The Ranger, himself, would start, at daybreak, for the peak, by that route; and would come back along the crest of the range, to find the artist.

At Carleton's, they told the officer that Aaron's horse had come in. Jack Carleton and his father arrived from the country above Lone Cabin and Burnt Pine, a few minutes after Brian Oakley reached the ranch. It was agreed that Henry should join the searchers at Pine Glen, at daybreak—lest any one should have seen the artist's camp-fire, that night, and so lose precious time going to it—and that Jack should accompany the Ranger to Granite Peak.

Henry Carleton had gone on his way to Pine Glen, and Brian Oakley and Jack were in the saddle, ready to start up the canyon, the next morning, when a messenger from the Sheriff arrived. An automobile had been seen returning from the mountains, about two o'clock that night. There was only one man in the car.

"Jack," said the Ranger, "Aaron has got hold of the right end of this, with his mirror flashes. You've got to go up the canyon alone. Get to Granite Peak as quick as God will let you, and pick up the trail of whoever signalled from there; keeping one eye open for Aaron. I'm going to trail that automobile as far as it went, and follow whatever met or left it. We'll likely meet somewhere, over in the Cold Water country."

A minute later the two men who had planned to ride together were going in opposite directions.

Following the Fairlands road until he came to where the Galena Valley road branches off from the Clear Creek way, three miles below the Power-House at the mouth of the canyon, Brian Oakley found the tracks of an automobile—made without doubt, during the night just past. The machine had gone up the Galena Valley road, and had returned.

A little before noon, the officer stood where the automobile had stopped and turned around for the return trip. The place was well up toward the head of the valley, near the mouth of a canyon that leads upward toward Granite Peak. An hour's careful work, and the Ranger uncovered a small store of supplies; hidden a quarter of a mile up the canyon. There were tracks leading away up the side of the mountain. Turning his horse loose to find its way home; Brian Oakley, without stopping for lunch, set out on the trail.

High up on Granite Peak, Aaron King was bending over the print of a slender shoe, beside the track of a heavy hob-nailed boot. Somewhere in Clear Creek canyon, Jack Carleton was riding to gain the point where the artist stood. At the foot of the mountain, on the other side of the range, Brian Oakley was setting out to follow the faint trail that started at the supplies brought by the automobile, in the night, from Fairlands.

Chapter XXXV
A Hard Way

When Sibyl Andrés left the studio, after meeting Mrs. Taine, her mind was dominated by one thought—that she must get away from the world that saw only evil in her friendship with Aaron King—a friendship that, to the mountain girl, was as pure as her relations to Myra Willard or Brian Oakley.

Under the watchful, experienced care of the woman with the disfigured face, only the worthy had been permitted to enter into the life of this child of the hills. Sibyl's character—mind and heart and body and soul—had been formed by the strength and purity of her mountain environment; by her association with her parents, with Myra Willard, and with her parents' life-long friends; and by her mental comradeship with the greatest spirits that music and literature have given to the world. As her physical strength and beauty was the gift of her free mountain life, the beauty and strength of her pure spirit was the gift of those kindred spirits that are as mountains in the mental and spiritual life of the race.

Love had come to Sibyl Andrés, not as it comes to those girls who, in the hot-house of passion we call civilization, are forced into premature and sickly bloom by an atmosphere of sensuality. Love had come to her so gently, so naturally, so like the opening of a wild flower, that she had not yet understood that it was love. Even as her womanhood had come to fulfill her girlhood, so Aaron King had come into her life to fulfill her womanhood. She had chosen her mate with an unconscious obedience to the laws of life that was divinely reckless of the world.

Myra Willard, wise in her experience, and in her more than mother love for Sibyl, saw and recognized that which the girl herself did not yet understand. Satisfied as to the character of Aaron King, as it had been tested in those days of unhampered companionship; and seeing, as well, his growing love for the girl, the woman had been content not to meddle with that which she conceived to be the work of God. And why not the work of God? Should the development, the blossoming, and the fruiting of human lives, that the race may flower and fruit, be held less a work of divinity than the plants that mature and blossom and reproduce themselves in their children?

The character of Mrs. Taine represented those forces in life that are, in every way, antagonistic to the forces that make the character of a Sibyl Andrés possible. In a spirit of wanton, selfish cruelty, that was born of her worldly environment and training, "The Age" had twisted and distorted the very virtues of "Nature" into something as hideously ugly and vile as her own thoughts. The woman—product of gross materialism and sensuality—had caught in her licentious hands God's human flower and had crushed its beauty with deliberate purpose. Wounded, frightened, dismayed, not understanding, unable to deny, the girl turned in reluctant flight from the place that was, to her, because of her love, holy ground.

It was impossible for Sibyl not to believe Mrs. Taine—the woman had spoken so kindly; had seemed so reluctant to speak at all; had appeared so to appreciate her innocence. A thousand trivial and unimportant incidents, that, in the light of the worldly woman's words, could be twisted to evidence the truth of the things she said, came crowding in upon the girl's mind. Instead of helping Aaron King with his work, instead of truly enjoying life with him, as she had thought, her friendship was to him a menace, a danger. She had believed—and the belief had brought her a strange happiness—that he had cared for her companionship. He had cared only to use her for his pictures—as he used his brushes. He had played with her—as she had seen him toy idly with a brush, while thinking over his work. He would throw her aside, when she had served his purpose, as she had seen him throw a worn-out brush aside.

The woman who was still a child could not blame the artist—she was too loyal to what she had thought was their friendship; she was too unselfish in her yet unrecognized love for her chosen mate. No, she could not blame him—only—only—she wished—oh how she wished—that she had understood. It would not have hurt so, perhaps, if she had understood.

In all the cruel tangle of her emotions, in all her confused and bewildering thoughts, in all her suffering one thing was clear; she must get away from the world that could see only evil—she must go at once. Conrad Lagrange and Aaron King might come at any moment. She could not face them; now that she knew. She wished Myra was home. But she would leave a little note and Myra—dear Myra with her disfigured face—would understand.

Quickly, the girl wrote her letter. Hurriedly, she dressed in her mountain costume. Still acting under her blind impulse to escape, she made no explanations to the neighbors, when she went for the horse. In her desire to avoid coming face to face with any one, she even chose the more unfrequented streets through the orange groves. In her humiliation and shame, she wished for the kindly darkness of the night. Not until she had left the city far behind, and, in the soft dusk, drew near the mouth of the canyon, did she regain some measure of her self-control.

As she was overtaking the Power Company's team and wagon of supplies, she turned in her saddle, for the first time, to look back. A mile away, on the road, she could see a cloud of dust and a dark, moving spot which she knew to be an automobile. One of the Company machines, she thought; and drew a breath of relief that Fairlands was so far away.

It was quite dark as she entered the canyon; but, as she drew near, she could see against the sky, those great gates, opening silently, majestically to receive her. From within the canyon, she watched, as she rode, to see them slowly close again. The sight of the encircling peaks and ridges, rising in solemn grandeur out of the darkness into the light of the stars, comforted her. The night wind, drawing down the canyon, was sweet and bracing with the odor of the hills. The roar of the tumbling Clear Creek, filling the night with its deep-toned music, soothed and calmed her troubled mind. Presently, she would be with her friends, and, somehow, all would be well.

The girl had ridden half the distance, perhaps, from the canyon gates to the Ranger Station when, above the roar of the mountain stream, her quick ear caught the sound of an automobile, behind her. Looking back, she saw the gleam of the lights, like two great eyes in the darkness. A Company machine, going up to the Head-Work, she thought. Or, perhaps the Doctor, to see some one of the mountain folk.

As the automobile drew nearer, she reined her horse out of the road, and halted in the thick chaparral to let it pass. The blazing lights, as her horse turned to face the approaching machine, blinded her. The animal restive under the ordeal, demanded all her attention. She scarcely noticed that the automobile had slowed down, when within a few feet of her, until a man, suddenly, stood at her horse's head; his hand on the bridle-rein as though to assist her. At the same instant, the machine moved past them, and stopped; its engine still running.

Still with the thought of the Company men in her mind, the girl saw only their usual courtesy. "Thank you," she said, "I can handle him very nicely."

But the man—whom she had not had time to see, blinded as

228

she had been by the light, and who was now only dimly visible in the darkness—stepped close to the horse's shoulder, as if to make himself more easily heard above the noise of the machine, his hand still holding the bridle-rein.

"It is Miss Andrés, is it not?" He spoke as though he was known to her; and the girl—still thinking that it was one of the Company men, and feeling that he expected her to recognize him—leaned forward to see his face, as she answered.

Instantly, the stranger—standing close and taking advantage of the girl's position as she stooped toward him from the saddle—caught her in his powerful arms and lifted her to the ground. At the same moment, the man's companion who, under cover of the darkness and the noise of the machine, had drawn close to the other side of the horse, caught the bridle-rein.

Before the girl, taken so off her guard could cry out, a softly-rolled, silk handkerchief was thrust between her lips and skillfully tied in place. She struggled desperately; but, against the powerful arms of her captor, her splendid, young strength was useless. As he bound her hands, the man spoke reassuringly; "Don't fight, Miss. I'm not going to hurt you. I've got to do this; but I'll be as easy as I can. It will do you no good to wear yourself out."

Frightened as she was, the girl felt that the stranger was as gentle as the circumstances permitted him to be. He had not, in fact, hurt her at all; and, in his voice, she caught a tone of genuine regret. He seemed to be acting wholly against his will; as if driven by some power that rendered him, in fact, as helpless as his victim.

The other man, still standing by the horse's head, spoke sharply; "All right there?"

"All right, sir," gruffly answered the man who held Sibyl, and lifting the helpless girl gently in his arms he seated her carefully in the machine. An automobile-coat was thrown around her, the high collar turned up to hide the handkerchief about her lips, and her hat was replaced by an "auto-cap," pulled low. Then her captor went back to the horse; the other man took the seat beside her; and the car moved forward.

The girl's fright now gave way to perfect coolness. Realizing the uselessness of any effort to escape, she wisely saved her strength; watchful to take quick advantage of any opportunity that might present itself. Silently, she worked at her bonds, and endeavored to release the bandage that prevented her from crying out. But the hands that had bound her had been too skillful. Turning her head, she tried to see her companion's face. But, in the darkness, with upturned collar and cap pulled low over "auto-glasses," the identity of the man driving the car was effectually hidden.

Only when they were passing the Ranger Station and Sibyl saw the lights through the trees, did she, for a moment, renew her struggle. With all her strength she strained to release her hands. One cry from her strong, young voice would bring Brian Oakley so quickly after the automobile that her safety would be assured. On that mountain road, the chestnut would soon run them down. She even tried to throw herself from the car; but, bound as she was, the hand of her companion easily prevented, and she sank back in the seat, exhausted by her useless exertion.

At the foot of the Oak Knoll trail the automobile stopped. The man who had been following on Sibyl's horse came up quickly. Swiftly, the two men worked; placing sacks of supplies and blankets—as the girl guessed—on the animal. Presently, the one who had bound her, lifted her gently from the automobile "Don't hurt yourself, Miss," he said in her ear, as he carried her toward the horse. "It will do you no good." And the girl did not again resist, as he lifted her to the saddle.

The driver of the car said something to his companion in a low tone, and Sibyl heard her captor answer, "The girl will be as safe with me as if she were in her own home."

Again, the other spoke, and the girl heard only the reply; "Don't worry; I understand that. I'll go through with it. You've left me no chance to do anything else."

Then, stepping to the horse's head and taking the bridle-rein, the man who seemed to be under orders, led the way up the canyon. Behind them, the girl heard the automobile starting on its return. The sound died away in the distance. The silence of the night was disturbed only by the sound of the man's hob-nailed boots and the horse's iron-shod feet on the road.

Once, her captor halted a moment, and, coming to the horse's shoulder, asked if she was comfortable. The girl bowed her head. "I'm sorry for that gag," he said. "As soon as it's safe, I'll remove it; but I dare not take chances." He turned abruptly away and they went on.

Dimly, Sibyl saw, in her companion's manner, a ray of hope. That no immediate danger threatened, she was assured. That the man was acting against his will, was as evident. Wisely, she resolved to bend her efforts toward enlisting his sympathies,—to make it hard for him to carry out the purpose of whoever controlled him,—

instead of antagonizing him by continued resistance and repeated attempts to escape, and so making it easier for him to do his master's bidding.

Leaving the canyon by the Laurel Creek trail, they reached Burnt Pine, where the man removed the handkerchief that sealed the girl's lips.

"Oh, thank you," she said quietly. "That is so much better."

"I'm sorry that I had to do it," he returned, as he unbound her arms. "There, you may get down now, and rest, while I fix a bit of lunch for you."

The girl sprang to the ground. "It is a relief to be free," she said. "But, really, I'm not a bit tired. Can't I help you with the pack?"

"No," returned the other, gruffly, as though he understood her purpose and put himself on his guard. "We'll only be here a few minutes, and it's a long road ahead. You must rest."

Obediently, she sat down on the ground, her back against a tree.

As they lunched, in the dim light of the stars, she said, "May I ask where you are taking me?"

"It's a long road, Miss Andrés. We'll be there to-morrow night," he answered reluctantly.

Again, she ventured timidly; "And is, is—some one waiting for—for us, at the end of our journey?"

The man's voice was kinder as he answered, "no, Miss Andrés; there'll he just you and me, for some time. And," he added, "you don't need to fear me."

"I am not at all afraid of you," she returned gently. "But I am—" she hesitated—"I am sorry for you—that you have to do this."

The man arose abruptly. "We must he going."

For some distance beyond Burnt Pine, they kept to the Laurel Creek trail, toward San Gorgonio; then they turned aside to follow some unmarked way, known only to the man. When the first soft tints of the day shone in the sky behind the peaks and ridges, while Sibyl's friends were assembling at the Carleton Ranch in Clear Creek Canyon, and Brian Oakley was directing the day's search, the girl was following her guide in the wild depths of the mountain wilderness, miles from any trail. The country was strange to her, but she knew that they were making their way, far above the canyon rim, on the side of the San Bernardino range, toward the distant Cold Water country that opened into the great desert beyond.

As the light grew stronger, Sibyl saw her companion a man of medium height, with powerful shoulders and arms; dressed in khaki, with mountain boots. Under his arm, as he led the way with a powerful stride that told of almost tireless strength, the girl saw the familiar stock of a Winchester rifle. Presently he halted, and as he turned, she saw his face. It was not a bad face. A heavy beard hid mouth and cheek and throat, but the nose was not coarse or brutal, and the brow was broad and intelligent. In the brown eyes there was, the girl thought, a look of wistful sadness, as though there were memories that could not be escaped.

"We will have breakfast here, if you please, Miss Andrés," he said gravely.

"I'm so hungry," she answered, dismounting. "May I make the coffee?"

He shook his head. "I'm sorry; but there must be no telltale smoke. The Ranger and his riders are out by now, as like as not."

"You seem very familiar with the country," she said, moving easily toward the rifle which he had leaned against a tree, while he busied himself with the pack of supplies.

"I am," he answered. "I have been forced to learn it thoroughly. By the way, Miss Andrés,"—he added, without turning his head, as he knelt on the ground to take food from the pack,— "that Winchester will do you no good. It is not loaded. I have the shells in my belt." He arose, facing her, and throwing open his coat, touched the butt of a Colt forty-five that hung in a shoulder holster under his left armpit. "This will serve in case quick action is needed, and it is always safely out of your reach, you see."

The girl laughed. "I admit that I was tempted," she said. "I might have known that you put the rifle within my reach to try me."

"I thought it would save you needless disappointment to make things clear at once," he answered. "Breakfast is ready."

The incident threw a strong light upon the character with which Sibyl had to deal. She realized, more than ever, that her only hope lay in so winning this man's sympathies and friendship that he would turn against whoever had forced him into his present position. The struggle was to be one of those silent battles of the spirit, where the forces that war are not seen but only felt, and where those who fight must often fight with smiling faces. The girl's part was to enlist her captor to fight for her, against himself. She saw, as clearly, the need of approaching her object with caution. Eager to know who it was that ruled this man, and by what peculiar power a character so strong could be so subjected, she dared not ask. Hour after hour, as they journeyed deeper and deeper into the mountain wilds, she watched and waited for some sign that her companion's mood would make it safe for her to approach him. Meanwhile, she exercised all her womanly tact to lead him to forget his distasteful position, and so to make his uncongenial task as pleasant as possible.

The girl did not realize how far her decision, in itself, aroused the admiring sympathy of her captor. Her coolness, self-possession, and bravery in meeting the situation with calm, watchful readiness, rather than with hysterical moaning and frantic pleading, did more than she realized toward accomplishing her purpose.

During that long forenoon, she sought to engage her guide in conversation, quite as though they were making a pleasure trip that was mutually agreeable. The man—as though he also desired his thoughts removed as far as might be from his real mission—responded readily, and succeeded in making himself a really interesting companion. Only once, did the girl venture to approach dangerous ground.

"Really," she said, "I wish I knew your name. It seems so stupid not to know how to address you. Is that asking too much?"

The man did not answer for some time, and the girl saw his face clouded with somber thought.

"I beg your pardon," she said gently. "I—I ought not to have asked."

"My name is Henry Marston, Miss Andrés," he said deliberately. "But it is not the name by which I am known these days," he added bitterly. "It is an honorable name, and I would like to hear it again—" he paused—"from you."

Sibyl returned gently, "Thank you, Mr. Marston—believe me, I do appreciate your confidence, and—" she in turn hesitated—"and I will keep the trust."

By noon, they had reached Granite Peak in the Galenas, having come by an unmarked way, through the wild country around the head of Clear Creek Canyon.

They had finished lunch, when Marston, looking at his watch, took a small mirror from his pocket and stood gazing expectantly toward the distant valley where Fairlands lay under the blue haze. Presently, a flash of light appeared; then another and another. It was the signal that Aaron King had seen and to which he had called Brian Oakley's attention, that first day of their search.

With his mirror, the man on Granite Peak answered and the girl, watching and understanding that he was communicating with some one, saw his face grow dark with anger. She did not speak.

They had traveled a half mile, perhaps, from the peak, when the man again stopped, saying, "You must dismount here, please."

Removing the things from the saddle, he led the horse a little way down the Galena Valley side of the ridge, and tied the reins to a tree. Then, slapping the animal about the head with his open hand, he forced the horse to break the reins, and started him off toward the distant valley. Again, the girl understood and made no comment.

Lifting the pack to his own strong shoulders, her companion—his eyes avoiding hers in shame—said gruffly, "Come."

Their way, now, led down from the higher levels of peak and ridge, into the canyons and gorges of the Cold Water country. There was no trail, but the man went forward as one entirely at home. At the head of a deep gorge, where their way seemed barred by the face of an impossible cliff that towered above their heads a thousand feet and dropped, another thousand, sheer to the tops of the pines below, he halted and faced the girl, enquiringly. "You have a good head, Miss Andrés?"

Sibyl smiled. "I was born in the mountains, Mr. Marston," she answered. "You need not fear for me."

Drawing near to the very brink of the precipice, he led her, by a narrow ledge, across the face of the cliff; and then, by an easier path, down the opposite wall of the gorge.

It was late in the afternoon when they arrived at a little log cabin that was so hidden in the wild tangle of mountain growth at the bottom of the narrow canyon as to be invisible from a distance of a hundred yards.

The girl knew that they had reached the end of their journey. Nearly exhausted by the hours of physical exertion, and worn with the mental and nervous strain, she sank down upon the blankets that her companion spread for her upon the ground.

"As soon as it is dark, I will cook a hot supper for you," he said, regarding her kindly. "Poor child, this has been a hard, hard, day for you. For me—"

Fighting to keep back the tears, she tried to thank him. For a moment he stood looking down at her. Then she saw his face grow black with rage, and, clenching his great fists, he turned away.

While waiting for the darkness that would hide the smoke of the fire, the man gathered cedar boughs from trees near-by, and made a comfortable bed in the cabin, for the girl. As soon as it was dark, he built a fire in the rude fire-place, and, in a few minutes, announced supper. The meal was really excellent; and Sibyl, in spite of her situation, ate heartily; which won an admiring comment from her captor.

The meal finished, he said awkwardly, "I want to thank you, Miss Andrés, for making this day as easy for me as you have. We will be alone here, until Friday, at least; perhaps longer. There is a bar to the cabin door. You may rest here as safely as though you were in your own room. Good night."

Before she could answer, he was gone.

A few minutes later, Sibyl stood in the open door. "Mr. Marston," she called.

"Yes, Miss Andrés," came, instantly, out of the darkness.

"Please come into the cabin."

There was no answer.

"It will be cold out there. Please come inside."

"Thank you, Miss Andrés; but I will do very nicely. Bar the door and go to sleep."

"But, Mr. Marston, I will sleep better if I know that you are comfortable."

The man came to her and she saw him in the dim light of the fire, standing hat in hand. He spoke wonderingly. "Do you mean, Miss Andrés, that you would not be afraid to sleep, if I occupied the cabin with you?"

"No," she answered, "I am not afraid. Come in."

But he did not move to cross the threshold. "And why are you not afraid?" he asked curiously.

"Because," she answered, "I know that you are a gentleman." .

The man laughed harshly—such a laugh as Sibyl had never before heard. "A gentleman! This is the first time I have heard that word in connection with myself for many a year, Miss Andrés. You have little reason for using it—after what I have done to you—and am doing."

"Oh, but you see, I know that you are forced to do what you are doing. You are a gentleman, Mr. Marston.—Won't you please come in and sleep by the fire? You will be so uncomfortable out there. And you have had such a hard day."

"God bless you, for your good heart, Miss Andrés," the man said brokenly. "But I will not intrude upon your privacy to-night. Don't you see," he added savagely, "don't you see that I—I can't? Bar your door, please, and let me play the part assigned to me. Your kindness to me, your confidence in me, is wasted."

He turned abruptly away and disappeared in the darkness.

235

Chapter XXXVI
What Should He Do

The next morning, it was evident to Sibyl Andrés that the man who said his name was Henry Marston had not slept.

All that day, she watched the battle—saw him fighting with himself. He kept apart from her, and spoke but little. When night came, as soon as supper was over, he again left the cabin, to spend the long, dark hours in a struggle that the girl could only dimly sense. She could not understand; but she felt him fighting, fighting; and she knew that he fought for her. What was it? What terrible unseen force mastered this man,—compelled him to do its bidding,—even while he hated and loathed himself for submitting?

Watchful, ready, hoping, despairing, the helpless girl could only pray that her companion might be given strength.

The following morning, at breakfast, he told her that he must go to Granite Peak to signal. His orders were to lock her in the cabin, and to go alone; but he would not. She might go with him, if she chose.

Even this crumb of encouragement—that he would so far disobey his master—filled the girl's heart with hope. "I would love to go with you, Mr. Marston," she said, "but if it is going to make trouble for you, I would rather stay."

"You mean that you would rather be locked up in the cabin all day, than to make trouble for me?" he asked.

"It wouldn't be so terrible," she answered, "and I would like to do something—something to—to show you that I appreciate your, kindness to me. There's nothing else I can do, is there?"

The man looked at her wonderingly. It was impossible to doubt her sincerity. And Sibyl, as she saw his face, knew that she had never before witnessed such mental and spiritual anguish. The eyes that looked into hers so questioningly, so pleadingly, were the eyes of a soul in torment. Her own eyes filled with tears that she could not hide, and she turned away.

At last he said slowly, "No, Miss Andrés, you shall not stay in the cabin to-day. Come; we must go on, or I shall be late."

At Granite Peak, Sibyl watched the signal flashes from distant Fairlands—the flashes that Aaron King was watching, from the peak where they had sat together that day of their last climb. As the man answered the signals with his mirror, and the girl beside him watched, the artist was training his glass upon the spot where they stood; but, partially concealed as they were, the distance was too great.

When Sibyl's captor turned, after receiving the message conveyed by the flashes of light, his face was terrible to see; and the girl, without asking, knew that the crisis was drawing near. Deadly fear gripped her heart; but she was strangely calm. On the way back to the cabin, the man scarcely spoke, but walked with bent head; and the girl felt him fighting, fighting. She longed to cry out, to plead with him, to demand that he tell her why he must do this thing; but she dared not. She knew, instinctively that he must fight alone. So she watched and waited and prayed. As they were crossing the face of the canyon wall, on the narrow ledge, the man stopped and, as though forgetting the girl's presence, stood looking moodily down into the depths below. Then they went on. That night, he did not leave the cabin as soon as they had finished their evening meal, but sat on one of the rude seats with which the little hut was furnished, gazing into the fire.

The girl's heart beat quicker, as he said, "Miss Andrés, I would like to ask your opinion in a matter that I cannot decide satisfactorily to myself."

She took the seat on the other side of the rude fireplace.

"What is it, Mr. Marston?"

"I will put it in the form of a story," he answered. Then, after a wait of some minutes, as though he found it hard to begin, he said, "It is an old story, Miss Andrés; a very common one, but with a difference. A young man, with every chance in the world to go right, went wrong. He was well-born. He was fairly well educated. His father was a man of influence and considerable means. He had many friends, good and bad. I do not think the man was intentionally bad, but I do not excuse him. He was a fool—that's all—a fool. And, as fools must, he paid the price of his foolishness.

"A sentence of thirty years in the penitentiary is a big price for a young man to pay for being a fool, Miss Andrés. He was twenty-five when he went in—strong and vigorous, with a good mind; the prospects years of prison life—but that's not the story. I could not hope to make you understand what a thirty years sentence to the penitentiary means to a man of twenty-five. But, at least, you will not wonder that the man watched for an opportunity to escape. He prayed for an opportunity. For ten years,—ten years,—Miss Andrés, the man watched and prayed for a chance to escape. Then he got away.

237

"He was never a criminal at heart, you must understand. He had no wish, now, to live a life of crime. He wished only to live a sane, orderly, useful, life of freedom. They hunted him to the mountains. They could not take him, but they made it impossible for him to escape—he was starving—dying. He would not give himself up to the twenty years of hell that waited him. He did not want to die—but he would die rather than go back.

"Then, one day, when he was very near the end, a man found him. The poor hunted devil of a convict aroused his pity. He offered help. He gave the wretched, starving creature food. He arranged to furnish him with supplies, until it would be safe for him to leave his hiding place. He brought him food and clothing and books. Later, when the convict's prison pallor was gone, when his hair and beard were grown, and the prison manner and walk were, in some measure, forgotten; when the officers, thinking that he had perished in the mountains, had given up looking for him; his benefactor gave him work—beautiful work in the orange groves—where he was safe and happy and useful and could feel himself a man.

"Do you wonder, Miss Andrés, that the man was grateful? Do you wonder that he worshipped his benefactor—that he looked upon his friend as upon his savior?"

"No," said the girl, "I do not wonder. It was a beautiful thing to do—to help the poor fellow who wanted to do right. I do not wonder that the man who had escaped, loved his friend."

"But listen," said the other, "when the convict was beginning to feel safe; when he saw that he was out of danger; when he was living an honorable, happy life, instead of spending his days in the hell they call prison; when he was looking forward to years of happiness instead of to years of torment; then his benefactor came to him suddenly, one day, and said, 'Unless you do what I tell you, now—unless you help me to something that I want, I will send you back to prison. Do as I say, and your life shall go on as it is—as you have planned. Refuse, and I will turn you over to the officers, and you will go back to your hell for the remainder of your life.'

"Do you wonder, Miss Andrés, that the convict obeyed his master?"

The girl's face was white with despair, but she did not lose her self-control. She answered the man, thoughtfully—as though they were discussing some situation in which neither had a vital interest. "I think, Mr. Marston," she said, "that it would depend upon what it was that the man wanted the convict to do. It seems to me that I can imagine the convict being happier in prison, knowing that he had not done what the man wanted, than he would he, free, remembering what he had done to gain his freedom. What was it the man wanted?"

Breathlessly, Sibyl waited the answer.

The man on the other side of the fire did not speak.

At last, in a voice hoarse with emotion, Henry Marston said, "Freedom and a life of honorable usefulness purchased at a price, or hell, with only the memory of a good deed—which should the man choose, Miss Andrés?"

"I think," she replied, "that you should tell me, plainly, what it was that the man wanted the convict to do."

"I will go on with the story," said the other.

"The convict's benefactor—or, perhaps I should say, master—loved a woman who refused to listen to him. The girl, for some reason, left home, very suddenly and unexpectedly to any one. She left a hurried note, saying, only, that she was going away. By accident, the man found the note and saw his opportunity. He guessed that the girl would go to friends in the mountains. He saw that if he could intercept her, and keep her hidden, no one would know what had become of her. He believed that she would marry him rather than face the world after spending so many days with him alone, because her manner of leaving home would lend color to the story that she had gone with him. Their marriage would save her good name. He wanted the man whom he could send back to prison to help him.

"The convict had known his benefactor's kindness of heart, you must remember, Miss Andrés. He knew that this man was able to give his wife everything that seems desirable in life—that thousands of women would have been glad to marry him. The man assured the convict that he desired only to make the girl his wife before all the world. He agreed that she should remain under the convict's protection until she was his wife, and that the convict should, himself, witness the ceremony." The man paused.

When the girl did not speak, he said again, "Do you wonder, Miss Andrés, that the convict obeyed his master?"

"No," said the girl, softly, "I do not wonder. But, Mr. Marston," she continued, hesitatingly, "what do you think the convict in your story would have done if the man had not—if he had not wanted to marry the girl?"

"I know what he would have done in that case," the other answered with conviction. "He would have gone back to his twenty years of hell. He would have gone back to fifty years of hell, if need be, rather than buy his freedom at such a price."

The girl leaned forward, eagerly; "And suppose—suppose—that after the convict had done his master's bidding—suppose that after he had taken the girl away from her friends—suppose, then, the man would not marry her?"

For a moment there was no sound in the little room, save the crackling of the fire in the fire-place, and the sound of a stick that had burned in two, falling in the ashes.

"What would the convict do if the man would not marry the girl?" persisted Sibyl.

Her companion spoke with the solemnity of a judge passing sentence; "If the man violated his word—if he lied to the convict—if his purpose toward the girl was anything less than an honorable marriage—if he refused to keep his promise after the convict had done his part—he would die, Miss Andrés. The convict would kill his benefactor—as surely as there is a just God who, alone, can say what is right and what is wrong."

The girl uttered a low cry.

The man did not seem to notice. "But the man will do as he promised, Miss Andrés. He wishes to make the girl his wife. He can give her all that women, these days, seem to desire in marriage. In the eyes of the world, she would be envied by thousands. And the convict would gain freedom and the right to live an honorable life—the right to earn his bread by doing an honest man's work. Freedom and a life of honorable service, at the price; or hell, with only the memory of a good deed—which should he choose, Miss Andrés? The convict is past deciding for himself."

The troubled answer came out of the honesty of the girl's heart; "Mr. Marston, I do not know."

A moment, the man on the other side of the fireplace waited. Then, rising, he quietly left the cabin. The girl did not know that he was gone, until she heard the door close.

In that log hut, hidden in the deep gorge, in the wild Cold Water country, Sibyl Andrés sat before the dying fire, waiting for the dawn. On a high, wind-swept ledge in the Galena mountains, Aaron King grimly walked his weary beat. In Clear Creek Canyon, Myra Willard and Conrad Lagrange waited, and Brian Oakley planned for the morrow. Over in the Galena Valley, an automobile from Fairlands stopped at the mouth of a canyon leading toward Granite Peak. Somewhere, in the darkness of the night, a man strove to know right from wrong.

Chapter XXXVII
The Man Was Insane

Neither Sibyl Andrés nor her companion, the next morning, reopened their conversation of the night before. Each was preoccupied and silent, with troubled thoughts that might not be spoken.

Often, as the forenoon passed, Sibyl saw the man listening, as though for a step on the mountainside above. She knew, without being told, that the convict was expecting his master. It was, perhaps, ten o'clock, when they heard a sound that told them some one was approaching.

The man caught up his rifle and slipped a round of cartridges into the magazine; saying to the girl, "Go into the cabin and bar the door; quick, do as I say! Don't come out until I call you."

She obeyed; and the convict, himself, rifle in hand, disappeared in the heavy underbrush.

A few minutes later, James Rutlidge parted the bushes and stepped into the little open space in front of the cabin. The convict reappeared, his rifle under his arm.

The new-comer greeted the man whom Sibyl knew as Henry Marston, with, "Hello, George, everything all right? Where is she?"

"Miss Andrés is in the cabin. When I heard you coming, I asked her to go inside, and took cover in the brush, myself, until I knew for sure that it was you."

Rutlidge laughed. "You are all right, George. But you needn't worry. Everything is as peaceful as a graveyard. They've found the horse, and they think now that the girl killed herself, or met with an accident while wandering around the hills in a state of mental aberration."

"You left the supplies at the same old place, I suppose?" said the convict.

"Yes, I brought what I could," Rutlidge indicated a pack which he had slipped from his shoulder as he was talking. "You better hike over there and bring in the rest to-night. If you leave at once, you will make it back by noon, to-morrow."

The girl in the cabin, listening, heard every word and trembled with fear. The convict spoke again.

"What are your plans, Mr. Rutlidge?"

"Never mind my plans, now. They can wait until you get back. You must start at once. You say Miss Andrés is in the cabin?" He turned toward the door.

But the other said, shortly, "Wait a minute, sir. I have a word to say, before I go."

"Well, out with it."

"You are not going to forget your promise to me?"

"Certainly not, George. You are safe."

"I mean regarding Miss Andrés."

"Oh, of course not! Why, what's the matter?"

"Nothing, only she is in my care until she is your wife."

James Rutlidge laughed. "I will take good care of her until you get back. You need have no fear. You're not doubting my word, are you?"

"If I doubted your word, I would take Miss Andrés with me," answered the convict, simply.

James Rutlidge looked at him, curiously; "Oh, you would?"

"Yes, sir, I would; and I think I should tell you, too, that if you should forget your promise—"

"Well, what would you do if I should forget?"

The answer came deliberately; "If you do not keep your promise I will kill you, Mr. Rutlidge."

James Rutlidge did not reply.

Stepping to the cabin door, the convict knocked.

Sibyl's voice answered, "Yes?"

"You may come out now, please, Miss Andrés."

As the girl opened the door, she spoke to him in a low tone. "Thank you, Mr. Marston. I heard."

"I meant you to hear," he returned in a whisper. "Do not be afraid." In a louder tone he continued. "I must go for supplies, Miss Andrés. I will be back to-morrow noon."

He stepped around the corner of the cabin, and was gone.

Sibyl Andrés faced James Rutlidge, without speaking. She was not afraid, now, as she had always been in his presence, until that day when he had so plainly declared himself to her and she met his advances with a gun. The convict's warning to the man who could send him back to prison for practically the remaining years of his life, had served its purpose in giving her courage. She did not believe that, for the present, Rutlidge would dare to do otherwise than heed the warning.

Still she did not speak.

James Rutlidge regarded her with a smile of triumphant

satisfaction. "Really," he said, at last, "you do not seem at all glad to see me."

She made no reply.

"I am frightfully hungry"—he continued, with a short laugh, moving toward her as she stood in the door of the cabin—"I've been walking since midnight I was in such a hurry to get here that I didn't even stop for breakfast."

She stepped out, and moved away from the door.

With another laugh, he entered the cabin.

Presently, when he had helped himself to food, he went back to the girl who had seated herself on a log, at the farther side of the little clearing. "You seem fairly comfortable here," he said.

She did not speak.

"You and my man get along nicely, I take it. He has been kind to you?"

Still she did not speak.

He spoke sharply, "Look here, my girl, you can't keep this up, you know. Say what you have to say, and let's get it over."

All the time, she had been regarding him intently—her wide, blue eyes filled with wondering pain. "How could you?" she said at last. "Oh, how could you do such a thing?"

His face flushed. "I did it because you have driven me mad, I guess. From the first time I saw you, I have wanted you. I have tried again and again, in the last three years, to approach you; but you would have nothing to do with me. The more you spurned me, the more I wanted you. Then this man, King, came. You were friendly enough, with him. It made me wild. From that day when I met you in the mountains above Lone Cabin, I have been ready for anything. I determined if I could not win you by fair means, I would take you in any way I could. When my opportunity came, I took advantage of it. I've got you. The story is already started that you were the painter's mistress, and that you have committed suicide. You shall stay here, a while, until the belief that you are dead has become a certainty; then you will go East with me."

"But you cannot do a thing so horrible!" she exclaimed "I would tell my story to the first people we met."

He laughed grimly, as he retorted with brutal meaning, "You do not seem to understand. You will be glad enough to keep the story a secret—when the time comes to go."

Bewildered by fear and shame, the girl could only stammer, "How could you—oh how could you! Why, why—"

"Why!" he echoed. Then, as he went a step toward her, he

exclaimed, with reckless profanity, "Ask the God who made me what I am, why I want you! Ask the God who made you so beautiful, why!"

He moved another step toward her, his face flushed with the insane passion that mastered him, his eyes burning with the reckless light of one past counting the cost; and the girl, seeing, sprang to her feet, in terror. Wheeling suddenly, she ran into the cabin, thinking to shut and bar the door. She reached the door, and swung it shut, but the bar was gone. While he was in the cabin he had placed it out of her reach. Putting his shoulder to the door, the man easily forced it open against her lighter weight. As he crossed the threshold, she sprang to the farthest corner of the little room, and cowered, trembling—too shaken with horror to cry out. A moment he paused; then started toward her.

At that instant, the convict burst through the underbrush into the little opening.

Hearing the sound, Rutlidge wheeled and sprang to the open door.

The convict was breathing heavily from the exertion of a hard run.

"What are you doing here?" demanded Rutlidge, sharply. "What's the matter?"

"Some one is following my trail down from Granite Peak."

"Well, what are you carrying that rifle for?" said Rutlidge, harshly, with an oath.

"There may be others near enough to hear a shot," answered the convict. "Besides, Mr. Rutlidge, this is your part of the game—not mine. I did not agree to commit murder for you."

"Where did you see him?"

"A half mile beyond the head of the gulch, where we turn off to go to the supply point."

Rutlidge, rifle in hand, stepped from the house. "You stay here and take care of the girl—and see that she doesn't scream." With the last word he set out at a run.

The convict sprang into the cabin, where Sibyl still crouched in the corner. The man's voice was imploring as he said, "Miss Andrés, Miss Andrés, what is the matter? Did he touch you? Tell me, did he harm you?"

Sobbing, the girl held out her hands, and he lifted her to her feet. "You—you came—just in time, Mr. Marston."

An instant he stood there, then muttering something under his breath, he turned, caught up his rifle, and started toward the door.

But, as he reached the threshold, she cried out, "Mr. Marston, don't, don't leave me again."

The convict stopped, hesitated, then he said solemnly "Miss Andrés, can you pray? I know you can. You are a good girl. If God can hear a prayer he will surely hear you. Come with me. Come—and pray girl—pray for me."

The most charitable construction that can be put upon the action of James Rutlidge, just related, is to accept the explanation of his conduct that he, himself made to Sibyl. The man was insane—as Mr. Taine was insane—as Mrs. Taine was insane.

What else can be said of a class of people who, in an age wedded to materialism, demand of their artists not that they shall set before them ideals of truth and purity and beauty, but that they shall feed their diseased minds with thoughts of lust and stimulate their abnormal passions with lascivious imaginings? Can a class—whatever its pretense to culture may be—can a class, that, in story and picture and music and play, counts greatest in art those who most effectively arouse the basest passions of which the human being is capable, be rightly judged sane?

James Rutlidge was bred, born, and reared in an atmosphere that does not tolerate purity of thought. It was literally impossible for him to think sanely of the holiest, most sacred, most fundamental facts of life. Education, culture, art, literature,—all that is commonly supposed to lift man above the level of the beasts,—are used by men and women of his kind to so pervert their own natures that they are able to descend to bestial depths that the dumb animals themselves are not capable of reaching. In what he called his love for Sibyl Andrés, James Rutlidge was insane—but no more so than thousands of others. The methods of securing the objects of their desires vary—the motive that prompts is the same—the end sought is identical.

As he hurriedly climbed the mountainside, out of the deep gorge that hid the cabin, the man's mind was in a whirl of emotions—rage at being interrupted at the moment of his triumph; dread lest the approaching one should be accompanied by others, and the girl be taken from him; fear that the convict would prove troublesome, even should the more immediate danger be averted; anger at himself for being so blindly precipitous; and a maddening indecision as to how he should check the man who was following the tracks that led from Granite Peak to the evident object of his search. The words of the convict rang in his ears. "This is your job. I did not agree to commit murder for you."

Murder had no place in the insanity of James Rutlidge To destroy innocence, to kill virtue, to murder a soul—these are commonplaces in the insane philosophy of his kind. But to kill—to take a life deliberately—the thought was abhorrent to him. He was not educated to the thought of taking life—he was trained to consider its perversion. The heroes in his fiction did not kill men—they betrayed women. The heroines in his stories did not desire the death of their betrayers—they loved them, and deserted their husbands for them.

But to stand idly aside and permit Sibyl Andrés to be taken from him—to face the exposure that would inevitably follow—was impossible. If the man who had struck the trail was alone, there might still be a chance—if he could be stopped. But how could he check him? What could he do? A rifle-shot might bring a dozen searchers.

While these thoughts were seething in his hot brain, he was climbing rapidly toward the cliff at the head of the gorge, across which, he knew, the man who was following the tracks that led to the cabin below, must come.

Gaining the end of the ledge that leads across the face of that mighty wall of rock, less than a hundred feet to the other side, he stopped. There was no one in sight. Looking down, he saw, a thousand feet below the tops of the trees in the bottom of the gorge. Lifting his head, he looked carefully about, searching the mountainsides that slope steeply back from the rim of the narrow canyon. He looked up at the frowning cliff that towered a thousand feet above his head. He listened. He was thinking, thinking. The best of him and the worst of him struggled for supremacy.

A sound on the mountainside, above the gorge, and beyond the other end of the ledge, caught his ear. With a quick step he moved behind a projecting corner of the cliff. Rifle in hand, he waited.

Chapter XXXVIII
An Inevitable Conflict

When Aaron King set out to follow the tracks he had found at Granite Peak, after his long, hard trip along the rugged crest of the Galenas, his weariness was forgotten. Eagerly, as if fresh and strong, but with careful eyes and every sense keenly alert, he went forward on the trail that he knew must lead him to Sibyl Andrés.

He did not attempt to solve the problem of how the girl came there, nor did he pause to wonder about her companion. He did not even ask himself if Sibyl were living or dead. He thought of nothing; knew nothing; was conscious of nothing; but the trail that led away into the depths of the mountain wilderness. Insensible to his own physical condition; without food; unacquainted with the wild country into which he was going; reckless of danger to himself but with all possible care and caution for the sake of the girl he loved, he went on.

Coming to the brink of the gorge in which the cabin was hidden, the trail, following the rim, soon led him to the ledge that lay across the face of the cliff at the head of the narrow canyon. A moment, he paused, to search the vicinity with careful eyes, then started to cross. As he set foot upon the ledge, a voice at the other end called sharply, "Stop."

At the word, Aaron King halted.

A moment passed. James Rutlidge stepped from behind the rocks at the other end of the ledge. He was covering the artist with a rifle.

In a flash, the man on the trail understood. The automobile, the mirror signals from Fairlands—it was all explained by the presence and by the menacing attitude of the man who barred his way. The artist's hand moved toward the weapon that hung at his hip.

"Don't do that," said the man with the rifle. "I can't murder you in cold blood; but if you attempt to draw your gun, I'll fire."

The other stood still.

James Rutlidge spoke again, his voice hoarse with emotion; "Listen to me, King. It's useless for me to deny what brought me here. The trail you are following leads to Sibyl Andrés. You had her all summer. I've got her now. If you hadn't stumbled onto the trail up there, I would have taken her out of the country, and you would never have seen her again. I might have killed you before you saw me, but I couldn't. I'm not that kind. Under the circumstances there is no possible compromise. I'll give you a fighting chance for your life and the girl. I'll take a fighting chance for my life and the girl. Throw your gun out of reach and I'll leave mine here. We'll meet on the ledge there."

James Rutlidge was no coward. Mr. Taine, also,—it will be remembered,—on the night of his death, boasted that he was game.

Without an instant's hesitation, Aaron King unbuckled the belt that held his weapon and, turning, tossed it behind him, with the gun still in its holster. At the other end of the ledge, James Rutlidge set his rifle behind the rock.

Deliberately, the two men removed their coats and threw aside their hats. For a moment they stood eyeing each other. Into Aaron King's mind flashed the memory of that scene at the Fairlands depot, when, moved by the distress of the woman with the disfigured face, he had first spoken to the man who faced him now. With startling vividness, the incidents of their acquaintance came to him in flash-like succession—the day that Rutlidge had met Sibyl in the studio; the time of his visit to the camp in the sycamore grove; the night of the Taine banquet—a hundred things that had strengthened the feeling of antagonism which had marked their first meeting. And, through it all, he seemed to hear Conrad Lagrange saying that in his story of life this character's name was "Sensual." The artist, in that instant, knew that this meeting was inevitable.

It was only for a moment that the two men—who in their lives and characters represented forces so antagonistic—stood regarding each other, each knowing that the duel would be—must be—to the death. Deliberately, they started toward the center of the ledge. Over their heads towered the great cliff. A thousand feet below were the tops of the trees in the bottom of the gorge. About them, on every hand, the silent, mighty hills watched—the wild and lonely wilderness waited.

As they drew closer together, they moved, as wrestlers, warily—crouching, silent, alert. Stripped to their shirts and trousers, they were both splendid physical types. James Rutlidge was the heavier, but Aaron King made up for his lack in weight by a more clean-cut, muscular firmness.

They grappled. As two primitive men in a savage age might have met, bare handed, they came together. Locked in each other's arms, their limbs entwined, with set faces, tugging muscles, straining sinews, and taut nerves they struggled. One moment they crushed against the rocky wall of the cliff—the next, and they swayed toward the edge of the ledge and hung over the dizzy precipice. With pounding hearts, laboring breath, and clenched teeth they wrestled.

James Rutlidge's foot slipped on the rocky floor; but, with a desperate effort, he regained his momentary loss. Aaron King—worn by his days of anxiety, by his sleepless nights and by the long hours of toil over the mountains, without sufficient food or rest—felt his strength going. Slowly, the weight and endurance of the heavier man told against him. James Rutlidge felt it, and his eyes were beginning to blaze with savage triumph.

They were breathing, now, with hoarse, sobbing gasps, that told of the nearness of the finish. Slowly, Aaron King weakened. Rutlidge, spurred to increase his effort, and exerting every ounce of his strength, was bearing the other downward and back.

At that instant, the convict and Sibyl Andrés reached the cliff. With a cry of horror, the girl stood as though turned to stone.

Motionless, without a word, the convict watched the struggling men.

With a sob, the girl stretched forth her hands. In a low voice she called, "Aaron! Aaron! Aaron!"

The two men on the ledge heard nothing—saw nothing.

Sibyl spoke again, almost in a whisper, but her companion heard. "Mr. Marston, Mr. Marston, it is Aaron King. I—I love him—I—love him."

Without taking his eyes from the struggling men, the convict answered, "Pray, girl; pray, pray for me." As he spoke, he steadily raised his rifle to his shoulder.

Aaron King went down upon one knee. Rutlidge his legs braced, his body inclined toward the edge of the precipice, was gathering his strength for the last triumphant effort.

The convict, looking along his steady rifle barrel, was saying again, "Pray, pray for me, girl." As the words left his lips, his finger pressed the trigger, and the quiet of the hills was broken by the sharp crack of the rifle.

James Rutlidge's hold upon the artist slipped. For a fraction of a second, his form half straightened and he stood nearly erect; then, as a weed cut by the sharp scythe of a mower falls, he fell; his body whirling downward toward the trees and rocks below. The sound of the crashing branches mingled with the reverberating report of the shot. On the ledge, Aaron King lay still.

The convict dropped his rifle and ran forward. Lifting the unconscious man in his arms, he carried him a little way down the mountain, toward the cabin; where he laid him gently on the ground. To Sibyl, who hung over the artist in an agony of loving fear, he said hurriedly, "He'll be all right, presently, Miss Andrés. I'll fetch his coat and hat."

Running back to the ledge, he caught up the dead man's rifle, coat, and hat, and threw them over the precipice, as he swiftly crossed for the artist's things. Recovering his own rifle, he ran back to the girl.

"Listen, Miss Andrés," said the convict, speaking quickly. "Mr. King will be all right in a few minutes. That rifle-shot will likely bring his friends; if not, you are safe, now, anyway. I dare not take chances. Good-by."

From where she sat with the unconscious man's head in her lap, she looked at him, wonderingly. "Good-by?" she repeated questioningly.

Henry Marston smiled grimly. "Certainly, good-by What else is there for me?"

A moment later, she saw him running swiftly down the mountainside, like some hunted creature of the wilderness.

Chapter XXXIX
The Better Way

Alone on the mountainside with the man who had awakened the pure passion of her woman heart, Sibyl Andrés bent over the unconscious object of her love. She saw his face, unshaven, grimy with the dirt of the trail and the sweat of the fight, drawn and thin with the mental torture that had driven him beyond the limit of his physical strength; she saw how his clothing was stained and torn by contact with sharp rocks and thorns and bushes; she saw his hands—the hands that she had watched at their work upon her portrait as she stood among the roses—cut and bruised, caked with blood and dirt—and, seeing these things, she understood.

In that brief moment when she had watched Aaron King in the struggle upon the ledge,—and, knowing that he was fighting for her, had realized her love for him,—all that Mrs. Taine had said to her in the studio was swept away. The cruel falsehoods, the heartless misrepresentations, the vile accusations that had caused her to seek the refuge of the mountains and the protection of her childhood friends were, in the blaze of her awakened passion, burned to ashes; her cry to the convict—"I love him, I love him"— was more than an expression of her love; it was a triumphant assertion of her belief in his love for her—it was her answer to the evil seeing world that could not comprehend their fellowship.

As the life within the man forced him slowly toward consciousness, the girl, natural as always in the full expression of herself, bent over him with tender solicitude. With endearing words, she kissed his brow, his hair, his hands. She called his name in tones of affection. "Aaron, Aaron, Aaron." But when she saw that he was about to awake, she deftly slipped off her jacket and, placing it under his head, drew a little back.

He opened his eyes and looked wonderingly up at the dark pines that clothed the mountainsides. His lips moved and she heard her name; "Sibyl, Sibyl."

She leaned forward, eagerly, her cheeks glowing with color. "Yes, Mr. King."

"Am I dreaming, again?" he said slowly, gazing at her as though struggling to command his senses.

"No, Mr. King," she answered cheerily, "you are not dreaming."

Carefully, as one striving to follow a thread of thought in a bewildering tangle of events, he went over the hours just past. "I was up on that peak where you and I ate lunch the day you tried to make me see the Golden State Limited coming down from the pass. Brian Oakley sent me there to watch for buzzards." For a moment he turned away his face, then continued, "I saw flashes of light in Fairlands and on Granite Peak. I left a note for Brian and came over the range. I spent one night on the way. I found tracks on the peak. There were two, a man and a woman. I followed them to a ledge of rock at the head of a canyon," he paused. Thus far the thread of his thought was clear. "Did some one stop me? Was there—was there a fight? Or is that part of my dream?"

"No," she said softly, "that is not part of your dream."

"And it was James Rutlidge who stopped me, as I was going to you?"

"Yes."

"Then where—" with quick energy he sat up and grasped her arm—"My God! Sibyl—Miss Andrés, did I, did I—" He could not finish the sentence, but sank back, overcome with emotion.

The girl spoke quickly, with a clear, insistent voice that rallied his mind and forced him to command himself.

"Think, Mr. King, think! Do you remember nothing more? You were struggling—your strength was going—can't you remember? You must, you must!"

Lifting his face he looked at her. "Was there a rifle-shot?" he asked slowly. "It seems to me that something in my brain snapped, and everything went black. Was there a rifle-shot?"

"Yes," she answered.

"And I did not—I did not—?"

"No. You did not kill James Rutlidge. He would have killed you, but for the shot that you heard."

"And Rutlidge is—?"

"He is dead," she answered simply.

"But who—?"

Briefly, she told him the story, from the time that she had met Mrs. Taine in the studio until the convict had left her, a few minutes before. "And now," she finished, rising quickly, "we must go down to the cabin. There is food there. You must be nearly starved. I will cook supper for you, and when you have had a night's sleep, we will start home."

"But first," he said, as he rose to his feet and stood before her, "I must tell you something. I should have told you before, but I was waiting until I thought you were ready to hear. I wonder if you know. I wonder if you are ready to hear, now."

She looked him frankly in the eyes as she answered, "Yes, I know what you want to tell me. But don't, don't tell me here." She shuddered, and the man remembering the dead body that lay at the foot of the cliff, understood. "Wait," she said, "until we are home."

"And you will come to me when you are ready? When you want me to tell you?" he said.

"Yes," she answered softly, "I will go to you when I am ready."

At the cabin in the gulch, the girl hastened to prepare a substantial meal. There was no one, now, to fear that the smoke would be seen. Later, with cedar boughs and blankets, she made a bed for him on the floor near the fire-place. When he would have helped her she forbade him; saying that he was her guest and that he must rest to be ready for the homeward trip.

Softly, the day slipped away over the mountain peaks and ridges that shut them in. Softly, the darkness of the night settled down. In the rude little hut, in the lonely gulch, the man and the woman whose lives were flowing together as two converging streams, sat by the fire, where, the night before, the convict had told that girl his story.

Very early, Sibyl insisted that her companion lie down to sleep upon the bed she had made. When he protested, she answered, laughing, "Very well, then, but you will be obliged to sit up alone," and, with a "Good night," she retired to her own bed in another corner of the cabin. Once or twice, he spoke to her, but when she did not answer he lay down upon his woodland couch and in a few minutes was fast asleep.

In the dim light of the embers, the girl slipped from her bed and stole quietly across the room to the fire-place, to lay another stick of wood upon the glowing coals. A moment she stood, in the ruddy light, looking toward the sleeping man. Then, without a sound, she stole to his side, and kneeling, softly touched his forehead with her lips. As silently, she crept back to her couch.

All that afternoon Brian Oakley had been following with trained eyes, the faintly marked trail of the man whose dead body was lying, now, at the foot of the cliff. When the darkness came, the mountaineer ate a cold supper and, under a rude shelter quickly improvised by his skill in woodcraft, slept beside the trail. Near the head of Clear Creek, Jack Carleton, on his way to Granite Peak, rolled in his blanket under the pines. Somewhere in the night, the man who had saved Sibyl Andrés and Aaron King, each for the other, fled like a fearful, hunted thing.

At daybreak, Sibyl was up, preparing their breakfast But so quietly did she move about her homely task that the artist did not awake. When the meal was ready, she called him, and he sprang to his feet, declaring that he felt himself a new man. Breakfast over, they set out at once.

When they came to the cliff at the head of the gulch, the girl halted and, shrinking back, covered her face with trembling hands; afraid, for the first time in her life, to set foot upon a mountain trail. Gently, her companion led her across the ledge, and a little way back from the rim of the gorge on the other side.

Five minutes later they heard a shout and saw Brian Oakley coming toward them. Laughing and crying, Sibyl ran to meet him; and the mountaineer, who had so many times looked death in the face, unafraid and unmoved, wept like a child as he held the girl in his arms.

When Sibyl and Aaron had related briefly the events that led up to their meeting with the Ranger, and he in turn had told them how he had followed the track of the automobile and, finding the hidden supplies, had followed the trail of James Rutlidge from that point, the officer asked the girl several questions. Then, for a little while he was silent, while they, guessing his thoughts, did not interrupt. Finally, he said, "Jack is due at Granite Peak, sometime about noon. He'll have his horse, and with Sibyl riding, we'll make it back down to the head of Clear Creek by dark. You young folks just wait for me here a little. I want to look around below there, a bit."

As he started toward the gulch, Sibyl sprang to her feet and threw herself into his arms. "No, no, Brian Oakley, you shall not— you shall not do it!"

Holding her close, the Ranger looked down into her pleading eyes, smilingly. "And what do you think I am going to do, girlie?"

"You are going down there to pick up the trail of the man who saved Aaron—who saved me. But you shall not do it. I don't care if you are an officer, and he is an escaped convict! I will not let you do anything that might lead to his capture."

"God bless you, child," answered Brian Oakley, "the only escaped convict I know anything about, this last year, according to my belief, died somewhere in the mountains. If you don't believe it, look up my official reports on the matter."

"And you're not going to find which way he went?"

"Listen, Sibyl," said the Ranger gravely. "The disappearance of James Rutlidge, prominent as he was, will be heralded from one end of the world to the other. The newspapers will make the most of it. The search is sure to be carried into these hills, for that automobile trip in the night will not go unquestioned, and Sheriff Walters knows too much of my suspicions. In a few days, the body will be safely past recognition, even should it be discovered through the buzzards. But I can't take chances of anything durable being found to identify the man who fell over the cliff."

When he returned to them, two hours later, he said, quietly, "It's a mighty good thing I went down. It wasn't a nice job, but I feel better. We can forget it, now, with perfect safety. Remember"—he charged them impressively—"even to Myra Willard and Conrad Lagrange, the story must be only that an unknown man took you, Sibyl, from your horse. The man escaped, when Aaron found you. We'll let the Sheriff, or whoever can, solve the mystery of that automobile and Jim Rutlidge's disappearance."

A half mile from Granite Peak, they met Jack Carleton and, by dark, as Brian Oakley had said, were safely down to the head of Clear Creek; having come by routes, known to the Ranger, that were easier and shorter than the roundabout way followed by the convict and the girl.

It was just past midnight when the three friends parted from young Carleton and crossed the canyon to Sibyl's old home.

Chapter XL
Facing the Truth

As Brian Oakley had predicted, the disappearance of James Rutlidge occupied columns in the newspapers, from coast to coast. In every article he was headlined as "A Distinguished Citizen;" "A Famous Critic;" "A Prominent Figure in the World of Art;" "One of the Greatest Living Authorities;" "Leader in the Modern School;" "Of Powerful Influence Upon the Artistic Production of the Age." The story of the unknown mountain girl's abduction and escape was a news item of a single day; but the disappearance of James Rutlidge kept the press busy for weeks. It may be dismissed here with the simple statement that the mystery has never been solved.

Of the unknown man who had taken Sibyl away into the mountains, and who had escaped, the world has never heard. Of the convict who died but did not die in the hills, the world knows nothing. That is, the world knows nothing of the man in this connection. But Aaron and Sibyl, some years later, knew what became of Henry Marston—which does not, at all, belong to this story.

Upon his return with Conrad Lagrange to their home in the orange groves, Aaron King plunged into his work with a purpose very different from the motive that had prompted him when first he took up his brushes in the studio that looked out upon the mountains and the rose garden.

Day after day, as he gave himself to his great picture,—"The Feast of Materialism,"—he knew the joy of the worker who, in his art, surrenders himself to a noble purpose—a joy that is very different from the light, passing pleasure that comes from the mere exercise of technical skill. The artist did not, now, need to drive himself to his task, as the begging musician on the street corner forces himself to play to the passing crowd, for the pennies that are dropped in his tin cup. Rather was he driven by the conviction of a great truth, and by the realization of its woeful need in the world, to such adequate expression as his mastery of the tools of his craft would permit He was not, now, the slave of his technical knowledge; striving to produce a something that should be merely technically good. He was a master, compelling the medium of his art to serve him; as he, in turn, was compelled to serve the truth that had mastered him.

Sometimes, with Conrad Lagrange, he went for an evening hour to the little house next door. Sometimes Sibyl and Myra Willard would drop in at the studio, in the afternoon. The girl never, now, came alone. But every day, as the artist worked, the music of her violin came to him, out of the orange grove, with its message from the hills. And the painter at his easel, reading aright the message, worked and waited; knowing surely that when she was ready she would come.

Letters from Mrs. Taine were frequent. Aaron King, reading them—nearly always under the quizzing eyes of Conrad Lagrange, whose custom it was to bring the daily mail—carefully tore them into little pieces and dropped them into the waste basket, without comment.

Once, the novelist asked with mock gravity, "Have you no thought for the day of judgment, young man? Do you not know that your sins will surely find you out?"

The artist laughed. "It is so written in the law, I believe."

The other continued solemnly, "Your recklessness is only hastening the end. If you don't answer those letters you will be forced, shortly, to meet the consequences face to face."

"I suppose so," returned the painter, indifferently. "But I have my answer ready, you know."

"You mean that portrait?"

"Yes."

The novelist laughed grimly. "I think it will do the trick. But, believe me, there will be consequences!"

The artist was in his studio, at work upon the big picture, when Mrs. Taine called, the day of her return to Fairlands.

It was well on in the afternoon. Conrad Lagrange and Czar had started for a walk, but had gone, as usual, only as far as the neighboring house. Yee Kee, meeting Mrs. Taine at the door, explained, doubtfully, that the artist was at his work. He would go tell Mr. King that Mrs. Taine was here.

"Never mind, Kee. I will tell him myself," she answered; and, before the Chinaman could protest, she was on her way to the studio.

"Damn!" said the Celestial eloquently; and retired to his kitchen to ruminate upon the ways of "Mellican women."

Mrs. Taine pushed open the door of the studio, so quietly, that the painter, standing at his easel and engrossed with his work, did not notice her presence. For several moments the woman stood watching him, paying no heed to the picture, seeing only the man.

When he did not look around, she said, "Are you too busy to even look at me?"

With an exclamation, he faced her; then, as quickly, turned again; with hand outstretched to draw the easel curtain. But, as though obeying a second thought that came quickly upon the heels of the first impulse, he did not complete the movement. Instead, he laid his palette and brushes beside his color-box, and greeted her with, "How do you do, Mrs. Taine? When did you return to Fairlands? Is Miss Taine with you?"

"Louise is abroad," she answered. "I—I preferred California. I arrived this afternoon." She went a step toward him. "You—you don't seem very glad to see me."

The painter colored, but she continued impulsively, without waiting for his reply. "If you only knew all that I have been doing for you!—the wires I have pulled; the influences I have interested; the critics and newspaper men that I have talked to! Of course I couldn't do anything in a large public way, so soon after Mr. Taine's death, you know; but I have been busy, just the same, and everything is fixed. When our picture is exhibited next season, you will find yourself not only a famous painter, but a social success as well." She paused. When he still did not speak, she went on, with an air of troubled sadness; "I do miss Jim's help though. Isn't it frightful the way he disappeared? Where do you suppose he is? I can't—I won't—believe that anything has happened to him. It's all just one of his schemes to get himself talked about. You'll see that he will appear again, safe and sound, when the papers stop filling their columns about him. I know Jim Rutlidge, too well."

Aaron King thought of those bones, picked bare by the carrion birds, at the foot of the cliff. "It seems to be one of the mysteries of the day," he said. "Commonplace enough, no doubt, if one only had the key to it."

Mrs. Taine had evidently not been in Fairlands long enough to hear the story of Sibyl's disappearance—for which the artist mentally gave thanks.

"I am glad for one thing," continued the woman, her mind intent upon the main purpose of her call. "Jim had already written a splendid criticism of your picture—before he went away—and I have it. All this newspaper talk about him will only help to attract attention to what he has said about you. They are saying such nice things of him and his devotion to art, you know—it is all bound to help you." She waited for his approval, and for some expression of his gratitude.

258

"I fear, Mrs. Taine," he said slowly, "that you are making a mistake."

She laughed nervously, and answered with forced gaiety. "Not me. I'm too old a hand at the game not to know just how far I dare or dare not go."

"I do not mean that"—he returned—"I mean that I can not do my part. I fear you are mistaken in me."

Again, she laughed. "What nonsense! I like for you to be modest, of course—that will be one of your greatest charms. But if you are worried about the quality of your work—forget it, my dear boy. Once I have made you the rage, no one will stop to think whether your pictures are good or bad. The art is not in what you do, but in how you get it before the world. Ask Conrad Lagrange if I am not right."

"As to that," returned the artist, "Mr. Lagrange agrees with you, perfectly."

"But what is this that you are doing now? Will it be ready for the exhibition too?" She looked past him, at the big canvas; and he, watching her curiously stepped aside.

Parts of the picture were little more than sketched in, but still, line and color spoke with accusing truth the spirit of the company that had gathered at the banquet in the home on Fairlands Heights, the night of Mr. Taine's death. The figures were not portraits, it is true, but they expressed with striking fidelity, the lives and characters of those who had, that night, been assembled by Mrs. Taine to meet the artist. The figure in the picture, standing with uplifted glass and drunken pose at the head of the table—with bestial, lust-worn face, disease-shrunken limbs, and dying, licentious eyes fixed upon the beautiful girl musician—might easily have been Mr. Taine himself. The distinguished writers, and critics; the representatives of the social world and of wealth; Conrad Lagrange with cold, cynical, mocking, smile; Mrs. Taine with her pretense of modest dress that only emphasized her immodesty; and, in the midst of the unclean minded crew, the lovely innocence and the unconscious purity of the mountain girl with her violin, offering to them that which they were incapable of receiving—it was all there upon the canvas, as the artist had seen it that night. The picture cried aloud the intellectual degradation and the spiritual depravity of that class who, arrogating to themselves the authority of leaders in culture and art, by their approval and patronage of dangerous falsehood and sham in picture or story, make possible such characters as James Rutlidge.

259

Aaron King, watching Mrs. Taine as she looked at the picture on the easel, saw a look of doubt and uncertainty come over her face. Once, she turned toward him, as if to speak; but, without a word, looked again at the canvas. She seemed perplexed and puzzled, as though she caught glimpses of something in the picture that she did not rightly understand Then, as she looked, her eyes kindled with contemptuous scorn, and there was a pronounced sneer in her cold tones as she said, "Really, I don't believe I care for you to do this sort of thing." She laughed shortly. "It reminds one a little of that dinner at our house. Don't you think? It's the girl with the violin, I suppose."

"There are no portraits in it, Mrs. Taine," said the artist, quietly.

"No? Well, I think you'd better stick to your portraits. This is a great picture though," she admitted thoughtfully. "It, it grips you so. I can't seem to get away from it. I can see that it will create a sensation. But just the same, I don't like it. It's not nice, like your portrait of me. By the way"—and she turned eagerly from the big canvas as though glad to escape a distasteful subject—"do you remember that I have never seen my picture yet? Where do you keep it?"

The painter indicated another easel, near the one upon which he was at work, "It is there, Mrs. Taine."

"Oh," she said with a pleased smile. "You keep it on the easel, still!" Playfully, she added, "Do you look at it often?—that you have it so handy?"

"Yes," said the artist, "I must admit that I have looked at it frequently." He did not explain why he looked at her portrait while he was working upon the larger picture.

"How nice of you," she answered "Please let me see it now. I remember when you wanted to repaint it, you said you would put on the canvas just what you thought of me; have you? I wonder!"

"I would rather that you judge for yourself, Mrs. Taine," he answered, and drew the curtain that hid the painting.

As the woman looked upon that portrait of herself, into which Aaron King had painted, with all the skill at his command, everything that he had seen in her face as she posed for him, she stood a moment as though stunned. Then, with a gesture of horror and shame, she shrank back, as though the painted thing accused her of being what, indeed, she really was.

Turning to the artist, imploringly, she whispered, "Is it—is it— true? Am I—am I that?"

260

Aaron King, remembering how she had sent the girl he loved so nearly to a shameful end, and thinking of those bones at the foot of the cliff, answered justly; "At least, madam, there is more truth in that picture than in the things you said to Miss Andrés, here in this room, the day you left Fairlands."

Her face went white with quick rage, but, controling herself, she said, "And where is the picture of your mistress? I should like to see it again, please."

"Gladly, madam," returned the artist. "Because you are a woman, it is the only answer I can make to your charge; which, permit me to say, is as false as that portrait of you is true."

Quickly he pushed another easel to a position beside the one that held Mrs. Taine's portrait, and drew the curtain.

The effect, for a moment, silenced even Mrs. Taine—but only for a moment. A character that is the product of certain years of schooling in the thought and spirit of the class in which Mrs. Taine belonged, is not transformed by a single exhibition of painted truth. From the two portraits, the woman turned to the larger canvas. Then she faced the artist.

"You fool!" she said with bitter rage. "O you fool! Do you think that you will ever be permitted to exhibit such trash as this?" she waved her hand to include the three paintings. "Do you think that I am going to drag you up the ladder of social position to fame and to wealth for such reward as that?" she singled out her own portrait. "Bah! you are impossible—impossible! I have been mad to think that I could make anything out of you. As for your idiotic claim that you have painted the truth—" She seized a large palette knife that lay with the artist's tools upon the table, and springing to her portrait, hacked and mutilated the canvas. The artist stood motionless making no effort to stop her. When the picture was utterly defaced she threw it at his feet. "That, for your truth, Mr. King!" With a quick motion, she turned toward the other portrait.

But the artist, who had guessed her purpose, caught her hand. "That picture was yours, madam—this one is mine." There was a significant ring of triumph in his voice.

Neither Aaron King nor Mrs. Taine had noticed three people who had entered the rose garden, from the orange grove, through the little gate in the corner of the hedge. Conrad Lagrange, Myra Willard and Sibyl were going to the studio; deliberately bent upon interrupting the artist at his work. They sometimes—as Conrad Lagrange put it—made, thus, a life-saving crew of three; dragging the painter to safety when the waves of inspiration were about to overwhelm him. Czar, of course, took an active part in these rescues.

As the three friends approached the trellised arch that opened from the garden into the yard, a few feet from the studio door, the sound of Mrs. Taine's angry voice, came clearly through the open window.

Conrad Lagrange stopped. "Evidently, Mr. King has company," he said, dryly.

"It is Mrs. Taine, is it not?" asked Sibyl, quietly, recognizing the woman's voice.

"Yes," answered the novelist.

The woman with the disfigured face said hurriedly, "Come, Sibyl, we must go back. We will not disturb Mr. King, now, Mr. Lagrange. You two come over this evening." They saw her face white and frightened.

"I believe I'll go back with you, if you don't mind," returned Conrad Lagrange, with his twisted grin; "I don't think I want any of that in there, either." To the dog who was moving toward the studio door, he added; "Here, Czar, you mustn't interrupt the lady. You're not in her class."

They were moving away, when Mrs. Taine's voice came again, clearly and distinctly, through the window.

"Oh, very well. I wish you joy of your possession. I promise you, though, that the world shall never hear of this portrait of your mistress. If you dare try to exhibit it, I shall see that the people to whom you must look for your patronage know how you found the original, an innocent, mountain girl, and brought her to your studio to live with you. Fairlands has already talked enough, but my influence has prevented it from going too far. You may be very sure that from now on I shall not exert myself to deny it."

The artist's friends in the rose garden, again, stopped involuntarily. Sibyl uttered a low exclamation.

Conrad Lagrange looked at Myra Willard. "I think," he said in a low tone, "that the time has come. Can you do it?"

"Yes. I—I—must," returned the woman. She spoke to the girl, who, being a little in advance, had not heard the novelist's words, "Sibyl, dear, will you go on home, please? Mr, Lagrange will stay with me. I—I will join you presently."

At a look from Conrad Lagrange, the girl obeyed.

"Go with Sibyl, Czar," said the novelist; and the girl and the dog went quickly away through the garden.

In the studio, Aaron King gazed at the angry woman in amazement. "Mrs. Taine," he said, with quiet dignity, "I must tell you that I hope to make Miss Andrés my wife."

She laughed harshly. "And what has that to do with it?"

"I thought that if you knew, it might help you to understand the situation," he answered simply.

"I understand the situation, very well," she retorted, "but you do not appear to. The situation is this: I—I was interested in you—as an artist. I, because my position in the world enabled me to help you, commissioned you to paint my portrait. You are unknown, with no name, no place in the world. I could have given you success. I could have introduced you to the people that you must know if you are to succeed. My influence would insure you a favorable reception from those who make the reputations of men like you. I could have made you the rage. I could have made you famous. And now—"

"Now," he said calmly, "you will exert your influence to hinder me in my work. Because I have not pleased you, you will use whatever power you have to ruin me. Is that what you mean, Mrs. Taine?"

"You have made your choice. You must take the consequences," she replied coldly, and turned to leave the studio.

In the doorway, stood the woman with the disfigured face.

Conrad Lagrange stood near.

XLI
Marks of the Beast

When Mrs. Taine would have passed out of the studio, the woman with the disfigured face said, "Wait madam, I must speak to you."

Aaron King recalled that strange scene at the depot, the day of his arrival in Fairlands.

"I have nothing to say to you"—returned Mrs. Taine, coldly— "stand aside please."

But Conrad Lagrange quietly closed the door. "I think, Mrs. Taine," he remarked dryly, "than you will be interested in what Miss Willard has to say."

"Oh, very well," returned the other, making the best of the situation. "Evidently, you heard what I just said to your protege."

The novelist answered, "We did. Accept my compliments madam; you did it very nicely."

"Thanks," she retorted, "I see you still play your role of protector. You might tell your charge whether or not I am mistaken as to the probable result of his—ah—artistic conscientiousness."

"Mr. King knows that you are not. You have, indeed, put the situation rather mildly. It is a sad fact, but, never-the-less, a fact, that the noblest work is often forced to remain unrecognized and unknown to the world by the same methods that are used to exalt the unworthy. You undoubtedly have the power of which you boast, Mrs. Taine, but—"

"But what?" she said triumphantly. "You think I will hesitate to use my influence?"

"I know you will not use it—in this case," came the unexpected answer.

She laughed mockingly, "And why not? What will prevent?"

"The one thing on earth, that you fear, madam"—answered Conrad Lagrange—"the eyes of the world."

Aaron King listened, amazed.

"I don't think I understand," said Mrs. Taine, coldly.

"No? That is what Miss Willard proposes to explain," returned the novelist.

She turned haughtily toward the woman with the disfigured face. "What can this poor creature say to anything I propose?"

264

Myra Willard answered gently, sadly, "Have you no kindness, no sympathy at all, madam? Is there nothing but cruel selfishness in your heart?"

"You are insolent," retorted the other, sharply. "Say what you have to say and be brief."

Myra Willard drew close to the woman and looked long and searchingly into her face. The other returned her gaze with contemptuous indifference.

"I have been sorry for you," said Myra Willard slowly. "I have not wished to speak. But I know what you said to Sibyl, here in the studio; and I overheard what you said to Mr. King, a few minutes ago. I cannot keep silent."

"Proceed," said Mrs. Taine, shortly. "Say what you have to say, and be done with it."

Myra Willard obeyed. "Mrs. Taine, twenty-six years ago, your guardian, the father of James Rutlidge won the love of a young girl. It does not matter who she was. She was beautiful and innocent That was her misfortune. Beauty and innocence often bring pain and sorrow, madam, in a world where there are too many men like Mr. Rutlidge, and his son. The girl thought the man—she did not know him by his real name—her lover. She thought that he became her husband. A baby was born to the girl who believed herself a wife; and the young mother was happy. For a short time, she was very happy.

"Then, the awakening came. The girl mother was holding her baby to her breast, and singing, as happy mothers do, when a strange woman appeared in the open door of the room. She was a beautiful woman, richly dressed; but her face was distorted with passion. The young mother did not understand. She did not know, then, that the woman was Mrs. Rutlidge—the true wife of the father of her child. She knew that, afterward. The woman, in the doorway lifted her hand as though to throw something, and the mother, instinctively, bowed her head to shield her baby. Then something that burned like fire struck her face and neck. She screamed in agony, and fainted.

"The rest of the story does not matter, I think. The injured mother was taken to the hospital. When she recovered, she learned that Mrs. Rutlidge was dead—a suicide. Later, Mr. Rutlidge took the baby to raise as his ward; telling the world that the child was the daughter of a relative who had died at its birth. You must understand that when the disfigured mother of the baby came to know the truth, she believed that it would be better for the little one if the facts of its birth were never known. The wealthy Mr. Rutlidge could give his ward every advantage of culture and social position. The child would grow to womanhood with no stain upon her name. Because she felt she owed her baby this, the only thing that she could give her, the mother consented and disappeared.

"Madam," finished Myra Willard, slowly, "a little of the acid that burned that mother's face fell upon the shoulder of her illegitimate baby."

"God!" exclaimed the artist.

Throughout Myra Willard's story, Mrs. Taine stood like a woman of stone. At the end, she gazed at the woman's disfigured face, as though fascinated with horror, while her hands moved to finger the buttons of her dress. Unconscious of what she was doing, as though under some strange spell, without removing her gaze from Myra Willard's marred features she opened the waist of her dress and bared to them her right shoulder. It was marked by a broad scar like the scars that disfigured the face of her mother.

Myra Willard started forward, impelled by the mother instinct. "My baby, my poor, poor girl!"

The words broke the spell. Drawing back with an air of cold, unconquerable pride, the woman looked at Conrad Lagrange. "And now," she said, as she swiftly rearranged her dress, "perhaps you will be good enough to tell me why you have done this."

Myra Willard turned away to sink into a chair, white and trembling. Aaron King stepped quickly to her side, and, placing his hand gently on her shoulder waited for the novelist to speak.

"Miss Willard told you this story because I asked her to," said Conrad Lagrange. "I asked her to tell you because it gives me the power to protect the two people who are dearer to me than all the world."

"Still in your role of protector, I see," sneered Mrs. Taine.

"Exactly, madam. It happens that I was a reporter on a certain newspaper when the incidents just related occurred. I wrote the story for the press. In fact, it was the story that gave me my start in yellow journalism, from which I graduated the novelist of your acquaintance. I know the newspaper game thoroughly, Mrs. Taine. I know the truth of this story that you have just heard. Permit me to say, that I know how to write in the approved newspaper style, and to add that my name insures a wide hearing. Proceed to carry out your threats, and I promise you that I will give this attractive bit of news, in all its colorful details, to every newspaper in the land. Can't you see the headlines? 'Startling Revelation,' 'The Secret of the

Beautiful Mrs. Taine's Shoulders,' 'Why a Leader in the Social World makes Modesty her Fad,' 'The Parentage of a Social Leader.' Do you understand, madam? Use your influence to interfere with or to hinder Mr. King in his work; or fail to use your influence to contradict the lies you have already started about the character of Miss Andrés; and I will use the influence of my pen and the prestige of my name to put you before the eyes of the world for what you are."

For a moment the woman looked at him, defiantly. Then, as she grasped the full significance of what he had said, she slowly bowed her head.

Conrad Lagrange opened the door.

As she went out, the woman with the disfigured face started forward, holding out her hands appealingly.

Mrs. Taine did not look back, but went quickly toward the big automobile that was waiting in front of the house.

Chapter XLII
Aaron King's Success

The winter months were past.

Aaron King was sitting before his finished picture. The colors were still fresh upon the canvas that, to-day, hangs in an honored place in one of the great galleries of the world. To the last careful touch, the artist had put into his painted message, the best he had to give. Back of every line and brush-stroke there was the deep conviction of a worthy motive. For an hour, he had been sitting there, before the easel, brush and palette in hand, without touching the canvas. He could do no more.

Laying aside his tools, he went to his desk, and took from the drawer, that package of his mother's letters. He pushed a deep arm-chair in front of his picture, and again seated himself. As he read letter after letter, he lifted his eyes, at almost every sentence from the written pages to his work. It was as though he were submitting his picture to a final test—as, indeed, he was. He had reached the last letter when Conrad Lagrange entered the studio; Czar at his heels.

Every day, while the picture was growing under the artist's hand, his friend had watched it take on beauty and power. He did not need to speak of the finished painting, now.

"Well, lad," he said, "the old letters again?"

The artist, caressing the dog's silky head as it was thrust against his knee, answered, "Yes, I finished the picture two hours ago. I have been having a private exhibition all on my own hook. Listen." From the letter in his hand he read:

"It is right for you to be ambitious, my son. I would not have you otherwise. Without a strong desire to reach some height that in the distance lifts above the level of the present, a man becomes a laggard on the highway of life—a mere loafer by the wayside—slothful, indolent—slipping easily, as the years go, into the most despicable of places—the place of a human parasite that, contributing nothing to the wealth of the race, feeds upon the strength of the multitude of toilers who pass him by. But ambition, my boy, is like to all the other gifts that lead men Godward. It must be a noble ambition, nobly controlled. A mere striving for place and power, without a saving sense of the responsibility conferred by that

268

place and power, is ignoble. Such an ambition, I know—as you will some day come to understand—is not a blessing but a curse. It is the curse from which our age is suffering sorely; and which, if it be not lifted, will continue to vitiate the strength and poison the life of the race.

"Because I would have your ambition, a safe and worthy ambition, Aaron, I ask that the supreme and final test of any work that comes from your hand may be this; that it satisfy you, yourself—that you may be not ashamed to sit down alone with your work, and thus to look it squarely in the face. Not critics, nor authorities, not popular opinion, not even law or religion, must be the court of final appeal when you are, by what you do, brought to bar; but by you, yourself, the judgment must be rendered. And this, too, is true, my son, by that judgment and that judgment alone, you will truly live or you will truly die."

"And that"—said the novelist—so famous in the eyes of the world, so infamous in his own sight—"and that is what she tried to make me believe, when she and I were young together. But I would not. I would not accept it. I thought if I could win fame that she—" he checked himself suddenly.

"But you have led me to accept it, old man," cried the artist heartily. "You have opened my eyes. You have helped me to understand my mother, as I never could have understood her, alone."

Conrad Lagrange smiled. "Perhaps," he admitted whimsically. "No doubt good may sometimes be accomplished by the presentation of a horrible example. But go on with your private exhibition. I'll not keep you longer. Come, Czar."

In spite of the artist's protests, he left the studio.

While the painter was putting away his letters, the novelist and the dog went through the rose garden and the orange grove, straight to the little house next door. They walked as though on a definite mission.

Sibyl and Myra Willard were sitting on the porch.

"Howdy, neighbor," called the girl, as the tall, ungainly form of the famous novelist appeared. "You seem to be the bearer of news. What is the latest word from the seat of war?"

"It is finished," said Conrad Lagrange, returning Myra's gentle greeting, and accepting the chair that Sibyl offered.

"The picture?" said the girl eagerly, a quick color flushing her cheeks. "Is the picture finished?"

"Finished," returned the novelist. "I just left him mooning over it like a mother over a brand-new baby."

They laughed together, and when, a moment later, the girl slipped into the house and did not return, the woman with the disfigured face and the famous novelist looked at each other with smiling eyes. When Czar, with sudden interest, started around the corner of the house, his master said suggestively, "Czar, you better stay here with the old folks."

Passing through the house, and out of the kitchen door, Sibyl ran, lightly, through the orange grove, to the little gate in the corner of the Ragged Robin hedge. A moment she paused, hesitating, then, stealing cautiously into the rose garden, she darted in quick flight to the shelter of the arbor; where she parted the screen of vines to gain a view of the studio.

Between the big, north window and the window that opened into the garden, she saw the artist. She saw, too, the big canvas upon the easel. But Aaron King was not, now, looking at his work just finished. He was sitting before that other picture into which he had unconsciously painted, not only the truth that he saw in the winsome loveliness of the girl who posed for him with outstretshed hands among the roses, but his love for her as well.

With a low laugh, Sibyl drew back. Swiftly, as she had reached the arbor, she crossed the garden, and a moment later, paused at the studio door. Again she hesitated—then, gently,—so gently that the artist, lost in his dreams, did not hear,—she opened the door. For a little, she stood watching him. Softly, she took a few steps toward him. The artist, as though sensing her presence, started and looked around.

She was standing as she stood in the picture; her hands outstretched, a smile of welcome on her lips, the light of gladness in her eyes.

As he rose from his chair before the easel, she went to him.

Not many days later, there was a quiet wedding, at Sibyl's old home in the hills. Besides the two young people and the clergyman, only Brian Oakley, Mrs. Oakley, Conrad Lagrange and Myra Willard were present. These friends who had prepared the old place for the mating ones, after a simple dinner following the ceremony, returned down the canyon to the Station.

Standing arm in arm, where the old road turns around the cedar thicket, and where the artist had first seen the girl, Sibyl and Aaron watched them go. From the other side of roaring Clear Creek, they turned to wave hats and handkerchiefs; the two in the shadow of the cedars answered; Czar barked joyful congratulations; and the wagon disappeared in the wilderness growth.

Instead of turning back to the house behind them, the two, without speaking, as though obeying a common impulse, set out down the canyon.

A little later they stood in the old spring glade, where the alders bore, still, in the smooth, gray bark of their trunks, the memories of long-ago lovers; where the light fell, slanting softly through the screen of leaf and branch and vine and virgin's-bower, upon the granite boulder and the cress-mottled waters of the spring, as through the window traceries of a vast and quiet cathedral; and where the distant roar of the mountain stream trembled in the air like the deep tones of some great organ.

Sibyl, dressed in her brown, mountain costume, was sitting on the boulder, when the artist said softly, "Look!"

Lifting her eyes, as he pointed, she saw two butterflies—it might almost have been the same two—with zigzag flight, through the opening in the draperies of virgin's-bower. With parted lips and flushed cheeks, the girl watched. Then—as the beautiful creatures, in their aerial waltz, whirled above her head—she rose, and lightly, gracefully,—almost as her winged companions,—accompanied them in their dance.

The winged emblems of innocence and purity flitted away over the willow wall. The girl, with bright eyes and smiling lips—half laughing, half serious—looked toward her mate. He held out his arms and she went to him.

The End